Georgia

A Trilogy

Part Three

Michael Boylan

PWI Books

Bethesda, Maryland

Copy edited by Joanna Jensen

Proof read by Lydia Johnson

The Archē Novels

Naked Reverse

Georgia (A Trilogy)

T-Rx: The History of a Radical Leader

The Long Fall of the Ball from the Wall

Epitome of Part One

Jefferson John Brown leaves the share-cropping farm of Marcel Beauchay after Jefferson's father dies. Marcel was a brutal man who beat Jefferson and stole Jefferson's inheritance (from his father, who ran Marcel's farm). Jefferson went north, trying to find less discrimination against people of African descent. He went to Boston, but got the same, though more subtle, treatment.

Then Jefferson travelled south to New York City and ended up getting a job with a crusading printer on the lower east side of Manhattan. This man, Mr. Peabody, who only lived with his cats (Matthew, Mark, Luke, and John), took a liking to Jefferson. He taught his charge reading, writing, and arithmetic. Jefferson was so talented that in time Peabody got him admitted to an Ivy League college in Ithaca, New York. Peabody paid all the fees, but Jefferson worked for his room and board. After four years, Jefferson (the only student of African descent at the school) became the first black man to earn a degree in philosophy at that college.

Jefferson returned to Peabody, who was on a campaign to clean up Tammany Hall. It was a failed mission and Peabody was murdered. Jefferson moved further south to Baltimore and labored in the ship yards among other workers of African descent. These workers had lower wages than their European descent counterparts.

Jefferson joined the NAACP and began working for union rights for African descent individuals. It became contentious. There was a riot, and a squad of anti-black unionists raided Jefferson's apartment and killed his wife and child.

Jefferson decided to move back to his old home and resided once more in Bella County at the Beauchay farm. This time the owner was Samuel Beauchay, with whom he had grown up. Jefferson was made steward of the farm. Under Jefferson it transitioned from share-cropping to hired farm labor.

Samuel became the surprise recipient of a foundling. People said the mother was Myra Dow, a mixed race worker at the shared farm store (between the Beauchays and the Vanderkamps) of Bella County. After some discussion, Beauchay decided to raise the child but discharged Myra from Bella County. The boy, John Dow, did not know whether he was white or mixed race (meaning black in the social climate at the time). He was raised with Samuel Beauchay's only child, who was born very soon after, with the result of Samuel's wife dying in childbirth.

Samuel was convinced by his sister to take a trip to Texas to try to re-coup after his wife's death. While they were in Texas, Dorthay found and married a man, George Dodson, who was too coarse for Samuel's taste. This led to antipathy between the two which culminated in Samuel setting a trap for George.

John Dow and Beauchay's biological child, Jason, grew up side by side, though Jason always carried a sense of superiority. They had a private tutor. Both boys especially liked Julia Vanderkamp from the neighboring farm. Actually, every boy around that age admired Julia— especially Victor Stuart. Victor was a confirmed racist who tormented John Dow. The two boys were the most athletically talented in the county in their age bracket. John endured much abuse from Victor.

Julia Vanderkamp favored John because of his natural gentleness. Rodney, Julia's brother, loved sports and dreamed of going to college so he might become a professional athlete.

There was some natural tension between these adolescents as they were growing up on their own. How far might some of these antagonisms go?

Behind it all is Jefferson who watches over John and everything else.

Epitome of Part Two

Things begin happily enough for idyllic Bella County as they celebrate their annual County Fair. There are baking and sewing contests for the women, a daily carnival with games and entertainment in tents, and the ending activities of the rifle shooting contest, cross-country horse race, and a dance. All goes as planned until the last day. Then the temperature rises as John Dow comes from behind to win the rifle shooting contest and has a down-to-the-wire sprint in the horse race. The officials gave the race to Victor Stuart. At the dance, Julia Vanderkamp had reserved three dances for John. Victor was furious. He almost started a fight on the dance floor. The older male chaperones intervened and Victor was led out.

The next morning, Victor Stuart was found dead. His body was in the town garbage dump. Suspicion immediately fell on John. Since John was mixed race (and considered to be black by prevailing standards), a posse was formed (really a lynch mob). John escapes the lynching with the help of Jefferson and Julia. Then John becomes a fugitive.

John's travels take him around the state and even into Tennessee.

Back in Bella County, two sub-plots develop. The first is Samuel Beauchay's purchase of the old golf course. He has various governmental experts on minerals come and do some tests. The rumor mill generates speculation on whether Beauchay will get rich on those rights. George Dodson wants the land. The two men bargain and George pays a high price for the land that later proves to have no valuable minerals. Has Samuel won?

Then there is the investment company that Oscar Whren (who secretly works for George Dodson) creates surreptitiously among the planters via a fake outsider who spreads dreams of participating in the riches of the 1920s. The group is formed and they put down more money than they can afford. Whren says he's also an investor, but it's sham money. Charles Vanderkamp has been in the investment group all along while Samuel Beauchay has not.

Meanwhile, John travels. First he lands with an immigrant Mexican share-cropping family. John likes the family and longs for stability, but violence make it impossible for him to stay. Then he travels and finds a job at a lumber mill. The mill only pays by the month and John is flat broke. He utilizes his woodsman skills by living in the forest for 28 days. On the 29th day, the workers at the mill declare a strike. John is two days from his first paycheck. He's mighty tired of the vegetarian lifestyle living in the woods. John shows up to work despite the strike, only to pay a price. There is then a strange interlude in which John cannot determine what is and is not real.

Finally, Jefferson gets extended time off from his job running the Beauchay farm to take up the criminal investigation of Victor Stuart's murder. He wants to uncover the evidence that will exonerate John. This requires travel to Savannah where Rod Dodson, George's brother, is overseeing their expanding criminal empire.

Will Jefferson be successful? The deck is certainly stacked against him.

We begin our journey with Book Nine.

Book Nine

The Quest of the Artist

The creative process is a very queer one because it often time happens without any apparent direction. There is a mystery about the creative act which defies any systematic analysis. One can talk about certain formal problems that face an author, or an overriding concern of an author, or of the nature of the audience, but in the end *the act itself* is no clearer. One way to discuss an aspect of the process is through a discussion of the tools that the author/artist has at his/her disposal in order to see how the final product is affected.

One must realize that to some extent, the artifact is the real product of an artistic endeavor. The *fact of* an object also implies an active process (which has already been discussed). What is of concern now is how that artifact, as a necessarily limited model, can help explain part of what the art *really is* and how it came about. In a play, the tools are used to create certain effects, e.g., a language is used to create a text which has a meaning that can be readily understood by others who can read the same language. This is a restriction that other arts do not have. Music requires only ears and hearing. Visual art (including costume design) requires only sight. But any written art requires that the audience can understand what is being *communicated*.

With language (vocabulary and grammar), the author can create illusions of characters by making up speeches for them to recite. These are spoken through the agency of the actors and give the appearance of actual life—they imitate life to some extent.

The speeches are the connection through *character* and *action*. These two elements are in turn woven into a plot which unites the whole. Now, in some dramas the plot is the principal element, while in others the parts (like set design, costume design, or lighting), rather than the whole, draw the attention of the audience. Stories of the latter variety may be termed *episodic*, unless they are completely disconnected, in which case they may be termed as *chaotic*.

Elements of the plot, character, and action work together either in presenting *similarities* between people and events or *differences*. In the first group there are two further categories: parallels and patterns. A parallel is when two characters are faced with similar circumstances that force them to act in a given way. The tension of one may inform upon the crises of the other. There may also be a parallel between some past and present action within a single character. This device is very powerful as it offers greater complexity in the reader's understanding of the nature of the problem concerned as well as creating more *real* characters who can respond with greater depth. A pattern may involve a reoccurrence of a symbol, image, metaphor, epithet, or phrase, or any other small unit that comes to be recognized in connection with something else. Again, the result is a juxtaposition of the symbol's first appearance with all its other appearances, as well as what it may stand for independently, i.e., with its analogue.

Patterns are not directly concerned with characters, but may function with a parallel to create more data from which the reader may apprehend a particular scene. Contrasts, or differences, may operate with characters or the smaller units and denote the complement as with "A or not-A." However, since life isn't a logician's table, there may be a third alternative so that the law of the excluded middle does not hold.

Scenes that try to communicate something must have sufficient complexity to accomplish this task, but not more than is necessary. The human mind can only remember so much data at one time, and art is not merely a puzzle that is only understood *a posteriori* through a careful reconstruction after the whole is known. Certainly, a good work of art bears greater returns to the careful reader, but there must be a significant impact during the process of audience apprehension for the work to be anything more than a mannequin (in the sense of a non-imitative, ersatz endeavor).

On the other hand, simplicity can reduce a problem to such an extent that it no longer interests an active mind. The artist's essential problem is to *show*, and not *tell*. The latter is the proper function of the essay. In order to *show*, the artist must be suggestive through the use of external devices, such as character and action which must be controlled so that the problems that they raise might relate to each other. If this is done effectively, the author can *anticipate* the types of reactions that the patrons will have and control them so that one plays against the other as in a chemical reaction. The author must guess as to the chemical formula and the reaction that will result, but with practice she will devise some reactions that she knows she can control, and so use them to create other reactions. This is not a pure modern chemical reaction, as per the Periodic Table of Elements set out by Dmitri Mendeleev. Rather, it is more akin to alchemy set out by Paracelsus.

All the time, the artist is trying to say the truest things that she can, as she fumbles about mixing things together in an attempt to get at essences. But since nothing can be said directly (as in analytic chemistry and philosophy), the artist is an alchemist seeking after the philosopher's stone—that pure unrestricted expression of meaning: pure, unpolluted, and potent.

The quest, then, is to get it *right* and to make it beautiful. These are not easy tasks. They cannot be willed. Plato said they were *a gift of the gods*. One can *will* competence, but one cannot *will* the pure, unpolluted, and potent. This is the philosopher's stone that turns base metal (the dross of everyday experience) into gold. It is the obsession of every true artist. It is what drives him forward in the quest.

I've felt this urge myself in my own small way for forty years. I think every artist feels it to some degree. Logically, it's nonsense. This is because the project is necessarily restricted by the very medium itself, but still we try; devoting ourselves wholly to that fantastic chimera. We give our lives (for artists must endure the quest). And it is upon that effort that all hope rests.

Exhibits:

What gave great Villers to th'assassin's knife,

And fixed disease on Harley's closing life?
What murder'd Wentworth, and what ex'd Hyde
By kings protected, and to kings ally'd?
What but their wish indulg'd in courts to shine,
And pow'r too great to keep, or to resign?

When first the college rolls receive his name
The young enthusiast quits his ease for fame;
Through all his veins the fever of renown
Spreads from the strong contagion of the gown;
O'er Bodley's dome his future labours spread,
And Bacon's mansion trembles o'er his head.
Are these views? Proceed, illustrious youth,
And virtue guard thee to the throne of Truth!

*****

There mark what ills the scholar's life assail,
Toil, envy, want, the patron, and the jail.
See nations slowly wise, and meanly just,
To buried merit raise the tardy bust.
If dreams yet flatter, once again attend,
Hear Lydiat's life, and Galileo's end.

Samuel Johnson, *The Vanity of Human Wishes,* 11.
129-142, 159-164.

Mr. Solmes came in before we had done tea. My Uncle
Antony presented him to me as a gentlemen he had a
particular friendship for. My Uncle Harlowe in terms
equally favourable for him. My father said, Mr Solmes is
my friend, Clarissa Harlowe. My mother looked at him,
and looked at me, now and then, as he sat near me, I
thought with concern—I at *her,* with eyes appealing for
pity. At *him,* when I could glance at him, with disgust little
short of affrightment. While my brother and sister Mr.
Solmes'd him, and *sirr'd* him up at every word. So
carressed, in short, by all—yet such a wretch! But I will at

present only add my humble thanks and duty to your honoured mother (to whom I will particularly write, to express the grateful sense I have of her goodness to me), and that I am/ your ever obliged/ Cl. Harlowe.

> Samuel Richardson, *Clarissa,* from letter from Harlowe Place, Feb. 20.

Mr. Blifil soon arrived; and Mr. Western soon after withdrawing, left the young couple together. Here a long silence of near a quarter of an hour ensued; for the gentleman who was to begin the conversation and all the unbecoming modesty which consists in bashfulness. He often attempted to speak, and as often suppressed his words just at the very point of utterance. At last out they broke in a torrent if far-fetched and high-strained compliments, which were answered on her side by downcast looks, half bows, and civil monosyllables. Blifil, from his inexperience in the ways of women, and from his conceit of himself, took this behaviour for a modest assent to his courtship; and when, to shorten a scene which she could no longer support, Sophia rose up and left the room, he imputed that too, merely to bashfulness, and comforted himself that he should soon have enough of her company.

He was indeed perfectly well satisfied with his prospect of success; for as to that entire and absolute possession of the heart of his mistress which romantic lovers require, the very idea of it never entered his head. Her fortune and her person were the sole objects of his wishes, of which he made no doubt soon to obtain the absolute property; as Mr. Western's mind was so earnestly bent on the match. . . From these reasons, therefore, Mr. Blifil saw no bar to his success with Sophia. He concluded her behaviour was like that of all other young ladies on a first visit from a lover, and it had indeed entirely answered his expectations.

> Henry Fielding, *Tom Jones,* VI, vii.

Not long after, a young man, who had for some time looked at us with a kind of negligent impertinence, advanced, on tiptoe, towards me; he had a set smile on his face, and his dress was so foppish, that I really believe he even wished to be stared at; and yet he was very ugly.

Bowing almost to the ground, with a sort of swing, and waving his hand with the greatest conceit, after a short and silly pause, he said, "Madam—may I presume?"—and stopt, offering to take my hand. I drew it back, but could scarce forbear laughing. "Allow me Madam," (continued he, affectedly breaking off every half moment) "the honour and happiness—if I am not so unhappy as to address you too late—to have the happiness and honour—"

Again he would have taken my hand, but, bowing my head, I begged to be excused, and turned to Miss Mirvan to conceal my laughter. He then desired to know if I had already engaged myself to some more fortunate man? I said no, and that I believed I should not dance at all. He would keep himself, he told me, disengaged, in hopes I should relent; and then, uttering some ridiculous speches of sorrow and disappointment, though his face still wore the same invariable smile he retreated.

Frances Burney, *Evelina*, letter xi.

—I am half distracted, captain Shandy, said Mrs. Wadman, holding up her cambrick handkerchief to her left eye, as she approach'd the door of my uncle Toby's sentry-box—a mote—or sand—or something—I know not what, has of into this eye of mine—do look into it—it is not in the white—

In saying which Mrs. Wadman edged herself close in beside my uncle Toby, and sqeezing herself down upon the corner of his bench, she gave him an opportunity of doing it without rising up— do look into it—she said.

Honest soul! thou didst look into it with as much innocency of heart, as ever child look'd into a raree-shew-box; and 'twere as much a sin to have hurt thee. —If a man will be peeping of his own accord into things of that nature—I've nothing to say to it—

My uncle Toby never did: and I will answer for him, that he would have sat quietly upon a sopha from June to January, (which, you know, takes in both the hot and cold months) with an eye as fine as the Thracian Rhodope's besides him, without being able to tell, whether it was a black or a blue one.

The difficulty was to get my unc le Toby, to look at one at all,

'Tis surmounted. And I see him yonder with his pipe pendulous in his hand, and the ashes falling out of it—looking—and looking—then rubbing his eyes—and looking again, with twice the good nature that ever Galileo look'd for a spot in the sun.

—In vain! for by all the powers which animate the organ

—Widow Wadman's left eye shines this moment as lucid as her right—there is neither mote, or sand, or dust, or chaff, or speck, or particle of opaque matter floating in it—There is nothing, my dear paternal uncle! but one lambent delicious fire, furtively shooting out from every part of it, in all directions, into thine—If thou lookest, uncle Toby, in search of this mote one moment longer—thou art undone.

Laurence Sterne, *Tristram Shandy, vol. viii, ch, 24.* Work ed.

He took her hand; whether she had not herself made the first motion she could not say—she might, perhaps, have rather offered it—but he took her hand, pressed it, and certainly was on the point of carrying to his lips—when, from some fancy or other, he suddenly let it go. Why he should feel such a scruple, why he should change his mind when it was all but done, she could not perceive. He would have judged better, she thought, if he had not stopped. The intention, however, was indubitable; and whether it was that his manners had in general so little gallantry, or however else it happened, but she thought nothing became him more. It was with him of so simple, yet so dignified a nature. She could not but recall the attempt with great satisfaction. It spoke such perfect amity. He left them immediately afterwards—gone in a moment. He always moved with the alertness of a mind which could neither be undecided nor dilatory, but now he seemed more sudden than usual in his disappearance.

Jane Austen, *Emma*, vol. 3. ch. 9.

The chief trick of the ascetic priest permitted himself for making the human soul resound with heart-rending, ecstatic music of all kinds was, as everyone knows, the exploitation of the *sense of guilt*. Its origin has been briefly suggested in the preceding essay—as a piece of animal psychology, no more: there we encountered the sense of guilt in its raw state, so to speak. It was only in the hands of the priest, that artist in guilt feelings, that it achieved form—oh, what a form! "Sin"—for this is priestly name for the animal's "bad conscience" (cruelty directed backward)—has been the greatest event so far in the history of the sick soul: we possess in it the most dangerous and fateful artifice of religious interpretation. Man, suffering from himself in some way or other but in any case physiologically like an animal shut up in a cage, uncertain why or wherefore, thirsting for reasons—reasons relieve—thirsting, too, for remedies and narcotics, at last takes counsel with one who knows hidden things, too—and behold! He receives a hint, he receives from his sorcerer, the ascetic priest, the *first* hint as to the "cause" of his suffering: he must seek it in *himself,* in some *guilt,* in a piece of the past, he must understand his suffering as a *punishment.*

Nietzsche, *Genealogy of Morals,* tr. Walter Kaufmann, 3rd essay, sect. 20.

With this renewed self-respect and self-dependence, the life of the Negro community is bound to enter a new dynamic phase, the buoyancy from within compensating for whatever pressure there may be of conditions from without. The migrant masses, shifting from countryside to city, hurdle several generations of experience at a leap, but more important, the same thing happens spiritually in the life-attitudes and self-expression of the Young Negro, in his poetry, his art, his education and his new outlook, with additional advantage, of course, of the poise and greater certainty of knowing what it is all about. From this comes the promise and warrant of a new leadership. As one of them [Langston Hughes] has discerningly put it:

We have tomorrow

Bright before us
Like a flame.

Yesterday, a night-gone thing
A sun-down name.

And dawn today
Broad arch above the road we came
We march!

Alain Locke, *The New Negro.* (1925)

Men of the Negro race, let me say to you that a greater future is in store for us; we have no cause to lose hope, to become faint-hearted. We must realize that upon ourselves depends our destiny, our future; we must carve out that future, that destiny, and we who make up the Universal Negro Improvement Association have pledged ourselves that nothing in the world shall stand in our way, nothing in the world shall discourage us, but opposition shall make us work harder, shall bring us closer together so that as one man the millions of us will march on toward that goal that we have set for ourselves. The new Negro shall not be deceived. The new Negro refuses to take advice from anyone who has not felt with him, and suffered with him. We have suffered for three hundred years, therefore, we feel that the time has come when only those who have suffered with us can interpret our feelings and our spirit. It takes the slave to interpret the feelings of the slave; it takes the unfortunate man to interpret the spirt of his unfortunate brother; and so it takes the suffering Negro to interpret the spirit of his comrade. It is strange that so many people are interested in the Negro now, willing to advise him how to act, and what organizations he should join, yet nobody was interested in the Negro to the extendt of not making him a slave for two hundred and fifty years, reducing him to industrial peonage and serfdom after he was freed; it is strange that the same people can be so interested in the Negro now, as to tell him what organizations he should follow and what leader he should support.

Whilst we are bordering on a future of brighter things, we are also at our danger period, when we must either accept the right philosophy, or go down by following deceptive progaganda which has hemmed us in for many centuries.

<blockquote>
Marcus Garvey, " 'Crocodiles' as Friends" in *The Future as I see It* (1923)
</blockquote>

Sagittarius

Ceration

Chapter 1

"In Which the Truth about Certain Matters is Revealed"

It was a bright noon-day sun that greeted the train when it pulled into the station. The light was almost beating down vertically, showing everything without shadows. It was not a warm summer sun but a cooler winter one, though the absence of clouds made the effect all the same, as if it had been a clear day in August. In the sunlight colors have a tendency to wash out slightly as white light—being composed of all the colors—does not take too kindly to a single component color trying to stand out from the community. And so with egalitarian equanimity the sun tries to bring the last errant hues back into the fold of transparent *whiteness*. But people don't usually happily accommodate the intentions of bright light as they try and counter the physical designs of the sun with personal desires of their own that stem from a desire to become individuals that require personalities that have their own distinctive hue. But the sun doesn't cater to this. And so it renders revenge at times like this upon the renegades who seek to break away from soft transparency of the spectrum of colors so thoroughly mixed that each individual is imperceptible from the others except under close examination with a glass. Its method of retribution is by washing everything in a bright intensity designed to lessen the degree of difference between individual colors.

    So it was that when Jefferson got off the train he had to squint some, as the light hurt his eyes and he could not see his home town, but had to cover his eyes to protect himself from the sun's painful rays.

He rented a horse at the stable and rode out to the old Rutherford Place to have a talk with Dorthay.

"Mama's ill right now," said Howard, who didn't like the idea of someone strange coming around to the house when his father was not home. For all the visitors who ever came to the farm were always for his father, and it bothered him that someone would call on his mother, especially when she was so ill.

"I think she'll see me," said Jefferson.

"She isn't supposed to see *anyone*, doctor's orders." The boy lied, but he would do anything to get this intruder (who was a *black* intruder, besides) away from their house and away from his sick mother.

But before Jefferson could reply, Dorthay Dodson appeared in the living room and said, "It's all right Howard, let the man in. He's an old friend of mine."

The boy didn't want to have any part of this and so opened the door and went out as the other man went inside.

"It's been a long time."

"The boy says you're sick."

"I haven't been very well, but it's nothing."

"He said the doctor said it was serious."

"Well you know boys at that age, they have quite an imagination."

"Yes, I know," said Jefferson, sitting down.

Jefferson looked at Dorthay. She didn't look as she used to when he remembered her before her marriage. She had changed, and her face and body bore the marks of long work and not much pleasure. Why had she stayed in that marriage if she was unhappy? But this supposition, of course, was an unfounded value judgment that Jefferson himself recognized immediately.

There was a silence which Jefferson finally broke. "We haven't seen you for quite some time. How are things on this side of the county?"

"Well, you know, we get the sunrise, you get the sunset. I suppose it all amounts to the same."

"I have been in Savanah recently," began Jefferson.

The clock on the wall began signaling the changing of the hour with its chimes.

"I used to love the town. Of course, I haven't been out too much lately. There's so much to do around here that I—well, you know this place doesn't look like much, but really it's quite a handful, believe me."

"You are alone, and have no servants?"

"Oh, it would be silly to have servants for a place as small as this, and yet there is just enough work to keep me quite occupied. Yes, it's surprising how much that I have to do. You'd be surprised."

"I met someone in Savannah, whom we both know," began Jefferson, trying to get back to the topic again, but not knowing exactly where he would press and what he would say. Dorthay, it seemed to him, was rather uneasy at his manner. She sensed, he thought, that he had something to say to her, but wanted to put him off as long as she could.

"You know, I've often talked to George about taking a vacation, but you know he works so hard that he says he can't take a vacation or things will fall apart. I swear, I don't know what it's good for if not for a little time off. What's the use of work if people can't enjoy themselves?"

"Yes, I suppose your husband works very hard," said Jefferson.

"This next weekend I had wanted him to stay here with me, but he has to go to some sort of big conference."

Suddenly Jefferson wondered whether perhaps there was some connection between Dodson and Wyse. They *had* been connected in the same enterprise: the gambling house. Perhaps there were other connections as well. The thought turned his mind away from his purpose momentarily as he said, "You must get very tired of all your husband's affairs."

"Oh, not really. I tell you he doesn't let me in on anything. The only things that I know are from what I hear in between delivering coffee to his friends when they come over."

"You know, one man I met—well didn't actually meet face-to-face, but heard about—was a fellow that you may remember around town named Sigmund Wyse. It seems that he's working out of Savannah now."

Dorthay's expression suddenly changed and she was no longer so jovial as she was before.

"I don't know anything about it," she said. "I try and never meddle in my husband's business." But by her tone, Jefferson could tell that she was not telling him the truth. He wanted to know.

"You know, it's not just idle curiosity that makes me mention his name to you. In fact, it's rather important that I find out something about this man Wyse, if I can, as he may have a considerable bearing upon a very important matter."

"I wish I could help you," said Dorthay, beginning to rise.

"I think you can, especially after I tell you about a visit that I had with a Myra Bakersfield, though you might recognize her better by her maiden name of *Dow*."

As Jefferson's words became sensible to Dorthay, it was as if she was reacting to a series of blows as first her expression changed (Jefferson thought) from one of resigning to rigidity, to surprise, but controlled surprise, to a softening of the features and then a collapsing of the arm that was supporting her intended exit so that she sat down again. She started to speak and then stopped and put her face in her hands momentarily before looking up with a contrived hardness that if nothing else, he thought, was designed to shield her feelings from him. Her silence indicated that she was unwilling to commit herself before he said anything further as she wanted to know just how much Jefferson knew.

"She was working as a cleaning woman, you know, a step down from the farm general store where she had been working at only a few years earlier."

Jefferson didn't know why he gave Dorthay these biographical details, but as he spoke there was a certain bitterness to his voice. Somehow this woman before him, he felt, was somehow to blame, at least in part, for much of the ill fortune that had befallen John, Myra, Samuel Beauchay, and even the very county itself.

This woman sitting before him had brought with her the virus that had infected the moral body of the town and had changed it from—but now that wasn't right either, he told himself, for if it hadn't been Dorthay Beauchay then it would have been another. The time had been ripe, and no single person can do anything at all unless other people and circumstances are willing to support her. The blame couldn't be properly attributed to Dorthay, for those men who readily volunteered hadn't been mere pawns of a power structure that seemed to be in some way strongly influenced by George Dodson, but were agents who as a result of a myriad of factors had become what they were. It would be easy to try and crystalize the source of the problem to one person, but to do so clearly wouldn't do justice to the actuality of what had happened and was happening.

"Yes, just a common cleaning woman, working because she was in a common situation of not having a job in a time when they seem to be getting dearer."

"Times aren't as rosy, I suppose, as they used to be for some people," said Dorthay with a tone of detachment that made Jefferson quite perturbed, so that he didn't even consider whether the words might have been designed to do just exactly that and so cover her previous retreat.

"No they aren't, for *most* people," replied Jefferson, pausing as he didn't wish to allow himself to be diverted from the vague plan of attack that he knew he must execute, though he was not exactly certain what it was. So he sought a direction embedded readily in his conscious sensibility. This was the method that he felt obliged to follow. It seemed to be an approach honest to his intentions and the vague ends that he wished to achieve.

"But that again isn't really to the point of the interesting account that Myra happened to stumble upon when we reminisced about old times. It seemed that there was some kind of story about a monetary natal exchange that took place and caused Myra to have to leave the county for something that she didn't do. She was covering up for someone." Jefferson stopped. He could see by Dorthay's face that she now fully believed that he knew all, if she had doubted any of it before, and in those lines that were set into her forehead and emanated from the corners of her eyes there was a sharpness as the ridges stood out with greater relief that gave her entire expression a cast of anxious waiting.

"Now I needn't tell you who the party was who sought to cover up the fact that she was an unwed mother, do I?"

"What are you after, blackmail?"

"No, not blackmail. I don't want money. My purpose is to find certain information you possess that can help me or not."

"Then why have you come?"

"I've told you already: *for information.*"

"Then you do intend to blackmail me."

"No, whatever I will do with the information that I have, I will do whether you tell me anything or not."

There was a pause as Dorthay opened up a candy dish and took out a peppermint, but didn't put it in her mouth, keeping it in her hand. "So what do you intend to do with your *information*, then?"

"There are two parties that deserve to be told about this: your son and your brother."

"Only two, that's indeed generous of you. And how do you suppose that this precious information will be kept to only those ears, may I ask?" replied Dorthay in a strident voice that portrayed much energy.

"They are honorable people. If there are any mistakes, it would not be done intentionally by them, you can be sure of that."

"No, I'm sure nothing would be done intentionally," said Dorthay, thinking that her brother disliked her enough that he just might take it upon himself to tell several people about it, and certainly she couldn't expect Dow to keep silent about his having at least one parent of respectable birth—why, he might expect some of their, Dodson's, money; a cut of the will that would come out of the pockets of her children. It seemed impossible to her that such a thing could be kept quiet. The secret that she had long since forgotten about would now again surface. There was nothing that she could do about it except try and stop Jefferson.

"The truth must come out," said Jefferson, reacting to Dorthay's animated conversation.

"Yes, at any cost, I suppose. You speak of truth as if it would be some sort of magic cure-all," she said as her voice cracked on the last words and she broke into a fit of coughing.

She was a sick woman and she was expending a lot of energy speaking to this visitor, but she never gave one thought about asking him to leave. She was involved in something more important than her health.

Jefferson offered to get her a glass of water, but Dorthay refused, saying that she would be all right, but she now sensed a weakness in herself. She was combatting with a man who already had the edge, and yet she was not up to capacity. "Do you know," she began again, this time in a strained whisper that still carried the same vitality, if not the volume of her previous speech, "what your so-called truth would cure? Yes, it might cure my children of the good impression that they have of their mother, and do a lot for them as they grow older. It might help my husband and his opinion of me and thereby put new life into our marriage. I'm just sure you know how easily a man likes to forgive and forget such things. Yes, it would do a lot for my life as a whole. I could walk down the streets again a respected woman. Yes, my dear friend, your honesty is really taking into consideration the parties involved. Think of how much I'll benefit from this windfall."

"Yes, but think of what effect it's had on others," said Jefferson, who would have been more lacerating, but Dorthay's obviously failing condition made him go rather gently on his adversary. He wanted to make his point, but he didn't want to totally destroy her in the process.

"Oh yes, I did a terrible thing, didn't I?" said Dorthay as she lifted the clenched hand with the candy in it to her cheek and her body began to tremble slightly. "What did I do, sir? I simply made a woman a proposition," began Dorthay, thinking that Jefferson had been referring to how she had ruined the girl's reputation.

"And she accepted, something I might add she was under no coercion to do. Not from me, not from anybody—she was a free agent in the matter and she chose to take some money and accept the blame. The child got a good home, certainly better than any of my children got here." As she talked, she gestured with the clenched hand as it shook slightly. Her body was in pain, but she had to make her case; there was much at stake.

"You talk about Myra," returned Jefferson, "as if she were the only party involved. Perhaps she is to some extent responsible for accepting your money, though to say that she wasn't coerced is a falsehood. This whole county judged her to be guilty, so that whether she accepted you or not she would have had to bear the brunt of an offense that you committed." Jefferson instantly regretted the choice of the word *offense*, but he wanted so to make his argument plainly to Dorthay and it seemed as if he was outlining it in juristic terms, and so he used the vocabulary of the same—though this didn't excuse but only explain his use of the word to himself.

"All *she* had to do was say 'no,' " replied Dorthay.

"All *you* had to do was tell the truth," replied Jefferson.

Dorthay didn't answer but began coughing again, this time much worse than before so that Jefferson went into the kitchen and got her a glass of water. When she was better, Jefferson cautiously added, "What's perhaps most damaging of all was what happened to John in the process."

"It does no good to talk about such things," she snapped.

"The only reason I mention it is not to chide you or to make you miserable, but your son, John, is now in serious trouble and you can now help him."

"He killed a man, didn't he?" asked Dorthay, who knew perfectly well the case against John.

"He's accused of killing a man, but he's innocent, and I'm going to prove it, but I need your help."

"What can I do? I don't know anything about such things."

Jefferson felt himself preparing to attack this obstinate woman. Despite her sickness, she was being her usual cagy, calculating self that he did not like. Wasn't there anything that could be done to move such a person?

"For starters, you can tell me who Sigmund Wyse is," said Jefferson directly.

"You mentioned that name before and said that you met him in Savannah. If that's so, why don't you ask him?"

"You know that I said I didn't see him face-to-face, but only heard about him, which is why I'm asking you."

"I never meddle in—"

"Mrs. Dodson, a boy's life is at stake, and the boy is your son!"

Dorthay held her clenched hand with her free hand to steady it. Jefferson's presence was starting to wear upon her. She wanted him to go now; the interview would be over. He was now beginning to become unpleasant, and why should she have to abide unpleasantness? She was just about to ask him to leave when the matter of Myra's story loomed again before her eyes. This matter hadn't been resolved. What were they to do? How was she to act?

"I'm sorry about the boy of course—" began Dorthay.

"Not *the* boy but *your* boy, Mrs. Dodson."

"I'm sorry about the boy, but what can I do? I know nothing about these men who you mention; how would I know them?"

"Mrs. Dodson, even you can't be so cold and insensible to your own child. I'm not asking for a lot, I'm only asking for you to tell me who a man is who has probably had a considerable exposure to your house here. I just want to know what Sigmund Wyse does."

Dorthay wasn't at all prepared for this further accusation that Sigmund had been a frequent visitor—meaning that she would have to have known him. The thought of Myra's son getting all of the money that was in her name (her Beauchay money) frightened her. That money would have been her legacy to whom she might have given it as she pleased. How she had protected *that money*, and now things were all becoming confused.

"What makes you think he comes here?" asked Dorthay.

"What does he do?"

"The man of whom you speak, I may say in all candor, does not come here."

"Dorthay."

"No, he doesn't," she repeated as she began to lightly cough.

"Your son's life, an innocent life, is in the balance."

"Mr. Wyse has no connection with my husband."

"Then you admit that you know him."

"Why, how—" began Dorthay, who believed that she must have made some tactical mistake that she, because of her weakened condition, could not control. She must be strong. It was strength that counted as in the end only this element endured. "I admit nothing of the kind. All I know is that my husband doesn't know him," she responded.

"But you just said that he had no connection with your husband in such positive terms that would have required that you knew just who and where he did have connections."

"Of course I've heard the name, just as you have," began Dorthay, trying to reverse directions and take the argument onto another track. "But this man is not at all connected with my husband."

"Who is he connected with?"

"He's not connected with George. I know this to be so. Please don't ask me any more questions. I'm tired, I want to rest."

"But Mrs. Dodson, if you know him and he doesn't come over here, then how do you explain your knowledge of him (as you yourself said you have no understanding of your husband's affairs)?"

"He has no connection with George, George doesn't know him—except through Rod. He has no connection with us at all. None."

Jefferson paused. Of course, Rod—George's brother. Could Sig be the connection between the brothers? No, this seemed too unlikely, especially since they were so relatively close together, if he were indeed in the area. Perhaps they were working together and

Sig was the connection between them as a partnership and someone else, or some other organization. This seemed the most likely explanation.

Dorthay still held her hand tightly. She was very tired. Jefferson's silence she took as a sign that he was retreating and that she had won a victory over him. Even in her weakened condition, she had thwarted the enemy.

Then the screen door opened and in came William, a strong boy of nineteen. His brother had reported to him that there was a visitor and that in the boy's opinion, their mother ought not be seeing visitors at this time of the day in her condition. William had come back to evict the unwelcomed visitor from the premises.

"Mother, are you all right?" asked William.

"Yes, dear, I'm just a little tired. This man here was just about to go, weren't you, Jefferson?"

"Yes, I'll go," replied Jefferson.

"Has he cause you any trouble, Mother?"

Dorthay paused, but it wasn't clear to William if she was pausing for a purpose or just because she had difficulty in forming a reply. "No, Son, he's fine."

"In that case, your horse is ready," said William to Jefferson. Jefferson got up to go and started for the door.

"Jefferson?" began Dorthay. "What about Myra's story?"

Jefferson turned around. "I told you what I was going to do."

"But is there no other way?"

"Yes," he replied. "If you did it first. I'd prefer that."

Dorthay didn't respond but sunk back into the sofa where she was sitting as the two men disappeared into the bright sunlight and she quickly fell asleep, drooping her head and relaxing her hand so that the fingers straightened, revealing the partially melted peppermint candy still sticking to her skin.

Chapter 2

"Concerning Various Matters"

The next stop for Jefferson was the Vanderkamp Estate, where he hoped to find Julia. As it turned out, she was at home and quite alone as the two sat on the front porch.

"And so I'm to go to Atlanta tomorrow. It is fortunate that you happened to come today and not tomorrow, for then I'd have been gone."

Jefferson listened to the account of John's telegram and the rendezvous that the two were to make and Julia's plans to stay with her aunt outside of Atlanta.

"Would you like to come along and see him? I'm sure that he would like to see you."

"I'd like to come, but I can't really. You see, I've gotten some important leads in the case."

"Case?"

"To try and fine Victor's real murderer," clarified Jefferson.

"That's wonderful," she replied. "John will be very anxious to hear that, I'm sure."

"Well, don't get his hopes up too high. I'm not sure that I have anything as of yet, but I'm getting into the mud and my hands are getting dirty, as the metaphor might go."

Julia was truly excited. Now there would be good news to give John when she saw him. His freedom was possibly close at hand. All of a sudden she felt as if a large burden had been lifted from her spirit. There was more reason to hope because she was that much closer to being permanently united with her love. How she had been living in a world of shadows, formless hopes that had no grounds. It had been a world where she longed for a particular future event, knowing all the time in her rational self that it could never be. And yet, even as she realized that it was impossible, the charm that this vision held became greater. It meant she wanted it all the more. In the center of the vision, she sensed that she was the tragic heroine that was fated to lose her love to forces beyond her control and that she would be obliged to yield to her fate.

But this news brought a change to all of this; now there was a good cause for her to be hopeful. No longer was her dream impossible—improbable perhaps, but she had faith in the capability of Jefferson and she knew that if anyone could make the situation turn out right, it was him. This man who seemed so wise to her was about to unravel the mystery that was preventing two people in love from uniting their lives in marriage (for so Julia was fully confident that John and she would be married if only John were free). Her mother had told her that she, Julia, should not give her heart to a man with no money and no job. Since Victor's death her mother had added: he's a criminal and he's rather *dark*, isn't he?

Julia couldn't respond to her mother, but silently told herself that she had to remain true to John no matter what happened, as only in such devotion would she ever find any happiness. Then Julia looked up again to Jefferson and smiled.

"You may tell him as well that I have some other important revelations to make to him that I'm sure will bring him some calm. I can't say anything more about it now, but he may know what I mean," said Jefferson.

Julia didn't stop to try and figure out what Jefferson meant by these words as they didn't bear directly on either the murder or her future with John (two thoughts that were predominant in her mind at the moment), though she did make a mental note of what had been said to her and she wouldn't forget. It was just that now she was enraptured by her vision that had some more concreteness to it where before it had been more longing and less fact.

Since her brother had left for college, Julia had been increasingly lonely at the farm. Many of her friends had gone too: either having gotten married or having left to try their luck in some larger place than Varner's Junction. There didn't seem to be the same kind of loyalty to the family that she believed existed in previous generations. Everyone, it seemed, was moving to make their fortune in a big city somewhere. What was wrong with Bella

County? Why couldn't people who grew up continue to live there until their natural death?

What made it necessary to try and spread one's wings and go somewhere else to see if things were any better? None of this made any sense to Julia, who wanted nothing more than to settle down in the county somewhere and carry on the life as it had been for generations. It seemed to be the natural order of things to settle down where one grew up, and highly unnatural to want to explore other areas of the country. Weren't all towns just like Varner's Junction, except that they had their own peculiarities? Wouldn't it take a person the same length of time to become used to different customs and traditions that it took them in their native soil? What was the purpose of leaving when the result would be just to become *established* somewhere else? This seemed like a great amount of wasted effort. Besides, there was something very basic about Bella County that made the very thought of moving to be unsettling. For in this county she had grown up, and had so many associations with certain pieces of ground and trees, the sounds of a private place in each of the seasons—all of these contributed to her being able to feel secure and at *home*. Her farm was located within the boundaries of this humble stretch of ground which, many years before, the first Vanderkamps had fought and scratched to establish the community.

There even seemed to be a collective sense of the consciousness of those first settlers that Julia could feel at times when she was alone on the land. It was a sense that she was sure she would lose if she ever went anywhere else.

"Well, I guess I'll be going," said Jefferson.

"I'll tell John everything that you've said," replied Julia.

"If you can set up another meeting, that would be a good idea, I think," added Jefferson as he mounted his horse and left.

Chapter 3

"The Rendezvous"

The next morning was a hectic one for Julia. She had found that she was slightly overburdened with things. She would only be spending a few weeks with her aunt, but it seemed to her that she had enough obligations to last her until next June. Though when she had packed with her mother, it had seemed that they had not put anything but what was essential into her cases, and that all would be kept to a bare minimum. It wasn't until she began loading the luggage that she realized the relativeness of the phrase 'bare minimum.'

Her father drove them to the station and stayed with her until the train came. Julia had had her bags tagged so that she wouldn't have to carry them once she got to the depot. There were the good-byes, which seemed overly emotional to Julia when she looked back to them once she was on the train. After all, she would only be going for a few weeks, not a lifetime; why all the ceremony? But even with these thoughts, there was a certain sadness as she passed out of the county while the mighty iron horse pressed onward to Atlanta and her John.

John was staying at a small hotel not very far away from the station. He had discretely gone and taken a train schedule so that he would be certain of when the train would be arriving. One thought worried John: What if she was being accompanied by someone else—her father or brother or someone like that? What could John do then? He knew that this would have to be the time, but if such a situation arrived, what would John be able to do? He couldn't very well go up to Julia with her father there, so what type of precautions could he take to safe-guard against such an eventuality?

He went to the station several times to try and figure out the layout. It was a rather ordinary one that was primarily enclosed, which didn't allow for easy escape or hiding. The platform at which the train from Varner's Junction would arrive was number two and it was out in the open so that he would have to be a long ways away in order to not be seen, unless there were a crowd that would conceal his movements sufficiently. As to exits, there was one large one directly adjacent and a long ramp that he didn't know where it lead, though it was marked "private" and he imagined that it might be some sort of loading dock for freight to be transferred to trucks.

What would he say to Julia? His thoughts were too confused as he went over many imaginary scenarios in his mind. He wanted to tell her about what he had done and all the things that he had seen. Somehow he had a desire to show Julia every place that he had been so that she could understand what had happened to him. John knew that his story was impossible to tell in only a few minutes.

What worried him was the prospect that he might not be able to say anything.

***

The local authorities handled the telegram of Varner Junction's sheriff with a calmness that bespoke of their routine attitude towards criminals of the more serious variety. They had come up against many unsavory types each month, so the case of John Dow would be just another of the standard jobs that a policeman was required to perform seven days a week.

Several days before the arrival, a patrol car and advance crew came to the terminal and checked out the area where the train would arrive. The supervisor decided that they would need five men (they never liked to use more than they had to) who would be stationed at strategic points around the platform and in the areas that led to the exits.

It was a task that they had performed many times before, and there was no question in their minds that they were more than capable of performing this rather simple task of apprehending the criminal. The last part of the message about not harming the girl was almost insulting. After all, they were Southerners and Atlanta's finest.

On the train, Julia was doing a little sewing that she had brought with her to pass the time, but often she would stop and think about what was about to happen. She would see her lover!

She didn't want to allow herself to become too excited as she knew that if she did, she wouldn't be able to stand it. She decided that it was better to try and suppress any thoughts about how she would react to him, but still she wondered whether she would throw her arms around him or simply shake his hand, or perhaps they would walk to some secret place where they might not be noticed.

Julia had carefully arranged to take a cab from the station to her aunt's house so that she wouldn't be met by her aunt at the station and thus ruin any chance she might have at seeing John. What a terrible calamity that would be!

Had John changed since she last saw him? Of course, he would have to have changed some. A person doesn't live several months in such circumstances without changing somewhat, but what she was anxious about was whether she would still feel the same way about him now. Was he the same man she had fallen in love with?

She tried to suppress these thoughts, but they were consistently present no matter what she tried to do to the contrary.

***

John had bought some new clothes as his old ones were in very bad condition. He also bought a hat that he hoped would help conceal his face some in the event of a freak recognition. He was seated inside the terminal on one of the long wooden benches provided for people waiting for arrivals. He was reading a newspaper and was in position to see the train—though he was a long way away, he would still be able to tell when it had arrived. Then he planned to walk carefully to meet the train where, in the crowd, he might be able to become lost if necessary.

Around the platform, five police in plain clothes were awaiting the arrival. All five of them were wearing light brown rain coats that fit loosely so that they could conceal their guns underneath. They were at perfect angles so that if John stepped onto the platform, he would have no chance to surrender. They planned to kill him on the spot (easier for everyone involved).

The unit of officers was relaxed, as it was the sixth such assignment they had had that week. They had been successful in four of the five previous cases. Their percentage was always very high. Each man in the group was an excellent shot and could hit a threat in a crowd without too much difficulty, though such tactics were discouraged by the force. Still, the special squad from which these men had been chosen was responsible for keeping serious crime *under control.* They took it as their personal responsibility that the criminal be taken no matter what the cost. If crime was to be managed, they felt, the police had to be just as ruthless as the criminal, otherwise there would be no question as to who would eventually come out on top.

***

The city of Atlanta was in view. Julia had never seen the city, but she deduced that it must be Atlanta by its size and the fact that the train was slowing slightly. What a city, she mused—so big and exciting. All her thoughts about Bella County instantly disappeared as she was captured by the magnitude of the metropolis. *How can all of this be one spot?* Her mind raced at all the things that might be located within such a place as this.

She had had ideas of what Atlanta might be like, but none of them matched the actuality of the real thing. It was stunning, she thought, as she put away her needlework and fixed her eyes to the window to try and take in all of the city. John was living somewhere in this big place. *I wonder what type of room he lives in*, she thought. *And whether he has a job? What he does he do for entertainment?* The train was slowing down even more, but Julia didn't perceive it as her eyes were glued to the city.

In the station, John sat. According to the clock the train was due to arrive, but there had been no call announcing it, and nothing on the arrival board. John waited impatiently. What if something had gone wrong? John's eyes began scanning the area around him for an exit. He spotted a bar that was also a little restaurant that might suit him very well if things got out of control.

The men on the platform one-by-one put their hands inside their coat pockets, checking their guns and releasing the safeties. They were becoming a little impatient that the train was late and began wondering what might be the matter.

John felt the urge to go to the lavatory and got up, leaving his newspaper on the seat.

The men in the raincoats began searching the terminal with their eyes to see if they could spot John, but he was not there. One man was sent to make another check. They had already made several checks, but John had arrived late enough to avoid all but one, and he had not been spotted because of the new clothes and newspaper.

"He's not there," said the man, returning.

Then a voice announced that the train was arriving but that the platform had been changed to number ten.

John heard the announcement and hurried out, only to see a group of men all dressed in tan raincoats rushing over to the same platform ten where he was headed.

One of the men spotted John and instantly recognized him, and he took out his pistol and fired a shot as John ducked back into the lavatory. The man tried to signal to his comrades, but they were already to platform ten.

The train was unloading and another of the group thought that *he* spotted John descending from the train. The man spotted was actually an insurance salesman standing in front of Julia and helping her to step down from the car. There was another shot, and the insurance man fell to the ground, wounded in the shoulder.

Meanwhile, John was back in the lavatory. He locked a stall door and opened a window to crawl out. The man who had shot at John, seeing that his comrades were not at hand, decided to take Dow himself and rushed into the lavatory.

Bursting through the door, the policeman said to the attendant, who also shined shoes and was at the moment involved with putting some of his things in order, "Did you just see a man come in here?"

The attendant was slightly caught off-guard by such a question as he didn't usually keep track of everyone who entered or exited, unless, of course, they decided to have their shoes shined. But even then, he would have been better at giving a description of the shoes that the man was wearing than of any clear description of anything else. The attendant turned around slowly to answer concerning the arrival of a man into the men's room. He paused. He wanted to know who this man with a gun was and what was behind the question. (The policeman, after all, was not in uniform.)

Because of the high cost of an error, the shoeblack pursed his lips and scratched his head. This was not going to work for the policeman, who was in a hurry. The policeman had a full appreciation of the importance of each second in the chase, and so he simply rushed to each stall, kicking it open, much to the chagrin of some of the occupants, who began to vocalize their complaints in an uproar that covered the sound of John, who was by this time out the window and onto the ground outside, running for his life.

Finally, the policeman made his way to the open windows to see if John had gotten out that way. He found the right one and saw John in the distance, running. He would have one shot. It had to be accurate.

Just then, John ran into the street and a bus passed between the officer's aim and his target. When the bus had passed, John was gone.

In the station, there was equal pandemonium as the police were trying to keep the people back away from the wounded man, who the police still believed to be John Dow.

"What have you done?" cried Julia.

"Don't worry, ma'am, we're the police. This man's name is John Dow, and he's a desperate murderer."

Another man with a big belly was shouting to the crowd, "Stand back, we're the police, stand away."

"Say, Clem?" said one officer, who was kneeling over the body of the man on the ground, twisting his head back to his fellow officer.

"Now, now, Hubert," said Clem, the leader of the squad, as he repeated his words of comfort to the crowd so that panic would not break out: "Don't worry, ladies and gentlemen, we are the police and we have this matter well under control."

"Clem!" repeated Hubert, anxious to tell his chief that the man on the ground had identification to prove that he wasn't John Dow. He also had a satchel of insurance papers that a hardened criminal wouldn't be carrying.

Meanwhile, Julia was trying to persuade the policeman that this man was no murderer, but simply a man who was trying to help her. "Sorry, ma'am, we know all about it."

"Know about what?"

"This man's planned meeting with you."

"But this man rode in the same train as I did. Search him, he must have some identification. You've shot the wrong man."

These last words of Julia didn't reach Clem's ears, but they did reach those of some people in the crowd who quickly circulated —*did you hear that that man isn't the criminal—how did you find that out—*

"Stand back everybody," shouted Clem.

— I heard that young Lady talking to the cop over there—you say that lady is a cop—yes and that man they shot is really a companion of hers, they shot the wrong man by mistake—

"This is all a dreadful mistake, Officer," repeated Julia, as the Clem turned around to ask Hubert if the man had any identification. *—the man shot was a federal marshal who was just about to capture a high ranking mobster when these fumble heads came in and shot the wrong man—stupid police, you have the wrong man!*

"Quiet everybody," shouted Clem as the crowd was beginning to get unruly.

"Help me," gasped the man on the ground, who in all the confusion about his identification and papers was now lying with his head on the pavement, bleeding. Julia rushed to him and lifted his head and put it on her jacket, then took out her handkerchief and, like a skilled nurse, applied pressure to the wound to stop the bleeding.

—you see that marshal was on an important mission and these police were supposed to be back-up only, but they wanted to get into the act—that girl is his co-worker—I think I read about her in the newspaper somewhere—she's his mistress and now look at her, she's trying to save his life.

"Will somebody call a doctor!" cried Julia.

"Clem?" said Hubert as he showed the man's information to the other officers in succession, but could not get Clem's attention as the other was intent on crowd control (which was becoming increasingly more difficult as people from the terminal were flocking to the spot to see what was the commotion). Word was even reaching the street, as some people were coming in to see a high-ranking mobster lying on the cement.

—where is he—you can't see him, he's on the ground—is it true that they shot the kingfisher?—the Kingfish?—you know Governor Long—I know who the Kingfish is, but you've got it all wrong, that's a top gangster from Chicago there, he was here to make a big sale of booze—

"Will somebody get a doctor, this man's dying!" screamed Julia as she grabbed a hold of the pant leg of one of the officers.

The officer turned around, not knowing quite what to do, except that it wasn't supposed to be happening like this.

"This man needs a doctor," cried Julia.

The message quickly sunk in, and one of the officers tried to make his way through the crowd. They couldn't let the man die; losing John Dow was bad enough, but all of this was awful.

"Will everybody please stand back?" yelled Clem.

"Clem, goddamnit, turn around."

Clem, hearing these profane words, turned angrily around to assess an official reprimand about the danger of police using vulgar and profane language and how they were to be the examples to children, who would be the leaders of tomorrow, when he saw instead a card which was thrust into his face. Taking the card, he quickly read a name that meant nothing to him.

"What did you give me this for? Hubert, you know what to do with lost identification. You turn it into the lost and found. Do I have to tell you everything? And another thing—" he was going to add about the foul language, when Hubert interrupted him, an offense that was far more serious than the language.

"This is the identification of him—that man," he said, pointing to the man on the ground.

Clem looked at the man being held by Julia. Why would she be so tender to a man she didn't know? Didn't the report say that the two were close friends and that she might give them some trouble? He was about to further remonstrate Hubert when the other added, "He's got a briefcase full of insurance papers, too. This man's an insurance salesman."

What was Hubert saying? The man perfectly fit the description that they had gotten of Dow, and now this underling was trying to tell him that they had made a mistake and shot the wrong man?

"Hubert, you're under suspension," barked Clem.

"But Clem," protested Hubert, but it was too late as his chief was back to crowd control.

Soon a doctor came along with more police, and a ranking member of the department. After they fought their way through the crowd, the ranking official snapped, "What's the idea of all this?"

"We're just doing our duty, sir. This crowd isn't my fault."

"It certainly is, mister. People love to gather around and see a policeman make an ass of himself. It's just the kind of thing that they like to put in the papers so that people don't have bad consciences the next time a municipal bond issue fails and we take a cut in salary."

"But sir—"

"What business did you have shooting before you knew for certain that you had the right man?"

"I thought he was going to take the girl as hostage and use her for protection. I saw it with my own eyes."

"Balls, man! This fellow's an insurance salesman. What would he want to take anyone hostage for?"

It then struck Clem that there may have been an error, though he hardly knew how he was to blame for it. After all, he was only discharging his duty as he saw fit.

"This could go very hard on you, son," said the other again.

Clem turned around and saw Hubert's face conveying a pleading look that said "I tried to tell you." Clem looked at the man on the ground being attended to by the doctor. He had been so sure.

The crowd and the noise began to push closer. Their man had gotten away.

Chapter 4

"A Few Matters in Passing"

I never thought t'was possible," said Ike.

"Me neither. Mitchell's been there for such a long time," said Ed.

"He said that his property was heavily mortgaged and that an old man like him couldn't continue to keep making payments on it so that it was either sell or be foreclosed," put in Jake.

"But you think they'd really go and foreclose? Maybe threats, but I'se never heard," Ike began as he pulled up a place near his friends as they were dealing rummy and it was the only game that Ike knew.

"Thar is no mere threats with George running the show. He wants something; he goes and gets it," declared Jake.

"I think he's still smartin' from that Beauchay deal, and now he wants to make it up."

"What do ya reckon he'll do with it? Farm it?" asked Ed.

"George doesn't know a plow from a mule," replied Jake.

"Then why da ya suppose he wants it?" asked Ike, who was the last to sort out his hand, as he was a very slow card player.

"Thars no telling with that 'un, thars no telling," said Jake with a kind of respect to his voice, not at all for Dodson, thought Ed and Ike, but for the craft by which the man operated, keeping them off guard so that they didn't know what would come next.

They started playing the hand again. It began with Ike, who had been the loser, as he said, "I'll sure be sorry to see Mitchell go."

"He may fist move into town. With the money he got from the place, he could live right comfortable for a time."

"He'd be closer to the church," added Ed, trying to make it seem like there was good that would be coming out of the transaction, but none of them, including Ed, really thought that there was anything good about one of the oldest places in the county being sold.

***

So they knew about it all along, thought Julia as she rode the taxi to her aunt's.

Now she wouldn't see John, and had inadvertently put him into danger. Had they just been following her? Or was it due to some mix-up that they only happened to mistake the insurance man for John? She thought that it could have easily been Dow lying on the pavement, bleeding before her. What would she have felt like then, with his life in her hands?

She wondered again whether she had been followed, and if there was anything that she could have done to have made things turn out better? How did they find out? How much did the authorities know? Did they know that John was supposed to meet her on the platform, or was it simply a case of tailing her until she led them to John?

In the first instance, there would have been nothing she could have done, she thought, but if it was the second, then perhaps she was to blame. Everything seemed ruined when just hours before it had seemed as if nothing could stand in the way of her happiness. How she had looked forward to this day as a time of happiness, and instead it was something else.

When she arrived at her aunt's, she was greeted with a loving hug and kiss on the cheek. Julia, though she was in very poor spirits, reciprocated as best she could, noticing that her aunt suffered badly from halitosis.

"Well darling, tell me about your trip. Was it pleasant?"

"Yes, quite pleasant," she replied, not wishing to tell her aunt about what had happened at the train station. If the time came when the incident had to be related, then so be it. But until then, she would keep her peace by avoiding the complicated questions that would inevitably result from such a disclosure.

Life at Aunt Margaret's was like an excursion into the world of people's sordid affairs, past and present. Having nothing better to occupy her time, Aunt Margaret would keep up on what everyone worth knowing was doing with their private lives in the way of lurid, salacious episodes. She would collect such stories and put them on display whenever guests came over.

Margaret carefully selected the news she thought to be appropriate for the guest involved. The purpose of this personalization of the gossip was to stimulate a further donation on the part of the guest to her collection: stories bred more stories. But as Julia had no such stories to tell her aunt, nor would have wanted to, her aunt showered her with expensive tales of the highest value, designed to elicit admiration from the young visitor, whom she fondly referred to as her *charge*.

"You see, Victor Stuart's wife, I mean Victor Stuart Sr., was Kathryn Vanderkamp, who you may have heard of as Kathy Smith as she was the daughter (covertly of course) of old Richard Vanderkamp and Margaret Rutherford. But since they couldn't keep the infant, Richard consented to take the child and bring it up as a Vanderkamp, and his wife, Jo Anna, who was six months pregnant herself when she married Richard, was hardly in a position to argue. But you know that Richard was quite a rogue. It was said of him that he had been in almost half the beds in the county! Isn't that awful? I know that I probably shouldn't be telling such things to a girl so young and innocent as you, Julia, but you know, sometimes a girl has to learn the ways of the world, doesn't she?" The old woman put on her glasses, which she wore on a chain around her neck, to look at her charge to see if she was as offended as she hoped.

Julia did not disappoint her aunt (though she had no conscious thought of doing anything to please anyone, and only listened to her aunt because it would be impolite to leave her in the middle of a story, but she did wish to display her displeasure, as she didn't like hearing things about other people behind their backs) and so she fidgeted and gave every appearance of wishing the story to be finished and the conversation to change course. But this, of course, is precisely what the aunt had wanted, and so seeing that the desired reaction was occurring, she continued with more fervor than ever.

"I only mention this because you know it is said that the offspring of such marriages are often like their parents in certain respects, and I only wanted to lessen the blame to Kathy Smith somewhat, even though some folks said she was forced unduly by Lucius Smith, whose own history is interesting as well, but then we won't go into that, will we. I mean, hardly a soul knows anything about any of this, and I often talk about it as if it were common knowledge."

"But Aunt Margaret, I believe that Mr. Stuart's parents were Rudolph Stuart and Margret Rutherford. It was a very prestigious match for its day, was it not?"

"Yes, or so people say. Who am I to dispute such a thing? Or to say that Sally Lou Thompson's parents weren't Kathryn Vanderkamp and Herald Thompson—at least I feel half justified in upholding that story, but you are quite right in keep up the appearance of things. Yes, quite right. But sometimes there is more to things than what simply appears to be the case."

"Life is very complicated," replied Julia, not quite knowing how to respond to her aunt, who seemed determined to get some kind of reaction from Julia, which she did not wish to give.

Aunt Margaret smiled at her charge and rang for tea.

Chapter 5

"Gaining the Point and Losing the Land"

The five men walked in and sat at the table in front of the room that was filled with tired people. This would be the last committee report of the session, and everyone was tired and anxious to get the whole thing over with. This attitude, Samuel Beauchay hoped, would be to his advantage as perhaps his proposal might be approved quickly, without discussion.

As the chairman handed his report to the speaker for his observation, Samuel thought about how many times he had tried to get his proposals through the committee and how each time he had failed. Once, he had gotten an open discussion on the committee's action and had been voted down on his proposal to force the committee to submit the proposition for a vote.

This time he was sure that they had approved his ideas—and why not? Were not the times proving him to have been right in his prediction of price levels? The prices during most of the twenties had been so solid that the growers hated to meddle with a good thing and tamper with the profits, even though Beauchay had predicted that this condition wouldn't last forever. *We've got to protect a fair price for our goods*, he had always said. *When the bottom of the market falls, we'll be in a sorry state unless we have protections, and the only way these are to be procured is through collective action.*

Now his predictions were coming to pass. Prices had dropped quickly, and it didn't look as if they were rising, at least not for a while. Everything seemed to be slowing down, and they would probably have a couple of bad years as the country tightened its belt a bit. These cycles always came about and when they did, there would be two or three bad years and then the boom would start over again. The problem was that there was a large number of farmers who operated on a marginal rate of return, and a couple of bad years might be just enough to bankrupt them. All this tragedy could be alleviated if only the board would take some action.

"Gentlemen," began the clerk, "it is the opinion of this board that resolution 2391 is basically a sound proposal and should be adopted by the council and the assembly with the following emendations and revisions: First clause four Section A should read, 'and this body will work within the given framework at the discretion of the Board of Governors.' Then the Third clause Section A should read 'this body, which will consist of a committee of three who will make recommendations for action to the Board of Governors, who will, in turn, send out notices to all members recommending that they only sell their products within the guidelines established as fair by the select board, but will be under no obligatory compulsion to do so, though it is understood that breeches of this agreement will make it harder for their comrades to get their desired price.'

"Section B should read, 'this board of governors will invite other southern associations to join with us in establishing regional prices to better compete with regional wholesalers who currently control the market.'

"Sections C and D have been omitted."

Then the report was handed back to the chairman who asked if anyone cared to make an affirmative or negative speech, of which there were two short speeches both for and against, after which the question was called and the vote overwhelmingly in favor.

As the meeting broke up, several men approached Beauchay: "Well, old boy, you finally got your proposal through."

"Yes," said Beauchay with a sigh.

"What's the matter, old boy? You talk as if you were defeated."

"I was. That wasn't my proposal. What they passed is worthless. It will do nothing. There are no enforcement clauses, nor the unified body provisions, and all they want to do is ask other states to join us. But how do they expect anyone to join something as loosely structured as that?"

"Got to keep government close to the people, old boy, you know that. That's what the Democratic Party's all about."

"It'll never work," replied Beauchay. "I wish it had died in committee like the others. This is worse than nothing."

"Oh, don't be so gloomy. You're just piqued because they didn't keep what you had proposed word-for-word. Every proposal gets changed a little in committee."

"I suppose so," replied Samuel softly.

"Are you coming to the bar for the Georgia Toast?"

"I don't know. I suppose so," Beauchay replied.

"Well, I've got to get there in a hurry. I'm in charge of a presentation, you know."

Samuel shuffled along slowly by himself. What they *had* done was to effectively silence him by passing a very weak version of his bill. In the bill that was passed, there was only a voluntary effort called for by each individual farmer, which would result in the same situation that existed at present. There would be no real change.

Samuel had envisioned a board that would have the collective resources of all the farmers in the state, and that they would be able to get a better price because they would be selling large bulks of goods instead of small personal, or Grange, supplies. The small producer and medium producer alike are presently at the mercy of the large buyers, who were organized. His proposal would create a large supply entity that could demand a fair price as far as they were concerned.

Currently the small and medium sized farms were operating near a loss as it was. If several of the states had grouped together as he had planned, then they could have established a floor price and farmers would always know how much to plant, depending on how close they thought the price they would get for their crops would be to the floor (which itself would be guaranteed and would not be subject to falling as commodity prices had been doing lately).

This vision would never be. His expected success was now a failure. He had fought for the proposal with vigor, he thought. But then, he told himself, perhaps he could have been more forceful than he had been. A person has to maneuver for things he wants to be done.

It was a simple fact, but he had never made time for such lobbying for his legislation. Not that he had never thought of doing such, but it seemed that each time he really thought he might so embark, something sidetracked him from his purpose. He would be called to another emergency that required his immediate attention.

So then why was he lamenting his losses? If he had applied himself properly, then he would have gotten his legislation passed. All this he had known, but he had spent much wasted time deluding himself into thinking that all he needed to do was draft a coherent bill, and that it would be judged by its merits. No amount of speeches in the convention ever helped either, because by that time everyone had made up their minds. What he should have done was taken his case to the members during the year and make his case and try and draw support in that way. But it had all seemed so plain that he need merely write a good resolution and argue it well. Why should it make any difference if he had campaigned for it or not? Was the bill not the same bill no matter what he did?

He stumbled down the hall, his hands in his pockets. He was alone now, and trying to fight off the conclusion that was forcing itself upon him—namely that people aren't rational, or rarely are, and that the majority of people are governed by something else, though whatever it was he was afraid to speculate.

He had failed because he had looked at the problem idealistically and not politically. If he had been more sensible, he would have taken his case to the farmers and estate owners alike and won support, as he would have appealed to whatever instinct it was that persuaded people to do something. But even as he decided that his course would have been another, he felt at the same moment that he had not been so bad for expecting others to judge his proposal by its merits. It's not a question of being wrong. *I wasn't wrong to expect that, but merely naïve. I may have been theoretically correct, but that has gotten me nowhere.* What is required to attain any goal worth reaching is a single mindedness that pushes aside all other problems and crises and only concentrates upon itself and it alone. A man cannot spread himself too thinly over several projects, or they will all result in failures.

Failures are fine for those who have no dreams, but for those who feel the inspiration of *possibility* beckoning them through the haze of everyday existence, they become intolerable. One learns to associate his own worth as a person with the success or failure of those endeavors. There are no excuses or explanations for such defeats. They are clearly not only defeats of proposals and hopes, but also defeats for the *self*; that which comprises identity, and leaves it battered and less than before.

As Samuel slowly walked down the long flight of stairs, a friend of his approached, bubbling with excitement as apparently they had already opened the booze and, upon seeing the form of his acquaintance (Beauchay), he raised his glass and declared in a loud voice, "There he is. There's our man who finally won! Yes, he's a jolly good fellow, he's a jolly good fellow, he's a jolly good fellow," began his friend in a broken bass voice, "which nobody can deny."

Chapter 6

"Containing a Few Letters"

Dear Julia,
    I know that I haven't written you since you left, and I received your letter the other day and was happy to hear from you, but rather disappointed that you aren't enjoying yourself as much as you thought you might. However, I cannot accept your plan about returning early, as things around here have made that impossible. I don't know where to begin, but to tell you right away that there have been some financial problems with the Estate and that it has been purchased by an unknown company who wishes me to leave within the month. As we haven't planted any new crops yet, we don't lose any money that way, but of course this is still quite a blow to us.
    How could I have done such a thing, you might ask? And to that I can only say that I didn't do it on purpose. I have been forced by the law to give up the land that has been in our family for such a long time. The story began when some of the members of the casino board were approached by a Mr. Johnston who told us about certain real estate investment companies that were springing up all over the South. The way he described it, the deal seemed to be fool-proof. We were all to invest a certain amount of money in the company and then the company would buy some land and sit

on it—waiting for it to mature. Well, we bought two pieces of land—the first was supposed to have mineral rights that fizzled out. The other was prime industrial land. Unfortunately, we bit off more than we could chew and the long and short of it is that we had to put more and more money down to keep our loan with the bank until it got to the point that with the money and business problems at present they wanted some security against the investment. So a few of us agreed to underwrite the loan with our property, thinking that it could never come to pass that we would ever be called upon to actually have to part with our property.

We had been given assurances of this by Mr. Johnston, but then the bank failed and its assets were purchased, which included this note on the loan, so that it was necessary to foreclose in the bankruptcy proceedings. Some company bought the deed to my land and Oscar Whren's property, and informed us that we had only thirty days to vacate the premises. Of course, I've been to our lawyer and he tells me that there isn't anything I can do, as I had been stupid to underwrite the property in the way that I did—I suppose that I was. I can't get over the fact that my life as a farmer will no longer be. How can we actually move away from the place in which we've spent so many happy occasions? It seems incomprehensible to me. At any rate, I'm writing Rodney and telling him that we are moving out of town. I couldn't bear to live in the county when I knew someone else was living on our land. I suggested to him that he change schools to Georgia, where we could all live close together. It would be cheaper and give your mother and I moral support, which we both need very badly at the present.

It is for this reason that I think that it would be a good idea for you to stay another couple of weeks with your aunt while we get some things sorted out here, and then you may return and help gather your things. I don't know how such events are allowed to happen. The paper that I signed I should have cleared with my attorney. I didn't understand some of the strongly worded irregular clauses at the time I signed, and perhaps there might be some hope for us to

regain possession on this ground? At any rate, all my love, and have pity on your foolish father who has made such a mess of things.
Papa

And on the same day, in the afternoon was the following letter.

Dear Julia,
Your father has written you concerning the robbery of our land by these crooked scalawags that are trying to steal a Southerner's estate. Some big company, I bet, who wants to bully their way into a few dollars at the expense of honest people. I don't know how or why your father signed some papers, but I still don't think they can just come and throw us off our land! After all, this is land that was handed down, and can't just be discarded at the whim of some businessmen. Was it our fault that a bank failed? Why should honest gentlemen have to suffer for the inadequacy of some incompetent half-wits in the bank? I don't know what we are to do. I just get flustered and headaches when I consider that we have to leave this lovely land that we've always called our home—isn't there some law or something that can protect us? Your father has been to see the local lawyer, but I say that he should go to Atlanta, but he will have none of it. I suggest that you tell your aunt and see if she'll let you see some Atlanta lawyer. I know that big city lawyers are slicker at handling things like this. Though we don't have very much money, we still could afford to pay something to retain our land. It's really important—please do what you can. I'm counting on you.
Love,
Mother

Losing the land, moving from Bella County? How could any of this be possible? Julia still hadn't gotten over the incident at the rail terminal and was fearful that any day the police would come knocking at the door in order to question her. But there was never a knock, only silence, which in a way was worse, as the anticipation of the event was far worse than the actual event could ever possibly be. How could they lose the land? A bank failed, and there was something to do with some paper that her father had signed. But these alone weren't sufficient to force a person to move, were they? What authority could they presume to do that? Julia didn't know the answers, but she was determined to find out.

***

"No, I have no opinion," said the man behind his large mahogany desk.

"But I've told you everything that I know," pleaded Julia to the lawyer. Her aunt Margaret, who had insisted upon coming along, was getting a little impatient, but had spent too much time in the realms of high society that she was unaccustomed to making her wishes known in a direct fashion, which was thought to be so unbecoming of a southern woman. Indeed, the lawyer himself was a little taken aback at the candor with which Julia presented her case, and this even increased the distance between the two as the lawyer didn't wish to overly expose himself to this woman who appeared to have quite a bit of moxie, as well as intelligence to back it up.

"You see, Miss. Vanderkamp, I can't issue an opinion unless I can see the document in question. Without the papers before me, plus a copy of the court order that was issued to evict your family, I cannot say anything. This is because a lawyer is bound to the facts as they are, and unless he sees the facts before him spelled out specifically, he can do nothing nor think anything. Do I make myself clear?"

"Quite clear sir. But in the meantime, my family will be run off their land by this money hungry company, and I'm sure that even if they are found to be in the right at some later date, we will have a very difficult time reclaiming our land. It seems much better to fight now, and we haven't much time. Surely you can suggest something as a stalling measure?"

"As far as that goes, Miss. Vanderkamp, I will as well need to have the precise documents in front of me, because for us to get a temporary restraining order from the court, we would have to have ample evidence that there had been something irregular in either the original document or in the court order calling for the eviction.

Upon presenting probable causes for these, we might obtain such a writ which would last until the higher court would hear our appeal and make a ruling."

"Then there's hope that we may not be moved off our land after all?"

"I didn't say that, Miss. Vanderkamp. Indeed, I can say nothing until I have seen the actual legal paper involved."

"Well I daresay that may take some time, sir," put Margaret, sensing that the conversation was nearing an end and determined not to be left entirely out of it.

"In that event, I must say that things do not look bright as to staying on the land," replied the lawyer.

"Well, *I never*," said Margaret, setting herself as if preparing to leave.

"I'll do what I can. Thank you very much, Mr. Reynolds," said Julia as they got up and made for the door.

"Good day, ladies."

Something must be done, and with great haste. This was no trifling matter, and Julia knew that her father might be a little stubborn.

"I didn't like the manner of that man," said Margaret when they had gotten outside.

"Yes, he was all business, wasn't he," replied Julia.

"Well, I don't mind that, I know several very successful businessmen who are all business, but at the same time are a little friendly as well. I daresay, he was raised without any money. You can always tell: junior partner or no junior partner."

It would be senseless to say anything to her aunt, so Julia was quiet and mulled over what she must do. Though all this worry, her concern for John never left. He was a constant comfort, and anxiety as well.

Chapter 7

"In which Certain Facts are Revealed about the Mansion"

—**a mansion** you say?—that's what I heard, George is going to build the biggest house next to the guvnor's himself—how did you find out?—well, Maybel's husband's second cousin's step father's nephew has been retained by Mr. Dodson to make him some plans for the house to be constructed on the old Mitchell Evan's Farm—that's disgusting, why he just moved out and now someone wants to build on the property that's barely a few weeks old, I think that for decency's sake he ought to keep it for at least a year or so—why property's not like a woman, can't expect it to go into mourning—I don't know, I still don't think it's right, that's all, and I have my ideas—Lord knows that when you git something inta your head there ain't nothin that can shake it luse—it was a shame about old Mitchell having to leave—they say that he hates it in town, too noisy for him—I don't know why he went and sold—those are questions that no one can answer—I suppose you're right, but I know that if I had some property like that I certainly wouldn't want to just give it up all of a sudden—they say that the new house is going to have a black iron balcony just like in Orleans—really?—what's that look like?—really Susan-Jean, you is backward, why everyone knows a black iron balcony, why they is famous—have you ever seen one—of course I have, they're very well-known—tell me where one is so that I can see one too—well, there's none that are so close as that, what do you think they are anyway, common? I mean if they was just a regular thing like that *do you suppose that someone as important as George Dodson would want to go and have them puts on his house? —I never thought of that—it's true, they're as rare as diamonds—like diamonds, yes that will be a marvelous house—*

Samuel Beauchay sat in his study. It was his time to go out for a ride, but he didn't have the stomach for it, as he thought about his good friend Vanderkamp. He had no doubt in his mind that the mysterious buyer was ultimately none other than the buyer of the Mitchell Evan's farm, George Dodson. He was trying to get back at Samuel for having put one over on him in the golf course land deal. It was Dodson's petty form of revenge, but what Samuel didn't see was where Dodson was getting all the money to finance these projects of his—after all, his salary at the bank wasn't extraordinary and he didn't make much from his gambling house and local bootleg sales. It didn't make sense that he would be able to make good such an outstanding debt as was owed by the Whren and Vanderkamp properties.

Samuel had told Charles that the land company would turn out to be no good. But Charles was fixated on how the casino project had become a good money maker though the shareholders didn't get an overly extravagant return on their original capital. Now things would change quite radically. If, for example, some people moved in, they could be a very disagreeable type who could make life most unpleasant. They might forbid Beauchay from riding on their (the old Vanderkamp) property. In that event, he would have no easy access to the woods. Things had been so good between the two families that it was almost as if he was being dispossessed along with his neighbor.

How long the two had known each other. And now for it all to end was unthinkable. Of course, there must be something that could be done that could prevent them from being evicted, but what exactly it was, Samuel was in no position to know. He could try some out of town lawyer, but he didn't like working behind Charles' back, which would be required as the other had made his views quite clear as to dealing with outsiders in the latter.

It was all due to Dodson, who was finally prepared to move and pollute their side of the county now with his nauseating presence. What if Dodson were behind this unknown company and intended to surround the Beauchay farm? There could be no more disagreeable prospect in his mind than for such a thing to come to pass. It would be like a siege in which he was the last defender inside the bastion and George was threatening to tear everything down.

It would be necessary to mount the energy for a real fight this time. There could be no dodging the fact that now he would have to summon up all and any resources that he had at his disposal, and concentrate it upon his adversary. This scourge at hand was the most threatening of all. This was because it was deteriorating the very base upon which everything had rested for such a long time. There had been enough time spent in the politics of trying to help the farmers of Georgia, now he must look to his home and try to keep all in order. This would be a very difficult task, but there could be no stopping once the project had begun. It must be an all or nothing effort, demanding full dedicated commitment on his part.

George Dodson must be stopped.

The way to do this would be to help his neighbor, who he wished to help anyway. He would go and see Charles the very next day and discuss with him what he, Samuel, thought the other should do, and then actively persuade him to follow his advice. Yes, this would be the best course of action. Samuel felt better and decided that it wasn't too late to take his afternoon ride after all.

Chapter 8

"A Discourse to the Reader on the Subject of Fairness"

It was difficult for anyone to budge Charles Vanderkamp. He felt a kind of fatalism about the entire endeavor that surprised many of his close friends and family. He had told his daughter that he wasn't interested in handing over family documents to some lawyer from Atlanta, and that he had perfect confidence in the local advice. As for his neighbor, Samuel, he didn't quite know how to tell him no, as this was something very foreign to their previous relationship. Even though the advice was exactly the same as Julia's, somehow coming from a man it seemed to be more sound, and he honestly considered Samuel's suggestions.

"There's no way that they can get you off the land if you've a mind to fight," said Samuel.

"Of course I don't just want to give it to them on a platter like that, but what am I to do? Sometimes I think it is the wiser man who knows when to give up."

"Give up? How can you say that? Just because the times aren't the best, that isn't any reason for pessimism. While you're still on the land there's a chance to save it, and you're a fool not to try."

"Of course you're probably right, Samuel, but you know, I have a feeling sometimes that maybe it isn't worth fighting for any longer. You know at first I was, I don't know: stunned, I suppose. But after a while, I became indignant and angry and went to see the lawyer. Well, Millsbourgh and I talked a while and it sounded more and more hopeless and almost in the midst of it all, I don't know when it happened, I felt a sense of calm, like I didn't have to fight any longer. It was as if the struggle was all over and now all I had to do was relax. I have a little money, you know, and all the effects of the equipment and such can be sold as they only own the property. Well, after that's all taken care of, I think I can live off the interest of it all if it's invested and Rodney gets the same scholarship offer that he got this summer from Georgia, though he might get *more* as he has had a very good season in Alabama. With all of that, I may be able to comfortably settle down and start enjoying things." As he spoke, Charles lit a pipe and puffed away and he gently rocked in the swing on the front porch.

Samuel felt a welling of sorrow for his friend as he saw him: a beaten man resigning himself to dying, in effect. He was talking about leaving the place of his birth and his life and going somewhere else—no longer living the only kind of life that he had ever known. Such words were foreign to Beauchay's understanding and meant only one thing to him: abdication. The Vanderkamp Estate, which was the largest estate in total acreage in the County, though his own was larger in actual useable acreage that was put under production, was a sort of symbol to him of everything that adherence to traditional values stood for. How could one believe in anything if there wasn't that? Society couldn't keep remaking itself every generation, there had to be an inheritance, otherwise how was anything to emerge? How could there be any progress (a concept that Samuel believed in)?

However, this could never occur without the continuity of social institutions and a strong sense of inherited tradition, a commodity that was increasingly being called into question. There was no conflict between such a prudent ordering of society and progress, as long as the progress that one was describing was that which held as given the very values that it was trying to better implement and not to tear down. This included any of the basic *intuited, felt codes* that comprised the very fabric of society. This was a constructive progress. But then there was the other progress that hides under the name of advancement and modernization. That was a *false progress* that sought to randomly replace old institutions and alter social structures with no regard *to what has been*. It operates under different sorts of imperatives, strange dictums that place individual interests beyond that which will benefit the whole—not the whole as a majority, but the whole which includes the minority as well: a true whole.

When the individual is elevated in his megalomania, he may legislate in divisive fashion, causing permanent changes in the established order and altering those subliminal verities that people have so long held as basic. The result is an overall loss of meaning for everyone as the prize to the one who has effected the change. In this event, the people as a whole can no longer look to the actualization of the established, commonly held values as a source of mutual and personal fulfillment. Nothing would seem worth attaining anymore because there were no real reinforcements for anything noble, as all previous sources of such reinforcement would have been removed. And so, all eyes turn away from their brothers and their State and focus on themselves and their own interest, and then the State as a political and social unit is broken. This, of course, happens by degrees and might never occur in whole, but such disillusionment causes degeneracy that can only be restored by a reassertion of the old values by energetic people who actually believe in them and have the power to make others believe as well.

Once, the South had united and fought a great war on principles alone. The war had nothing to offer economically, as most were well off, but the evolutionary process had developed to such a degree that men were willing to risk their lives for the sake of a principle, and yet how many men would do such a thing today?

"I don't agree with you, Charles. I think that you were made for this land and it was made for you. If you move, I won't know just what to do, as you and I have been, well, more than just neighbors in the usual sense."

Charles puffed long into his pipe. He didn't want to let Samuel bring the return of the torturing conflict of feelings that he had been going through in the past days. It was necessary to learn to accept what happens to one. Reality can't always be fought, and fighting wasn't always the answer. "You have to believe me when I say that the years that we've spent here near you have been—"

"There you go again, saying *have been* and *was*—why are you always talking in the past tense? You're not licked yet. Everyone agrees with me. Just ask your wife, or your daughter—"

"My daughter's in Atlanta," corrected Charles.

"You know her wishes from her letter." Charles looked at Beauchay with surprise. He hadn't shown Samuel the letter, and he wondered how he had known. Beauchay, seeing this, quickly added,

"Your wife told me about you daughter's letter and your stubborn refusal to comply with her wishes. I think you're making a mistake. What can it hurt?"

"I'm only putting off the inevitable."

"But perhaps it isn't inevitable."

"I feel it is."

"But darn it man, don't you want to make sure before you roll over and play dead?"

Charles knocked out his pipe to re-pack it. "I don't think I'd call—"

"All right, maybe my language was a bit strong, but don't you think that it would be worth a try? I mean, you want to do what is right, and I can appreciate that you don't want to make a fuss if you think that you are in the wrong, and that is very decent of you; something I'd expect only of a man of your character. But I also know that you wouldn't want to make a sacrifice that wasn't called for or was unnecessary. Why, that's plain foolish. Perhaps there was some mistake in the way that this transaction was set down. For example, if they really weren't entitled to your land, or if you could get off by paying a certain amount each year out of your harvest, then wouldn't you consent to staying on?"

Vanderkamp didn't answer. He had made up his mind and accepted what was to befall him, and now his neighbor, his friend, was trying to tell him that all this might be unnecessary and that he might be simply giving his land away unless he more fully explored the possibilities. He didn't want to be one who left his land clinging on to it as if it was the only thing that he needed to live. He had always told himself that if he ever lost what he had—completely— then he could start over again somewhere else and would be the same person. Because what defines a person are not his surroundings, but his feelings. And feelings can never be taken away, not by any external force. They could be polluted from within by avarice and greed, or self-pity. That might be occasioned by the unfortunate experience of his land. The bank would never have foreclosed on its own, he had been assured of that. But no one had ever envisioned that the bank would fold and thereby actually jeopardize his holdings. Old Jackson had been the smart one, but now he, Charles Vanderkamp, had to pay for his mistake. When one makes a mistake, it must be rectified. He had gambled for high stakes and lost. Now the only gentlemanly thing to do, the only thing he could do and still preserve his self-respect and honor (the bastion which held those private feelings), would be to pay up and not to welch.

"You know, I don't like to be a Jew about this," began his neighbor, but stopped. Samuel merely felt that his friend didn't have the situation in proper perspective.

Charles didn't finish his statement. Instead he put the finishing touches on packing his pipe.

"All a lawyer would do, Charles, would be to see that everything is fair. That's all you want, I'm sure. If the land has to go to someone else, then let it go, but only let it go if it is *supposed* to go. I'm not advocating that you cheat anyone out of what is supposed to be theirs, but merely that you make sure that it really *is* theirs before you go and waltz away."

"Of course, Samuel. If I didn't feel confident that I had no clear claim to the land, I wouldn't be acting like this." There was a reluctance that Samuel thought he detected in his neighbor's voice. He had put some doubt where before there had been none. Samuel was certain that Charles would yield.

Chapter 9

"Another Turn of the Roulette Wheel"

"Is there anything else that I can get for you, Mother?" asked William as he left his mother's bedroom.

"No, dear, I'm quite fine, thank you."

Dorthay sank down into her bed, which now felt rough and chafed her skin. The smell of the room, too, was of sickness as she had had different things that she had tried to cure her, all home remedies that had failed. She hadn't called for the doctor and her husband had left the judgment up to her as to what she should do, as he was very busy at present with his various deals.

She had called in her son to bring her paper and ink so that she could write a letter to her brother. It had been a long time since she had contacted him. But on the other hand, the time didn't seem that long since she and her brother had played together and talked about what it would be like to be rich and full of leisure. What an ideal that had seemed as a child. Money was thought of as desirable because it could buy shiny things that glittered in the sun. Play jewelry and candy could be purchased with money. A pony as well would come with the ownership of that mysterious commodity. But soon she had learned that the real power of money was not what it could merely buy but the power that one could exercise with the possession of it. Her husband had taught her that, not through words but through actions. He knew what money was all about and how it affected men in various ways.

When she had been a child she had worshipped money and what it could buy, and so it had a grip over her. But she soon learned that the only way to master money and to put it absolutely in one's power was to renounce it for what it could buy and come to terms with it in the abstract. That was what her husband had done. He had gone after money, but not for what money could buy, as he was very wealthy. And yet despite his wealth, he lived quite modestly: they had no servants nor an expensive home nor even clothes that would be expected of people that had much money. They lived the same way that they had lived when they *really* didn't have any money at all. Their mode of life hadn't changed much over the years, except for the purchase of the automobile, which was a Ford Model-T. George still wore the same Arrow Collars and string ties that he wore at the beginning. They ate the same meals and did the same things. No, money hadn't changed their lives materially (though now they were planning to move into a proposed house on some new property, that was, again, part of the process) as George had started after money as a means to power. Power is something that a person can concretely understand. It isn't complicated, like possessing things can be.

Power can be understood, pure and simply, for itself as itself. When one admits that he desires it, then there has to be a kind of commitment of the spirit to it, towards itself, as it must be pure in its pursuit and not settle for anything less than the full exercise—an ideal which, of course, can never be realized. So the metaphor of a ladder is discarded in favor of a conception of the ego and its extension of its dominion over other things (*people* for this example may be thought of as *things*, too). For this to happen, a man must be perfectly honest with himself and admit all his weaknesses so that he might fortify against them and assess his strengths, so that he might build an arsenal which can be mobile and versatile.

Such a man sees money as the key to power and so seeks it— not for what it can buy but as the completion of a grand design (though after a time when the process runs its course and one may, as a matter of fact, alter his standard of living). But then such alterations run the risk of engaging in a meaningless gesture. For excessive material consumption should only be for the sake of manipulating others via their envy and greed.

Such moves must be taken cautiously and only when the opposition has been effectively muted. One must never lose the power of presenting the general allure of money and what most people imagine they would die for. Keep up the illusion and gain control of their souls. The program is a sure winner every time.

This was the gospel of George Dodson. He played on the foibles of others in order to crush them. He knew the allure of money as goods attainment. But a greater attraction was the power of controlling others. It was a gambling proposition that sought to gain control and come out on top.

Everything is for the sake of winning that big stake. They continue to play, looking for some combination of bets that will make their fortune so that they will never have to listen to the metal ball rolling on the roulette wheel again. But they always lose; and men like George Dodson play upon their appetites, gaining influence as more and more people succumb to the prize promised to the fortunate and gifted.

George didn't actually cheat people; they lost their own money. George merely gave them an attractive way to do it. No one had to take the bait. George never forced them. They did it to themselves.

Now was the big opportunity when her husband, George, was about to make his move from a local figure to a larger arena. She knew that he would be a man of destiny and that there would be nothing that could hold him back. And she was witnessing it all come true. Soon, he will have achieved what he had set out to do, but if he was true to his spirit; he wouldn't stop there. The state wasn't big enough to hold George, nor even the country. The only limits that he would have to deal with would be physical ones: how fast he could go given natural restrictions of travel, time, and death. Certainly wherever it was, it would have been as far as he would have been able to go. But even there he had somewhat provided for himself as he had been instructing William in much of what he was doing so that when the time came for him to go, there might be another Dodson—an extension of George— to take his place.

How much William reminded Dorthay of her husband. He was George's favorite, and George intended William to be just like himself. The boy was a very good learner, and had already mastered himself within the rivalry of the family to a position just below his father, who he may have even schemed to overthrow as soon as he thought himself ready, and this, too, George knew. The father made sure that there was never that opportunity. This was because George knew how to manage his power.

And where did she fit into this picture? The question troubled Dorthay, for she had asked herself that question often, but now it had lay dormant for such a long time that she was surprised at its entrance. Perhaps it was her fever that made her carry on so. Activity dulls the mind, and she longed to stop with all these musings and return to the hard work that had been her purpose for so many years. But *had* that been her purpose? How could she ever admit that her purpose in life was to start fires and cook food—to have babies and to clean diapers? What kind of purpose was that for a woman who wanted to be an active part of the new South? She had always wanted to be a player in the revitalization of Georgia, a dream that she had held since she had been a little girl playing in the fields with her brother. But had she done anything constructive towards that?

She had brought George Dodson to Georgia, but that was mere action by association. She had supported him in his rise, giving him advice at times and standing by him as she had always been excited by the strength and power that seemed to emanate from his very presence. But was this enough? Did she feel satisfied after all these years? The question remained unanswered as she turned over and was about to go to sleep. The day seemed long and time stretched endlessly before her as if the divisions that were marked for common usage (day and night) would never succeed each other as the oppressive weight of all those durations that within her experience burdened her. She thought from the time that she was a little girl listening to Marcel Beauchay tell her what it was like in the grand old days, or Col. Rutherford who told her—but no, he had died so suddenly. Had she killed him? Of course not—at least not with her own hand. But she confronted him with the failure of the South in its quest against the North. But that wasn't what she wanted to think about either. Was it the time that had never been but which she had once dreamed? A peaceful time so that when she would awake, her thoughts would be purged of all the distasteful elements and she could get on with the business of being a—what? But then again, all would be better if only she could let herself relax and fall into that renewing state of ultimate passivity that is the sanity of us all.

There was a disturbance outside, a noise that she tried to shut out as she pulled the pillow up over her head. The linen seemed to tear at her face as her skin, w o r n raw from nothing, now forced her to grip her pillow more tightly as she wished to shut it all out from her mind, to make all the sounds go away so that she could be in that relaxing peace that she so desperately yearned for with an all-consuming passion that at the same time worked against its own professed end.

"Mother," cried the high voice of young Howard as he stood by the bed. He was all of fourteen, but his mother still liked to think of him as a little boy so he remained so. He was the youngest-acting member of family, though he had a sister and brother chronologically younger than himself. But at this moment, Dorthay Dodson didn't see her little boy as she was beneath her pillow, her hands gripping it so tightly that her veins stood out and her knuckles looked as if they were going to break through the skin in their bony whiteness. Howard was afraid—he didn't know what to do so he screamed louder: "Mother, Mommy!"

But the effect was that his mother didn't move or change her pose, so the boy jumped into the bed and grabbed his mother by the shoulders. But when he put his fingers upon her skin, he could feel that it was wet and very warm. It was as if she had been working all day in the hot sun instead of resting quietly in bed. Little Howard didn't know what to do. He became a statue, shaking and trying to decide whether it would be better to try and locate one of his brothers or to stay with his mother. Both seemed like the right and the wrong thing to do, so he stayed where he was, trying to make up his mind.

Finally, he decided that a loud scream would be the best course of action, but even when he opened his mouth he felt as if he were making a mistake because as his vocal cords vibrated with his cry, his mother threw her pillow on the floor. Then she sat up with a crazed look on her face, as if she was not herself but someone else. She cuffed the boy with the back of her arm so that he was thrown onto the ground with considerable force. This was his mummy, little Howard told himself, the one he had always thought loved him best. Why was she doing this? She looked like someone else, and she had hit him! Though he felt no pain from the blow, he felt sorrow from the act. Howard sat staring at his mother who was still sitting up. She was staring forward at nothing in particular, or rather through everything in general. Then she jerked back, hitting her head against the wooden headboard, but she didn't seem to record any noticeable reaction to the blow. She moved in bed, arranging herself to a sitting position at a 120 degree angle from the plane of the bed. But then she stopped. She was no longer moving, but obviously stiff.

The teenage boy sat on the floor, waiting for his mother to say something to him. He no longer felt afraid. The sensation that had come over him just moments before was gone. And so he sat in obedient silence, watching, waiting—until it became clear that she would move no more.

Chapter 10

"Further Events on the Road"

When John had escaped on the bus, he had only one thought in mind, and that was to get to his hotel room, gather his old clothes, and get out of town. The police would be looking for him and he must avoid their nets if he could.

However, when John actually reached his room, he decided that detection by daylight would be much easier than at night, though admittedly travel at night was harder (he knew that he couldn't try the bus or trains, as they would be watched, and that meant thumbing a ride).

Soon, however, sitting in his room, he couldn't resist any longer the thought that had been forcing itself upon him—but he wouldn't—couldn't accept: Julia had betrayed him. But that thought transmuted into the conjecture that somehow the law had gotten on to her, and that they were using her to betray him.

Nothing seemed appealing to him at that moment. He was running, but why? What was there to run for—what was the point of it all? Wasn't one place as good as another? On the wall there was a spider that was crawling up a thin thread to the ceiling. How easy it would be to knock that spider down, he thought, knowing that if he did it the spider would simply begin again as if nothing had happened. Spiders are not impatient creatures. They have one task at hand and will continue with it as long as they can.

For the first time in a long while, John felt the weight of the chain that Jefferson had given him around his neck. The chain wasn't in one piece, but was obviously two chains joined together; a very small one and then the larger one. John marveled at the oddly shaped cross at the end with its inscription on the reverse side. Where had it come from, he half-wondered as he thought about his friend, the only one who had been true to him. Jefferson was really the father he never had. Jefferson was loyal and trustworthy. That's what any boy would want of a father.

Despite everything that had happened, John knew that Jefferson was still trying to help him in any way that he could. That thought alone gave John something to cling to as he thought about where he was to go once it became dark.

Strangely enough, there wasn't any heavy police build-up on the streets, as John had no idea how common it was for the Atlanta police to have a murderer to deal with that they didn't feel it necessary to do anything out of the ordinary to try and apprehend him. Perhaps he would have no trouble after all?

There was a truck stop near a large intersection that was only a few blocks away. John went inside and ordered some grits and a coffee. It didn't take too long before a tough, heavy-set black man came in and sat next to John.

"You got a cigarette?" asked the man.

"No I don't, sorry," replied John, wishing that he did so that he could have a possible ride with the man.

"No need to be sorry," replied the man, who motioned to the waitress to come over and bring him some coffee and cigarettes. When he got his order, the man lit his cigarette and then offered one to John. John didn't usually smoke, but felt that he should accept the man's offer.

"Thanks," responded John as he lit his cigarette from the man's.

"You lookin' for a ride or something?" asked the man right away.

"Why yes, how did you know?" asked John.

"It isn't too hard to figure out: a man with a bundle at his feet and sitting over a cup of coffee at a truck stop."

John laughed. This man saw more than John had given him credit for.

"Where are you going?" asked the man.

"I don't know, nowhere in particular I guess."

The man paused as he took some of his coffee. John felt as if he was being inspected as to whether he would be suitable for a ride.

"Well, I'm going north. If you want to ride I can take you to all the way to Chattanooga, but that's all."

This sounded fine to John and he gladly accepted the ride.

As they rode, the man didn't say much to John but kept to himself, occasionally humming, but never singing or making a loud noise of any kind. "You running away from the law?" asked the man in a tone that startled John.

"Why no, why should I—" began John, hardly knowing what to say except that he was surprised that this fellow should seem to know everything about him; was it all so evident?

"Look, I've got no time to play games about this. I ask you for a reason. There's a road block ahead, maybe you'd better climb behind the seats."

"But I—" began John, knowing that if he did as he was told, that it would be a sure admission of his guilt. But on the other hand if he didn't accept this suggestion, he might be recognized and apprehended.

"Get behind the seat, damn it, you can explain it to me later, if you want," the man said as his truck began to deaccelerate.

John did as he was told and crawled behind the large seats. All this was rather humiliating to him. He realized in another way just what it meant to be a fugitive: he would do anything to avoid capture. He was so afraid of being caught that it seemed that he would submit to any indignity in order to preserve his safety and freedom.

The police officer walked to the cab. "You have any riders in there?"

"No sir, just driving to Chattanooga, that's all."

"You seen anyone trying to hitch on the road?"

"There were a few, I can't remember anything about them though, it was too dark."

"That's the trouble with you coons, you can't tell one spook from another at night," said the sheriff.

The sheriff opened the cab door and looked around for a second or two then shut it. "All right go on, and watch who you pick up. There are three bank robbers and a murderer out on the roads tonight."

"Yes sir," replied the truck driver half-heartedly in a tone that John thought was almost mocking, but just at that point of ambiguity in which the distinction would not be made with any exact certainty.

The truck pulled out again and they were on the road once more. John crawled out from his hiding place and sat down again.

"What are you, the bank robber or the murderer?"

"Well I've never robbed any banks," said John, "so I guess I'm the other." John didn't know why he told the truck driver this information, as he generally remained much more secretive about such things, but it seemed to him that this man probably knew that he was a criminal and it didn't seem to matter one way or the other. Also, there was something about the situation and the manner of speech of the driver that put him at ease and almost compelled him to talk.

"That so? And did you do it?" asked the driver, sounding as if he was asking about the weather or inquiring about an operation scar, or some such routine question. Again, this made John want to be completely candid, but he almost felt that this man would respect him more if he was guilty than if he wasn't, so that John felt reluctant about telling him that he was innocent.

"No."

"But they was going to string you up anyway, so you run?" asked the man.

What insight this man must have, or perhaps he was just making lucky guesses. "You certainly have it down. Did you read about it somewhere?"

"Certainly. It's in all the papers."

"Really?" responded Dow, surprised that his case had received so much notoriety.

"Oh not your case in particular, I don't know you from a horse's ass, but the story is common enough. You read about it all the time: some po nigger gets blamed with a killing that he didn't do so that white folks don't have to be bothered with the law."

The driver took out another cigarette and lit it. "Who was the victim? A white boy?"

John felt as if he was in the presence of a sage who knew all there was to know about life, who so accurately could describe his situation. John liked the way he said "po' nigger." Somehow from his lips the epithet didn't seem the same as when Victor Stuart had used it—suddenly John became aware that it was the first time that he had consciously thought about Victor Stuart in his yellow car for a long time. It was because he was called a po' nigger by this amiable man, who seemed to be able to see through all the facades that he, John, and everyone else lived behind. Dow wanted to sit at this fellow's feet and listen to him talk about the way things were.

"You ain't really out of d'ordinary, you know. Why, I know many guys like you in the same situation. There ain't nothin' you can do neither, 'cept go to another state and try to start it again.

"You know white folks have a hard time recognizing one colored from another; you get far enough away and they won't know you from Stepin Fetchit."

John laughed. He enjoyed being accepted by someone and not questioned. He didn't feel like telling the other man that he had blue eyes. In fact, after the dwarf, John no longer believed that his eye color made any difference. He was colored. And right now that felt *all right*.

John badly wanted to look at this man's strong black face, but he didn't dare look at him directly. John felt ashamed that he couldn't be *really black,* like his friend, and then he could laugh loudly at his jokes and they could both revel in what it meant to be themselves. But John was afraid that the other would turn around and see that maybe John wasn't really black enough to count. Maybe he wasn't black enough to be allowed to hear the jokes and be treated to the familiarity that he was being given.

"Why you know, I nearly killed a man once myself. It was an old white man who was messing with my old lady, and I didn't like it. So I goes and tell him to keep away from her and he laughs at me like I was some kind of field nigger of his and then I lost all my temper and hit the man real good. He fell back to the ground and I jist left him there. Yep, the old white bag of skin was laid up for about a month. But he pulled through in the end."

"Did you get any time for it?" asked John, hardly knowing what he was saying but yearning to become a part of the conversation.

"Yeah, I got about a year fer it, and when I gets out I found my old lady done gone off and left me. Can't blame her though; a year is a long time to wait for anyone."

How calmly this man took things, what detachment he had, John thought. If only I could view life with such objectivity and have such a strong control over my emotions, then I'd be in better shape than I am now. But I'm just weak; there's no getting around it. I can't make it alone. I know that I need support from somewhere, but where can I go? I can't just start driving a truck like this. Why, I imagine that these jobs are pretty hard to come by.

But for a moment, John tried to imagine himself behind the wheel driving several tons of goods into the night each day, living on coffee and truck stop food—never having anyone to care about. Never having anyone to torture him with betrayal and ingratitude.

No, John said to himself. He'd simply sit stoically behind that large wheel, humming to himself as he kept himself company.

The two didn't talk much more, as all too soon the truck slowed and pulled to the shoulder. It was very early in the morning and there was little traffic. The other man turned and said, "I've got to take in this cargo in a few hours, but I'm only about an hour or so away so I think I'm going to take some sleep. If you want to stay, that's fine, or if you want to go, the same. But after I start up again, you can only go to the beginning of town, cause I have to turn in this rig and I'm not supposed to have any passengers, do you get me?"

"Yeah, I follow," replied John. "If you don't mind, I think I'll take a little sleep with you here; there's not much out this time of night."

"Suit yourself."

After their sleep, the man dropped off John as expected and John watched the truck get smaller and smaller until it disappeared. Somehow John was very sad. He had imagined that he and the truck driver were getting to be good friends, but the other man hadn't offered to see him after he delivered his rig. But that was understandable. The man probably had things to do, and besides, associating with a suspected murderer isn't the best risk to take in a town where you are known. No, John didn't in any way blame the truck driver for anything, but still he felt a lost emptiness.

Now it was incumbent upon John to decide what exactly he was going to do with himself. He couldn't very well just stay where he was. The key thing for a fugitive to do is to keep moving so that no one ever knows who you are and what you're about. A man can't afford to stop because when he does that, he begins to think about life and living, and nothing is more destructive to the spirit of a man on the road than to contemplate personal attachments to anything. He had had Julia, whom he had dreamed about, but now she had turned against him and he must rejoice in his new freedom. He was tied to no woman; only to Jefferson and to that truck driver. They were his friends, and as he would probably never see either of them again, he needn't worry himself about people at all. Maybe he would go to another state and take the advice of the midnight sage. But did he look enough like a black to live in their community? John thought not, though his skin was dark for a white, it was light for a Negro. The only thing to do was to get another ride and let it take him where it will. He went back to the road to try and thumb a ride, but there weren't many cars yet.

The chain felt heavy around his neck, and so he lifted it up with his fingers so that he could look at it. The names of Douglas, Du Bois, and Garvey suddenly came to mind. Where had he heard of them before? Were they people that he knew, or were they famous people—he couldn't tell in what context the names came to him. But he felt that they had been associated with some dreams that he had had, symbols that had once frightened him, but suddenly seemed to gleam, even as the cross that he was holding was reflecting the sun just rising over the trees.

John decided to take the road south again.

He soon got a ride with a fellow who promised to take him East and South, but that he might take a while as he had to make several business stops. But as John was in no particular hurry, the arrangement seemed fine to him. He had to go somewhere and alight for a time so that he could regain his strength and again continue.

The first stop was near a hotel that stood by a lagoon. As John sat in the car, a cat jumped up upon the car hood and stared at him for a time through the front window. The cat was a tabby and had bewitching eyes that were slanted green ovals. Though John knew that they were simply dumb beasts, still that stare was like some knowing being who understood more than John wanted anyone to know about himself. For a moment, he felt like a child again.

Then the thought of Victor Stuart played before him. Everyone, if seemed, thought that he, John, had killed young Stuart. But the only reason that they thought this was because of the events of the previous day—no, he couldn't go over those again. But one thing did puzzle him, something that he had never exactly gone over before himself: had he ever really wanted to kill Victor? There had been much animosity between the two, as John had often wished to smash the other's face, but this was in an abstract way, a way that would make up for all the hurt that Victor had caused him. There had been times, especially in his early teens, when his frustration over the hurt that Victor inflicted upon him was unbearable, and he wanted to do something about it. But this something would never be in the form of killing Victor. No, John could never be that violent, or at least not to Victor. This was because the more Victor had done to him the more he found it impossible to do anything in return to him, except to retreat into solitude and let the hurt feelings well up inside. Then when they became excruciating, he would allow himself to think about the person who had caused it all. He would conjure up this vision of Victor almost as if he, John, were bringing the other there to witness the pain that he, Victor, had inflicted upon the body of Dow. This ephemeral Victor Stuart would be made to witness the terrible pain that he had caused John and would be very sorry and beg John's forgiveness, which John would instantly give, and so affect Victor even more. This demonstrated the contrast between *his* generosity and the *other's* cruelty. But then, was such benevolence really kindness when so conceived and plotted to make it harder on one's adversary? Wouldn't it be more honest to say to the spirit that Victor had caused this pain, and that Victor had his just reward—at the hand of another. Victor had brought himself down by his own cruel comments to Dow? This would certainly be more honest, but John wondered if honesty was what human suffering was all about.

John then tried to link together several bits of stories that Jefferson had told John about Baltimore. Jefferson had taken a job at the new NAACP as a labor organizer in the ship yards that were segregated. They were not only segregated in work teams, but with wages and benefits tilted greatly towards the white workers. Jefferson had tried to change that. Jefferson had lost. Jefferson came back to Bella County in defeat. But it wasn't total defeat. He found John. And John found a father figure—something an orphan longs for.

Then John's thoughts returned to Victor. Perhaps it was better to simply take everything upon himself, John thought, knowing that no one would ever understand how he suffered. Perhaps he should just be silent about the whole thing? But what was being accomplished by this silence? Certainly, he would have the comfort of suffering nobly, as a true man should not bother anyone with his troubles. But then was such action healthy? Was it normal? Didn't the world call such people masochists and martyrs, and wasn't this realization that he *would be*, falling into such a trap and so make this alternative unbearable? Weren't all the alternatives unbearable once the individual started thinking about them?

This process of analysis was something that was just beginning in his life and was like a powerful potion—once taken one felt the need to keep taking it until he had drunk the dregs and experienced the *all*. But when he thought about his situation, it always turned out hopeless, and so what was the use of trying to figure out the proper course of action? If when one thought of consequences (which he had done when he went to the Martinez's) then where does one draw the line between consequence-speculation about concrete things and mere abstract thinking about disconnected lines of thought which often times could be quite disagreeable to him. A person could work themselves into quite a fit by just thinking about what they did, or might do, or are doing about anything in particular.

A line must be drawn somewhere about such speculation so that it didn't become unpleasant. But then is unpleasantness a correct criterion?

Just then the man returned to the car.

"I hope I didn't keep you waiting long, I had a spot of breakfast."

John wondered why this man didn't invite him inside to have some breakfast. Did they have an exclusive dining room that didn't serve anyone who might be suspected as having colored blood in them? Did this driver think him colored, or was it that John was dressed so poorly, or did the man simply forget?

At any rate, the man didn't explain and John didn't ask him. They drove on and John tried quietly humming to himself to attempt to drive the painful thoughts away. Through the car window, he tried to absorb himself in the scenery as they sped along the old back roads of northern Georgia. The land was beautiful and John wished that they could stop so that he could just get out and walk about to feel the ground, smell the fresh natural odors of the vital flora that so distinctly let him know where he was. Even in the winter, the grandeur of the land drew him. How he longed to go out into the woods of Varner's Junction and fish a stream again where he would wade into the water with the current running against his legs. In this way, he could feel as if he were a part of nature and not some unnatural appendage.

This was a reality that had existed for him once, just months before when he had simmered in the August heat, before horse races and county fairs—but this was incorrect too. No, he had changed before that, but when? Was it when he had met Cindy Pancroft? That sounded like a good date to affix, but even while he was endeavoring to do this he realized that again this was wrong, as he had been somewhat restless before, and in a state of uncertainty that had no clear beginnings. But somewhere, there seemed to John that there was a time when he was more or less carefree, or rather able to master any cares that he did have and to lose them in his pursuit of sport, or some other pastime. Though there was no clear line of demarcation between the two, he knew that the two phases did exist and somehow he had passed from one into the other without being cognizant of the transition.

"Well, I've got to get some gas," said the man behind the wheel. "Care to take a rest stop?"

"Sure," replied John.

They pulled over to a store that had a petrol pump outside and John got out and stretched his legs a bit. He had been in the front seat for a few hours and he hadn't realized how stiff a person's legs can get in those circumstances, but he was happy for the opportunity to sense his muscles again. It had been a long time since he had had a real opportunity to exercise—free from the compulsion to make money or complete a task assigned to him, but just exercise pure and for itself alone. John imagined that life for a man living in a small band or tribe of people must afford great time for this when hunting or tracking, for example. Man's enjoyment was incorporated into his work, in a full way; not like at the lumber mill where he would only use a certain set of muscles and neglect the rest, day after day. No, when out hunting and tracking, a person must rely on all his instincts and the development of the body as an instrument that is within the natural structure of things. This seemed to be the best or ideal existence where a man could fully realize himself.

Perhaps he could go and become a hermit somewhere and live such a life, but the thought of this was frightful to him. For as a hermit he would be completely away from everybody, and though this seemed like an idealistic paradise, the reality of all his loneliness of the past months made the occasional company of people seem more of a necessity than a luxury.

Still, he could never abide too many people—not that he didn't like people, on the contrary he cherished people for what they were to quite a degree. But often times he would find that he used people to merely back away from the kinds of problems that he was now facing. Why hadn't he ever asked himself some of the kinds of questions that he was facing now? Perhaps it was because whenever the problems became grave, he retreated into others for refuge from himself. Perhaps this was an overstatement, he wondered, but he didn't doubt that there was at least a measure (and a large one) of truth in what he had hypothesized.

They got back into the car and started out on the road again. The night was falling when John got the feeling that he knew this area. He was returning to the region of the lumber mill. After a few minutes, John was confirmed in his suspicion and asked the driver if he had any business in that area, and upon hearing that he didn't, John asked to be let off in a few miles for he knew the area and had friends there.

"Suit yourself," said the man.

John stepped onto the pavement and heard the car go, but what was occupying his mind was the old house. He felt that somehow he must return. There was something there that was drawing him. He didn't know what it was, but it was the same element that had made him leave before and now was affecting him strongly again, this time making him want to come back and discover whatever it was that so enchanted him.

Would he return to the lumber mill? Was the strike over? He imagined so, for it was unlikely that it would be still continuing. They'd probably take him back, as he remembered the friendly telegram that Charles Dumount had sent to the sheriff, getting him out of jail. But whether he did that or not was of secondary importance, what counted now was his getting to that house. He searched in his mind to try and remember where he had gone with the dwarf, as the trails in the forest weren't very well marked and the house was a little out of the way. John walked to the spot where he had been struck and tried to retrace his steps. He saw no one and could tell by the noise and smell that the mill was again operative.

To attempt to follow the trail in the woods that he had only negotiated but once was like entering a dream world and trying to see clearly shapes and forms only half distinct. All was undefined in its maze of incomprehensibility, but then he was in no hurry as he wandered about for a long time until he finally admitted to himself that he was lost. Perhaps, he thought, if he tried again in the morning, he would have better luck in his journey. So John sat down and made himself a little nest amidst the weeds and rubble near an old log that must have fallen in some windstorm many years ago and was now covered with moss and was a trellis and host for other types of small forest inhabitants. John slept fitfully and awoke twice from dreams, and for a time would stare about him into the blackness. He was hungry and it bothered him. Other times he had been hungry, especially during that month at the mill, and he was able to control it by eating plants that he knew were safe, but this time he could not control his hunger, so he roused himself for the last time an hour or so before sunrise.

When the light slanted through the trees, giving him a path to walk, he set out and soon found that he recognized certain little things that he somehow felt as being familiar to his walk with the dwarf. It was only a few hours before he gazed on the field that hosted the ruins.

John wished to sit in the woods for a while and just simply stare at the old place. What was it about it that drew him towards it? Then John remembered the cat that had jumped upon the car hood while he had been waiting; that cat's eyes were certainly haunting. Wouldn't it be something, John thought, if cats had intelligence just as humans do and that they were simply handicapped in that they couldn't communicate their thoughts in language like humans did? What a frustrating existence that would be, always wanting to say something but never being able to articulate what you wanted to be known. It was almost the reverse of the problem that he was facing: he was quite able and in fact desperately trying to limit this urge he had to communicate with himself. But he didn't know what he wanted to say. The words were there, but he didn't know what arrangement he wished to choose.

The ugly structure slumped before him. It was really just an ordinary ruined house, nothing unique in it; he could do perfectly well if he never saw it again and turned around and went back to the mill. But John rose and started into the field towards the grotesque shambles of what was once grand. As he strode decisively forward, his chain swung freely about his neck, and his hands hung relaxed at his sides.

Chapter 11

"The Reader is Taken on Another Train Ride"

When Jefferson got onto the train, he felt that he had accomplished all that he ever hoped to do in Varner's Junction. Dorthay Beauchay had been most helpful to him and he now felt that he knew that the two Dodson brothers were in this together, and that Sig Wyse had something to do with the other brother. There was the possibility, of course, that Rod Dodson didn't have anything to do at all with his brother and in that case any associations that Jefferson might make were false. But there was the suspicion that he, George, must be in on it, and if that was true, then there might be an arm of his organization that was working in conjunction with Georgia Tom and so have some link with Victor's murder. The key connection was whether there was a working relationship between the two brothers or not, because if there wasn't, then Georgia Tom might have simply made book in Varner's Junction like he might have in any number of other local races around the state where there was a lot of money being wagered (local and outside as well), in which case there might be no connection between the victim, Victor Stuart, and the gambling consortium, whoever they were.

Jefferson was fast approaching the limit that could be ascertained under this method. He knew enough, perhaps, to stir things up. He had a minion of Georgia Tom under his and Myra's control. Now, he needed a further lever. This might get him into a larger network and eventually to the killer.

All this was based upon a conjecture and was the result of Jefferson trying to fit together the pieces of the situation as he saw them. Of course, another person examining the same facts might see things differently, so Jefferson was trusting in his own resources. Next would be the problem of what to do with the thug that they had already. He would not be missed for a few days, but what then? Wouldn't his buddies be looking for him? And suppose that he had overcome Myra in some way back in her room. What would he, Jefferson, do then?

The train, which could have been going at any pace when they left in the morning, now couldn't move fast enough for Jefferson, who kept looking at his clock. Things might start happening, but he, Jefferson, knew that he would have to be alert so that he could be on top of the events and have some control over them. His position at the moment, he determined, was one of power, but blind power—he only knew fragments of the actual situation, and in order to act with perfect equity one must have perfect knowledge. With this ratio, he knew that he could act only haphazardly at best. But perhaps Jefferson could improve this by using what he did know to his best advantage.

Julia would be going to Atlanta soon to meet John. Jefferson hoped that all would go fine with her and that she could arrange to meet John at regular intervals so that he might keep abreast of the ongoing status of various events as they happened.

This had been the longest time that he had been away from the Beauchay Estate in many a year, as he had told Mr. Beauchay simply that he needed to take a rest and get away for a while. He would have told Samuel everything, but he knew that Samuel would have been afraid for him and tried to dissuade him or else join him, something that Jefferson couldn't allow, knowing that Samuel would have had to forego his trip to the annual planters' convention, an event that was of great importance to him. Besides these practical considerations, this quest had been something of a personal endeavor. Thus, he, Jefferson, preferred to undertake it on his own without interference or aid. It was important that he do something for his young friend who he often thought of as a son. It was for this reason that it was never a *choice* for Jefferson to do all he could for John. There was nothing else that he could do.

At least he was trying with vigor against very stiff odds. The very act of making such an effort was something he had not tried since—well, for a very long time. There had almost been a sleepiness about his person that didn't wish to stir, preferring to stay where it was in warm comfort—no, that wasn't right, there was much more to it than that: painful fragments that he could not bring himself to fit together about what it meant to believe in something and fight for it—yes, even what it meant to fight at all.

The question was, he thought, properly framed: if x believes in y, then will x do everything in its power to bring about y? Of course, the question was not well-formed; there were other considerations. For example, to what extremes would x go to in trying to bring about y, and if these amounted to severe gestures on x's part, then how is x to come to terms with y? By what does he judge its essential nature? How does x *know* that he is right? Where is the method by which one can check one's intuition of a just action? If he said that he could test his opinion against that of his peers, he would get no further, because his peers frequently had contradictory ideas about what was right, even about the same instance or example. Should he rely on general popular consensus if it could be measured? But what authority would this have?

Surely a group of people can be just as wrong as one person, and why should ninety-nine people be any more infallible than the one who opposes them? There didn't seem to be any real logical reason for supposing that they might. Even if one supposed that the ninety-nine had that many more chances to check themselves for error, and that the one person had only one opportunity, still this would not lead to the desired conclusion because surely the act of checking for error is an independent event happening ninety-nine separate times. In probability logic, these are treated uniquely each time. Each one has as much opportunity (*ceteris paribus*) of making a mistake as the one person singly did. If this reasoning is correct, then one person cannot be judged against the collective ninety nine. Instead, one person is judged against one person, ninety-nine times. There is no additivity involved.

So nix that means of epistemic testing. Intersubjective reporting only works when one is dealing with empirical facts that require simple judgments, such as q being red or not. Here, the collective judgment creates an externalist context that makes sense. However, for more complicated problems in verifying a knowledge claim, the only thing a person can do is to utilize reliable criteria for the examination of the data to be affirmed or denied. This was the approach that Jefferson had used all his life, even before his study of philosophy.

Once one moves over to ethics, it is important to assert that the rightness or wrongness of the action is not simply relative, but can be judged absolutely by such a completely impartial, all-knowing, rational examiner to be *what it is*. This is true even when the ethical is transcendent. This examiner could ascertain all the facts and determine whether the action was right and whether the intuition which prompted the action (assuming that actions are prompted by intuitions) was correct or not.

This, sadly enough, though it affords an absoluteness to the probity of action does nothing to further the individual's understanding of any particular action and whether it was (is) based upon a correct intuition, since no such observer as was described above actually exists (or has office hours for consultation). Then the problem is still how does one verify one's intuitions to ascertain whether he is right or not? Is such a check possible?

These questions bothered Jefferson as he felt a calm at having tried to formalize one of his worries in such a way that it was no longer a restless incantation that agitated the formless relations within his breast, but became one more sordid subject for his confused cranium.

Despite these careful reflections, there was no peace as again the tempest began to blow.

Chapter 12

"Philosophical Reflections From a Cracker Barrel"

"I tell ya Ike," began Jake after having just entered, "that old Dodson is smarter than all of us put together."

"I'se always knew he was crafty," returned Ike, eating an apple.

"I mean here we was all a thinkin' about how he had really been out-foxed by Samuel Beauchay by being forced to buy that oil field which wasn't really no oil field. But all along he knows the same exact thing hisself, and he then makes plans to put up a tract of homes there and subdivide the whole thing, and sell them all so that he'll make a profit out of it yet."

"It's a good idea," began Ike, who again felt that he had known all along that the field would have been a good investment despite what his friends had insisted. "But the one thing that I don't see is who's going to buy all them houses?"

"You know," responded Jake, "that's there's lots of new folk who come here every month, almost. I don't think he'll have too much problem."

"But thar ain't *that* many families, I hear he wants to build a whole lot of houses on little plots of ground so as he can get more money that way. You forget that thar are a lot of people who leave each year as well."

"You're right there, Ike, I can't rightly say as I know where he's going to git all the families, but you can be sure of one thing: a man like George Dodson ain't going to go to all the trouble of puttin' up a bunch of houses without knowin' whar he's going to git the people who is to occupy them."

"Ya thinks he has a trick up his sleeve somewhere?"

"Well," put Jake as he ambled over to the cracker barrel and sat down, slowly, as befitted his stiff back. "I've never played poker with him, as I don't really go in for it much you know. Checkers is more my game," he motioned with his hand to the checker board lying against the wall. "But from what I hears about his table manner, he always seems to have something up his sleeve sides his arm, cause when he needs an ace, strange enough he always seems ta get it."

Ike laughed at that as he finished his apple.

"Yep," Jake repeated, "he always seems ta git it."

Then the door opened and Ed walked in with a large grin that bespoke of some information that he had just received and that he was anxious to tell, but not overly anxious, as he wanted to hold his precious secret for a while.

"Well, what you grinning fer?" asked Ike, knowing perfectly well, as did Jake, that they were to be treated to some choice tidbits of information, but that they would have to wait for it and not seem too eager or the wait would be prolonged.

"Nothin' in particular," responded Ed as he put his hands in his pockets and strutted about the store a few times, lifting his legs high in exaggerated motions and smiling a big smile that was just waiting for someone to ask him again what was the big news.

"You want to play checkers?" asked Jake, determined not to ask Ed what he was grinning about, and knowing that if he did, it would be all morning before he got an answer from him.

"Sure, Jake, jist a minute," said Ed, a little put-off at the apparent indifference of his friends to his important news that he was just busting to tell.

"I think I'll go out back and bring in those bags of feed. Maclin said he'd send his boy after them today sometime, and I suppose now is as good a time as any." Ike started toward the back door.

"Say, do you want any help?" asked Jake, standing up.

"Much obliged," responded Ike.

Jake got up and started walking towards the counter. Ed didn't know what the matter with the other two was. Didn't they see that *he* had something important that *he* wanted to tell them and that *they* weren't going to hear it unless *they* started asking him what it was and where he heard it? He wanted to be coaxed. So maybe he'd let out a little bit.

"You'd never guess what happened," started Ed, hoping to stimulate their curiosity (just in case they hadn't picked up on the visual cues of his grinning and extra energy).

Jake stopped and turned his head, though not all the way, "Really?" Then Jake paused as if waiting for something, and then proceeded to go behind the counter and go out back with Ike.

The two of them brought in the sacks one by one, and perhaps under different circumstances, Ed might have lent a hand, but he wasn't budging until they asked him about his special news. He was getting rather hurt that they didn't seem to care one way or the other. Perhaps he should go somewhere where people did care: to the barbershop or somewhere else. That would serve them right for pretending not to care.

But Ed stayed where he was and soon the bags were all in and Jake sat down again and said immediately, "All right Ed, what's the news?"

The casual manner of Jake's voice slightly offended Ed, who thought that the other man just expected him to hand over his information without being cajoled. Where was their sense of mystery?

"Nothin' much," responded Ed.

"Oh, c'mon Ed," said Ike, "you come in here grinnin' from ear to ear and a walkin' about like a horse just put to stud. Now you tell us what you know."

"Well, I do know something, thar. You're right. A little economy is coming to this area, and guess what it is?"

"I don't know," said Jake in a straight-man's voice, "what?"

"Guess."

"I don't know."

"Guess."

"All right, President Hoover's coming to town."

"No, be serious, Jake."

"I am being serious. I just thought the other day that I'd like that Republican to come to town so that I could throw an egg in his face."

"Now, you wouldn't do that and you know it," replied Ike.

"I know it," said Jake, "but do you know how long it's been since we had a Democrat as President?"

"When was Appomattox?" replied Ike.

"A big textile plant," said Ed.

"What?" the other two said as if it was meant as a response to their dialog.

"Jist that," repeated Ed.

"What on earth you talkin' about Ed?" asked Jake.

"They're going to construct a plant that takes our cotton and makes it into cloth. It'd be on the Vanderkamp property as soon as they get them off it."

"I don't believe it," said Ike.

"I heard it from over in the records office. They got some kind of official permit jist today saying that they had permission to build it there."

"They'll never get the Vanderkamps off the land," said Jake.

"All they need is some fancy-dan lawyer from the big city. They'll stop it."

"I don't know, but wouldn't that be something, to have a big factory right in Bella County?"

"It would sure push the price of them houses sky high," put Ike, who was getting more and more angry with himself for not following his first instincts and buying a piece of the property. Just think of the money he'd have with a factory going up.

"I don't like it," said Jake. "All dat smoke and clouds of smell, this place would get to be jist like Birmingham."

"Don't know, never been thar," replied Ed.

"Well believe me, it's no pretty sight. I tell you, this county is being turned over to the dogs. I can't believe that such a thing as that could ever happen here, and I won't believe it until I sees it with my own eyes. And the minute I do, I'm leavin' 'cause I ain't stayin' in a town with no big factory."

"But this is your home, Jake," said Ed, who liked the idea of there being a factory and the town of Varner's Junction becoming important.

"Not anymore it won't be. It'll have changed so much that it won't be the same place. I knows the place where I call home; I'se got a picture of it in my mind, and I also knows what factories is like and the two don't go together at all. No, if they decide to put up a factory, then I'm goin'."

"I think you're being a little uppity there Jake," put Ike, who was thinking of the expansion that he might get to do on his store if a factory moved in and brought a lot of new jobs and more money.

"I don't think so, Ike, and I'll tell you something else, I think that Dodson's behind the whole thing. Ever since he came he's wanted to wreck this place and change it into *his* kind of town. And he won't rest happy until he'd done jist that. Well, I tell you, I'm not going to sit by and let 'em do it. We can pass zoning ordinances or somethin' to keep him out."

"'Cept he controls the city council, they won't do nothin' 'gainst Dobson," said Ike.

"You may be right, but somebody sides me has to hate this, and I'm going to go and find 'em, and if we can't change it, then we'll leave together."

"Dodson may be in on it, Jake, but that doesn't mean that it has to be bad," said Ed, remembering that he once liked George, and now fancied that perhaps he wasn't altogether against the fellow after all.

"I'm a stubborn man; my mind's made up," said Jake. "Now git out the board, I only have time for one game of checkers."

In the street outside stood the old sheriff, who was leaning against a parked automobile. There was some dust blowing onto the paved Main St. from Magnolia, which was still a dirt road. The city council had surprised everyone when they had decided to pave Main Street. It was controversial in its time, a month ago. Proponents were claiming that all the big streets of the important towns were becoming modern. The pavement only lasted for three blocks from the railroad tracks to Magnolia Street. They had future plans of joining it up to Sawyer's Bridge and so linking it with the state highway.

As he stood there chewing on his tobacco, he had an urge to shuffle across the newly paved street and kick up the dust that, on a windy day like this one, would travel quite a distance. He remembered how when he was young they used to kick up dust on days such as this and bring the women folk to near fits as they complained about all the dirt that would be flying about. They would go on and on about all the trouble that went to boiling and washing clothes. But now with this pavement, there was nothing for the kids to do—least not on these three blocks, but the point was that soon everything would be paved and there wouldn't be any of the old innocent pastimes that used to occupy so much of a boy's life. Everything was being made so modern, and efficient, but somehow there seemed to be a trade-off somewhere. Even chewin' tobaccy seemed dirtier than the old spittle because it just sat on the pavement, whereas *before* it always seemed to be absorbed into the dirt, kind of like watering the ground, making it fertile, or something like that.

Sometimes all the action made him feel lonely and old. There never used to be much for a sheriff to do except mediate between disputes as an impartial party and keep the men from getting too drunk on Saturday night. But now there was no drinking even, at least not officially (and that would be the only kind that he would have jurisdiction over anyways). Now there were only stupid things that people would have never thought of doing twenty years before. Why, it was getting to the point where petty theft was rising so much that people in town had to consider locking their doors when they weren't at home, or when they went to sleep at night! Perhaps the town was getting *too big*. Perhaps it was just the times—he didn't know, but what he did understand was that it wasn't the same being sheriff any more. Things were getting too complicated. He would be getting a part-time deputy in the spring if the motion passed the city council. He felt that this might relieve much of the bother that was beginning to accumulate. Some young man who liked the idea of wearing a badge would apply. Yes, *the badge* was attractive, it glittered so when he was younger. But now, he was sorry to say, the shine seemed to be dulled, even though he cleaned it religiously once a week.

There was never time any more for anything. Everyone was trying to squeeze more things into a shorter stretch so that they could do things better than they were done the day before. But what was so wrong with the day before? Or the month, year or decade before, as far as that went? Why was there so much confounded emphasis upon improving, improving, improving? It seemed to him that people could spend so much time changing things that they might never have time to *enjoy* what it was they changed. In the old days, changes came slowly and one at a time so that everyone could determine the full effects of what had happened to see if the change was good or bad, for just because there is a change doesn't mean that the new situation is any better than the old. "Change" as a word doesn't carry in its definition "for the better." It seemed dumb just to embrace change and *then* go and judge the outcome.

Another thing that bothered him was that he was expected to become a young, spry man to suit the interests of each constituent who wanted this person or that person investigated and brought to justice or arrested for something or other. Why couldn't people understand that a sheriff isn't around to try and stir up trouble?

He's there to keep things going smoothly. Sure, there might be some abuses by a few people who get out of hand, but most of these could be worked out by the people themselves. And when they couldn't, the answer was for him, the sheriff, to talk to both sides and help them settle it themselves, not to call in the law on everything. The more the law could stay out of things directly, the better life would be for everybody. People complained that they never saw their sheriff, but isn't a good sheriff one who tries to prevent abuses of the law by keeping everyone in the right frame of mind, and understanding that when one person thought that he had been cheated, that there was always another side to it and that probably one party acted with provocation of some sort and if they could only go down and have a drink or go fishing together, that nine times out of ten the problem would work itself out?

The sheriff was there to remember that both parties weren't nameless criminals, but people who wouldn't respond to shouting, but might be surprisingly accommodating if approached in the right way. And if the citizens thought that he was too old and lackadaisical, they were only describing the objectivity that he had to display. For the last person who should ever allow himself to become angry was the sheriff. He had to be the man who could look out for everyone's interest at the same time, despite it all. And if people were more impatient than they used to be about getting things settled right now and less willing to *talk things out* because they didn't have the time, or because they were afraid that somehow they weren't getting everything that was entitled to them (oh yes, greed is something that came too, along with the rise in everyone's pay—"you give 'em meat twice a week and they want it thrice") so that it would be all thrown back on the sheriff who was supposed to take someone into custody or bring someone to court. But all they do in court is force the people to talk it out in such a formal setting designed to get their grievances out. But it rarely worked that way. Going to court was a journey to hard feelings. So, consequently when "it's all over in court" instead of two friends reconciled, you have two enemies partially satisfied that they got their "fair share." It all seemed twisted to the sheriff.

If only we weren't in such a darnn hurry, he thought, and weren't so all fired eager to pull down the accomplishments of the past to start all over each time, then maybe we'd get somewhere, but instead we keep laying a new foundation every twenty years or so.

The wind continued to blow over the new paved street as some of the dirt from Magnolia Street gathered near one side and began to lightly swirl about. The sheriff chewed his tobacco, deliberately.

Book Ten

Why?

In asking the question 'why' in reference to a piece of art, I am not talking about why the author decided to make it, e.g. that he had some personal problems that needed a kind of therapy, or that he had a weak Oedipal complex and so wanted to be creative in a way that a male can never be, using art as a surrogate child—but rather the question is directed to the artifact itself. What can that silent thing tell me? Obviously dead men tell no lies, and play scripts tell nothing, but only lie there. The proof must come from the reaction that one receives when confronted with the datum. It has been suggested earlier that there are numerous reasons why one work excels another, centering around the good, the true, and the beautiful. Some scripts excel in one, though all have to be beautiful in order to qualify as high art. This, however, doesn't tell us why one work is better than another. The ultimate question of what the artifact satisfies, its *reason* or its *why,* is unanswered. Perhaps this can be illumined indirectly through an example from my own past.

When I had gotten my first job on the West End, I thought that life was full and beautiful. I was completely satisfied and earning the best money of my life. I had more than I needed, and so my Barclay's account was growing quite quickly. Suddenly, the show that I had been working on closed, and the theater itself shut down (became dark). I was out of a job. This coincided, poorly enough, with a crises in my personal life. The two incidents together drove me to fits of despair so low that I began using up my bank account for alcohol that would make the depression easier to bear— sometimes. Well, I might have ended up at Charing Cross, but for an article I read about someone or other who had just made a big success of himself and had also had a falling off and because of it had killed himself. In addition to this (as I was reading) a man came up to me and begged for some money. It seems that he was down on his luck and wanted something to buy himself some booze so that he could sleep it off. The two incidents had a profound effect upon me. I took the man by the shoulder and told him that I was going to find him a job so that he would have more than enough money to support any kind of recreation that he saw fit. The man was a mason, and I knew someone in Wapping who needed people for construction. This poor soul didn't like the idea at first, but as soon as he saw that I wasn't "balmy" he readily accepted. I was successful in placing the chap in the position and he has been employed ever since. (I get a Christmas card from him every year.) This incident worked on me as a miracle cure. I felt as if a large load was lifted from me and I got a job with a tailor on Oxford Street until an opening in the West End came along. The point of all this is that I was experiencing some collection of profound human dilemmas which I was unable to cope with, and through two examples which I experienced that were parallel in some respects to my situation, I was able to undergo a learning experience.

It wasn't as if I logically reasoned out of my condition, nor was there anything particularly rational about what happened. Instead, it was an apprehension that "rang true to my condition." Some people with more education than I have called this *moral intuitionism* when I told them this tale.

I think that much the same thing happens in good art. It rings true to something in life so that the audience goes through some kind of experience in which they are changed in some respect. All this depends upon the vision of the artist. The artist need not be brilliant, nor extremely learned to have such a vision (indeed oftentimes such education gets in the way of a pure response to some problem), but he needs to be able to react to a dilemma and produce an artifact which solves, makes coherent, or somehow indicates a reaction to his inciting impulse. The artist reacts to something and his reaction is what is captured by his created artifact.

Now it is clear that some of these reactions may have a distinctly limited appeal, but the nature of their appeal is usually gauged by the two factors mentioned earlier, namely the sensory appeal and the intellectual response. According to the particular bent of the patron, he will be inclined to like one more than another. Artistic excellence is therefore a function of the reaction of a single patron in a particular historical setting. Nothing can be gained by adding numbers except as a sum of figures. Merit has nothing to do with popularity, since what is involved in the process is one reaction to a problem set out by the artist to create an artificial event that in some way resembles life, which in turn causes some kind of reaction on the part of the observer.

When this observer reacts favorably, *that* observer judges first that the imitation is worthy as an artifact and that the world created on stage is one worthy to get lost in. The worldview thus created allows the observer to project herself into it and be glad for the experience.

Sometimes it isn't an "on" or "off" reaction. The experience of the drama may occasion positive attitudes in some areas but not in others. She may have a qualified reaction, e.g., "I loved the sets, costumes, and lighting, but the main character's voice put me on edge." This, of course, is an example of comments on the execution of the drama. Others may have different sorts of mixed reactions relating to the plot or themes set out in the script and the director's presentation of the same. It is from these sorts of reactions that the patron comes to know the artist's vision through his treatment of the particular problem, or collection of problems set in the work: the *why*. The author's/director's vision is immediately known. All the parts of the presentation must work together toward some end. It is this to end that the patron reacts. If queried after the show by another patron, it is very important for there to be some common understanding on the purpose behind the presentation. Though there may be argument about how well it is set out and whether the numerous elements work together or not, still it is important for an audience to be able to articulate what it this presentation was all about. Why was it staged? Was it a good use of resources?

The only way to answer such a question is by reference to the problem that the production addresses and whether audience members, critics, and the production team, itself, really believes that they have adequately answered the promise of the play: addressing itself to the purpose that it raised and consequently put forth some causal consequence as a resolution. It need not be the case that the play shuts the door on other interpretations of the central problem, but it does seek to rise as one of the valiant attempts. There are many "why" questions connected to living in the world. Has this artistic endeavor defined a problem and then made comment or a coherent response? If the answer is "yes," then the drama has fulfilled the minimum necessary to call itself *art*.

Exhibits:

Of the Sleep of Ulro! and of the passage through
Eternal Death! and of the awaking to Eternal Life.

This theme calls me in sleep night after night, & ev'ry m o r n
Awakes me at sunrise; then I see the Saviour over me
Spreading his beams of love & dictating the words of this mild song:

"Awake! awake! o sleeper of the land of shadows, wake! expand!
I am in you and you in me, mutual in love divine:
Fibres of love from man to man through Albion's pleasant land.
In all the dark Atlantic vale down from the hills of Surrey
A black water accumulates; return, Albion! return!
Thy brethren call thee, and thy fathers, and thy sons;
Thy nurses and thy mothers, thy sisters and thy daughters
Weep at thy soul's disease, and the Divine Vision is darkened;
Thy Emanation, that was wont to play before thy face,
Beaming forth with her daughters into the Divine bosom—
Where hast thou hidden thy Emanation, lovely Jerusalem,
From the vision and fruition of the Holy one?"

       William Blake, from *Jerusalem: The Emanation of
       the Giant Albion*, ch. 1, plate 4

          Away, my soul away!
     In vain, in vain the Birds of warning sing—
And hark! I hear the famish'd brood of prey
Flap their lank pennons on the groaning wind!
         Away, my soul, away!
     I unpartaking of the evil thing,
       With daily prayer and daily toil
       Soliciting for food my scanty soil,
    Have wail'd my country with a loud Lament.

Now I recentre my immortal mind
    In the deep Sabbath of meek self-content;
Cleans's from the vaporous passions that beaming
God's Image, sister of the Seraphim.

Samuel Taylor Coleridge, *Ode to the Departing Year*, Stanza IX

Four seasons fill the measure of the year;
There are four seasons in the mind of man:
He has his lusty Spring, when fancy clear
Takes in all beauty with an easy span:
He has his Summer, when luxuriously
Spring's honied cud of youthful thought he loves
To ruminate, and by such dreaming nigh
His nearest unto heaven: quiet coves
His soul has in its Autumn, when his wings
He furleth close; contented so to look
On mists in idleness—to let fair things
Pass by unheeded as a threshold brook.
He has his Winter too of pale misfeature,
Or else he would forgo his mortal nature.

John Keats, *The Human Seasons*.

Prometheus. Monarch of Gods and Daemons, and all Spirits
But One, who throng those bright and rolling worlds
Which Thou and I alone of living things
Behold with sleepless eyes! regard this Earth
Made multitudinous with thy slaves, whom thou
Requitest for knee-worship, prayer, and praise,
And toil, and hecatombs of broken hearts,
With fear and self-contempt and barren hope.
Whilst me, who am thy foe, eyeless in hate,
Hast thou made reign and triumph, to thy scorn,
O'er mine own misery and thy vain revenge,
Three thousand years of sleep-unsheltered hours,
And moments aye divided by keen pangs

Till they seemed years, torture and solitude,
Scorn and despair,—these are mine empire.
More glorious far than that which thou surveyest
From thine unenvied throne, O, Mighty God!
Almighty, had I deigned to share the shame
Of thine ill tyranny, and hung not here
Nailed to this wall of eagle-baffling mountain,
Black wintry, dead, unmeasured; without herb,
Insect, or beast, or shape or sound of life.
Ah me, alas! pain, pain ever, forever!

No change, no pause, no hope! Yet I endure.
I ask the Earth, have not the mountains felt?
I ask yon Heaven, the all-beholding Sun,
Has it not seen? The Sea, in storm or calm,
Heaven's ever-changing Shadow, spread below,
Have its deaf waves not heard my agony?
Ah me! alas, pain, pain ever, for ever!

The crawling glaciers pierce me with the spears
Of their moon-freezing crystals, the bright chains
Eat with their burning cold into my bones.
Heaven's winged hound, polluting from thy lips
His beak in poison not his own, tears up
My heart; and shapeless sights come wandering by,
The ghastly people of the realm of dream,
Mocking me: and the Earthquake-fiends are charged
To wrench the rivets from my quivering wounds
When the rocks split and close again behind:
While from their loud abysses howling throng
The genii of the storm, urging the rage
Of whirlwind, and afflict me with keen hail.
And yet to me welcome is day and night,
Whether one breaks the hoar frost of the morn,
Or starry, dim, and slow, the other climbs
The leaden-coloured east; for then they lead
Their wingless, crawling hours, one among whom
—As some dark Priest hales the reluctant victim—
Shall drag thee, cruel King, to kiss the blood
From these pale feet, which then might trample thee
If they disdained not such a prostrate slave.

Disdain! Ah no! I pity thee. What ruin
Will hunt thee undefended thro' wide Heaven!
How will thy soul, cloven to its depth with terror,
Gape like a hell within! I speak in grief,
Not exultation, for I hate no mere,
As then ere misery made me wise. The curse
Once breathed on thee I would recall.

Percy Bysshe Shelley, *Prometheus Unbound*, I, i

Finally, and above all, O Friend! (I speak
With due regret) how much is overlooked
In human nature and her subtle ways,
As studied first in our own hearts, and then
In life among the passions of mankind,
Varying their composition and their hue,
Where'er we move, under the diverse shapes
That individual character presents
To an attentive eye. For progress meet,
Along this intricate and difficult path,
Whate'er was wanting, something had I gained,
As one of many schoolfellows compelled,
In hardy independence, to stand up
Amid conflicting interests, and the shock
Of various tempers; to endure and note
What was not understood, though known to be;
Among the mysteries of love and hate,
Honour and shame, looking to right and left,
Unchecked by innocence too delicate,
And moral notions too intolerant,
Sympathies too contracted. Hence, when called
To take a station among men, the step
Was easier, the transition more secure,
More profitable also; for, the mind
Learns from such timely exercise to keep
In wholesome separation the two natures,
The one that feels, the other that observes.
            William Wordsworth, *The Prelude,* bk. 14, ll. 321-
            347.

Where organizations have appeared under a cooperative principle they have taken one of three forms, sometimes known as consumers, productive and credit cooperation. Societies of consumers are established to buy and sell commodities. The profits from which are to go to the members of the associations. Such organizations have been remarkably successful creating an organized market for the products made by productive societies.

Frank L. McVey, *Modern Industrialism*, (N.Y., 1904): 174.

This mortgage system still continues to some extent and has been an important factor in the continuance of a one-crop agriculture in which very few supply crops are grown, so that even the hay eaten by the mule that plows the cotton is often imported in bales from north of the Ohio or west of the Mississippi. The man who advances the money to the cotton grower does not encourage the growth of other crops, nor the development of a more rational agriculture, because no other crop is so easily mortgaged, so easily kept or so readily salable as cotton. Thus the South, which has excellent natural facilities for the development of live-stock industries and the growth of forage crops, continues to import mules, hay, corn, butter, cheese, and pork, which it might produce as cheaply as any other part of the world, if not more cheaply (see chapter on live stock). . . .

With the continued rapid spread of more scientific agriculture, with crop rotation and animal husbandry in the cotton belt of the United States, the production can be increased several fold during the present century. The invention of a successful cotton-picking machine which now seems assured would work a great revolution by removing the greatest labor element in its production and putting it on a par with wheat, oats, and corn, all of which crops machinery has made possible the working of many acres by a single individual.

Fig. 130: Amount of Cotton Grown and as a percentage of total economy

States:	Texas	Georgia	Ala.	S. Carol.	Miss.	Ark.	Ok.	N. Carol.	Others
Percentage:	26.6	16.9	10.5	10.5	9.7	6.4	6.4	6.4	6.6

| Million of bales | 3.3 | 2.1 | 1.3 | 1.3 | 1.2 | .8 | .8 | .8 | .8 |

/12.4 total bales produced (by millions)

(1908-1910)

. . . In the United States the manufacture of cotton is concentrated in the region east of the Appalachians, in a long belt from Maine to Alabama, with its greatest centers in New England and at the eastern base of the Appalachians in the Carolinas and Georgia, with a lesser center in Philadelphia. New England, with 17 million spindles, is the leader in cotton manufacturing and is likely to be for an indefinite time to come, although the southern states with 11.5 million spindles are already consuming more cotton in a single year than does New England.

> J. Russell Smith, *Commerce and Industry,* (N.Y., 1916): 214-5, 220-1.

A marked characteristic of the South was that income received from the export of cotton (and sugar, rice and tobacco) flowed directly out of the regional economy again in the purchase of goods and services. The South provided neither the services to market its own exports nor the consumer goods and services to supply its own needs, and had a very high propensity to import. . . .The Northeast provided not only the services to finance, transport, insure, and market the South's cotton, but also supplied the South with manufactured goods, either from its own industry or imported and reshipped to the south. . . . Underlying the uneven pattern of development was the shape of the supply curve of cotton (or grain) and the way in which the supply curve shifted. During each period of expansion, millions of acres of new land were purchased from the government for cotton production. Once this land had been cleared and a crop or two of corn planted to prepare the soil, the amount of cotton available could be substantially increased, and the supply curve of cotton shifted very sharply to the right. With the depressed cotton prices that followed such an expansion, a good deal of this land was devoted to alternative uses.

> Douglass C. North, "Aspects of Economic Growth in the United States, 1815-1860," in *The Experience of Economic Growth*, Barry E. Supple ed., (N.Y., 1963): 246, 249-50.

One of the most mischievous superstitions in connection with the coming of industrial civilization is the assumption that the greater and greater use of machinery tends to standardize or to mechanize human life. The notion is utterly contrary to the facts, but this does not keep certain highly intellectual persons, and even some eminent scholars, from entertaining it. They believe in "robots" today quite as childishly as they once believed in Santa Claus, and quite as naively as the eminent intellectuals of the middle ages believed in witches and demons. Fortunately, they are not keeping us from inventing new machinery; they are simply keeping us from appreciating it, and from using it as effectively and as happily as we might be using it. These croakers remind me of a certain type of mother who, in her love for her children, has come to love their childishness, and is therefore dismayed at the discovery that they are growing up. The youngsters are learning new words, new phrases, are even beginning to read books and evince a taste for literature, all of which so encroaches on their baby talk that the doting parent is utterly distracted. Such a mother, to be sure, cannot quite keep her children from becoming men and women, but she can and does create no end of mischief. She can keep them sometimes, from wanting to grow. She can keep them from appreciating the new developments and the new, responsibilities of life. It is much the same with these intellectual kill-joys. They cannot keep the machine civilization from advancing, and they often wistfully admit that they cannot: but they can and do sour the lives of those who take them seriously. Why curse the sunrise because it obscures the stars? True, the sunrise does obscure the stars; and the machine civilization compels us to see things which were out of sight before, and to observe many of the old familiar things in an entirely new light. But why be sour about it?

Edward A. Filene, *Successful Living in this Machine Age* (N.Y., 1931): 181-2.

I am colored but I offer nothing in the way of extenuating circumstances except the fact that I am the only Negro in the United States whose grandfather on the mother's side was *not* an Indian chief.

I remember the very day that I became colored. Up to my thirteenth year I lived in the little Negro town of Eatonville, Florida. It is exclusively a colored town. The only white people I knew passed through the town going to or coming from Orlando. . . . During this period white people differed from colored to me only in that they rode through town and never lived there. They like to hear me "speak pieces" and sing and wanted to see me dance the parse-me-la, and gave me generously of their small silver for doing these things, which seemed strange to me for I wanted to do them so much that I needed bribing to stop. Only they didn't know it. The colored people gave no dimes. They deplored any joyful tendencies in me, but I was their Zora nevertheless. I belonged to them to the nearby hotels, to the county—everybody's Zora.

But changes came in the family when I was thirteen, and I was sent to school in Jacksonville. I left Eatonville, the town of the oleanders, as Zora. When I disembarked from the river-boat at Jacksonville, she was no more. It seemed that I had suffered a sea change. I was not Zora of Orange County any more. I was now a little colored girl. I found it out in certain ways. In my heart as well as in the mirror. I became a [color] fast brown—warranted not to rub nor run. . . .

Zora Neale Hurston, "How it Feels to be Colored Me" (1928)

I am a Negro. The origin of the Negro is African. It would therefore seem an easy matter for me to assume African nationality.

Instead it is an extremely complicated matter, fraught with the gravest importance to me and some millions of coloured folk.

Africa is a Dark Continent not merely because its people are dark-skinned or by reason if its extreme impenetrability, but because its history is lost. We have an amazingly vivid reconstruction of the culture of ancient Egypt, but the roots of almost the whole remainder of Africa are buried in antiquity.

They are, however, rediscoverable; and they will in time be rediscovered. I am confirmed in this faith by recent researches linking the *culture* of the Negro with that of many peoples of the East . . . . I realize that this will never be accomplished by viewing from afar the dark rites of the witch-doctor . . . [but] it may be accomplished, or at least furthered by patient inquiry. To this end I am learning Swahili, Tivi, and other African dialects—which come easily to me *because their rhythm is the same as that employed by the American Negro speaking English.* . . Meanwhile in my music, my plays, my films I want to carry always this central idea: to be African.

Multitudes of man have died for less worthy ideals; it is even more eminently worth fighting for.

Paul Robeson, "I Want to Be African" (1934)

death surrounds itself with the living
i watch them take the body from the house
i'm a young kid maybe five years old
the whole thing makes no sense to me
i hear my father say
        lord jesus—what she go and do this for
i watch him walk out the backdoor of the house
i watch him walk around the garden
kick the dirt

stare at the flowers
& shake his head shake his head
he shake his head all night long

yazoo
jackson
vicksburg
we must have family in almost every city
i spent more time traveling than growing up
guess that's why I'm still shorter than my old man
he don't like to stay in one place much
he tell me

soon as people get to know your last name
seem like they want to call you by your first
boy if someone ask you your name
tell them to call you mississippi
not sippi or sip but mississippi.

> E. Ethelbert Miller, "mississippi" from
> his volume *where are the love poems for
> dictators* (Washington, D.C., 1986): 62.

De railroad bridge's
A sad song in de air.
De railroad bridge's
A sad song in de air.
Ever time de trains pass
I wants to go somewhere.

I went down to de station
Ma heart was in ma mouth.
Went down to de station
Heart was in ma mouth
Lookin for box car
To roll me to de South.

Homesick blues, Lawd.
'S a terrible thing to have.
Homesick blues is

A terrible thing to have.
To keep from cryin'
I opens ma mouth an' laughs.

Langston Hughes "Homesick Blues"
(1926)

♑ Capricorn

Fermentation

Chapter 1

"Jefferson and Myra have a Few Words"

And again Night's course began over heaven-inducing darkness. A grateful truce was imposed once more, with the Sun creating the setting for the departing train from Varner's Junction. The iron horse pulled slowly away from the station, and still staring out the window was Jefferson, contemplating what he should do in the hours and days ahead. Now the odious din which had plagued him, as a fury, had now transitioned to silence.

A time of climax was approaching.

He had brought with him half of his total financial resources which he intended to use wisely in his cause for Justice. Righteous was his purpose. But he had been there before, and it had been bloody. First, in New York with Peabody (who was brutally murdered), and then second in Baltimore with his wife and family (who were savagely killed). If God's on the side of Justice, then why doesn't He protect His servants?

When they had reached Savannah, Jefferson stepped down from the Jim Crow car, alone amidst the somber blackness. He proceeded toward his destination where he knew that he was compelled to go. His task would be more serious than anything he had undertaken in many years. It was his life's purpose.

Jefferson made it back by foot to Myra's place in a half-hour. He went up the back way by the fire escape. She heard him knocking on the rear door and rushed to open it.

"I'm glad you're back," said Myra, stepping outside to Jefferson but then pausing as if afraid to put her arms around him, as he might not approve or enjoy the embrace of one of her station.

But Jefferson, sensing her hesitancy, took the initiative and gave her a hug of welcome.

"Did you think I'd forget to come back?" asked Jefferson with a smile.

"No, never," said Myra, not realizing that Jefferson was only joking, but then adding lightly, "I thought that I might have to finish this thing all by myself, or maybe bail you out again."

The two laughed and then Jefferson told Myra all that he had heard. "The only question I have, and I admit that it's a big question, is whether the two Dodsons work together, and if Sig Wyse is the link between them? Or whether Sig is the link between them and Daniels? However, as I said, I don't even know whether Rod Dodson has a partner. But one thing is for certain, that he wants Daniels dead, and that must mean that Daniels and he are involved in some sort of power struggle in which Rod thinks that he will make short work of his rival.

"The key to the other brother is important, because if this has anything to do with the killing of Victor, and if the killer is still about, then our only hope is if the two brothers *are* working together. That might imply that the killer is associated with the organization."

"That all seems to make sense, but what if the killer isn't in the organization?" asked Myra.

"Then he'll never be caught, or at least not by us. He's probably in another state living under a false name. I don't think we could trace him."

"But even if the killer were in the organization, don't you think that he might have done the same and be impossible to trace?" Myra asked her question as she took her arms away from Jefferson.

"He could have, but I'm gambling on the fact that there's a difference between a hired gun that doesn't work for an organization and a hit man within one. I think that they might consider themselves protected, especially if the killer wasn't a regular killer. He might figure that as the police have a suspect already (and a good one), that there wouldn't be any use in leaving, which might have drawn unnecessary attention to them. This would be especially true if they were local. This wouldn't have been necessary if they are part of the Savannah branch. In that case they figure that they are fully protected and so would have no reason to leave. In either event, an *inside hit man* has no reason to high tail it.

Besides, the only way an organization, like this one, can work is if they have a high degree of loyalty, real or otherwise, and so reduce their turnover and keep their secrecy high. I think that if our killer is a part of the Dodson organization, then he is probably still where we can get our hands on him."

"Well, I sure hope that you're right," said Myra.

Jefferson looked at the woman standing across from him in the fire escape in front of the back door. Perhaps it was the flickering light of the night, but it seemed to him that some of her former beauty, that had been so admired by so many when she lived in Bella County, was returning to her face. It was like a transformation, and at that moment he felt a warm closeness that he hadn't felt since one early summer day in Baltimore many years before—before all his dreams lay breathless upon the floor as a sign for him to follow. There was within him an emotional response that he had been sure had died with that young woman that was now rekindled, not in the same young way, but in a different way: very quiet and profoundly moving.

He took her hand in his old bony one and nodded his assent.

The next morning, Jefferson arose and discovered that their food supply was barely existent, so he took it upon himself to refurbish it. When he returned, he had made up his mind that he would meet the man, who was from Detroit, himself.

"What are you, crazy?" asked Myra when he told her about his scheme.

"Not at all, at least I don't think so."

"Then what are you doing, are you trying to get yourself killed?" her voice was plaintive, and showing her vain attempt to control it.

"Look, if there is a link between the two Dodsons, then maybe I can find out about it. It's my only chance of breaking this thing open."

"The only thing you'll break open is your head," replied Myra.

"I know it's a risk, and that you are in this thing with me, and that hence you are taking as big as risk as I am. I've thought about that and I came to the conclusion that you should probably leave."

"Leave? You mean you're going to have let me go to all this trouble of watching this fellow, helping you escape, with all the danger that entailed, and now you are going to let me go? Well, tell me, sir, where do you think I should go?" Her voice was harsh and sarcastic. Jefferson didn't expect such a violent reaction from his suggestion. It had seemed like the only thing that he could do to keep everything open and operating.

"Well, you could go to Bella County, for one thing."

"Oh, sure, and do what, go back and work at my old place in the store?"

Why was she being so hostile? This antagonistic energy of hers was unsettling. "I don't care if you don't want to go to Bella County. You can go anywhere you please, but you shouldn't stay around here. It's too dangerous."

Myra stared at him for a long moment. Jefferson felt her stare, but couldn't bring his eyes to meet hers, they were too intense. What did she want from him? Couldn't she see that he had to find the killer and that nothing else mattered? But even as he wanted to express this to her, he felt himself unable to look at her and leaned back against the railing of the fire escape. His eyes stared downward to the peeling sky-blue paint shards that curled up from the wood planks that hadn't been maintained for years.

"You know," she began in a very calm voice, "for a man who's so intelligent, you can certainly be thick-headed sometimes." Then she turned around and entered the apartment.

What did she mean? And where was she going? Jefferson followed her into the apartment. Myra had departed. She hadn't taken any of her things, not even a coat, and it was chilly today. Where was she going? And what did she mean by 'thick-headed?'

Jefferson's mind was confused. Didn't she see that it was important for him to find the killer or at least try as hard as he could? Didn't she see that he was only trying to look out for her safety when he suggested that she go away? It wasn't that he thought she'd make things clumsy or bother him in any way (he enjoyed and needed her assistance), it was just that he didn't want to feel responsible for her injury. He couldn't let that happen. Not to Myra; because he, he—cared for her.

Jefferson sat down in a chair and put his face into his open hands.

"So your woman's run out on you," Coody said from his position on the floor. "Hey, why don't you let me go," said the man again. "I won't cause you any trouble. I'll leave town, yeah, that's what I'll do I'll leave town, and then I won't be of any more trouble."

"Shut up, and eat something," said Jefferson, throwing the man some pieces of bread and a portion of salami.

"Salami? I hate salami."

"Eat."

"Nigger, you is shit clear through. Shit, do you hear me? Shit clear through. That octoroon woman you got ain't never comin' back, because she's tired of you and your smell."

Chapter 2

"Waiting for a Man"

It was late afternoon and Jefferson was sitting in the same chair, doing nothing except sleeping and thinking about whether he should let the man go and call it quits to the entire endeavor. Perhaps he had been too ambitious. A person can't make up for lost time; there's no coming back, they say, and perhaps it's true. One time you've had it, and you failed. Now, you're through.

Perhaps the best thing to do would be simply to let the man go and then to take off, perhaps to Texas or somewhere. Sure, he was old, but he could never go back to Bella County again, not like this. The thought of such a thing would be too unbearable. But there didn't seem to be any real purpose to it all any more. Man was made to relax, not to keep himself tense all the time and try to do things that he wasn't made to do. Jefferson felt that now he was merely experiencing what he should have realized a long time before, that he was only good for nothing. . . .

But before he could finish his thought, he heard something, like a cat scratching at the door. He looked up and went to investigate. The noise repeated itself. There was a cat out there. He could tell by the noise of its claws and other cat sounds that were felt rather than distinctly recognized. Jefferson rushed to the door and opened it, but saw nothing; there was no cat, but he did hear someone coming up the stairs. He walked to the landing and saw Myra.

He couldn't express the excitement that he felt upon seeing her as he ran to meet her and greeted her with a big hug.

"Careful," said Myra. "We got to keep our comings and goings secret." Her voice was not hard, but it was firm.

Jefferson put her down and they went back to the room. "I'm glad you came back," he said.

"It was *dangerous*," she replied with a hint of sarcasm.

"I know, but I'm still glad to see you. I was always glad to see you. It was just that I didn't want anything to happen to you. I didn't express it very well, I suppose."

He took her hand, but she drew it away.

"I came back, but I'll leave again in an instant unless one thing is clear, and that is, if I intend to stay here, I do so knowing fully the risks and must be allowed to live as dangerously as you. This is nonsense about you're always trying to *protect me* and *guard me*. I can decide what risks I want to take, and if they ever get too much for me, believe it, you'll be the first one I'll tell."

"Oh, Myra, —" began Jefferson.

"I mean it," she repeated. "I've been around enough to know when I should be careful, and if you think I'm throwing my life away or some garbage like that, then all I have to say is that it's *my life* to throw away, just as it was *my risk* to help you git out of that cat house you was trapped in."

Having said her piece, she sat down, and Jefferson sat next to her and took her hand, and she didn't take it away.

"Aw, ain't that sweet," said Coody from his spot on the floor before moaning and turning over to sleep.

Jefferson just smiled and turned to Myra, "Have you eaten? I should be leaving soon."

"You still have time," she said.

"Yes, but I want to look the place over as well as buy another gun so that we can each have one."

"I don't want to carry a gun. One is all right for now while I guard Charlie over there, but I wouldn't want to make it a regular thing."

"Well, I think I will buy one anyway, and if you don't want to carry it, then I'll carry two. Besides, I have to get a good look at this place before I go inside in case there's something suspicious."

They ate and Jefferson went on his errands, which went according to the allotted time that he had anticipated in his mind.

Jefferson went to a gambling place he had been told about a few days before. The corner table was perhaps the best seat, as far as Jefferson was concerned, in the whole place, as it afforded a view of everyone in the room. As he had his back to the wall he could concentrate on what was happening in front of him.

The room was rather dark and filled with different types of smoke. Jefferson surmised that perhaps there were some West Indian cigarettes about. At any rate, the atmosphere was one of medium noise and intoxicated indulgence; nobody seemed to care what the other was doing and this was very good for Jefferson's purposes, as he was reading a newspaper, which would have been farcical except for the fact that there was a lamp just over his head so that if he really had been intent on reading he might have done so. The person who envisioned this knew everything down to the last detail, thought Jefferson. He looked up and quickly spotted a door near him for quick exit if he so desired.

A man plopped down at the table across from Jefferson. It was obvious to Jefferson that the man was drunk.

"Say, there, do you remember the Maine?" said the man in a faltering voice.

"I do, but you don't look like you can remember anything," responded Jefferson, anxious that the drunk should leave so that his contact might not be scared away by the uninvited company.

"How about buying me a drink, and then I'll tell you how I helped lead the charge up San Juan Hill, with Teddy."

"Some other time, friend," said Jefferson, politely trying to extricate himself from the dilemma.

"But it's a fascinating story, and it's true!" declared the man.

Just then it entered Jefferson's mind that this might indeed be the man he was supposed to meet, simply trying out different things until he, Jefferson, made the first move.

"Ever been to—Detroit?" asked Jefferson cagily.

"Detroit, Detroit, sure lots of times, why there was the time back in aught-nine when we was a bumming around together and I met this little Spanish dish, wow was she a handful, know what I mean?" said the man, holding himself to indicate large breasts.

"Look friend, some other time I'd be more than willing to listen to these tales of true adventure, but just now—"

"You don't want to hear my stories?" said the man rather loudly.

Jefferson was afraid of the man making a scene and scaring the real man away so he thought that perhaps if he gave the man some money, that he would be quiet.

"Here old man, buy yourself a whiskey," said Jefferson, bossing him a quarter. The old man caught the coin in the air as if he had reflexes that had been trained from long experience and smiled and tipped his hat to Jefferson.

"Thank you kindly, you're a real gentleman, sir, and if you ever want to hear about the charge up San Juan Hill—"

"Yes, I know where to find you," said Jefferson as the man staggered away.

Jefferson looked down to his newspaper and lifted it up again, when he saw something slip into his lap. It was a note of some kind. He carefully lifted it up so that he appeared to be only turning the page of his newspaper.

Down the block to Jeb Stuart, in ten minutes

Jefferson didn't know the meaning of the note except that the drunk was indeed the man that he was supposed to meet, but that for some reason, he didn't want to meet him in the arranged spot. Was it a trap? Did he simply want to get him out of the crowded place so that they could take him down? Jefferson was somewhat apprehensive. He had the thousand dollars that was to be the payoff to the man, in an envelope in his coat pocket. Perhaps this man was only a common thief and suspected that Jefferson had a lot of money—but this thought seemed too ludicrous and Jefferson was faced with the decision of going after the man or else waiting where he was or thirdly going back and forgetting about it.

Were there lots of Dodson's people here? Is that why the man wanted to change the place? Jefferson put the paper in his pocket and took out his clock and pretended to be impatient. After a few minutes he got up and walked out. He strode carefully around the block to where the street lamp on the corner of *Jeb Stuart* burned brightly.

Jefferson saw a figure in the dark next to the building. It was a drunk lying against the wall; perhaps it was his man. Jefferson walked over to look. Then he heard footsteps. There were two men following him. It was a trap. Jefferson took off running down the street and into an alley, then into a crowded speakeasy and out the back way.

The men weren't anywhere in sight. Just then Jefferson heard the footsteps again, and this time there was nowhere to go. He was trapped in a blind alley, though it was dark enough so that he couldn't easily be seen. The figure could not be distinguished except by the long dark shadow that he cast near the entrance to the alley where a wedge of reflected light from the street lamp fell on the oily pavement near to where the alley met the sidewalk. He was waiting around the corner, waiting to see whether Jefferson was going to make a move. There was, of course, his gun. But it was one that he'd never used before. He knew that when he bought it, he could possibly be wild. A man has to get to know his gun. If he tries to respond with a weapon with which he was unfamiliar, he might accidentally kill the man. Or—even worse, fail to kill or injure an attacker against his own personal safety.

Jefferson could hear the faint sound of the muffled band music inside the club, for it was the only sound that could be heard. They were on a back street in a tough section and if anything happened the police would simply chalk it up to *that area of town*. One or more dead blacks here didn't amount to anything. It was just like a few bodies of junkyard dogs who were hungry and got into it.

The figure was stopped at the entrance, his shadow looming large in the light, but his presence was indistinguishable. Jefferson put his hand on the pistol and slid it slowly from his coat. He had already loaded it, and now held the gun unsteadily as if he wasn't sure what he wanted to do with it. Soon the men would be crashing up the stairs with their machine guns and make short work of him. His only chance was in escaping through the alley, but possibly there was more than one man at the end of the alley; maybe the whole lot of them were waiting for him.

Across the street was a small park, if he could get over to it. The noise from the band seemed to be getting louder; he took a step forward. His shoe squeaked; the shadow moved. Jefferson cocked his pistol, it made a loud click, and the figure crouched as the shadow betrayed his movements. Jefferson inched forward, pistol in front of him. It would be one of them. Jefferson felt that now was the time. There could be no backing away from this fight— everything depended on his getting out.

Just then a voice called him, "Hurry up and get out of there, if it's only you."

It was the voice at the end of the alley. Jefferson glanced at the shadow, which was standing again.

"C'mon, hurry, they'll be out soon."

"Detroit?"

"Hurry up, now."

The shadow disappeared. It could be a trap, they might all be waiting for him at the end of the alley, but then this figure might be the one that he was looking for. It was a single figure, at least that was all that he saw. Jefferson couldn't hear the band music any longer so he decided to risk it as he ran to the edge of the alley and looked cautiously around: there was no one there, so he stepped out of the alley and again looked around him. There was a noise across the street. Jefferson, still holding his gun, made his way to the other side of the street and into the park when he heard a burst of machine gun fire from what he thought must have been the alley.

"Down here," said the voice from a group of bushes.

Jefferson hurried to join the voice.

"Your friends are in a hurry," said the voice.

"Things are a bit tight just now," replied Jefferson.

They were silent as the men ran out to the street and split up, only one man heading for the park. The man was obviously not one of the best men for the job, for he just walked a ways into the park and perhaps, Jefferson thought, because of the darkness being an ideal place to be ambushed, decided quickly that there was no one there.

When all the men were gone, the stranger suggested they move to the park bench. Jefferson agreed and when they were seated, he remembered his gun and un-cocked it. As he did so, he heard a corresponding click—this man was not too trusting.

"What's the job exactly?" said the man, his face covered to his nose by the brim of his wide hat that was turned down for that purpose, and the shadow that it caused seemed to hide all but the man's lips from plain view.

"You've got to kill for us, to relieve a little situation that we have."

The man didn't respond. How could Jefferson go through with this? He was actually assigning a death warrant to someone's life, but then that person would have been commissioned whether he, Jefferson, did anything or not. However, the plain fact remained that it was Jefferson who was commissioning the killing. He would be responsible for the resultant deaths. He couldn't go through with it, but if he was to find the killer whose place John was filling at present, then wouldn't it all be worth it? No, he couldn't justify saving one life at the expense of another, even if the other was a criminal who might have justly deserved such a fate. No, it couldn't be done, and yet, might there be some middle ground?

"We have a little trouble here, and what we want exactly is to stir things up a bit, do you understand?"

The man didn't respond.

"We're not sure whether we *actually* want to hit anybody or not, but what we do want is to make some noise so that some parties can get a little anxious about it, do you understand?"

"You don't want a hit right now, but you want me to make it known that someone's out for somebody else?" the man paraphrased.

"That's it exactly. Now, the man we want harassed is a man named Rod Dodson. The man setting the contract is George Dodson. This is the rumor I want you to spread. For the moment, we are in the advertising business only. Things might require us to fulfill the mission—depending upon how things stir up. Now here's a thousand dollars. I'll be here next week. Right here on this bench. I'll tell you then if you have to finish the job or whether you can high tail it out of town."

"So for now, you just want some buzz and for me to lie low," repeated the man.

"And if I'm not here next week, right here, then take off."

The man didn't say another word, but took the envelope and put it into his coat and got up and walked away into the darkness.

Jefferson sat, wondering whether what he had done was the best thing. In all the confusion, Rod will think that someone's out to get him, and if he hears that it's George, and if they're working together, then perhaps this can start a little commotion that will smoke out a few people who might not otherwise have surfaced. As it is, everything is too tight. Things have to become more harried so that I can get some information. If I can shake things up a little, then maybe I can get my information before the two of them get together and find out that the whole thing was just a hoax.

What I'm trying to buy is a little time, when maybe Rod will become a little shaken up about the whole thing and then maybe some of his men might get a bit shaken as well; it's then that I might be able to get through to one of them, perhaps acquire some names from the fellow we're holding right now and then approach them with a deal of some sort, whereby we can get some information. Everything depends on whether Rod believes in the rumor that George sent out a killer to get him. If they aren't in this together, then of course he'll think nothing of it, and that will be the end of it. But if they really are partners, perhaps he will get a little suspicious about the whole thing and then maybe there will be a little commotion—especially since George is out of town, securing plans for something or other, and won't be back for a few days. We'll have all the time we will require for a split or defection of just a man or two who can give us information.

But everything depends upon finding the exact moment to approach the men. If it's too early, they might realize that it is a hoax. If it is too late, they may have had time to contact George personally and so dismiss it. At most, Jefferson thought they'd have a week to ten days.

Timing was everything.

Jefferson sat back on the bench. Things were in motion, and he was totally involved. He no longer considered turning back. He was in until they all had to lay their cards down on the table.

Chapter 3

"A Curious Encounter"

John entered the old house and searched for the lever to open the wall. But he couldn't find it. He looked around the ground floor but it wasn't there. He couldn't leave so he found a chair that was covered with a sheet. John lifted the sheet off the chair, shook off the dust, and decided to sit down. Soon he fell asleep.

"So you've decided to come back. I knew you would."

John recognized the voice of the dwarf.

"Why didn't you come to the lower level? I showed you how."

John turned around and saw the dwarf dressed in a green costume consisting of a tunic and a light-weight coat, with green tights and what appeared to be green felt shoes that were turned up at the toes. In such dress, the dwarf looked like a boy dressed up for Halloween.

"My, my, don't we look fancy, are you going to a masked ball?"

"No, my good man, but unless you get those filthy clothes off of you, you will be fit for nothing."

"I'm hungry, I think I'll have something to eat," said John. He wanted to see how far he could push this little man to obey him. The dwarf saw that John no longer seemed to be afraid of him and this realization, John thought, was bothering the little man to no end.

"But of course, if your highness is hungry, he must certainly eat," said the dwarf. There was a smile on the dwarf's face, which puzzled John. Perhaps the dwarf thought that he knew something that John didn't—it was the food, there was something to do with the food. Those strange effects—perhaps he had been drugged in some manner. The little man was smiling because he thought that he could once again put John under his dominion through the drug. It was all clear to him.

John nodded his head again and then when he heard a noise he woke up. He was in the subterranean room where he had been before. How did he get there? John blinked hard to right his consciousness. When Martin returned with the food, John sat at a table and prepared to cut a bite. "Perhaps you should taste my food, since you are my servant," began John. He remembered that all princes had their food tasted by their court fools.

"Perhaps you would prefer to eat in solitude," replied Martin.

"As you wish, my little man," replied John. He was determined to show this fellow that he would not cow him with any of his insults or vain threats.

Martin left and John disposed of his food, hiding it in various places around the room, and then lay down as if he were overcome by the urge to sleep. He lay for quite a while, and actually did fall asleep, when he awoke it was with the most noxious odor in his nose. He was about to sit up when he remembered where he was, so he carefully rolled over instead and opened his eye just a little. In the center of the room was Martin with a small orb in front of him that was emitting greenish smoke that John took to be the origination of the horrible smell. The smoke was having its own effect upon John, despite the fact that he had eaten no food (a fact which his stomach was sorely protesting at the moment).

Springing out of bed John cried, "Be away with you, you will be gone!" and so yelling he kicked the orb and it rolled around. However, where it had been lying were several worms that were flat and ugly.

Instantly John was nauseated and jumped backwards. What was happening? He was very hungry.

The dwarf laughed, "These worms, they are my friends. They bore into your skin and live in your intestines."

John wasn't laughing, but had retreated to the bed as he saw the worms move about slowly on the floor.

"They are parasites, my dear—just like you."

The dwarf started walking around the room, to the places where John had hidden his bits of food, and collected them in a large bin.

"You know the worms appreciate food like this, but they'd rather have it when it's inside you because then they can be sure of a good sized meal."

"What are you?" cried John. He was suddenly aware that he felt utterly fatigued. He wanted to move, but his body would not respond. This made him anxious.

"What do you want me to be?" asked the little man.

"I want you to take those worms away."

"What's the matter, you're not afraid of my little pets, are you?"

Pets? Who could this man be? John knew that he wasn't under the influence of any drug now, but simply disoriented. His disdain had transformed into confusion: the thought of something living inside of him seemed utterly hideous, and whereas he wasn't afraid of anything that might attack him openly, the thought of something boring its way into him and slyly attacking him was unbearable. He had had too much of that already. Why couldn't any of his foes meet him openly, but always through some small and ugly means?

"You know, if you really wanted to eat, you certainly show it in a strange way," said Martin, finishing in his collection of the food. He knew where all of it was, as if he had seen John hide it. "Perhaps you don't trust us, is that it? You know we feel offended when people don't trust us."

What was the *we* referring to? Was it to the worms or that old lady, if there really was an old lady?

"I want to be alone, and I want you to take the worms."

By now the worms had moved a foot or two from where they had been grouped together as they slithered slowly along on the carpet.

"You know you must learn to ask for things in a nicer way than that, if you ever want someone to wait on you. I pleased you before because you were hungry, but now I see that you weren't really hungry at all, and I'm hurt." The little man was standing next to his pail, smiling.

John thought about Julia and how she must have laughed at his note that he had sent her concerning the meeting in Atlanta. "I was a fool to believe that someone like her could ever love someone like me," he told himself. All the old thoughts returned to him. His eyes pleaded with the little man.

"Now how do we ask for things?" asked the little man, walking over and picking up a worm with tweezers and taking it to John's bed. All the while on the train she had been sitting there, probably enjoying herself in the thought that John would be sitting like a dumb fool waiting for her, if indeed she had taken the train at all.

"Now what do you say?" asked Martin again as he lowered the worm slowly so that it touched John's arm.

I'm not going to break, he can't try and scare me with some little worm, he thought, so John pulled himself away and rolled out of bed. But he didn't have any shoes on and they had been removed. He would have to walk through the worms. Then he felt his head ache. Had the little man given him some drug after all without his even knowing it? Could that have been possible? If John left, where would he go? What would he do?

"Leave me alone, will you?"

"You know, that's more polite," said Martin. "The harshness has gone out of your voice." The little man turned around and put the worms into a jar, which he left next to John's bed.

To betray is perhaps the cruelest thing that a woman can do. It is bad to go and leave someone, but to *betray them* at the same time is doubly cruel. Then he remembered sitting and watching Cindy Pancroft talking with Billy Thompson. Had Cindy been experiencing the same pain that he, John, was just feeling now? On the road, he had been able to shut it out to some extent, but now, the depression of it hit him all at once. How cruel he must have been to Cindy. John was ashamed. He should have offered to protect her, to do something, but instead he had treated her as if she were—a worm sitting in a jar ready to bore into the skin of any willing host. Was he paying now for that injustice? If he could only believe that, then perhaps there would be some sense, some reason for his suffering, but he knew that there was no connection except in his own guilty feelings about it. What he was feeling had no logical tie with the other except for the fact that both happened to be in his realm of experience.

This part of his life must be accepted for what it was, but that reality was too terrible to be fully imagined, for what that implied was that he wasn't really worthy of Julia's love after all. He had betrayed *her*. So what was his complaint if she had turned his letter over to the police? Wasn't that just retribution? He had been thoughtless. He had acted as an animal. He was not up to the standard of Jefferson. Oh, if only he could be half the man that Jefferson is. But that was not to be because he had chosen the worms. They were his only true companions.

Nothing could be too decadent for him: the worms, the dwarf, the old woman, any and all the drugs that they gave him to keep him passive and in their control. He would give himself wholly to everything that they had to offer, and sacrifice himself. Yes he would make a sacrifice of himself. He would be whatever they wanted him to be and not complain.

There was no real light. What allowed him to see within the room was artificial light. This made his visions copies of that which were unreal. It was as if he were in a subterranean cave looking at shadows and believing that they were *real*.

This reflection made him laugh raucously out loud. Then he stopped laughing. Was he going mad? What was he doing, just laughing because he felt so estranged by it all? If he let himself go, would he ever be able to come back again? Would he ever really know himself again? Where was that boy who used to go fishing when he should have been at lessons? John picked up the bottle of worms and lifted it to his face so that he could see them closely.

He was so hungry.

Chapter 4

"An Exotic Turn to Our Narrative"

When the dwarf came in, he brought with him a gramophone and cranked it up and put on a record. Then he sat down and began to read a book.

"I'm hungry," said John. "I want some food."

"Ah, yes, so you said before."

"I need something to eat. I haven't eaten for a long time."

The record began to repeat itself as the needle was caught in a groove, so the dwarf gave it a tap and soon it was back to normal.

John didn't know what the little man wanted. John's head was dizzy from everything, and he only felt like taking small naps and listening to the noises of the house, which weren't many. Then the dwarf walked over to John and put a book next to him on the bed and left the room. John picked up the book, it was by W.E.B Dubois, who John had never heard of, but when he read a few lines, he could tell that the man was black. Why did he bring me this? He expects that I won't read it— that I'm afraid to read it. Well, I'll not give him the satisfaction of thinking that. I know that he can see me somehow, just as he could see when I hid my food.

The thought of someone looking at him all the time didn't sink in at first to John. It was rather difficult to become accustomed to, as he didn't know how he should behave, or on which side he was being observed. Where and how did they see him?

John felt ashamed; he didn't know what to do. He had to use his chamber pot, but he was not in the mood for someone to be observing his every movement so he stripped the sheets from the bed and draped them over him as he performed his bodily duty. I hope they're getting a good show, he thought to himself, but what if they can't see me and I'm only afraid of nothing! This thought struck him the same way that the rational explanations that he used to give to himself when he was a boy and he was afraid of there being strange men (robbers and killers) in his room waiting to jump him and kill him at the first opportunity. He would often search his room from top to bottom to assure himself that no such villains were in hiding, but other times he would refuse to allow himself that luxury and forced himself to go to sleep without a search on the argument that it was absurd to think that there were dangerous bandits hiding for him in his room. Was this merely the same type of case? Was he afraid of mere illusions of the mind that he had manufactured to torture himself?

Surely he had proof to distinguish this case from the others: the fact that the dwarf knew where everything was and went to the places immediately. But was this really proof, couldn't the dwarf have come in while John was asleep and found the hiding places one-by-one? But how would he have even known that the food had been hidden?

Perhaps he could tell that John was not drugged, or maybe some of the food had been hidden badly, or even began to smell. There were numerous hints that he could have had, but none of these explanations seemed to shed any light on the question of whether he was being watched or not.

John wanted to go back to sleep, but now the project seemed utterly impossible. He picked up the book. John would read it. There wasn't any reason why he could be afraid of it. His host didn't know him very well. He could read anything that he pleased and wasn't affected by who or what a book was about. He wasn't that far gone.

"I thought that you might wish a little refreshment," said the little man, entering after John had been reading for a time.

"Thank you, you may put it on the bed," said John. The dwarf went about cleaning up the room and when he was through he vacated the chamber, leaving John with his food. There wasn't much, only cakes and sweet things. The thought of sweets when he was yearning for solid food was somewhat distasteful, but John decided to give it a try. He couldn't eat too much, as he had guessed. This was due to his feeling of revulsion at the very thought of ingesting something sweet when he had a yearning for basic food. When a person is hungry, he wants what naturally comes first, not what is meant for last. And so John stopped after only a few bites. He knew that soon he would be overcome by the drugs. Then he would be under Martin's power.

It was as if he saw things about himself that weren't right, not appropriate. It was the exercise of his power from an inauthentic source, and somehow the sight of the dwarf, the worms, and eating the dessert brought this all to his mind. But what was the disgust? Was it simply a nausea over asserting his power falsely? But what was all this talk? John tried to stop his thoughts, but his feeling or visceral sentiment kept on the same tract, whether he would allow himself to think it or not.

All the running, all the running, who was running, who was doing the running—John tried to read, but his body was hungry and wouldn't allow his mind to wander. There could be submission of the immediate consciousness to the will of the individual, but there was no submission of the body—it acted on its own.

Who was W.E.B. Dubois? What did he have to say? These are the kinds of questions that made John anxious. His thoughts were mush, though for some reason he thought himself profound. John wished to orient himself, but even though he could begin to engage with some thoughts, clear lines of reasoning wouldn't come. There was no serial ordering of consecutive impressions, so that there wasn't any real coherence at all. All sugar and sweetness, the cakes and worms were both laughing in a chorus. John was alone in the room, but he felt as if he were in a circus, for not only did the aforementioned chorus clap at his writhing dance of mental torment, but they cried for more!

John leaped from the bed and ran about the room, trying to find the spot on the wall where the eyes were watching him. Frantic, he climbed up on top of table to search for the cracks in the wall where those eyes were observing all that he did. He searched for his jailer, who was making careful records of everything that he did— what were they thinking behind their plaster façade?

"I don't care," he cried. He was talking not to the wall, though he was in fact facing the wall. But his intention was to address those that he couldn't see, who he was convinced were lurking behind the wall, keeping careful watch on him.

"What have I done to you?" asked John, retreating to the center of the room. If he couldn't find their secret, at least he could perform for his masters. "Would you like me to do a dance for you?" said John, bowing low to the wall. Then John lifted up his arms to the ceiling and stretched himself until his muscles hurt. Almost on cue, he switched positions into a small ball and rolled about on the floor. Then, thinking about the possibility of a stray worm slithering about he leaped up and grasped one of the bed posts and hugged it. It was then that John decided to attend to the large mirror. From his position wrapped around the bed post, he observed the surface of the mirror: smooth and clear, except for one brown spot in the corner.

Perhaps they were watching him through the mirror, from behind? John didn't know how this would be possible scientifically, but he was intrigued by the idea and walked over and stepped directly in front of the mirror. Dow started making funny faces, distorting his mouth so that his audience would know that he was mocking them. His hands pushed about the skin of his face so that he would look like a mutant. Then they will know, he thought, that I'm on to them and they will have to give up their spying and leave me alone. But then why did he want to be alone? The prospect of being alone hit John with a full and terrifying force. All this time he thought that the thing that was disgusting him was the smell of the place, or the dessert or the worms or most of all being watched, but these weren't at all terrible to him—not in themselves. This was because each of them had a proper place in the world that was useful. And John was prepared to embrace their worth within their own sphere. The problem was that they were out of place. That was the cause of the irritation.

There was no clock in the room, so he turned again to the mirror. He stood in front of the mirror. Who was behind that mirror watching him make faces? Could it be no one? Was he really alone? If this was so, then the only person who could see him making faces was himself. It was at that moment that he began to look at himself making faces in a different perspective than before. He became attentive that the person who he was watching was himself, separated from himself. This conjecture frightened him, and then disgusted him. He decided to run back to the bed and throw himself under the covers. There he curled up, trying to be born again.

Where was the certainty that he longed for? He remembered studying geometry with Mr. Russell. It was very satisfying. One did proofs and got results that were certain. There was no possible room to doubt it. Why couldn't life be like a geometry proof?

John got up again from the bed and walked to the mirror. He faced the glass but this time there was no reflection of John Dow looking back. He looked into the mirror and saw nothing but glass and the silver that was painted behind it.

John reluctantly walked back to his bed. He mechanically pulled back the covers and got inside. But then his body bumped into another body. He wasn't alone in bed! He turned over to find the old woman again, clothed in a red nightgown.

John jumped out of bed and ran toward to door to the room. It was locked. It was a heavy door that he couldn't break down. John turned back to the bed and saw the dwarf standing there with a silver tray and a glass.

"It's time for your cognac," said Martin.

John walked forward and took the glass and emptied its contents on the floor. Then he walked back to the bed. The old woman had changed to a young woman. And she was entirely naked.

The woman reached out her right arm to him and beckoned him to return to bed with her index finger.

John fell to his knees and began to cry. He sobbed until he fell asleep. When he awoke he was standing outside of the old house as dawn was breaking. John looked at the old house and wondered about all the ghosts that lived there.

Then John turned away. It was time to go home. Would he be able to make the journey?

Chapter 5

"A Short Chapter with a Long Reach"

John Dow was now aware that he could not continue running his entire life. The life of a fugitive was a dead end. While one was out of jail (because he was not behind bars), he was confined in a different sense. This confinement had to do with being imprisoned in a narrative in which one had to be continually on-the-run. There was no chance to make friends or establish a permanent life somewhere. Everything was temporary.

Temporary was a hellish thought to John. He always sought something *more*. When he first turned away from the old house, he thought about going back to the lumber mill to work a couple of days to earn his fifty dollar salary, which had never been paid to him. But since he had magically gotten fifty dollars in his first journey to the old house, John felt on some level that he had been paid. There was no use going back there. It was part of the realm of the temporary. And that was what John wanted to obliterate in his life.

When he thought of the permanent, his thoughts went again to Julia. Perhaps there had been some mistake? Surely she would have never betrayed him. Certainly not. But John in his *stinkin' thinkin'* had supposed she had. Someone could have spied on their correspondence and informed the police. Julia was a trusting person and could easily have been duped. Why wasn't she more conniving? But then, if she were, would John love her as he did?

It was very complicated.

But then there was life on the road. John thought of the truck driver who had made such an impression on him. Surely that man's life was continual change as he drove from various places to other ports of call. Could continual change be a kind of permanence?

John didn't think so. He wanted a quiet rural life with a wife and children. He could work on a farm (he knew some of the business from Jefferson's tutelage). Or perhaps he could work with horses in the racing business. He didn't want to be a jockey (he was too tall and muscular for the big time), but he could care for them as a stable manager. This was also a life he could endure.

Finally, there was the life that Jefferson often talked about: doing good for one's fellow man. Though John had heard bits and pieces of Jefferson's years in Baltimore from rather obscure references, John had put together that Jefferson had moved to Baltimore to work in the shipyards. He found contact with the new organization: The National Association for the Advancement of Colored People (NAACP). Jefferson wanted to be an activist and advance the cause of black people who were doing the same job as white people but paid half the salary. This was the situation in Baltimore's shipyards. Jefferson saw this as unjust and wanted to get blacks into the same union as whites and paid the same wages for the same work. It seemed like a simple concept, but Jefferson couldn't bring it about. His family was killed and he was to be next. He could stay and die or go somewhere else. Jefferson decided to go back home to Bella County. Was John enough of a fighter to join the NAACP? Was it worth the risk?

John didn't know what he wanted to do, but he did know that he didn't want to be forever on the run. If he went back, he might be put on trial and hung. If he ran forever, he might lose his soul. Both were about the same. Like Jefferson, John decided it was time to go home.

Chapter 6

"A Young Lady Surveys the Situation"

—*He hasn't wasted* *any time, has he—I think it's a crime the
way he's just started building that house—what with Mitchell
Evans hardly just leaving and all—he seems pretty anxious to
move off his land—and why should he be, I don't know what you
two are caterwauling about, I think George Dodson has every
right to start his house as soon as he wants to, you know he has to
move off his land, because it's going to be part of the new
subdivision —oh, get off your high horse Henrietta, you know that
the only reason that you don't want to give George a kick in the
pants is because your husband is getting a good deal of money to
help build that monstrosity of a mansion that our former Bank
President wants to move into. Your husband will most likely get as
much work as he likes when they start on them houses as well—
that isn't true, Maybel and you know it—isn't it, just ask Wilma
here, what do you think Wilma?—don't bring me in on it, my views
are completely neutral, but I do think it rather strange that
Henrietta, who joined the Casino club, which we all know was
anti-Dodson, should now turn and become one of his champions all
of a sudden—there's nothing all of a sudden about anything I've
done; you don't have to be anti-Dodson to be a member of the
Casino club—well, I suppose there was no oath to that effect, but it
was certainly thought about that way when the club was
organized—Maybel's right, everyone thought that our Mr. George
was getting a little too big for his breeches and so we thought we'd
trim him down to size a little and form a respectable club to take
business away from him—but now what's going to happen to it all*

when Oscar is forced to leave—Lord knows but my husband says that they can't take the casino annex because it's part of a separate holding and not in the hotel assets—we all hate to see him go—if times were better, I'm sure folks would take up a collection to help him keep his place, everyone likes Oscar—yes, he was such a fine man, not like your Mr. Bank President who ran the bank into the ground—Well, some people say that the bad economy and the run on the bank did it in—Maybe, but I'd bet you a dollar to a doughnut that George Dodson landed on his feet. You don't go building a mansion, a textile mill, and a large residential sub-division with nickels and dimes.

"How long do yer suppose they can keep a body like that?" asked Ed.

"Don't rightly know what you mean," said Ike.

"I mean before the stink gets too bad and all," replied Ed.

"Well they can keep the stink down by putting a little lime on her, no problem in that," said Ike.

"But you'd think George'd come home so that they could have the funeral," said Jake.

"They say that they can't get a hold of him. He's out a town on business or somethin'," replied Ike again.

"Yeah, he's always out of the way when he shouldn't be," replied Jake.   -

"Don't ya think that's a little hard?" returned Ed.

"All I knows is that it doesn't seem right for someone's old lady to have to lie there stinking in some box while her husband is out galavantin' around the country and can't be contacted."

As Jake finished, he took a cracker to indicate that he didn't want to respond, and that he'd spoken his last words.

"I agree with you, Jake," said Ike from behind the counter, "don't hardly seem right, does it, to have your misses just a rotten away without no burial."

"Well, they can't bury her without him, can they?" responded Ed, somewhat defending Dodson.

"Maybe he's fixin' up more industries to come here and dirty up our sky," put Jake, unable to control his urge for one more last word, though his mouth was full of crackers.

***

Though it was a bright day with the sun out and the temperature warm for the time of the year, Julia wasn't happy as she looked out the window of her aunt's living room onto the small garden that she had in back. Her life had gone from one of all happiness just a few months before to one of despondency and despair. If only John were there right now, she was sure that he would give her added strength just by his presence. There was no way that she could account for the mix-up at the train station, except that someone at the telegraph office must have read and guessed the meaning of the messages, because no one but herself had read the messages. Then she had burned them for safety's sake and the house had been vacated when the messenger had come. She wasn't sure whether the messenger could have opened the message, but she felt that the most likely possibility was that the telegraph operator was the one who had guessed the meaning of the message and had betrayed him.

But where had John been all this time? She had checked the newspapers carefully and there was no report of his being captured, as there would have been if it had come about. Therefore, he must have gotten away. But where had he been all the time and what did he think? Could he have guessed that the telegraph operator might have been the one, or did he suspect her? This second possibility greatly troubled Julia as she speculated about how John, who was out of contact with her, might be interpreting the episode. Would this be reason for him to leave the state altogether if he thought that he was being deserted by both his friends and closest companions? How much she would give, she thought, for the opportunity of consoling John and explaining to him all that had happened and that it wasn't her fault. Explaining that she never would, never could betray his trust, and that all she wanted—no, not exactly all, but what would make her extremely happy would be for John to be again safe and able to love and marry her, if he so desired.

Then there was the question of her father's land and what was going to happen, as well as her own struggle to free herself from her aunt's house. Though her aunt Margaret meant well, she had a different conception of what it meant to carry oneself in a crises than Julia did. Aunt Margaret didn't know about her love for John and how she was despondent about his situation. At least Julia had never told her. Though it must be admitted that the old woman seemed to have information on so many personal matters; she might also have known about this. Though her aunt had never mentioned it to Julia before, but she was quite aware of the urgency of the situation in regard to her father, whose letter she was anxiously awaiting in the mail which was due to arrive shortly.

If her aunt really felt as Julia did, then she would know that when things weren't right, she wouldn't press Julia onto the social scene. Assuming her aunt knew nothing about John, she should surely know that for Julia to indulge in a social pleasure spree when the family estate was about to change hands would make Julia a shallow person, indeed.

Julia had been obliged to do some socializing as her aunt had, even before her arrival, planned a great number of outings for her niece, but Julia had persisted against her aunt to excuse herself from as many as would be possible. She couldn't face people night after night feeling as she did, and to her credit, Margaret did make some cancelations, but then there were the others which just "couldn't be cancelled." And so there was some that she had to endure.

Julia sighed. With her sweetheart at her side she would happily endure anything, even if it meant the life of a fugitive. But then, she also loved her father and wouldn't like to act contrary to his will, as he would not approve of her marrying a criminal. Though as she thought back to the conversation that they had on the subject, he had used all his arguments to try and show how miserable it would be to live the life of the road, always running, and then Julia could talk about how strong she would be. But the facts of the situation were that Julia had been brought-up in material comfort and that it would be very difficult for her to ever adapt to a life of extreme poverty. The strains would be so great that they would be felt in their relationship and the relationship would suffer as a result. There might be some truth in these words, she thought, but she knew that in herself there was a resourcefulness that neither of her parents saw, and that she was independent enough to be able to fight the world on her own. She wouldn't be simply clinging to John as they probably imagined. She was or at least felt she could be very strong if the situation required it. And so she was able to put her parent's advice into context.

"But what if he wasn't a fugitive?" she had asked.

"Well, that would be a different case, then, wouldn't it?" replied the father.

"Would you give us your blessing in that case?"

"It's difficult to deal in hypotheticals. It would depend on the situation."

"Then you aren't unilaterally opposed to the idea of my marrying who I please."

"My dear Julia, I always want what you want. But I also have to consider who I think will make you happy," her father had responded.

"So then you have no objections, *per se,* to my marrying John Dow."

"Well, he hasn't got a family—"

"Is that your objection?"

"Well, no, I guess, but it would be nice if he did have a family."

"But he does have a family, the Beauchays."

"Julia, there would be nothing I'd like better than for you to marry someone that was a member of the Beauchay family, as they have been so close to us, and I so love Samuel Beauchay, like my own brother. But your Mr. Dow isn't a blood member of their family, and so can't be really considered to be a member of their family."

This had bothered Julia, but still she had persisted.

"Does anything else bother you?"

"Well, I don't wish to put it into those terms, my dear. Oh bother, this all makes me sound like an old goat, doesn't it?"

"You know I don't think of you as an old goat, I'm asking your opinion because I care about what you and mother think about marriage."

"I know dear, I was only joking. Both your mother and myself know that we have two of the finest children in the world and we feel truly blessed."

Then they had hugged and it seemed as if the conversation might have ended, except Julia then added the coda to clarify matters, "Then I'm right in assuming that your only objections are that he's a fugitive and that he doesn't really have a blood family."

"Well, it would be nice if he had some prospects and a job, or a little money, but I suppose that's mostly it."

As she thought back on it, she felt sure that her father would relent, if only John were to be found to be innocent. That was the one point that he wouldn't ever go back on—but if it was impossible for John to ever be found innocent, and if he wanted her, she would become his wife even above her father's objections, though it would make her very sad to do so.

Then there was the sound outside of the mail box closing, and Julia was running as fast as she could out the door and down the steps to see if there was anything for her, but sadly enough there wasn't—no letter from her father. She wished he would write her. She wrote him every few days to see how he was and to hear if there were any new developments. As she walked back up the steps, she could see her aunt in the window, motioning her with animated gestures.

"They've done it!" said Aunt Margaret.

By the tone of her voice, Julia knew that she must be talking about her father and the Estate. Had they beaten the private company who wanted to take their land away from them?

"Done what, Aunt Margaret? Done what?"

"The land! They've saved it!"

This news made Julia extremely happy, as might be expected, and she hugged her aunt. But what had happened exactly, she wished to know as the momentary euphoria wore away.

"How did you find out?" questioned Julia.

"Come in the kitchen and have some tea, and I'll tell you all about it," said her aunt, who was really enjoying her role as the bringer of glad tidings.

"I got a telephone call from Mr. Reynolds just a few moments ago," began her aunt as she was fixing the tea. "And he told me the good news." She set the cups on the table, and put out the sugar.

"But what sort of action did they get?" asked Julia anxiously.

"Oh, I don't know; I wrote it down on a slip of paper somewhere, but I didn't really understand it, so I asked him what it meant and he said that they couldn't kick the Vanderkamps from their land until the foreclosure went through a full court hearing, which Mr. Reynolds felt sure he would win."

"Where's the piece of paper?" asked Julia, as she wanted to see just exactly what kind of order had been issued. Aunt Margaret promised to get the paper after they had finished tea, but then she saw the worry on her young charge's face so she went and brought the scrap that had the information on it.

Julia could barely read her aunt's scrawl, but from what she could make out it seemed as if there had only been issued a temporary order of restraint and not the full one that she had hoped for.

"According to this letter you've written, they've issued only an injunction, is that correct?"

"I don't know, it's all down on the paper," said the aunt, determined not to have the good mood miffed by anything.

"But you know this only means that we will have another couple of weeks to give just cause that we should not forfeit title of the property."

"I don't know anything about the law, Julia, I leave that to the realm of men. What I do know is that our lawyer said that my brother didn't have to move and I took that as good news."

She brought the tea over and filled the cups.

Julia didn't want to spoil her aunt's good mood and so she kept smiling, but what the telephone call meant was that there was only a stay of the order and that there was still no decision. Julia thought that things didn't look very bright at that moment. She wished John was next to her so that she could rest her head on his shoulder and they could think about it together.

Chapter 7

"A Chapter in which the Reader is Led a Step Closer to the Truth"

As time dragged on, Jefferson became impatient as to whether anything was happening to his plan. He couldn't very well go out on the streets and begin asking questions as to whether anything was happening, as he was a hunted man. By now, the Link would know that Jefferson hadn't been killed, and that one of his men was missing, so it was necessary to stay very quiet. But the boredom of this type of life was taking its toll on the residents of that small apartment. For once, the prisoner was really making himself genuinely obnoxious, as he would be complaining continually as well as singing songs that he thought that Jefferson or Myra wouldn't like. In truth, he was driven to such tactics as the confinement was making him extremely nervous. He wanted more than anything to escape, and was almost to the point of trying it, even if it meant a bullet in the back.

Myra became quickly tired of the man's chattering, but knew that she and Jefferson wouldn't be safe walking the streets until this part of the puzzle was put in its proper place.

If they played it wrong and their whereabouts were found out, they would be trapped with no escape. Their provisions were again running low, and they would have to make a trip for more food soon.

Jefferson tried to think about problems which had always interested him, but that he had never had the time to really pursue. He would also draw pictures and do some problems in math for the practice, but his patience was short, too. Frequently, Jefferson and Myra would have short disagreements about something that would inevitably be intensified by the prisoner, who made caustic comments from the floor.

"You shut up," said Jefferson once, "or I'm taking you to jail."

"Go ahead. I'd rather be there than cooped up here all the time."

"I think you ought to take him," said Myra.

"He might still be useful to us," replied Jefferson.

"I think he's a nuisance," said Myra. "He's told us all he knows, what can we do with him?"

"Yeah, I said all I'm going to say."

"Which isn't much, believe me," returned Myra.

"Well I love you too, doll," said Coody.

"Why that—" began Myra, when Jefferson checked her with his arm.

"Why can't you two get a blind so that you can go a kissin' instead of pretendin' jist cause of me?" he returned.

Jefferson put on his evil face to the man, and Coody responded, "Go ahead. I'd be hot to put my hands on her myself."

Jefferson felt like kicking the fellow's face, but he knew that if he let himself become angry then the prisoner would become the jailer and Jefferson would become the prisoner. Jefferson was not willing to exchange roles so easily.

Jefferson and Myra were sitting at the table when Myra tossed a bowl full of water at the man sitting on the floor.

"Thank you," he said, dripping wet.

"What did you do that for?" said Jefferson, irritated that Myra had allowed the man to get the better of her temper.

"I'll do what I please, mister, and don't you forget it," she snapped as she started for the door, but Jefferson was up right away to stop her.

"Where are you going?" he asked.

"Out," she said.

"Where out? You know you can't be taking risks," he replied.

"I'll go wherever I feel like. You aren't going to order me around. I'm a free woman."

"You aren't free so long as your life and my life are in danger." Jefferson grabbed her arm.

"Let go of me," she said, taking his hand from her arm.

"Where are you going?"

"I don't have to tell you."

"Tell me," he said, taking her arm again and holding it tightly so that she couldn't move.

She looked into his eyes and didn't move momentarily. He could see that she was tired of all the tension. He should get rid of the prisoner and turn him over to the police. The strain was getting too great. She was right, and he knew it. Jefferson let go of her arm and turned away.

"I'll take him back as soon as I've talked to the police," said Jefferson.

"Don't take him to the police. They'll not be able to help us, because they're only interested in city crimes. What we want is to help John, isn't that right? Take him to the federal marshal instead. He has jurisdiction. Besides, he's always interested in gamblers and bootleggers," said Myra at the door.

"What—no more fight?" taunted Coody.

Then Jefferson turned and ran to Myra and hugged her. She also held him fast in her arms.

"Naw ain't that sweet," said the prisoner. "Don't you wish you had a curtain now?"

It was decided that the best time for Jefferson to try the United States Marshal's office would be in the evening when moving about was more concealed. Jefferson had his reservations. It was at night that most of the criminal men would be on the streets. He thought that the early morning might be best, however, he deferred to Myra, who was very afraid for him in the daylight, so he left that night to try and negotiate a deal.

***

"No that's B-R-O-W-N, Jefferson John Brown," he repeated for the man at the desk, who turned around to the man sitting next to him at a typewriter and said, "Mister Bran would like to see the sergeant."

"That's not exactly correct," put Jefferson, anxious that he be allowed to see the Marshal himself.

"Does he have an appointment?" asked the other, completely ignoring Jefferson.

"I don't know; I don't think so."

"Well, tell him that he can't see anybody unless he has an appointment. If it's urgent, he should contact the local police."

The man turned around to Jefferson again and asked, "What exactly is the nature of your business?"

"I can't tell you, I can only divulge that to the Marshal."

"Well, you can't see anybody unless you have an appointment and you can't make an appointment unless you specify the exact nature of your visit."

"That's ridiculous. I am a tax paying citizen of this state and I think I have the right to see the United States Marshal if I want to!"

The man behind the desk changed his expression. Jefferson had made a mistake, and he knew it. There was nothing police or authority-types liked less than what they might term as uppity niggers, and the expression that the man was giving Jefferson right now told him that he was being placed in that category.

"Look, I'm sorry, I'm a little excited I suppose," began Jefferson, who didn't care about protocol, but just wanted to get something done. "But I do have some very important information to give to the United States Marshal. Wouldn't it be possible for me to see him for just a minute? I wouldn't take too much of his time."

The man behind the desk immediately responded to Jefferson's change in tone and smiled in a smug sort of way saying, "Well, you see rules are rules, and we can't break them. Besides, the Marshal on duty tonight isn't in."

"Could I make an appointment to see someone tomorrow morning?"

"Certainly, who would you like to see?"

This was difficult. Jefferson didn't know that there was more than one Marshal to a district, and would apparently have to choose between several.

"Who would you suggest?" asked Jefferson, trying to make the desk man feel important.

"That would depend on what you wanted him for," responded the man mechanically.

"But who do *you* think would give me the most, *sympathetic,* hearing?" What Jefferson wanted to know was which Marshal had the fewest inhibitions about talking to a stranger. Who was the most open minded.

The man smiled as if he might help Jefferson, but then replied in the same manner as before, though with some hesitation at first, "I think all our men try to be open minded and racially unbiased."

This little twit behind the counter was glorifying his little position of power which Jefferson had given him so that he could get an appointment. But this charade had gone far enough, so Jefferson said, almost a little impatiently, "Well, then put me down for someone, whoever you think is best, for ten o'clock."

"Ten o'clock," repeated the man, "and what is your reason for the appointment?"

"I told you, to give him some information."

"You have to be more specific."

"I can't be more specific."

"Well the rules specify that—"

"The matter is very confidential, I can't just tell—" he was going to say *anyone*, or *only some office clerk*, but he checked himself.

"—I can only tell the Marshal because a man's life may be at stake."

"If it's a case of local murder, then the police are the ones to call."

"I tell you, I have to see the Marshal."

"All right, then what shall I put down for your reason for the appointment?"

Jefferson saw that he was going to get nowhere with this man; he couldn't see beyond the narrow rules that he was bound by and could be called on to make no exceptions, unless there was some other motivation for his action and he was trying to be difficult for some reason, a question that Jefferson didn't feel worth his consideration, so he said in a hushed tone, "I'm a relay from Washington, and I have some information about the latest civil service appointments in the area and some of them are quite surprising, so you can see why I have to keep this private."

The man behind the desk leaned forward to listen to Jefferson and carefully wrote down what he said.

"Don't worry," he said in a new tone of respect, as if Jefferson might have some information about *his* job (a possible raise or RIF). Maybe he should be nice to this man who might be able to affect his job. "Of course, mister, this will be kept in the highest secrecy."

Jefferson leaned forward, too, so that his head was almost touching the other's and said in most somber and serious tones, "Thank you, I appreciate this."

"You know I'd let you see someone tonight, but there's nobody in."

"Yes, I understand," replied Jefferson.

"Here's your appointment card," said the man, handing Jefferson the piece of paper. "My name's Fish, Frank Fish G.S. 3."

"Thank you, Fish, I think I'll be off," said Jefferson as he made his way to the exit, carefully controlling his urge to laugh.

The next morning Jefferson had no trouble getting right in. "Oh *yes,* step right in Mr. Brown. I understand you have a little news for us." The man was all smiles and Jefferson could tell that he might not be in the mood to hear what he actually had to tell him.

"Would you like some coffee?" asked the man, with the same smile on his face.

"No thank you; let me get right to the point. I don't have any news about Civil Service rankings, I only said that so that I could gain entrance to your office, the man at the desk last night was very insistent about having a precise reason for an appointment. But what I have to say is quite confidential—" Jefferson began.

The marshal across from him dropped his jaw so that he sat there open mouthed.

The marshal was a stocky man with a heavy-set jaw. This made his reaction even more dramatic. It was several moments before he could regain his composure to an adequate degree so that he could interrupt Jefferson.

"—Now see here, boy, this ain't a place where you can just play games like that."

"I understand your position," began Jefferson, seeing that this man wasn't at all pleased with his tactic, and wasn't going to be the most receptive audience. "But you must understand that—"

"No, *you* understand that the United States Government isn't a place to play games. Did you know that you came here under false pretenses and that constitutes fraud, which is a crime in this state punishable by up to ten years in prison?"

"What was this man's problem?" thought Jefferson. He wasn't even going to let Jefferson talk. Besides, there was no question of fraud, who did he think he was talking to? The man took Jefferson's arm and began to lead him out of his office.

"Now I'm a reasonable man, and I won't bother you any further if you don't bother us any further. We don't have time for fun and games around here." He opened the door to his office, but Jefferson, whose arm was still in the grip of the man, wasn't going to be pushed out without a struggles.

"I have important information for you, sir, that I'm sure you'd be interested in."

"Not from *you* it wouldn't be. Get out of my sight, boy, before I change my mind."

"But I can help you break a bootlegging ring!" cried Jefferson as he was being forced out of the door.

"You know when they took your kind off the plantations, you forgot all your manners; now I've been about as patient as I kin be. But if I hear one more word, that will be it, colored boy, do you understand?"

Jefferson tried to stay in the office—it was his last chance. *Why* was he being so pushy, if only he hadn't told him about the civil service so soon, maybe he could have presented his case first. The man forced Jefferson into the hall and quickly closed his door.

His only chance was gone with the noise of the door closing. Of course there was the police, but with them there were several problems: first, they wouldn't care about what happened in Bella County and would have no jurisdiction. Second, they might think that bootlegging and gambling were for federal officials and therefore would refuse to hold the man, Coody. And third, there was more corruption in the police force and therefore the man would not be as secure. But it was the only alternative left to him. Jefferson turned slowly and started down the hall when he heard a voice behind him call, "Hey, you there."

Jefferson didn't notice the call until it was repeated, and then he turned his head to see who the man who was calling him was. At the far end of the hall was a short, thin man who wore a light blue shirt that wasn't a policeman's shirt, but closer to a woolen sports shirt on which he wore his silver badge.

Jefferson cocked his head in surprise.

"Yes, you," he repeated, motioning Jefferson to come to his office.

"Now what did they want?" thought Jefferson. "Do, they want to find some other fault with him, or was this just another man who had heard that he had some appointments and wanted to see if his name was on the list?"

"I heard Callahan chewing you out down there and you trying to say something to him," said the slight man, who paused as he motioned for Jefferson to sit down in the chair. "Well, you know Jim has a lot of troubles, and is a little gruff at times, but I don't want to give you the impression that we're all like that. My name's Timay. Paul Timay." Paul reached out his hand to Jefferson and shook it firmly. "Please sit down. Now if you've got a story, let's hear it."

This man looked like a country fellow to Jefferson, who sat down and told the man about the killing in Varner's Junction and how he was sure that the wrong man was accused and how he had tracked down the case to Savannah and the gambling ring of Georgia Tom and the bootlegging of (he made a guess) Rod Dodson. Then he told the Marshal that he had a man in his custody that might be able to give them information so that they could break up the organization, but that his primary interest was getting the real killer in the Varner's Junction case. He would appreciate working with the Marshal so that they could extract this information before they closed down the operation and caused everyone to scatter.

Jefferson told his story slowly and truthfully, only leaving out some of the details concerning Myra, as well as his helping John to escape. The man behind the desk listened patiently, only occasionally interrupting Jefferson for clarification on several points.

When Jefferson was finished the man replied, "Well, you know, the city has been under our surveillance for some time, as you might have known, and though we do have information on some of the men you've mentioned, like Wyse and Daniels, the others haven't really appeared in our files up to now, which doesn't mean that they aren't involved, but only that we don't have any information about them. It would certainly be a plumb for us if we could shut these gangsters down, because that's all they are, you know, just common gangsters, no better than their Northern counterparts—you know, if you ask me. I think that most of the people who want to fight federal crime come to us from the North. This is especially true with the big ones. The Northerners come and organize our little Southern sections of the bureau into sub-organizations, without real power. Since the South is not on the scale of Chicago, naturally, they treat us as rubes. But I want to change that. You probably don't know, but I'm the boss around here. And I want respect for what we're doing. I'm not just some southern bumpkin who is only about the pre-War era. We are modernizing, too. I'd like nothing better than to arrest a major bootlegging-gambling ring. And if you can make that happen, then brother, we will be a team.

"It's not going to be easy, but that doesn't mean that we shouldn't try. And perhaps this is just the right time to move, because word is out that there is going to be a big meeting soon between Daniels and some other big cats that we don't know about—you call this man Dodson?"

"There might be two of them in the game. Two Dodsons, I mean. That's something I don't know yet for sure."

"All right, say we have these two Dodsons and Daniels with Wyse in the middle as a link between Daniels and this Dodson or Dodsons, whatever. Then what you were talking about when you said that you heard that there was a gang war starting could work to our advantage.

"This could be dangerous for you, Brown. I don't want you to risk your life. You seem like an educated man and a decent man. We've got to protect the few we have."

Timay got up and started pacing his office. As he did so, Jefferson saw that the name plate on his desk said *Paul Timay, Chief U.S. Marshal.* Jefferson had certainly gotten lucky. And this case, if it went down right, could be a feather in Mr. Timay's cap.

"Of course there are killers out for the big men in each camp. This might mean that someone is trying to get a little bigger portion of the pot so that when the big meeting comes, with whomever it is—say some outside money, then they might be able to speak from a more powerful position than if they were merely alone. You follow me? One less partner, one less person to split your money with, and one less temperament to worry about.

"Now we know that Daniels is connected with gambling and prostitution with a guy they call Georgia Tom, but we don't know who's running the bootlegging operations, or loan sharking, which is getting dangerous, especially in the shape of financial credit. I mean, the banks are dropping one-by-one all over the place. I don't keep my money in the bank; do you?"

Jefferson admitted that he had until the trouble had started with the banks. He took out all his money and had it in a locked box at home. Lucky thing, too, since the local bank failed three months later. George Dodson used to be the president of that bank.

"You don't say? That is interesting." Timay was rubbing his hands together. "If there was anything fishy there, we could pile on extra charges.

"Well, you watch it or you'll lose every cent you have. I put my money in gold. You know it's been the most secure standard for two thousand years."

Jefferson admitted that the idea was a safe one, which pleased the man who offered to give Jefferson some literature on the dealers he recommended. Jefferson took all of the brochures graciously, as this man Timay, in his blue shirt, seemed rather nice.

"Yes, in fact I could even give them a ring and tell them your name."

"Well, Paul, that would be very neighborly of you."

"Not at all, I'm happy to help. I can tell we're going to be doing some important work together." Paul Timay paused as he walked over to his desk, "Care for a cigar?"

Timay made his call. Then the two of them had a good conversation as the Marshal agreed to take custody of their prisoner, Coody, on gambling and bootlegging (this is because if he charged him with breaking and entering or attempted murder, owing to the episode in the room of Myra Dow, then it would have been a matter for the Savannah Police).

They agreed to keep in touch and work together as the situation progressed in its intrigue toward the possible turbulent episodes that proved to be ahead.

Chapter 8

"The Turn of a Screw"

"Where did you git that?" asked Rod Dodson in a fast, excited voice.

"Listen, I ain't telling you no bull, Mr. Dodson," said Georgia Tom in a supplicating tone. "You know how I works fer Mr. Daniels, but when I heard about what was happenin', I wanted to come and tells you right away, cause it was your influence that got me where I is. I owe everything to your generosity, sir."

"Don't give me any of this sentimental crap. I'm not as dumb as Daniels. I didn't get you any job, Big George did. I don't give a damn about you and don't you forget it."

"Yes sir," he replied.

"But you say that you heard that someone put a contract out for me? How did you find this out?"

"There's a gun around town from Detroit, I hear. He's been trying to get a few boys to help him with the job, and naturally he's let the word slip who he's after. Honest, boss, I wouldn't—"

"Only two people knew about that contract—three, me, Big George, and the man I sent as messenger; who hasn't come back." Rod reached for Tom's shirt collar and grabbed it, pulling Tom across the table violently. "Only three people knew about the man from Detroit. Now how come he's out to get *me*, when he was sent to get *someone else*?"

"I don't know, boss, I don't know—all that I can tell you is what I hear, and I wanted to come to you first. I haven't told nobody else about this, honest."

"Honesty? You're about as *straight and honest* as a pig's tail, you came to me instead of Daniels because you know that Daniels is washed up, and you want to jump out of the sinking ship as fast as you can. You make me sick, Tom. Get out of here." He let go of the man, who meekly left and immediately Rod penned a telegram to his brother.

What's this about a contract on me; do you know anything?
Rod

This little worm was probably talking through his hat, and didn't know a thing and just didn't want to be in the cold when Daniels got hit. They were all like that, the little underlings that worked for them. Just little insects that tried to bloat themselves as much as they could for as long as they could, so that they always had to be listened to. Rod noted these details with that reservation in mind. But whenever a rumor went around, it was always good policy to check it out, so Rod sent one of his better flunkies to go find out just what was being said and by whom.

"There's a contract out for you all right," said the man when he came back to report to his magister. Rod, who didn't smoke, but consumed a great quantity of chewing gum, unwrapped a piece and put it in his mouth. This new report didn't look very good. This man he sent out was first-rate, and he would get the story and tell it to him straight. Rod knew that.

"How did you find out?"

"I talked to a fellow who was recruiting extra fellows for the job."

"The man from Detroit?"

"Naw, he wasn't from Detroit, but then he wasn't the one behind it neither, just workin' for him."

So the man was a professional and planning a raid of some sort with what he could pick up on the streets, or was this merely a ruse to throw Rod off guard?

"Who set the contract, do you know?"

"Don't know, but there was a fellow named George Dodson that has been mentioned."

Rod was terrified when he heard this. This messenger didn't know the significance of what he was saying, because almost no one knew that his own last name was Dodson. And few had any inkling of his brother's existence. And the few who did only knew him as *Big George.* Whoever it was who set the contract must know everything, but then how could they? No one knew, or could know. It was too well guarded. George had made sure of that. He was excellent on security. He was the great planner, whose mind Rod respected immensely. But someone must know, or else—the conclusion couldn't be considered. It was too unthinkable that his brother, his own brother—no, this idea must be put out of his mind. If the deal with Daniels had fallen through, then he'd just have to get one of his local guns to try the job, but he couldn't let suspicion enter his mind, not with his brother. George wouldn't do such a thing. If someone was out to get him, it had to be Daniels.

"Go get Mitchells and Ewing right away," said Rod.

He was going to get Daniels another way. George had planned that if they got Daniels out of the way immediately, then they would be able to take over the entire Savannah operation, which included the entire eastern part of the state. They had to kill Daniels quickly, because speed was essential. *After the meeting will be too late—they needed him out of the way before then because with Daniels out of the way there would be one less partner, one less hand to take the profits.* Yes, everything had to be done before the meeting: all the housecleaning completed—but he couldn't have meant—Rod's own hand. A hundred thousand split three ways is thirty-three thousand a piece; split two ways it is fifty thousand apiece, quite a sizeable gain—but split one way. . . .

The men came in and Rod said, "I want Daniels killed before the week is out. You get a thousand dollars apiece for the job and a hundred dollars bonus for each day before a week when you kill him."

This man was getting expensive. These two men shouldn't be paid such high sums; the money will go to their heads. But then, this situation was a little desperate. They had to get Daniels out of the way. That was the only thing that should be concerning him, Daniels. But still one partner, two partners. . . .

His own brother—such a thought was so unthinkable that Rod became determined to put it out of his mind. The concept could only lead to destructive ends. Rod took out some papers on the money that they had taken in and was determined to check their accountant's work to see whether the books were correct, but still he could not get through a single column of figures before his mind returned to the tantalizing question.

Then he took out a piece of paper and hurriedly wrote a note and sealed it without reading it over.

There's some trouble here, come immediately, I'll meet you at the usual place—alone.
Rod

He couldn't believe such a thing from his brother, but it would help to hear from his brother, himself. George had such a calm, reassuring way to him. The entire thing would probably straighten itself out, he was sure of it—there would be no problem.

Rod went back to his figures, but soon decided that what he needed was some entertainment on the second floor.

Chapter 9

"A Preoccupied Mind"

With at least temporary good news, Julia decided to return to Varner's Junction, and made arrangements with her aunt. She didn't like to see Julia go, but she knew that if anyone would be able to keep the fire under her brother, it was her niece, who was a very strong-willed, determined young lady.

What a sad thing it would be, thought Margaret, if her brother had to give up his land. Why, a southerner's land was as precious to him as his life, at least that was what their father had always professed. How would her brother get on? What would he do? Would he have to go to work—and get a horribly common job? All these questions shuffled through the mind of Margaret as she tried to finally ascertain whether her own social standing might in some way be affected. But finally deciding that it would not— particularly since so many good banks around were having trouble, she thought that she was on firm ground with her brother and nothing that might happen in regards to the loss of his land would affect the way others thought of her. With this reassurance in mind, she went in the living room where Julia was sitting in an effort to make her last day comfortable before her return to Bella County.

"It's lovely weather for this time of year," began Margaret, as she made her entrance into the living room.

"I suppose," replied Julia absently.

"You know things will be very quiet here when you leave," said Margaret, trying to show Julia how much she enjoyed having her niece as a visitor and if she could, to intimate that if she ever wanted to return that she would have a home with her. But Julia didn't quite understand, as she spent most of her time just sitting and thinking of what she was to do, and the various ramifications of all that was happening to her (going over the same things often times with great frequency in an attempt to find some new angle that she might have forgotten to save the farm). She was reluctant to resign herself to having the estate vanish from Vanderkamp control. It was interesting that she had not heard from Rodney. She wrote him a single letter, but he did not respond. Perhaps the letter was not delivered. Still, it gave Julia even more consternation.

It hardly seemed possible that the house could become any quieter for her leaving than it was during her occupancy. Perhaps, she thought, this was her aunt's way of telling her that she was displeased at her conduct, or that she wished that Julia would show a little more life. So Julia, taking this last possibility as the probable intention of her aunt, summoned all her effort to carry on a conversation with her so that she might not seem a sullen house guest.

If her aunt was unhappy with her company, then Julia was sorry. This was because Julia didn't dislike her aunt. It was just that her aunt was a different type of person and that the things that interested her aunt didn't happen to coincide with those that interested her.

"Yes," she replied. "I suppose you will have to come to Bella County some time, especially if we are forced to—move."

"Of course," said her aunt in overly enthusiastic tones that she put on because she had the mental impression (though she wouldn't have admitted it to herself) that the more she became enthusiastic about the prospect of visiting her brother's estate, then the less likelihood there would be of its being offered for sale.

"You know it's been ages since I've visited your father on the farm. It's such a delicious place. I really don't know. I remember when my father, your grandfather, was still alive he used to talk about the possibility of my having half of the farm, if I found a husband who was good enough to run it. You know in some ways it is a rather natural thing to do, with the two heirs side-by-side. I like the people of the county, too. I always remember them as very warm, affectionate people. Yes, I would have liked it there."

"I imagine that you'd notice quite a few changes since you were a girl," said Julia.

"Well, don't make me seem too ancient!" put Margaret, smiling.

"No, that's not what I meant," returned Julia, a little flustered at having made such an ambiguous comment. "It's just that I've noticed a lot changing even in the small time that I've been alive, and I know that my father has seen a great deal more than I have in regards to the changes of people and customs. I supposed you to be somewhere in the middle."

"Bravo, that was handled very well," returned Margaret, admiring Julia's verbal dexterity at avoiding the trap which she had set for her. "But you know, I think that the *people* are one thing that can't really change about the county, the people: they stay the same."

"What do you mean?

"I don't know. You just put people all together against the same kinds of conditions and the natural elements bring out the same kinds of traits in people when seen as a whole, like that."

Julia didn't reply as she didn't quite understand her aunt's clarification, and thought it best not to ask for any further.

"You know the best thing that ever happened to the county was Prohibition," said her aunt, without noticing Julia's silence, as she prepared to launch onto one of her favorite subjects.

"Prohibition?"

"Yes. You know, that town seemed to be one of the purest, most God fearing places you'd ever want to live in, but you know, underneath, it was really rotten, and you know what was the cause was?"

Though it was evident what the answer was going to be, Julia invited the response, obviously seeing that her aunt was waiting for it with a searching expression of her eyes.

"Alcohol, that's what did it. Yes, that's the devil's curse. It brought all sorts of pain to countless people. It twisted their lives so that they couldn't see the way to a good moral life, as they had to depend on their liquor for artificial feelings because they weren't strong enough to face life without it." Aunt Margaret paused, but Julia didn't speak as she felt that the speech wasn't over yet. "And don't think that was the only thing that was twisting the lives of some people. You may not remember a man named Lucius Smith?"

Julia shook her head.

"Well, he used to be a respectable worker. Not very special, but a hard, clean liver, until he began to drink, and that's not all. They say that he took other drugs, as well, and that he formed an addiction to them so that he had to involve himself in all sorts of shady deals to avoid the pitfall of not having enough money for his habit. He solved his alcohol supply problem by becoming the bartender at the saloon, but that didn't solve his other problem. No, he led a miserable life, and it all ended when he was killed with a bullet through his head."

"Yes, I remember that," responded Julia.

"If you ask me, it all comes back to the bottle. And believe you me, I think this country is a sight better *without* alcohol than it was *with* it."

Julia tried to concentrate on what her aunt said after that, but it seemed that all her thoughts focused on the two major problems of her life: John and the farm. Why couldn't everything work out in her life as it did in the books that she read? Was there no Douglas Fairbanks to save her from what she might have to bear?

"—And you know they said that there was Negro blood in Lucius as well, you know there's no telling what his background was. There was such a commotion in the bedrooms in those days. . . ."

What did she think about John and his parents? Were they really Myra Dow and Samuel Beauchay, as her own father had said? Or was the father some patron of the store in which she used to work? Might it have been one of the share croppers on the estate? If it had been Beauchay, then John might have only a little colored blood in him. But how much? He had to have less than one eighth to be considered white. But would this be true if his parents were Myra Dow and the shop keeper or one of the share croppers?

"—But what I could never understand was about people who talked about Lucius being Sally Lou's father. Why, Herald and Kathy Thompson would never consent to bringing up Sally Lou as their daughter if she were the offspring of a colored man. It doesn't make sense, because certainly Kathy wasn't a generous sort and Herald was a God-fearing man who never would associate with a drug user like Lucius. Mind you, though, not that Herald would probably know, he didn't ever suspect anything behind the appearance of what he saw. I don't know why he never guessed. For instance, about the affair that his wife was having with Rudolph Stuart, not that it's agreed to by everybody, you understand, but. . . ."

Julia had never really considered what she thought of inter-racial marriage before, she had merely accepted what her patents had said. But if she really considered marrying John, wouldn't *that* be interracial? It would be if *he* were one-eighth black or more. All her life she had just assumed that blacks married their own kind while the whites their own. But now she was faced with a real test of the theory in practice, and she might be called on to make some kind of decision one way or the other.

This thought paradigm bothered Julia. She loved John Dow. Why should anything else present itself in her mind? But what she wanted to do was not think about the question at all, as it seemed to be such a disagreeable issue. *Why* should she have to contend with it? The probability was that the issue would never arise, but even if it did, she would prefer not to think about John being black or white, but just to think of him as being John. To think in any other way would be confusing. She wouldn't question the doctrine of interracial marriage. She would not discuss it with her parents. But then she wouldn't think about whether John was black or white, because if she did and if she found that John was really black, then she would have to work through the entire issue, something she could not do objectively as she already had her mind made up on the subject.

". . . Now you know if that were true, then perhaps that's why she came back and killed poor Lucius." Then her aunt cleared her throat, "She found out that he was really her father, and she hated the fact that she was illegitimate. I can't blame her for that. It has to gnaw at you sooner or later. I think it catches up to a person when they don't know who their parents were, or exactly where they came from. Sally Lou might have thought she'd known for a long time and then suddenly had a realization to the contrary, which must have been quite a shock for her, no wonder that she. . . ."

But as to the question of John not having any money or coming from a family as her father had mentioned, she was still unsure. What did her father mean? How could it make any difference coming from a good family or no family at all? Wasn't the Beauchay family his own? He'd grown up among them just as if he were a Beauchay. Surely that was more important than any blood tie.

"No, I think he was fated to the end that he got, and he deserved it. Yes he did. I've even though he came from unstable origins. He chose to take to the bottle, and those nasty drugs of his— a crutch. That is what it really was. And look all the harm it caused. No I'm not saying that he was absolutely fated to do what he did. He did choose somewhat, but let me put it this way: a person who starts out on the wrong foot in life is more likely to end up that way than one who starts out right. Lucius had a bad beginning, which caused another bad, illegitimate beginning, namely Sally Lou's, and so he was fated to the same force which brought him into the world—a force he might have escaped from, but the odds were against it. . . ."

What if John had had a violent father? Might that affect the way he was or would it affect his children? Could this *not having a blood family* have any real bad effects on him? To this question she felt she could answer a resounding *no*. Why, orphans weren't to be despised for what they were. They couldn't help it, and even though she knew that her father didn't despise John, she still felt it more convenient to put the argument into extreme terms as the resolution was always so much more resounding when phrased that way. Julia was sure that her father would not hold that against John. For what did a man's past have to do what he was today?

A person should be judged by what he was at the moment, she thought, but then she became confused as she began to think about how often she judged people by how they had acted to her in the past, and how really it was a common practice—yes, perhaps even a necessary one, which might leave the whole thing in a muddle. She felt sure that this couldn't matter—it mustn't. But then when she tried to reason it out, the answers weren't in accord with what she felt, and so she judged that her reasoning must be at fault.

Chapter 10

"An Assortment of Amusing Scenes"

As John turned over once more, his back told him how much harder the ground felt when one has been away from it for a while. His muscles were a little stiff and he was still very tired as he pulled himself up from what was left of his shelter that he was able to gather the night before. He felt awe at the brightness of the sun and how wonderful it was to see the sun in all its human warmth as it signaled another day for him. But it was not just a day like any other, but a day in which he would look on all the old objects in a new way. For he had finally decided what he was to do with himself.

He knew that he must go back and find Jefferson and join him. Perhaps Jefferson was indeed still on the quest? If so, they might work together in order to discover the truth. If not, then at least John might profit from Jefferson's advice.

There would be risk. John knew that. But he also knew he must face that risk, because in life one must always take certain gambles and accept the outcomes. His body's tiredness seemed to hang on him as if he were carrying extra weight. The day might be difficult, but what comforted him was that the next day would be better because he had now committed himself to a permanent solution over the transitory existence of the fugitive.

The wild flavor of the forest suddenly came vividly to his senses as he stood and tried to summon his body to activity. Even in the winter, there were odors of bark and limb that made it unique. John was in his element. He could now decide with certainty that he was never going back to the mill.

John hiked to the stream and washed. The cold water seemed to stimulate some of the life back into his limbs, and he suddenly had a wonderful thought: Julia hadn't betrayed him. It wasn't in her nature. No. The fault rested with someone else. The supposition was not critically analyzed, but simply registered for what it was: a wild, hopeful dream. And then he tucked it away in a place where the comforting aspects of the vision might shield him, but its ephemeral qualities wouldn't depress him.

John thought about who could have killed Victor Stuart. It was a problem very much to his own interest, but hitherto he had not really been able to speculate about it in a constructive fashion. This is because John was not in any of the communication links in the county. John talked to Julia, Jessy, and Jefferson. Those were his only regular community. Mr. Beauchay was distant to him. Jason hated him. Rodney lived in his sports fantasies. The Vanderkamp parents treated their son with benign neglect.

So how would he ever be able to effectively to engage in an investigation of Victor's murder? Victor Stuart had been the fair-haired boy. Everyone in the county doted on him as they doted on Julia. This was why they were the obvious choice for a couple. The only problem with this scenario was that Victor was a mean person. He lived for himself and his glory. Jefferson called such people narcissists. John didn't have the high education that Jefferson had— no one in the county had. But if he remembered correctly, the word 'narcissism' came from a story long ago about two lovers: one was focused upon himself and the other always wanted to have the last word. This was a terrible combination and ended badly for both. If Victor was truly a narcissist, then perhaps he received his just deserts. The question was *who* he encountered that brought about his end.

The only three facts that John knew about Victor were: 1. He considered himself to be the best young man in the county—perhaps in all of Georgia, 2. He loved riding horses and gambling (about which he was constantly bragging), and 3. He fancied Julia and wanted to marry her. Now John entered into Victor's fantasy world in all three categories. First, John was always better in sports than Victor. He was stronger and could best him in a physical contest if it came to it. This must have either made Victor furious or, if he were too far gone as a narcissist, then he might have created delusional scenarios about his power. Second, John was almost as good a rider as Victor and would have beaten him in the county horse race had it been run and judged fairly. Third, they both loved the same woman. Somewhere in there was undoubtedly a motive of murder. John hadn't gotten back home at his usual hour, so there was space for his possibly having committed the crime. But since Julia had clearly shown a preference to him at the dance, there was no motive on John's part there.

Sometimes John had imagined that Jason also fancied Julia. Jason was not in Victor's league regarding sports and manly virtues such as horse riding. But Jason was always a false kind of guy. There were so many times growing up that he had treated him, John, trecherously. Jason had created lies and artificially incriminating situations that would put John in a poor light with Mr. Beauchay or Mr. Russell, his and Jason's tutor. John did not understand the animus that Jason felt for him. Surely, Jason was the heir. That was not in question. So what problem did John pose to the boy with whom he was raised? Julia Vanderkamp.

Surely, this gave Jason a motive against John for years. But what about Victor? If Victor was the popular favorite for Julia's hand, then that would mean that Jason would be denied that prize. Could it have been the case that Jason used his craftiness against Victor somehow, just as he had for years against John? Might Jason have been involved in Victor's demise?

There was some real possibility in this. In the past six months or so before the county fair, Jason and Victor had been a pair of sorts. John didn't know any of the details, but as Jefferson used to say, "The devil is in the details."

Chapter 11

"Making Time"

John walked into town and boarded the bus that would take him to the nearest railroad station. From there, John would get on the train to the stop just before Varner's Junction. John would walk the rest of the way so that he could protect his security.

He looked out the window of the coach and stared at the scenery. The only difference between his activity on the bus and the train to which he transferred was that of not having to fan the cigarette smoke from his face on the train as he had to on the bus, otherwise his positions were interchangeable. He stared out the window and watched the scenery go by. It seemed to John that it was impossible to ever notice anything as they were just passing it. Since the rail track had telegraph polls adjacent, John would try to stare at a single pole in the distance and retain his focus as the pole approached, but when it came within twenty yards, it suddenly seemed to accelerate and zip by in a blur. Then he would turn his head back again and the poles regained their clarity.

Perhaps this is a little bit like life, thought John. Though John didn't know what further he could surmise about that. Like so many events in life, John often felt he recognized some moment of significance. But then he was unable to specify *just why* it was significant.

When the train was going around a bend, this phenomenon of the *approaching telegraph pole becoming invisible and then visible again* was even more exaggerated so that John could see poles that had been passed long before and now were quite small, and indistinct to the details, but then coming into full relief for just a blink before giving way to the landscape backdrop. Had they disappeared? Almost. But then they reappeared. The zoetrope was magical.

John was mesmerized. But then the conductor walked through the car declaring that Statesboro was the next stop. John was getting closer to his exit. It would be the second stop. John decided to pop into the men's room. All of a sudden his mind was filled with anxious thoughts. He was still twenty miles from Varner's Junction (he had taken a circuitous route), but already his safety zone had vanished. Again, he felt the role of the fugitive.

What John might have seen if he hadn't gone to the men's room was the figure of his Julia, walking through his car to the dining car for a snack. She was making her trip home, as well.

When the train pulled out, John returned to his seat and picked up a newspaper that someone had left on the seat opposite him. It had been a long while since John had read a newspaper. He literally devoured it from first to last. He read everything including the small fillers that told how many eggs an average Australian mongoose laid last leap year as compared to a normal year. He was anxious to fill in all the holes that were in his consciousness about the world since he had left Bella County.

It was as if he suddenly had become attuned to the necessity of his again caring about what was happening about him. This sharpened his awareness. He could not merely sit enclosed in his preoccupation with something trivial when the *real* world was about him.

It was in this spirit that John sat absorbed in his paper, his hands covering his ears so that he might not be distracted, while at the other end of the car, Julia re-entered on her way back to her seat. She stopped halfway down the car as she saw the conductor, who told her that they would be at Possum Holler in twenty minutes. Poor John, of course, didn't hear a thing as he was trying to read the newspaper with his hands over his ears. Only a half a car separated the two lovers, and yet they didn't see each other as they went their separate ways.

Now it wouldn't do for John to get out right at the terminal in Varner's Junction. That was too risky, so he had already decided to disembark at Possum Holler and walk the difference (around 7 miles). It seemed the safest plan to him, so that when he arrived at the appointed station, he hopped down onto the platform and stood momentarily as the train pulled away. What a tremendous adventure life could be, he thought. All it takes is the fortitude to go through it.

What he had to do was to be attentive to every opportunity that was open to him and make use of it in a decisive way. A person could get nowhere if he merely lets himself float about like some driftwood in the ocean. A person has got to see life's opportunities. Because there were a myriad of coincidences that happen (some good and some bad), a person had to create strategies of dealing with the bad and seizing upon the good. This was a continual process as one confronted a life for fortune. The world was rather random in this way so that the only way a person deserved anything was the way one handled what was given to him.

So John was deeply absorbed in thought, even as he disembarked and the train pulled slowly away from the platform. Julia had finished her snack and was now stationed with her sewing at the window seat. She stopped her work momentarily to make sure that the station they had arrived at wasn't her own, when suddenly she noticed a familiar shape on the platform. It couldn't be! Was it John? The train was moving forward again so that she wouldn't get an exact picture, but the man resembled John in all proportions. She struggled vainly with the window to try and lower it, but it was stuck. She knocked on the glass, but to no avail.

The train was pulling away from the platform and the man standing there with his head turned was her John! What could she do? She pounded on the glass, when an elderly man who had been watching her and thought that she wished assistance in opening her window came over and offered his aid. Naturally, his interference blocked Julia's view of the window and John, so that when the stubborn window was finally opened, both the platform and John were long gone.

It was a considerable walk for John back into the area which he knew so well, but he didn't mind as the exercise gave him time to think further on his speculations concerning Jason and the role he might have had in Victor's murder. Victor had been crowing a bit about his knowledge of pari-mutuel betting. Might Victor and Jason have engaged together in betting?

This seemed impossible to John since Jason was such a careful animal. He rarely went outside his comfort zone. He rarely took any chances. Then why go to the horse tracks to place bets? Betting establishments are profitable. They would not be profitable if betting were a legitimate business. There had to be a considerable edge to the owners. This seemed so simple that John had never questioned it. Jason was much more practically prudent than John. Therefore, it was probable that this line of thought was fruitless. John would have to start again.

It was dusk when he finally arrived, via the longest, most cautious route possible to the outskirts of the Beauchay Estate. Under the cover of the night, he would steal to the house and see whether he could see Jefferson's light, which he faithfully turned on for reading just after supper. But though he got in perfect position, there was no light. John waited, and nothing happened.

Perhaps he's out doing something, or in town, thought John, but these possibilities seemed remote. Then a terrible thought flashed through his mind: what if Jefferson was dead? The thought suddenly made him feel weak and nauseous. Jefferson dead, how could such a possibility be accepted? The coldness of the air chilled him as he experienced visions of never again being able to talk to Jefferson. Jefferson raised him. Jefferson was his hero. The emptiness of there being NO JEFFERSON, EVER! No person that lived in the body that he so easily recognized, and that he had come to know from a distance over the years as the temple of the spirit that he so loved—that person might not any longer be, and then what was to become of him, what was there left for John but death as well? To be or not?

But no, his friend wasn't dead, he couldn't be. Somehow John would know if it was true, and it wasn't—no, there wasn't any way that it *could* be. Jefferson *must* not be dead. Such a thing was unthinkable. Perhaps he had the flu or something, anything, but then John's mind froze. There was no way he could actually consider life without Jefferson. So John decided it was all a mistake. Jefferson was somewhere doing something. John would just have to live with that idea. John would go to the servant's house and call on Jessy. She would know where Jefferson was if anyone did, and she would be the only one that John could trust.

Jessy lived on the bottom floor and had a door to her own apartment, which was soon opened as the robed figure opened the locked door.

"'Lawd preserve me, it's master Johnny," began Jessy in a rather loud tone that quickly hushed as she became aware that his position was not one in which loud publicity was a desirable thing. "Come in son, and haves a chair, while I makes you some tea and gets you something to eat."

"I'm not really hungry," began John, not wanting to put Jessy to any trouble.

"Listen boy, I've raised you since you was this high, and I knows what and when you needs some nourishment."

John, knowing from long experience that he could never win an argument with Jessy once her mind was made up about something, quickly surrendered to some tea and a large meat sandwich.

"Now tell me why you is here," she said finally, sitting down across from him, her old portly figure assuming that dignity that he had grown so accustomed to.

"Well, to tell you the truth, I've come to help Jefferson track down the fellow who killed Victor, so that I can be a free man."

The words *free man* seemed to have a tremendous influence upon Jessy as she sat listening with as much intensity as if she were delivering an important message herself.

"Jefferson said to me once that he would try to look into the matter; well, I'm back to help him if he wants to give it a try."

The old woman sat back with these words, which were delivered slow and hesitantly. When they were finally out, she considered carefully what was before her.

"You cain't join him, Johnny. Fo' he done started in some manhunt, hisself." She paused, as John feared that her next words would be—because he *died*. But instead she said, "He's already out a lookin' for that man hisself. Has been for quite a spell. You'll have a devil of a time trying to locate him."

"I don't mind," John wanted to say, but before he had the chance Jessy continued, "He's going to git that man, Johnny, if he can be got."

"I want to help him," said John.

"Well, all that I know is that he's got hisself in Savannah. I don't know nothin' more."

John was encouraged and discouraged by this news. It was good to know that Jefferson was safe and that he was in a particular place, but on the other hand, John had expected to see Jefferson that night, and certainly he, John, could go to Savannah and spend all his time and money and never locate his friend.

"Now you listen to me a minute, Johnny. I wants ta tell you somethin;' that you mights find that killer and you mights not, but you gots to keep on goin'."

"Keep on going?"

"Now you jist listen ta me, an old lady who doesn't claim to be any wiser fer it, but no dumber neither. Ya jist gots ta keep makin' the best of whats ya got, that's all thar is, boy, that's all thar is. Thar's no use ta lookin' back and cryin' bout what should been or this or dat. What's important, is ta try and stay free and make da best, 'cause dat what the good Lawd gave us minds fer: so as ta keep a goin' whiles our heart's try and keep a pace."

John put one hand on the table while the other he put over his eyes. He had a headache and felt the sudden urge to cry, but knew that he wouldn't.

He listened to Jessy.

Chapter 12

"Entering a New City: A Tour of Major Sights"

The next morning John walked back to Possum Holler and took a bus to Savannah. When the bus stopped for a rest stop and as they got out, one of the passengers, whom John didn't recognize, suddenly looked at John in the way that bespoke to John that he was recognized.

The man vanished, and John knew that the police would be there in minutes. He had to think fast. He hadn't come all this way to be stopped at the last minute by some freak recognition.

"Why hadn't he taken the train?" he thought. But he knew that what he had to do now was to escape. A truck, that would be it. He climbed onto an open-ended truck that was just at the exit waiting to find a break in the traffic. He didn't think, but merely acted, swiftly trying as best he could to avoid detection. He would ride a while and then when they slowed down some, he could perhaps jump out and make his way to the rails, which he could see were running parallel to the highway. If the highway patrol was called, then they might have road blocks up and stop the truck, meaning the train would have been safest.

But the truck never slowed enough for John to get out, and he had a safe ride into Savannah. The city was certainly different than Atlanta. John had never seen the place before and found that he wasn't as awed by the size of this city as he had been by the other.

It seemed to be a bit of a large town or a very small city to him. But when he thought of how he was going to find Jefferson, suddenly the size of the place increased a great extent. What would he do? How would he manage? The enormity of the task dispirited him.

He also had to be very careful about the police, as they knew that he had been heading for Savannah and would be on the lookout for him. All his movements must be carefully planned so that he wouldn't make any foolish mistakes. As soon as he found Jefferson, they could establish some place as a headquarters from which they might operate to try and catch the quarry.

John had no idea what, if any, leads Jefferson might be working, but he tried to reason that if he were Jefferson, and he was looking for a murderer who might be trying to keep out of sight, that he would go to the poorer section of the city, where all the blacks lived.

As John approached the part of the city where he thought that he would have the best chance of finding his friend, he kept an eye out for a place where he could stay for a while. The aura of the city came into his immediate sensibility and he felt a hopefulness as he walked down the streets on the cracked sidewalks that were so dirty with refuse, tobacco juice (dried and decaying), and open ripening garbage within unattended cans. The attendant flies were fewer in number because of the cool temperature. There were children playing in the street as they used garbage can lids for shields and knocked each other's teeth out in the process. There were children playing on scooters, and there was a game of stick ball in progress as the players screamed that someone was cheating and that the play should be taken over while the other side was just as violent in their protestations. It was an open question as to whether they were playing more stickball or arguing about alleged violations of the rules.

From the alley in which John turned, he could see and smell fresh laundry being put up to dry in the sooty air. How hard she worked to knock out the dirt, he thought, thinking back to his own experience with the stones for the Dumont "party," and how long it had taken him just to wash the things he was wearing, much less the wash of an entire family. The cement was filled with small pools of dirty water that were miniature lakes, each with its own personality and foul smell. A dog came running down the alley, barking at another dog that it must have seen as it was making its rounds. The sound of the barking created a pitched cacophony with the ten or fifteen odd babies that he could hear crying for attention from their mothers who were already overworked, and near the point of listless exhaustion. There had been little traffic on the streets where John had come from, but the end of the alley was on a busy street where the smell of exhaust temporarily covered the smells of a paper mill that was nearby. John thought that he had the taste of oil in his mouth.

On this sidewalk, there were some white businessmen, who looked as if they were all late for some appointment. There were a few black teens sitting on the steps of adjacent row houses. Their leisure in the midst of the bustle was a perfect counterpoint.

Then the neighborhood transitioned to some quiet of the backstreets. But soon John emerged again to the bustling that he was unaccustomed to seeing. Everyone was going somewhere, doing something, unless it were all a trick and no one had anything really to do at all—perhaps it was one grand illusion!

All the people, the smells, the little pools of water, and the cats that he saw chasing rats contributed to making John suddenly feel quite alone. It seemed strange to him that when he was in the woods with no one around, he felt less isolated than here on this busy sidewalk with all these people.

A man at a bus stop glanced at John in a peculiar way—I suppose he's making his mental guess as to whether I'm white or black, thought John, who was at that moment rather amused by the thought, even as the man gaped at him again in a most indiscrete fashion. The whole thing was quite funny, John thought. It was like one big zoo with all the noises and smells. At the end of the block a dog was fouling on the cement. That dog, John thought, is bringing industry to this town, he's creating a job for someone. How John wished to walk up to the dog and kiss it or perhaps bite it, but of course he merely walked by the animal. Then John began to laugh, uncontrollably, out loud.

***

Having received no answer from his first inquiries, Rod sent the following letter,

Why won't you contact me? I've heard some things about you that I find hard to believe. Please come to

Savannah and clear things up. It's getting very hot around here.

    Rod

Dodson called up one of his boys: "You deliver this personally to the address shown here, and ask for Mr. Dodson, do you understand? Mr. Dodson, and I want you to wait for a reply."

The man left. Perhaps George would be angry at his letting someone else know the identity of his private dwelling, though the man had been so instructed so that he should have no idea to who he was delivering the letter. How could his messenger possibly make the connection between Big George and Mr. Dodson to whom he was delivering the note? Rod concluded that the secrecy had been maintained. There would be no problem. All would be cleared up in a matter of days. Meanwhile, he waited anxiously for news of Daniels' death.

Book Eleven

Professing What We Know

I was once hired as head designer of costumes for a production of *Antigone* at the Haymarket Theatre in London. It had been the first classical Greek drama that I had worked on. I hadn't a clue what I should do. I went to the early production meetings, both because my contract required I do so and because I hoped to get some ideas on themes that would drive my designs.

The artistic director, Sylvia Sneed, was very new to the business and not overly confident in her vision for the production. Her dramaturge, Michael Snit, was very interested in showing how *Antigone* was topical to the political climate of the day. He had a great blurb for the program on how the character Antigone was the rebel pushing the socialist policies of the Labor government, and Ismene was an apologist for the Tories.

Since the dramaturge was a personal selection from the producer, he had some weight in decision-making for the show. I happened to be moving some linen stock from point A to point B when I overheard the following conversation. It occasioned some reflection on my part. Ms. Sneed was sitting backstage on some materials that had been ordered for the set while Mr. Snit was pacing back and forth in front of her.

"You know, having an *Antigone* that is staged as it might have been in Ancient Greece is ridiculous," said Snit, gesticulating grandly.

"How so, noble Snit?" replied Sneed.

"Well, it's pretty well agreed that we know very little about the Ancient Greeks, much less how they might perform a drama." Snit put his hands to his side and began to strut from side-to-side.

"Well we do know some things. We have all the history of the time and commentary on the drama. We might not get it exactly, but we might not be too terribly far off," Sylvia said. Sylvia didn't tell Michael that she had a first in Classics at Cambridge.

"But *we* aren't ancient Greeks, are we?"

Sylvia lifted up her eyebrows and rolled her eyes.

"Well, *we aren't*," returned Michael. "This is important. For example. I was a dramaturge recently for a revival of *Showboat*. They wanted to re-create the African American experience in a totally artificial way that I found offensive."

"How so? Paul Robson's dead. But *he* believed in the show."

"Well, he was an African American, wasn't he?"

"Quite," returned Sneed. "But what has that to do with my point?"

"As a dramaturge, I am hired by Mr. Tops to make sure that this play resonates intellectually within some chamber of high art and will honestly present a picture of the verities of the text to a contemporary audience." Snit took out a cigarette and lit it with a wooden match that he pulled out of his tight jeans. With one deft turn of his wrist, the match head struck his pant zipper. The flame shot upwards and initiated his smoke.

Sylvia smiled. "As the artistic director of this production, also hired by Mr. Tops, I have complete artistic control of this play. But because I am a cooperative person, I want there to be teamwork in this rendition of *Antigone*." Sylvia smiled again and took out a breath mint from a very small wrist purse that she carried with her. "Therefore, I'm willing to listen to your arguments. And I'll return rejoinders to you. First of all, there is the script. We are using a standard version of the play with emendations of my own. I studied classical Greek at university."

"I rather assumed as much. I was Philosophy, Politics, and Economics at Oxford."

"Fine university. I was Cambridge. But all of that doesn't matter much, does it? What counts is the strength of our arguments. Now, what I think you are getting at is the standard assertion that one can only create art about which she knows individually."

"*Rather*. What I'm bothered about is some aftermath of colonialism. Here in Britain we try to be ever so *right minded* with respect to the people we have enslaved and now want to enshrine. Take Richard Attenborough (from your Cambridge, by the way). He made this movie, 'Gandhi' that was supposed to show how open-minded a British Colonialist could be. This is an inauthentic movie. A white British person cannot possibly get into the worldview of India post-1900, which was the object of the movie. It is insulting! Sure, lots of white Americans and other white Commonwealth folks can *feel good* about their expedition into exotic lands and peoples. This work, if it is done at all, should be undertaken by people of the oppressed socio-political group. They are the only ones who really *know* what the shared community worldview really was. "

"Well said, Michael," returned Sylvia as she took a swig at her bottled water. "I thought that this might be where you were coming from. But then, as a philosopher, you should have honed in on the word 'knows.'"

"It seems fairly simple to me," began Snit. "Each of us *knows* just what is presented to us in our own life's experience. For example, we just jousted on Oxford versus Cambridge. I cannot know what it is like to do a classics degree at Cambridge, just as you cannot know what it is like to do a philosophy, politics, and economics degree at Oxford."

"True enough. But what level of experiential understanding is sufficient? For example, say I had a boyfriend who took a PPE degree at Oxford and talked about the experience at length. Might I have enough understanding to write a short story? Or to direct a satirical play? The word 'know' is crucial here."

Michael scrunched up his nose. This was not a response he wanted to hear. "What I'm saying is that only the *oppressed* can tell the story of the *oppressed* because there is some element of actually living that existence that gives an authenticity which cannot be had by books and study."

"Well, then you will cut out a great deal of drama. We couldn't do *Antigone* because none of us is an ancient Greek. Method acting would also be jettisoned since it is based upon the principle that *analogy* is possible from one's own life to the life of the character one wishes to perform. You can *become* the character even though you have not lived her life experience."

Michael Snit pursed his lips.

Sylvia continued, "In fact, isn't the very possibility of language usage itself dependent upon people being able to converse, argue, and come to understandings despite our disparate life experiences?"

"But those who have walked the walk know best," returned Snit.

"Direct empirical experience is important. It's not to be discounted. That's why I'm directing an ancient Greek play having studied classics (a sort of second-hand experience). But it isn't *everything*. All of us have to *contemplate* the significance of what happens to us and others in the world. And drama is one vehicle that allows this to happen."

Snit knit his eyebrows together.

"It seems to me that we *know* in a variety of ways and in a variety of contexts. I may *know* that the Americans put a man on the moon from watching a news reel. That's a sort of experience, but the only ones who really *know* were the two chaps who did it. If I were a philosophical bloke like you, I'd probably transition to other cognitive terms such as *belief*, *hunch*, and *reasonable guess*. If Richard Attenborough got it terribly wrong, then let others join the discussion and have a debate. I'm sure that spirited debate on a play or film is every director's dream. It certainly is mine."

"I'll have to think about it."

"Wonderful! So let's get on to *Antigone*, natural law, and the power of women! We'll light up a debate of our own."

I smiled. I was going to like working with Ms. Sneed. And with a lightened step I returned to the costume wardrobe, determined to do the same.

Exhibits:

Come, dear children, let us away;
Down and away below!
Now my brothers call from the bay,
Now the great winds shoreward blow,
Now the salt tides seaward flow;
Now the wild white horses play,
Champ and chafe and toss in the spray.
Children dear, let us away!
This way, this way!

Call her once before you go—
Call once yet!
In *a* voice that she will know:
"Margaret! Margaret!"
Children's voices should be dear
(Call once more) to a mother's ear;
Children's voices, wild with pain—
Surely she will come again!
Call her once and come away;
This way, this way!
"Mother dear, we cannot stay!
The wild white horses foam and fret,"
 Margaret! Margaret!

Matthew Arnold from "The Forsaken Merman"

8

And broader and brighter
The Gleam flying onward,
Wed to the melody,
Sang thro' the world;
And slower and fainter,
Old and weary,
But eager to follow,
I saw, whenever
In passing it glanced upon
Hamlet or city,
That under the Crosses
The dead man's garden,
The mortal hillock,
Would break into blossom;
And so to the land's
Last limit I came—
And can no longer,
But die rejoicing,
For thro' the Magic
Of Him the Mighty,
Who taught me in childhood,

There on the border
Of boundless Ocean,
And all but in Heaven
Hovers the Gleam.

9

Not of the sunlight,
Not of the moonlight,
Not of the starlight!
O young Mariner,
Down to the haven,
Call your companions,
Launch your vessel
And crowd your canvas,
And, ere it vanishes
Over the margin,
After it, follow it,
Follow the Gleam.

Alfred Tennyson from "Merlin and the Gleam"

Lady Alice,
Alice the Queen, and Louise the Queen,
Two damozels wearing purple and green,
Four lone ladies dwelling here
From day to day and year to year;
And there is none to let us go;
To break the locks of the doors below,
Or shovel away the heaped-up snow;
And when we die no man will know
That we are dead; but they give us leave,
Once every year on Christmas-eve,
To sing in the Closet Blue one song;
And we should be so long, so long,
If we dared, in singing; for dream on dream,
They float on in a happy stream;
Float from the gold strings, float from the keys,
Float from the open'd lips of Louise;
But, alas! the sea-salt oozes through

The chinks of the tiles of the Closet Blue;
And ever the great bell overhead
Booms in the wind a knell for the dead,
The wind plays on it a knell for the dead.

    They sing all together.
How long ago was it, how long ago,
He came to this tower with hands full of snow?

        William Morris, from "The Blue Closet"

    xxx
Burningly it came on me all at once,
This was the place! those two hills on the right
Crouched like two bulls locked horn in horn in fight;
While to the left, a tall scalped mountain. . . Dunce,
Fool, to be dozing at the very nonce,
After a life spent training for the sight!

    xxxi
What in the midst lay but the Tower itself?
The round squat turret, blind as the fool's heart,
Built of brown stone, without a counterpart
In the whole world. The tempest's mocking elf
Points to the shipman thus the unseen shelf
He strikes on, only when the timbers start.

    xxxii
Not see? because of night perhaps?—Why, day
Came back again for that before it left,
The dying sunset kindled through a cleft:
The hills, like giants at a hunting, lay,
Chin upon hand, to see the game at bay,—
"Now stab and end the creature—to the heft!"

    xxxiii
Not hear? When noise was everywhere! It tolled
Increasing like a bell. Names in my ears,
Of all the lost adventurers; my peers,—
How such a one was strong, and such was bold,
And such was fortunate, yet each of old

Lost, lost! One moment knelled the woe of years.

    xxxiv
There they stood, ranged along the hill-sides, met
To view the last of me, a living frame
For one more picture! in a sheet of flame
I saw when and I knew them all. And yet
Dauntless the slug-to my lips I set,
And blew."*Childe Roland to the Dark Tower came.*"

        Robert Browning from "Childe Roland to the Dark
        Tower Came"

The following are excerpts from periodicals circa 1927 and 1928

    Last week, eight years after leaving under a politically-brewed cloud, Theodore Gilmore Bilbo returned in triumph to the State Capitol of Mississippi, for his second four-year term as governor. Once tried and acquitted of bribery, Mr. Bilbo had re-carved his career, whetting the fighting edge of his ambition on the grindstone of his persecution. Inaugurated once more, he reiterated all the things he wanted to do for Mississippi.
    January, 30, 1928

    There was no warrant or written complaint against Frederick Jockell, attorney of Mount Vernon, N.Y. Yet he was arrested in Manhattan on a charge of grand larceny, clapped into jail with "a howling Chinaman." So, claiming that he had been humiliated, Mr. Jockell sued Detective John J. Quinn (who arrested him) for $25,000. Last week a jury upheld Mr. Jockell to the extent of $1,000. Presiding Justice Joseph Morschauser of the New York Supreme Court added "The verdict should have been ten times as much, so as to teach New York police officers to be more careful in making arrests. Whenever I go into that city I do not know whether or not I'll get out again without being arrested. As a result I take the first train out into the country again that I can.
    March 12, 1928

The solace of many a dowager at Paris is the ubiquitous gigolo, a male who lurks in smart dancing places and is ready, for a modest tip, to offer gallantries to ladies whose age or ugliness induces them to buy what others can command.

Last fortnight M. le Prefect of Paris Policee Jean Chiappe released an interesting survey of the life of the gigolo based upon police investigation.

Points: 1. The earnings in tips per gigolo per night generally range between 70 francs ($2.80) and 200 francs ($8.00); 2. A large percentage of Paris gigolos are not French; 3. French law does not permit the arrest or restraint of a French gigolo, as such; 4. The Ministry of Labor has announced an intention to scrutinize more closely in future the applications of foreign males who seek permits to work as "dancers" in France. M. Chiappe expressed the hope that much good will be done by refusing permits to "foreign dancers" who appear in reality to be gigolos.

April 2, 1928

He was perhaps eleven, and he made his request with elaborate carelessness. "Gimme a ticket to Texas." "Where to in Texas?" the ticket seller asked smiling. "Oh, anywhere in Texas." "Half fare to Texas," he was informed with mock gravity, "will cost you $35." The young man produced a roll of bills. Later, under the kindly but firm question of station authorities, he confessed that he had taken French leave from home after scraping together enough cash to get to Texas. He was, he said, going to fight Indians. He, with the money, was returned to his parents. . . . Hundreds of such cases come to the ticket agent's office on the floor of the Pennsylvania Station in New York. . . . But this is only one phase of the varied and complex work of the ticket agents and ticket sellers. . . . Such men must be travel experts as well as diplomats of unusual tact and discernment. They are. With them Pennsylvania service starts. . . .

April 16, 1928

To W.S. Craig, president of the State Bank and Trust Co, at Tallulah, La., came last week a farmer. Last year this farmer had raised 500 bales of cotton. This year he hoped he might make ten bales. That same morning another farmer had talked to Mr. Craig, had said that not a single bale of cotton would grow on his land this year. His 1926 production had been 300 bales. "Dixie" may still be the "land of cotton," but that portion of "Dixie" hit by the Mississippi flood has become the land of the cotton-less.

July 25, 1927

The Sacco-Vanzetti case became even more an international affair with a rumor last week that a committee of noted Frenchmen was coming to the U.S. to aid the condemned men. On this committee were reported to be Georges Lecomte, of the French Academy, Louise Loucheur, the Countess de Noailles, onetime Minister of the Interior, Louis Malvy, Professor Paul Langevin and Lieutenant Colonel Alfred Dreyfus.

August 8, 1927

Has life been easy for "Willie" Hearst? Success is all around him. It is true he had the ten-year start on life which family millions give to any man. Unlike many a man he has worked hard with them. His success has meant ceaseless work; and that (for the few men who like it) is easy. Politically life has been hard. He wanted to see "President Hearst" streaming across the pages of his newspapers. He did not see it. Socially, who can say whether life has been hard or easy?

August 15, 1927

For 21 years Florenz Ziegfeld has produced the Follies according to one formula: to frame the most beautiful show girls discoverable against the most gorgeous backgrounds conceivable. His formula has never failed. But as nothing subscribes more unreservedly to the law of diminishing returns than succession of splendors, this last superbly heralded Follies achieves only another anti-climax. Though Eddie Cantor (eyes big as baseballs, and lugubrious) paces the stage with a repertory of "wisecracks," the tone of metropolitan criticism seemed to be, condescendingly: "The Ziegfeld Follies is the World's Most Beautiful Dumb Show."

March 29, 1927

The President and family attended church, accompanied by U.S. Senator from Connecticut Hiram Bingham and the Senator's son Woodbridge Bingham, Rolf Lium, student preacher of the Hermosa Church, gave his last sermon of the summer. When the collection plate was passed, the Coolidges, consistently impressed by the young man's ability, contributed to a $50 purse which members of the parish tendered Rolf Lium in addition to his monthly salary of $50. Mrs. Coolidge shook hands with Rolf Lium after the service and secured his mother's address.

September 12, 1927

Herbert Hoover, Secretary of Commerce, before leaving New Orleans after his ninth tour of the Mississippi flood areas, said: "I will not say one word about politics as long as I am engaged in flood relief work. . . Every crevasse in the Mississippi valley is being closed. . . and by Dec 1, I expect, the work will be completed. The War Department is going ahead with the work. . . I feel certain the money to pay for it will be found. . ."

September 19, 1927

Are you sure that unconsciously you do not use slipshod grammar and incorrect pronunciation? Through study of the MILLER SYSTEM OF CORRECT ENGLISH for cultured speech—business or social—you can eliminate all doubt and speak with assurance in any company. . . DO YOU SAY—in'kwirry for inqui'ry, ad'dress for address, cu-pon for cou-pon. . . . CAN YOU PRONOUNCE FOREIGN WORDS LIKE—masseuse, cello, lingerie, décolleté, faux pas, hor d'oeuvre. . . .

October 3, 1927

If the approaching automobile war between Henry Ford and General. Motors Corp. were symbolized in armaments, Mr. Ford would be a cannon and General Motors a machine gun. When a Ford product strikes the market squarely as did Model-T when first shot into the world of pedestrians, the battle is over. But when the Ford product misses, as Model-T has been missing ever since economic prosperity in the U.S. caused the public to shift from mere transportation to touring with style, it misses by a mile.

October 10, 1927

Governor Albert Cabell Ritchie of Maryland, wed Democrat, ate haggis with the St. Andrew's Society last week in Manhattan. Said he: "About the only things that make eyes flash and stir human emotions now are Prohibition, the K.K.K., religious intolerance and Fundamentalism. . . . The real question is not whether you are 'wet' or 'dry' to use the inept phrases of the hour, but whether there should be a national, blanket law governing any such question of personal conduct when that law receives neither sanction nor regard among large communities and groups of the people.'"

December 12, 1927

They cooped you in their kitchens,
They penned you in their factories,
They gave you the jobs that they were too good for,
They tried to guarantee happiness to themselves
By shunting dirt and misery to you.

You sang:
  Me an' muh baby gonna shine, shine
  Me an' muh baby gonna shine.
    The strong men keep a-commin' on
    The strong men git stronger. . . .

   Sterling A. Brown, from "Strong Men" (1931)

To fling my arms wide
In some place of the sun,

To whirl and to dance
Till the white day is done.
Then rest at cool evening
Beneath a tall tree
While night comes on gently,
      Dark like me—
That is my dream!

To fling my arms wide
In the face of the sun,
Dance! Whirl! Whirl!
Till the quick day is done.
Rest at pale evening . . .
A tall, slim tree . . .
Night coming tenderly
      Black like me.

        Langston Hughes, "Dream Variations" (1924)

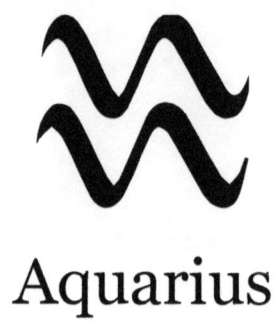

Aquarius

Multiplication

Chapter 1

"An Event from the Past and a Message from the Present"

When George Dodson was a boy, one event made a profound impression upon him. It was a foot race that several of the fellows, older than George, but still part of the group in which he associated, would bet money on the results and then they would race it out. The winner of the last race would decide the course and how the event would be run. Since George, who never took part in the running, would be at the finish, he was one of the judges who could decide the places in a close one. One time after one such race, George overheard one of the boys who had finished fourth laughing and joking as if he had won.

"It was sure something," said the boy.

"I've never seen you race as well," said the other.

"Imagine fourth, that's really something."

"Never thought you'd do it."

"Me neither."

"I hope you don't git to become braggart 'bout it."

What could the one boy be so happy about, thought George; he'd lost. In fact, he hadn't done very well, finishing fourth in a seven person race. How could anyone be happy about that? It seemed completely incomprehensible to little George that a person could ever be satisfied with anything less than first place and the money in the pot.

"Never thought you'd do it."

"Me neither."

The words just seemed to echo in George's head. The boy was not only satisfied with what he had done, but he was happy about it! He proclaimed that he never thought that he'd ever do as well. That fellow, George thought, was a sucker. The winner of the race had gotten his money, and the fourth place finisher wasn't mad as hell about it. He merely sat back and talked with one of his buddies about how well he thought he'd done. It all depended upon what perspective one viewed from to determine whether it was a success or a failure. Regardless, oftentimes the absolute standards that society uses to judge a man (namely economic betterment) is the best measure. It is quantitative and easy to compare.

All that one had to do was somehow convince people that they were actually better off under one situation than another. Comparatively, they might bear any sort of burden that might be imposed. Offer them a substitute goal and soon the real ones will be forgotten.

This maxim had stayed with George all of his life, and he could never forget the scene of the race down to the expressions of joy on the loser's face. All situations are judged by some particular individual. The trick for the one who wanted to be the master was to control the reactions of the slaves (here understood as anyone under the master's power). The goal in life for anyone of merit is to become a master. This was what life was all about. One's essential nature had to be expressed in a leadership role over others. Only the leaders were fully developed humans. Their minions were machine parts that allowed the masters to work out what they wanted to achieve.

The new era of industrialization was built upon this reality. George was going to transform not just Bella County, but the entire state of Georgia with his energetic vision of development. The old agrarian economy only worked when cotton prices were high. The old South with slave labor was profitable. Now the money is in finished goods: textiles (in the case of cotton). He would transform this sleepy county to an industrial powerhouse that would rival cities in the North.

So it was that George set out on a business venture with Oscar Whren, a fellow who had been loosely connected with his brother since his Texas days and who, along with Bill Marsh, had been the only real business associates who could say they really "knew" George Dodson. As his tool to manage public sentiment, Whren took up a public stance that was anti-George Dodson. This allowed Whren to gain credibility during the phony land investment company, which was only a sham to get real estate in the county on the cheap. Whren would lose his hotel in the deal, which was another cover for the felonious venture. The suckers in the investment company would see Whren as another victim (rather than a collaborator). In the end, Whren would be the real estate manager of the new industrial park.

"Who are you going to have to take over the hotel?" asked Oscar.

"I'm not sure yet,'" said George. "We have to get a neutral man in there, perhaps a man from the 'new company' who now owns the property." They both laughed at their little game of phony companies and front organizations.

"Now you say that we aren't selling the land to this company," began Oscar.

"Yes, that's the whole beauty of the plan. We lease for fifty years, and when renegotiation comes and everything is too costly to move, then we have them where we want them."

"And if they decide to move?"

"Then we have got a lot of saleable scrap material in addition to the land."

The two men then left their Atlanta hotel room to meet with representatives of the company to discuss details of the proposed deal. Of course, all this was done in tight secrecy. No one knew where George had gone, as Dodson was a very secretive man.

So it was that when the messenger came to Varner's Junction from Rod, he found no one at home except William, who angrily guarded the house against this stranger.

Now it must be remembered that Dorthay Dodson, William's mother, had just died and was lying in a box, slowly decaying as they waited for their father to return. These circumstances weighted on William so that he wasn't in a friendly mood for the messenger.

"I've got a message for your father, son."

"He's not in right now." The coldness in which these words were spoken by a teen-aged boy was unsettling to the messenger.

"Well, when do you expect him back?" returned the messenger, trying to gain common ground.

"If you have a message, then leave it with me," snapped William.

"I'm sorry, I can't do that. You see, I was instructed that I must leave it with your father personally."

"Well, he won't see you, he's not seeing anyone lately, especially not a messenger boy."

This wasn't taken too well by the man who didn't like the term *messenger boy* at all. He felt for his gun, but then checked himself. "I don't think you understand, this is quite important that I deliver this letter in person and get an answer."

"You can't deliver the letter in person, and he won't give you no answer. So if those are your instructions, you'll have to leave now. If you want him to see it, then you had better give the letter to me. I will give it to him in good time."

"I don't think you understand, boy."

"No I don't think *you* understand. I said you can't see my father just now, and that is that. Now would you either give me the letter, or kindly get off our land, or I'll call the sheriff and get you off."

Again the man felt the urge to do something, but much experience in his profession had taught him a patience that even surprised himself at times, and so he turned and didn't give the boy the letter. Next stop: Savannah.

***

"What do you mean you couldn't deliver the letter? Did you tell him it was important?"

"The boy said that Mr. Dodson wasn't seeing anyone, that he was very busy, and couldn't be bothered."

"Couldn't be bothered, eh? Couldn't be bothered?"

Rod was in a fit of excitement, and instantly wrote another letter.

Why won't you see me, eh? Do you have a little surprise for me that you didn't think I'd hear about? Well, it may surprise you, but I'm capable of giving surprises too!
Rod

The letter was sealed and Rod gave it back to the other man and said "You deliver this in person if you can. If not, give it to the boy, but make certain that you tell him that it is from Rod—do you understand? There must be no mistake."

Rod was seething mad. His brother was planning something that he hadn't informed Rod about. George had been planning something behind his back. He had always known that money was the common denominator between the two, but Rod still liked to feel that there was something about blood. They were brothers, after all. And blood trumped money.

But if George was going to play rough, then Rod could be just as rough. His brother would be sorry that he tried to cut him out of the picture—one less partner, one less cut of the money. Rod got up and took a thin cigar and lit it. He puffed just enough to get it going and then returned to his obsession. But then again, money couldn't be the reason. Rod had never been greedy. There must be something else to it. But what?

If George was trying to bring about a power play, what was his ultimate purpose? If he wants me out of the active operations of the business, then I'm willing to be the silent partner—but not the stone-silent partner.

Chapter 2

"A Quick Chapter in which There is Less than Meets the Eye"

The rumor of the contract on Rod by his associate Big George had the makings of a gang war. That contract, along with the contract on Daniels by Rod, brought another contract reputed to be from Daniels, himself. The atmosphere around the city was getting very tense and no one was taking any risks that they might have taken previously. Instead, they waited for some break in quiet before the storm. Each of the principals and their lieutenants planned for the various eventualities and how he would get out alive.

The most fearful were those who worked *between* the two men, that is the men who worked between Daniels and Rod and the men who worked between Rod and Big George; these men were loosely associated with Wyse.

So it was after Jefferson turned his prisoner over to Marshal Timay. This was an event that caused considerable stirs in the rumor circles around town. Timay was generally known as some kind of lawman on a mission. His mission was to arrest gamblers, bootleggers, pimps, and those engaging in grand larceny. Because of his leadership stature, he was a dangerous man to deal with. This caused perpetrators in his areas of interest to be cautious of this source of potential chaos.

Jefferson, for his part, was still lying low, waiting for something to break. He hadn't kept his rendezvous with the man from Detroit so he knew at least that no murders would be carried out on *his* direction. But he did know that the situation was getting heated from his daily talks with Marshal Timay. Something would break soon. It had to. There was too much tension for equilibrium. One day after one of these discussions, Jefferson was walking back to Myra's flat when suddenly he felt a gun in his back as a man who had simply been walking next to him pulled the weapon and told Jefferson to walk into an alley.

"Look, I know who you are," said the man.

Jefferson was somewhat apprehensive and kept thinking about how Myra had tried to convince Jefferson to use the phone to make his contacts with the sheriff instead of going on foot, but Jefferson had pigheadedly stuck to his established mode, overruling the wise advice of his good friend.

"What do you—" began Jefferson, but the man wouldn't let him continue.

"This place is like a powder keg and it's going to explode any minute. I don't want to be a casualty of the explosion, understand?"

Jefferson suddenly lost his fear of the man. He wasn't being sent by one of the gangs for revenge, or trying to "get Jefferson," but was acting as a private agent. The man himself was expressing his own fear to Jefferson.

"Now I hears that you have connections with the police," began the man again.

"—Not the police, the U.S. Marshal's office," corrected Jefferson, though it was completely unnecessary. The man's facial expression cringed at the world *U.S. Marshal*. This indicated that Jefferson had *more* power.

"Now, I have some connections too, and I was thinkin' that maybe we coulds make some sorts a deal?"

"What did you have in mind?"

"Well, I'd gives you some information, in exchange for some easy sentence, you know six months or somethin' like that."

"Yes?"

"An' after that, perhaps a lift to some other part of th' country."

"So your friends wouldn't pay their respects?"

"Look, I'm not a song bird, but I just don't wants to get caught up in a lot of shootin'. Better alive in the pokey for six months than in the ground: cold before I'm old."

Jefferson slowly turned around. This man was offering him a very interesting proposition, and of course, Jefferson didn't have the authority to make any deals of any kind, but he did have a rather strong voice with the Marshal behind him. This meant that he might be able to get a deal of some kind for this man, provided he could give Jefferson some useful information.

"Why didn't you go directly to the police yourself?" asked Jefferson.

"Are you crazy? You know what they'd do to someone like me?"

"What makes you think I'd be any different?"

"Well, for one thing we is both black skinned."

"What makes you think that makes any difference to me?"

"I'm not saying that it does, but it does tell me that you can probably be trusted more than some cracker dick with a stick."

Jefferson kind of enjoyed listening to this rather strange fellow who was not really visible as they were in the dark corner and angled such that the sun was in Jefferson's eyes, so that he had to squint. "Well, I might be able to help you. What kind of information do you have?"

"I worked with Sig."

"The Link."

The man nodded.

"What did you do?"

"I reported things between Sig and a guy named Marsh."

"Bill Marsh?"

"Yeah, that's him, you know him?"

"Listen, you can be useful, quite useful. Do you know anyone else who might want to give us some information who were in the same area as yourself?"

The man made some involuntary sounds of distress, "Hey man, I give you some information, for a price, but I ain't going around advertising the fact until I'm safely locked away. 'Cause if I did, then my life wouldn't be worth much, would it?"

Jefferson made arrangements with the man to meet him tomorrow at the same time and the same place and he would tell him if they had a deal or not. It was agreed and the man left as quickly as he had come.

Meanwhile, In Varner's Junction, the messenger for Rod Dodson was making another visit to the house. This time he was greeted by a twelve gauge shotgun as William instantly ordered him off the land.

"Hey kid, why don't you put that thing down, you might hurt somebody."

"I know perfectly well how to use this thing," said William, though he'd never fired a twelve gauge shotgun before in his life. But he was still convincing enough in his act to make the messenger have no doubt at all that if he didn't do as this boy said, that he would be quickly full of buck shot.

"I don't want no trouble, kid."

"Then, git."

"But I have some important information for your father. It's from Rod."

"From Rod?" repeated the boy, understanding immediately who had sent the message and how his father *would* want to see such a message, though William knew that Rod was only the lower partner in a business relationship. Only William alone among the sons was aware of this fact—though he knew none of the details of the business.

"Yes, from Rod, and he told me to deliver it personally and get a reply."

"Well, you can give it to me. I will see that he gets it."

"But Rod wants a reply right away.

"Rod will get a reply when my father is good and ready to give it to him and not before."

Now if George Dodson were actually watching this scene as if it were a play or written in a book, then he would have doubtless understood his son's tact in not revealing his absence from the house. For this would be telling outsiders something which is none of their business. But from the messenger's point of view it seemed as if Mr. Dodson were in the house and didn't want to see anyone and so sent his boy outside to ward them off so that he could do whatever he was doing without any interruptions.

The messenger assumed that the mere mention of Rod's name would have availed him instant access to the house, but apparently this name didn't make any difference, or rather, perhaps even greater opposition, as he had noticed the boy's manner change when he mentioned Rod's name, a change that the messenger took as the recognition of a name that Mr. Dodson had carefully instructed his son *not* to admit under any circumstances. It was the most forbidden of names.

Thus the two characters in this mini-drama viewed the action rather differently, though they were first-hand eyewitnesses to the very same phenomenon.

George lived by a truth of caution. He inculcated this caution to his entire family. The world was full of predators who want to take you down. But if you wanted to run *first* in the race of life, you didn't want to give your adversaries any advantages. Let them get their information the hard way. But surely *he* would not put the dagger into an enemy's hand. The protection against this was secrecy.

William was a good soldier. He followed his commanding officer's directives—not just in deed, but in his heart as well.

And so the messenger gave the boy the note, but was sure that it would never reach Mr. Dodson. But because he was also a good soldier, but not a rubber stamp of his c.o., he had only the *letter* of his commission that needed to be fulfilled. Along these lines he returned to Savannah.

***

"*What*, you say what?"

"That's right Rod, the boy when I told him that it was from Rod, he got especially belligerent, as if he had been told that he wouldn't have anything to do with such messages. I do believe the boy tore it up while I was leaving; I think I heard paper rip. But of course, I could be wrong about that detail. It seemed to me that George was in the house and had carefully told his boy to blow me off. In fact, he answered the door carrying a shotgun, which he stuck in my face."

"You say the boy changed when he heard my name?"

"That's right, boss."

"Thank you, that's all. You may go."

Rod was now convinced that his brother had sent a man to kill him. There was no doubt. Now there was only one thing to do, and that was to defend himself. In survival, it comes down to kill or be killed. It was rather simple. He had to get his adversary before his adversary got him.

Rodney didn't like the idea of sending out a gun after his own brother, but what else could he do? His life was in danger. The reports of someone out to get him (besides the man from Daniels, who had come as a result of the ineptitude of the handling of the job by his own men) made him shake. Two guns aimed at his heart. Rod couldn't get his mind around this.

Rod should have gotten another hired gun for the Daniels hit. This was a mistake, but it was one which he believed he was capable of handling. The threat from his brother was rather more serious. Now was the time to respond. First, he would double his body guard. Then he would commission another hired gun to take care of Daniels. But what would he do about George? Simple logic said that he should take him out, too. But he was his brother and had created much of this business empire himself. Rod had been along for the ride. With George dead, would Rod be able to handle it all? Of course he could.

The paths ahead were simple: he would win or he would die trying.

Chapter 3

"Concerning the Outcome of a Scheme that is of Interest to the Reader"

The deal was approved in a slightly modified form by Marshal Timay. If the man proved to have valuable information, then he would be used as a witness, and anything that he might say on the witness stand, he would be excused for. If he had had any personal involvement, in other words, if he had a lot to say, then he would have little time that he would be obliged to serve—along the lines of the six months. It was a plea bargain with limited immunity.

But if he had nothing, then he would get only the usual leniency granted to those who give themselves up rather than relying on being captured by the law. This generally meant the minimum rather than the maximum sentence. However, it seemed that though the man did have much to say about the organization, he did *not* have any direct knowledge of the affairs of Bella County. Though he did tell them that a man named Gale would know everything that happened, as he was the contact between Marsh and himself directly and spent most of his time in the area that Jefferson was interested in. Thus, Jefferson wanted to know where they might find this Gale and very reluctantly was told that he lived in the section of town near the garbage dump.

The dump—the coincidence rang in Jefferson's head. Of course, that was where Victor had been trashed after he was shot. Perhaps this Gale himself was the killer? But they couldn't be sure, so they had to capture Gale without arousing suspicion among the others in the town, just in case the real killer was still there. They wouldn't want to scare the actual killer (just in case it wasn't Gale) and so give him the cue to run away and out of their grasp forever.

It was decided that Jefferson would go and help bait the trap, which Marshal Timay would help with. They would go to Varner's Junction and send Gale the usual note via their caged bird. Then, when Gale responded, seeing Jefferson at the usual place instead of his expected colleague, he would be off-guard and easily arrested.

"I still don't see why it wouldn't be better to simply arrest the man without all this cloak and dagger," said Marshal Timay.

"This way we may get the killer."

"But Gale is the killer, from what has been said so far. It seems a certainty."

"Well, I think so too, but there may be more people with him, or maybe Gale just did the dumping of the body. I don't know, but I want to be sure," responded Jefferson. His own passion for the truth demanded nothing less.

***

The plan was set in motion by Timay. The scene was set: Jefferson lying under a tree with a hat over his face in the Varner's Junction Park. Though he was dressed like Gale's confederate, Gale noticed that this man wasn't the fellow who he knew, and started to dash away, but he was stopped by three pain clothes deputies.

Now time was critical, and Jefferson knew it. They would take Gale back to Savannah for questioning, but two of the officers were left in town (in plain clothes, so as not to attract suspicion) so that they might be ready to act if the phone call came to them.

In only a couple of days, at the most, the organization in town would know that he was gone. And even if they attributed it to a binge or some gallivanting, as was common among many in the organization, it couldn't last for more than a couple of days without arousing suspicion. They had to get Gale to talk. This was the object, but it was more easily said than done, as Gale was not disposed to tell anyone anything.

Paul Timay wanted to instigate a rough-style interrogation, but Jefferson persuaded him not to.

"I think we'll get him to talk once he's seen the entire situation."

Timay deferred, though he thought that Jefferson was just being soft on Gale because Gale was black, and that Jefferson didn't like to hurt his own kind.

However, when Bogs was brought forward (the one who had voluntarily given himself up) and he was given an opportunity to talk privately with Gale, there was some changes in the latter's attitude.

"So you've decided to talk?" said the Marshal.

"Only with Bogs present," said Gale, who was rather young and had seen two men in his life who he was afraid of: one was Marsh and the other was Bogs, but as Bogs came from a place so far away and was a part of something that Gale saw as more powerful, he feared Bogs more than Marsh. But he insisted that Bogs be with him when he was questioned (almost like an attorney who would tell his client which questions to answer and not to answer). Bogs had convinced Gale that he wasn't breaking any code of honor to the greater organization by testifying about what went on in Varner's Junction, which Bogs had described to Gale as *small stuff*.

Gale would not answer a single question unless he first looked at Bogs to see if it was all right to do so. Bogs wouldn't really do anything, but his lack of expression usually meant that it was fine to proceed.

So under these guidelines they began the investigation.

***

The interrogation room was a small room, 10 x 12 foot. It also had a low, 7 foot ceiling. There was no window. The only light came from two dangling wires from the ceiling that had at their ends light sockets that held 100 watt bulbs. These wires that came down only a foot or so gave the place a rather claustrophobic atmosphere.

In the center of the room was a small rectangular table, 4 x 3 foot. On one side of the table was Gale. On the other side were Timay and Bogs. Jefferson and an armed deputy stood behind Timay and Bogs. Back in the corner at a small desk (that resembled a primary school child's desk) was the court stenographer, a woman of 50 or so with greying blonde hair and very thick glasses. She was an expert in short hand and could handle up to 100 words a minute.

"Do you know Bill Marsh?" asked Timay.

"Yes." replied Gale without looking at Bogs.

"What does he do?"

"He runs a store and a gambling house. Well, really, he doesn't really run the house. I think that's more Miles' business." Gale was relaxed and didn't look at Bogs.

"Who's Miles?" asked Timay.

But there was a pause. The reason for the pause was unclear to everyone. In the midst, jumped in the philosopher-amateur detective, "Is he the black man who thinks he's king of that place?"

"I don't know about that," said Gale, not wanting to say anything really bad about anyone—especially to Jefferson.

"Yeah, that's him," offered Bogs, who knew Miles Bon very well.

"And what was your connection with these two men?" asked Timay.

"I ran messages, carried money to Bogs, and did any dirty assignments that needed doing."

"And what did that include?" asked the Marshal.

"You know, roughing up people who didn't pay their debts to the gambling house."

"Yet didn't this place have illegal games?" asked the Marshal as his voice got rather higher in octave by a fifth.

"Illegal? I don't know. It was just gambling."

"Let's not press that just yet," cautioned Jefferson.

"Is it true that the place was also a bootlegging operation?" asked Timay.

"Yes," replied Gale as the words caught in his mouth.

The Marshal poured a glass of water for Gale and passed it over to him. Gale took a short look at it and then pushed the water away.

"Yes, it was," said Bogs to Marshal Timay. And then he turned to Gale, "Listen, you've got to tell them everything, or else they throw the book at you. If you cooperate, then you get less time—don't you see?"

Gale didn't reply but it was clear by his expression that he didn't quite understand the situation as Bogs had outlined it.

"I'll repeat that last question," repeated Paul Timay, "were you a bootlegging operation or not?"

"Yes," said Gale quietly.

"What?"

"Yes," repeated Gale.

"And whom did you supply?"

"The gambling house, what else?"

"Anywhere else?"

"We also sold at the drug store to *special clients*."

"Anywhere else?"

"No."

"Are you sure?"

"Sure I'm sure."

"We also sold to another gambling house down the street," put Bogs. He had already given most of this information before, so it wasn't any new information to the Marshal.

"But I thought that the casino was run by Whren," put Jefferson as he lifted the palms of his hands upwards.

"*Was* run by him. He went broke on some business deal and had to sell."

"Who's taking his place?" asked Timay. Jefferson wanted to follow-up on the other question but deferred to the Marshal.

"Why would Whren buy Dodson alcohol?"

No answer.

Jefferson repeated, "Why would Whren buy from a man whom he was trying to stop?"

"Dodson didn't run the gambling house. I know everyone thinks he does, but he doesn't. Marsh runs it and he's backed by you, Bogs, and the guys from the city."

"And I'm backed by Sig; that's all I know," said Bogs.

"And so you don't think Dodson was in on it at all?" said Jefferson to Bogs.

"Certainly not. As for Whren buying from Marsh, why shouldn't he?" returned Bogs.

Then Gale said, "Whren and Marsh were good friends. It was Dodson that Whren didn't like, or at least he pretended to dislike him. The way I see it, I think that Dodson was behind Marsh. And so Whren tried make everyone think that he was his own man by publicizing his hatred of Dodson to build up his own business. Whren is a clever man." Gale was almost eloquent. He felt proud of the way he had put together a complicated picture. Bogs smiled back at Gale.

"Why did you kill Victor Stuart?"

Instantly, the mild euphoria that had existed only a moment before quickly left the room. Gale was speechless momentarily, which of course was interpreted immediately as a sign of guilt by the Marshal.

"You might as well tell us all about it," said Timay as he repositioned himself in his chair.

"I can't."

"C'mon kid, come clean, it will be better for you."

"But I didn't do it."

"Yes, yes, we know. Listen, you have been truthful with us so far, why ruin your perfect record?" the Marshal smiled and licked his lips.

"But I didn't do it. I helped afterwards, I admit, but I had nothing to do with the shooting."

"Well, if *you* didn't, then who do you claim did?"

Gale looked panic stricken as if he didn't know what exactly to say in response to this. He looked to Bogs, but there was no answer from him. He was going to have to face this one alone. Gale lifted his hands to the level of his face. His hands were shaking.

"I just helped them dump the body, that's all I did. I had nothing to do with the actual shooting."

"Who helped you?"

"Who?"

"You said that you helped *them*. Who were the others?"

"Old Moses Smith got me to help him, but Moses didn't have none to do with it neither."

"Well, then, who did?"

"I don't know."

"Liar!" exclaimed the Marshal as he slapped his hands hard on the table.

"No, I honestly don't; you've got to believe me."

"You know we have enough on you to send you away for the murder; do you know that?"

"Yes sir," replied Gale, who honestly thought that they probably could put any charge they wanted to on him and make it stick. Gale brought his hands down and hugged himself.

"Now, you don't want to suffer for a crime that you didn't commit, do you?"

Gale shook his head. He held himself tightly and began to cry.

"Who are you afraid of, Gale?" asked Timay in an altogether different voice. Now he was the good Marshal whom we all trust.

Gale continued shaking his head. His tears had stopped when he tightly shut his eyes. He couldn't talk. His tongue was getting hard and pulling back as his stomach and body felt extremely weak. He was going to be sick and he knew it.

"C'mon Gale, it will go better for you if you talk. No one can hurt you once you've told us. We'll protect you."

Then Gale vomited as he fell from his chair. He hit the floor hard, as he seemed not to be in control of himself. His body rolled into his own mess. When they lifted him up and began wiping him off, the words, *Miles Bon,* could be heard barely audibly, but clearly enough. He repeated the name several times, "Miles. Miles Bon."

Chapter 4

"Trying to Fit All the Pieces Together"

"Who is this Miles Bon?" asked the Marshal when Gale had been taken back to his cell. The three men, Bogs, Timay, and Jefferson, had moved to the Marshal's office.

"You were pretty rough on the kid," said Bogs as he sat down.

"A man was killed," returned Timay.

"He's only just a young boy."

"Old enough to bury dead bodies," said the Marshal. Then Jefferson interjected. "This Miles Bon, he's the one we were talking about before."

"Yes, that's the one."

"I take it you two don't get on especially well together."

"You might say that."

"What's his job, exactly?" Timay asked as he regained his appointed role as interrogator.

"He looks over the gambling house and makes some of the sales of booze."

"Is he important?"

"I think he isn't worth the dust to spit on, but then that's my opinion of him. If you want to know what he does, if that's what you're after, then I can tell you—he works for Marsh and he reports to me through some messenger boy there, like Gale. Marsh is the big bootlegger in town. He supplies everyone in the neighboring counties, from that drugstore where he has crates shipped to various points after they're brought in by rail in phony cases."

"But who is this Bon? Where did he come from?" asked Jefferson.

"Who knows? He came in right after Sig left, which was after someone got knocked off—that was when everything was just beginning. I was just getting into things then. Sig was a little man, who became a big man in a hurry. I guess the guy there before had been a part of some small time operation that was really falling apart when someone came in and killed him."

"Do you know who did it?" asked the Marshal.

"Haven't any idea. Somebody told me that someone from Daniels' group did it, but I wouldn't know. All I do know is that it made it a hell of a lot easier establishing ourselves when we were the only supplier in the town."

"So the gambling and the bootlegging were connected?" asked Jefferson.

"That's right, and some small-time loan sharking."

"Who ran that?"

"Don't know for sure, but some say that it was an extension of the real bank that Dodson ran."

"Do you think that Miles Bon killed Victor Stuart?" asked Paul Timay as he pointed his right index finger at Bogs.

Bogs shifted in his chair, "I don't know. I think he could have. He's the type: real secretive, you know what I mean? A real queer sort of fellow if you ask me, I wouldn't put anything past him."

"But you have no knowledge for certain."

"No."

"Thank you, that will be all for now."

Bogs was taken to a special holding cell which was constructed for informants who needed secrecy and protection.

Paul Timay stood up and motioned to Jefferson to move to the large sofa that stood in the corner of the office. In front of the sofa was a coffee table. Next to the sofa where Timay sat was a mahogany chest that Timay opened. The Marshal took out a box of cigars and offered one to Jefferson, though he declined.

"What do you make of it?" asked the Marshal.

"Well, one thing is for certain. John Dow is innocent of the murder of Victor Stuart," replied Jefferson.

"That's agreed, and I'll get a court order nullifying the warrant."

"As to who actually did it, I have some theories—nothing concrete really, but little threads of things that I've seen and observed. For one thing, those betting tickets that I told you about. They were for the county race. Victor couldn't place the bets himself because of the state restriction. So Victor had Jason place the bets. However, what is strange is why Victor didn't bet everything on himself? If you are in a bind, wouldn't you go for it all?

"Jason Beauchay placed the bets. He either acted on Victor's advice or on his own. If the latter, then it was to keep Victor under the thumb of whoever was lending him the money. That's a muddy part of the story." Then Jefferson got up and started pacing back and forth.

"What seems probable is that perhaps Victor met Bon that night and tried to get the money for his winnings that Jason had bet for him. But the problem was that something was mixed-up. Victor thought he was clear: debt free.

"But Victor was a careless lad. He didn't even examine his ticket. He trusted Jason, but when he went in to get his money, there were several horses on the ticket and perhaps they all didn't come in or something, I don't know, but at any rate, there was some kind of disagreement and a fight broke out in which Victor got the worst of it and was killed by Bon. Then Bon sent for this Moses fellow who got our friend Gale to help him dispose of the body. It was a Saturday night, and probably quite late, and they figured that they wouldn't have time to get rid of it properly so they put it in the dump temporarily until they could do a better job on the following evening, except that someone discovered it.

"It shouldn't have been found, no garbage service on the weekends, and who would go to the garbage dump on a Sunday? But apparently someone did, and then the whole thing changed directions. Circumstances pointed to John as the killer, and so with a suspect who also happened to run, the real killer felt safe and thought he had nothing to fear. Who would know? It was a safe plan of action; just as safe as storing the body in the dump.

"But what I'm puzzled about is why Bon didn't kill the two men who knew that he was the real killer."

"Perhaps they didn't know," said the Marshal.

"What?"

"Perhaps our boy Gale is only using some educated guesses that he put together from what he knew from the inside? And perhaps he's still covering something up."

"I don't think so," returned Jefferson. "It's hard to say, but even if he *did* know, Bon wouldn't have wanted another murder—you don't know how much that shakes up a town like Varner's Junction. Their whole business model depends upon *quiet*. Another killing might have created too much commotion," suggested Jefferson.

"Well, at any rate, we have our killer, and we also know that your friend is innocent," concluded the Marshal.

"Yes, we know *that*," agreed Jefferson. "Are you going after Bon right away?"

"I think I should. Things are a bit sensitive, and I think that we should move before the whole thing blows up in our face. I'll send warrants for Bon and Marsh in Bella County, and in the city, for Wyse—that's all that we can get right now, I'm afraid. We could wait and try and get the Dodsons and Whren as you suggested, but I think that they've covered up their tracks pretty well and so getting them would take time—something that we haven't got right now. This whole city is on the edge—"

Just then there was a knock on the door and a young man dressed in plain clothes burst into the room. "Marshal, some big news, first there was a shootout in a bar on the east end."

"Who did it?"

"Don't know, but they were after Daniels, that was sure enough."

"Did they get him?"

"No, that's just it, there was someone there as a decoy or something—I don't know. The whole thing's too confusing, but they got twelve persons."

"All hoods?"

"Hoods, and a few kickers."

"What's the other news?"

"That prisoner that you sent in last week?"

"Yes. His name is Coody. What about him?"

"Well, there was an escape attempt in block-C where he was being kept. Well, four men managed to get out and he was one of them."

The Marshal put out his cigar and sprang to his feet. "Can't our jails even hold anyone anymore? What's the matter with those knuckle heads? I bring them the men and they lose them again—this is the third escape in less than a year. I tell you, heads are going to roll over this one. You can spread that around; there's going to be an inquiry!"

The young messenger didn't quite know what to do as the Marshal ranted at him in the strongest possible terms. After all, he was only the one bringing the news, it wasn't *his* fault.

"Yes sir," he finally stammered and stumbled back outside again.

"I tell you, Jefferson, I don't know how they expect me to keep any order in this state when they let all the men in our jails just waltz away whenever their little hearts feel restless."

The situation was indeed bad, and Jefferson recognized this. Things were in chaos in the city and people were being murdered. How much was he, Jefferson, responsible for this? True, he had tried to mix things up a bit, but then hadn't the plan to kill Daniels been in the works before he had even entered the scene? All he had done was to start the rumor that Rod was being sought by his brother, known as Big George. He had directed the man to circulate for a week or so and then leave town unless he, Jefferson, showed up at a particular rendezvous which, naturally, Jefferson had not done. Essentially, all that had been done was to start a little rumor, nothing more. He certainly wasn't responsible for the Daniels affair. If anything, he had stopped one killer from his objective. But what worried Jefferson was whether the climate, which he felt he *did* have a hand in creating, would mean that he was responsible for any or all of the lives of those who were killed.

The Marshal had assured Jefferson that everything he had done was within the law—especially as he had been working in conjunction with the federal marshals (agents of the Attorney General of the United States) and with their advice. They frequently tried to plant men within these organizations to do just what Jefferson had done by himself.

"Those men," the Marshal had said, "are men who every day break the law and ruin countless numbers of lives. But they do so in the name of security. The end is so essential that it requires unconventional means now and again. The law gives us broad latitude in how we are to deal with these men, but our primary responsibility is to get the guilty parties off of the streets so that decent people might be protected."

So as to his immunity from criminal misdoings, Jefferson felt safe. But criminal responsibility was only a small part of what he felt he had to face. The larger moral questions didn't leave so much freedom or "latitude" in dealing with other human beings, be they criminal or otherwise. Jefferson had tried to disrupt an organization which itself had murdered a boy and tried to foist the blame on another. The persons responsible directly were at the bottom of this scale, but they were put there by the Dodsons, who created the structure which put people like Miles Bon in a position to kill others, so that these men weren't in any way blameless themselves. *He that lives by the sword*—the old words rang true, just as if Peabody had been sitting right next to him. By creating the organization of crime that they had and by presiding over that which had been responsible for at least one murder and the framing of another for the crime, the leaders had accepted some sense of the total blame for the crime.

But what was most important was that if they had constructed an organization based on fear and hatred, and all those attributes that appeal to the un-Christian sides of our person, then those systems, organizations, when disturbed, will or may bring about a series of events of equal ugliness, because the system merely responds to stimuli that resonate on the community worldview upon which it has been built. If Jefferson had disrupted the system so that evil results might follow, might not this evil be really attributed to the system, which deals with special occurrences, i.e., said disturbance, and those who created it?

This again came out technically to comfort Jefferson. But still now—especially now—that John would be freed, he no longer felt a desire to disrupt things anymore and would be perfectly willing to undo, if he could undo, everything disruptive that had been done. True, the Marshal was out to break any organizations of crime in the area, and his responsibility was towards the people of the state as a whole; but his, Jefferson's, duty was to his friend who was his surrogate son. Thus, having completed *this*—having cleared John's good name—he had no malice towards anyone and prayed that no more people might die.

Chapter 5

"A Mixture of Several Conversations"

Understandably, Julia was very shaken when she arrived in Varner's Junction. She had just seen her John on a train platform and could do nothing to tell him that she saw him, and that she wanted to talk with him. They had been separated for so long that much of the immediacy of what it means to love someone was missing. Though none of the real, that is to say the primary, emotion and attachment that loving another forms *was* or *could be* lost: that always remained. But what was damaged was that part of a person that longs to have some contact with her loved ones. Julia longed to be able to be near John and listen to him talk about the woods or what had happened to him. She didn't care about the topic. Whatever he wanted to bring forward was of interest to her. She missed the way he approached life on earth: his manner, style, and the way he organized thoughts. These were what she missed, as well as the way he communicated merely by the happy way in which he would stroll about, with a peaceful detachment and gay abandon that so characterized him to her.

John was a free spirit who was wild and noble (everything that Julia wanted to devote her entire life towards). So it was when she had seen John and couldn't open the window or in any way indicate to him that she had seen him and wanted him in all these ways, and others too. She was, to use an understatement, somewhat upset.

Everything seemed to be working against her. First, the accusations which made John flee. Then the situation in Atlanta, which might be construed as her complicity in an effort to capture or kill him. And *now* her family farm was being confiscated. All seemed to be driven by blind fate. It all seemed so unfair.

Before Julia were visions of people renting their clothing and lying in ashes dressed in sack cloth and bemoaning their condition. These and other nightmares vibrated through her imagination with vivid intensity, as she tried vainly to summons any hope that remained within her tender heart of ever seeing John again.

So when her father walked up to her on the platform and greeted her with open arms, she tried to put on the bravest front that was possible. She knew how much he needed encouragement in his own time of trouble and crisis. But despite all of this, Charles Vanderkamp, who loved his daughter very deeply, would understand that something was wrong and so when they were in the car driving back he asked, "What's the matter, Julia? Tell your father."

"Why father," Julia tried to start as if surprised that he should say such a thing to her, but her strong emotion overcame her and she fell onto his shoulder and began to cry.

Charles Vanderkamp was a strong man. Though he was kind, often times he found it difficult to really be able to express himself in highly charged emotional situations (which were rare around the Vanderkamp household). But under the circumstances he thought it best to pull the car over to the side of the road next to his lower field and comfort his little girl.

"Tell me what's wrong. Is it the land? Are you sad about giving up the land?"

Julia couldn't respond. Certainly she hated the idea of giving up the land and it was an issue that was close to her heart, and had John not been in difficulty, it would be the subject closest to her heart at that moment. It had already occasioned a few tears, but to hear her father guess wrongly only served to make the pain worse. She wanted to tell him, but how could she tell him that something was more important than her own family's land, their heritage? It wasn't that it *wasn't* important to her, but she knew there was no way that she could explain any of this to her father.

Mr. Charles Vanderkamp held his daughter's head against his shoulder. As he listened to her tears, he almost automatically began to stroke her hair just as he did when she was a little girl. Her father used to bounce her on his lap until she became tired and went to sleep.

"It's John, isn't it?" he said as he felt the little body throb. This was a body which never used to cry when it was hurt or wanted attention, as many little girls had done. No, this was his baby girl, small and big at the same time. She had tipped the scales respecting his agreeing to hire the Atlanta lawyer who had gotten them a temporary injunction against the company.

This woman, his daughter, was a mature and a full woman in every way, but was yet to her father also the little girl who used to fall asleep in his lap. He remembered stroking her in the same way that he was stroking her now.

"Oh, father, what am I going to do?"

"Hey, now," he said without really knowing what he was going to say. "Things aren't as bad as they may seem. In my experience on the earth, they never are. There's much good you know, good that you never see when you feel so sad."

Julia didn't say anything, but her crying stopped.

"You know, who'd have guessed that I would be fighting to save the farm only six months ago? I tell you, things can change very quickly, and unexpectedly. What we have to do is to be able to roll with the punches, so that they don't flatten us. You know my mother used to tell me that no matter how bad things got, they could always get worse. They lived through very hard times: a terrible loss in the War and then Reconstruction. We've been more fortunate, but the same still holds true, I think. What l mean is that after all that Fortune can toss our way, it cannot break apart our family and our honor. That's something that's sacred.

"Let them try and take anything else away from us that they want—all of our things and our loved ones, but don't ever let them have our honor, our self-respect, or our Christian decency. This is because that's what keeps us going. That's what keeps us alive."

Julia listened to her father. She knew that he was an old idealist; he always had been. He never ceased to be stirred by emotions that others discarded as overly sentimental and ridiculous, but say what they might, there was something very noble about him and the way that he held to those beliefs in a steadfast way. He never lost his faith. If nothing else, just this testimony of devotion was enough to give her some sort of hope.

Her father understood what was bothering her, and she knew his thoughts on the matter: he didn't approve of her loving a fugitive with no family, but still he loved her more than his sentiments against these two aspects of John, and that allowed him to give her words of hope and comfort, without mentioning John's name at all.

Somehow, the experience of viewing her lover on the railway platform, but unable to communicate with him, could have been a sign of resignation or of hope. Without overthinking the proposition as Jefferson was prone to do, Julia was filled with hope. Without any real evidence, she still believed that she would see John and see him soon.

Julia wasn't sure whether she really believed all of this, but she so wanted to at that moment that it didn't matter. Would they be able to keep the farm? She also wanted to believe in that, too.

Julia felt that her father believed that it might be possible to keep the farm in the family, and that was all that mattered at that moment.

Julia rubbed her eyes with her hands and straightened her hair. She was ready again to try and go home.

**

That day and night, Julia totally threw herself into the issue concerning the house, and talked about ways in which they might be able to save the land.

It was the next afternoon when she was busy in the kitchen baking a cake that she was startled by the phone ringing. Her intense state of concentration was shattered and she dreaded to answer it even though she knew that it was a local call, probably for her mother.

"Hello, Julia Vanderkamp speaking."

"Hello, Julia, this is Jefferson." Julia trembled. She fumbled the phone receiver in her hand so that it almost dropped. "Julia, I want to tell you that *we've done it*! We've got the real murderer of Victor Stuart. He's being taken into custody right away. . . ."

Julia was completely unprepared for this. How could it be possible? Her mind was racing, though she made herself listen to the whole story which Jefferson related as quickly as possible (as the phone call was long distance). "You can tell your family if you want, but make sure that it stays there for the time being, as not all of the men have been apprehended just yet and we don't want to tip them off."

Julia hung up the phone. She was completely dazed. She sat down in a chair and stared at the mixing bowl, but her mind was not on the cake.

The *words,* the *meaning*—was this a terrible joke? But she knew Jefferson would not joke about this. But still she didn't really believe that she had gotten the phone call until her mother came into the kitchen and asked her who was it who called (as she had heard it ringing outside in· her garden).

There was little that Julia could do for the rest of the day as her imagination was completely deranged, spinning about, and her chest sighed deeply with the strong emotion.

She went back to her cake. She had relied upon her faith as her father had suggested, but now there was something more, something extra which she had not any longer counted upon—the frosting. The cake was to have lemon frosting.

Jefferson made another phone call that afternoon to Samuel Beauchay, who was at home, quiet as he was feeling a bit ill. The news, however, seemed to buoy his spirits. Jefferson's call was essentially the same as the one that he had made to Julia, with one important exception, an inclusion of some of his conversation with Samuel's sister, who he was informed just moments before by the bereaved brother had recently passed away. They were all waiting for George to come home so that they could bury her.

Hearing this, Jefferson thought it best to tell Samuel everything, which the other listened to with careful attention and much emotion.

Chapter 6

"A Chapter Devoted to the Events Surrounding
George Dodson's Return Home"

Later that same afternoon, George Dodson drove into town in his new car. He had been with Oscar, who he dropped off at Vidalia Street where he could walk home since their connection must not be made explicit as yet. He was stopped by someone who used to work in the bank, who wasn't sure whether he'd been home yet.

"George, I'm glad to see you—gee. I'm sorry."

George wanted to question the fellow to see what he meant. This sense of uneasiness continued as he made his way into town. As he drove on the newly paved streets, a number of people turned Their heads towards his vehicle and reacted with uneasiness and mournful expressions. George parked his car and walked into the defunct bank. George had bought the property and now used the space for his private headquarters.

George rushed to his secretary and asked her, "What the hell has happened around here, everyone looks like they're going to a funeral or something?"

To this the secretary could only burst out into tears which made George become increasingly frustrated trying to shake her so that she could talk, but to no avail. So George rushed out of his office and grabbed the first thing that he saw, which happened to be the stack of letters recently sent.

George sat at his desk and settled in.

Then his secretary came in. She had brought him his cup of coffee that was his routine charge for her. But the middle-aged woman spilled some of the coffee on the floor.

"What's all the fuss?" demanded George.

The custodian, who had noticed all of what had happened, thought that George was angry at his secretary. There had been a page boy who had walked behind the secretary during her accident. Was George going to blame him?

"I don't rightly know, boss," was the other man's cautious reply.

"What do you mean you don't know?"

"Listen, Mr. Dodson, sir, I is just a broom pusher and—"

George didn't bother to listen to any more. He was frantic. Something had happened and he was going to find out what it was. George slammed his fist onto his desk and exited the office. He got back into his car and rode out to his house. It was then that he discovered that his Dorthay was dead.

Though she was in back in the shed, and chemicals had been put on her so that the decay would be slowed, still there was an odor that disgusted George. Standing on his front yard, he could smell the rotting corpse. This caused him to storm into the house in search of his son, William. He found him in the kitchen, eating a sausage and drinking some whiskey.

"Why didn't you bury her? That's terrible that she should be made just to lie there like that."

"I didn't know what you wanted done with her, so we had her body prepared by the undertaker, and then he suggested that we keep her here until you returned," William said (with his mouth full of sausage). He paused and knocked-off what was left in his glass. "The undertaker said that a wife shouldn't be buried without her husband," said William solemnly.

George tried processing this, and then nodded his head, "You're right there. That's very true. You know, I've had a very stressful business negotiation in Atlanta. If things go right—but let's not talk about that now. We've got to get your mother in the ground."

William nodded. He poured himself a short shot and then exited with the car keys for their old Ford Model-T.

After his son departed, George sat back on the sofa and put his feet up on the coffee table. He was tired. Oscar and he had been going to meeting after meeting and then staying up to all hours of the day and night to make their plans, and seeing how they would swing certain propositions. He wasn't as young as he used to be and such hard work took a much heavier toll on him than it used to.

Why, he remembered when he was young that he could stay up playing cards to all hours of the night, come home drunk, and the next morning be fit enough to go to work at seven o'clock. Those were times when his body responded to everything that was demanded of it and not flag at all, but now, though he could still make the effort required, his fatigue factor was higher than it used to be, making him work slower. And when he finished, suddenly he became utterly exhausted so that he could do nothing else except rest himself. So he was at this moment. He hadn't realized how wasted he really was until he lay back in the soft cushions and let his body become loose. It was as if some powerful force had been unleashed and he was the object of this unmitigated drowsiness. He wanted to go to sleep, so that he barely heard his boy tell him that he had some letters for him.

"Yes, I'll look at them when I wake up," he said, "I want to take a little nap just now."

"But they are important," said the boy.

"Nothing's more important to me just now than a little shut eye," replied George as he curled up on the sofa and was soon fast asleep. The boy put the letters on the coffee table where his father could read them when he awoke, and then went outside to chop some firewood.

George hadn't slept more than a couple hours when he opened his eyes and saw the letters on the table. He didn't know whether he wanted to go back to sleep, or look at the letters. He decided to go back to sleep, but as he tried to do this he seemed to remember something about them being important.

Were the letters important? What if they were? Was it more important to read some letters than to get some badly needed rejuvenation? After all, why does one break his back for money all the time? Couldn't a person take just a little time off for sleep? What was it all about if not to enjoy life occasionally, and that meant sleep?

George lay back and shut his eyes. But he couldn't rest. He sat up again and decided to look at the letters. They had been set down in order received, except for the one that was delivered personally. George decided to open that one first.

As his eyes scanned the short note, George quickly forgot his fatigue. He popped up and went outside to call William. His other children would be coming home from school soon, and he wanted to talk to William before they arrived. When William came into the room, George sat down on a stiff-backed oak chair and beckoned his eldest to come over to him.

"These letters, when did you get them?"

"The last one arrived a couple days ago," said the boy. "Do you know what is in them?"

"No sir."

"Trouble. That's what. *Big* trouble."

William didn't answer. He stood erect without any physical movement.

"Here boy, you sit down, I'm going to make a phone call."

William took the chair that his father vacated.

George went over to the phone and tried to call his brother, but unfortunately the other man had gone out just a half hour before and couldn't be reached.

"Just as I feared. I've got to go again, son. I know I just got back, but believe me, something very important has come up." Then George paused as if he were carefully considering whether he should divulge anything else to his son. Then he walked over to his boy and rested his right hand on William's left shoulder. The boy looked up at his father.

"Listen, William, I'm in some trouble. Some of my business associates are trying to make it very difficult for me just now, do you understand?"

William nodded, though he had no idea what his father meant exactly.

"Now I'm going to Savannah, and there may be trouble, and I might not—" he stopped. "I've got to straighten a few things up, but I think that before I go, I've got something that I want to do, something that I've meant to do for a long time. What I want to do is to make you acquainted with some of my holdings in business, so that if anything should ever happen to me, you'd know what exactly the family owned and what its assets were."

George went to his case and got out some scattered papers. Then he got out a key and unlocked his desk file drawer and removed an old blue leather covered leger. "Now these are only unofficial. I have other records about our clear titles and that file is over at my office in the old bank in a special safety deposit box. In there are the deeds for this property, the golf course, the Vanderkamp farm lein, and the property we bought for our new home."

George moved about rather uneasily. William was rather nervous, but at the same time terribly excited that his father had decided that he'd finally come of age and could be trusted with such important secrets. For secrets, the whole family knew, were the most precious commodities that George ever possessed.

"Now here are some other holdings I have. You see we operate several companies, which aren't real companies at all, in other words we created them so that we wouldn't have to pay any tax, or less tax, on them and also, it helps to conceal your movements so that your opponents never know where you are. That's so important, son, to keep your activities under the table as long as possible so that you can watch the other fellows make their mistakes and then be ready to make your move when you have to." George paused. He half expected William to say, "Isn't that dishonest, Daddy?" or "Is that against the law?" or some such naïve response, but instead, much to George's satisfaction, William only smiled and said, "Yes, go on."

And so, George outlined the various relationships between his company that bought the Vanderkamp land for the new textile mill, and the enterprise that was going to build the houses on the golf course, and others which he controlled in many of the eastern counties of the state. After he finished, he watched his son beam with pride over his father's achievements.

"It's an empire,'" said William.

"It can be. Right now we're only localized in the eastern part of the state, but soon we'll expand to the entire state of Georgia and then when we are finished we will move west. That is the goal."

George took out the key to the safe in the old bank and handed it over to his son, confident in the knowledge that he had the essential records and would be a valuable asset in the times to come. He might do less work himself and leave some to his son, who showed a remarkable ability to see financial moves that could be made. George was proud and confident in his son. Before leaving Varner's Junction he sent a telegram to Rod:

Stop! There's been some mistake; I've been out of town on some business and didn't get your notes. Let's talk; I'm driving to your place right now.
George

And so George left in his car, speeding for Savannah, to clear up all the nonsense that had developed, and get on with the real work."

Chapter 7

"Looking for Jefferson"

Though Savannah was a comparatively smaller city than Atlanta, there would still be problems locating Jefferson, thought John. His first idea was to ask some local shopkeepers whether they had seen anyone matching the description of Jefferson, but due to the tense climate of that section of town brought on by the anticipated violence between Rod and Daniels, no one was very willing to talk and the only answers John got were vague and not helpful.

"Sorry, I got a lot of customers," said a balding young middle-aged shop keeper who wore a white apron.

"But surely you must have some idea—" John tried to follow the shopkeeper who was trying to walk away from John.

"I don't have no idea about nothin'. I run a simple little store, and I don't see nothin'."

"But this is terribly important." John finally had the shopkeeper cornered.

"Listen mister, I have a wife and three children, I don't want no trouble."

This was typical. John would shuffle out of one place after another with the same result. John felt terribly alone at that moment. There was nothing really for him to do but to keep trying, knowing full well that he would get no answers as everyone seemed to be terribly afraid of something. Were there criminals who were tormenting these poor people, or were they just very timid, and selfishly looking after their own interests? A small group of people could certainly terrorize a community, he realized as he thought back to the Martinez family.

Then John saw a little boy sitting in the gutter, crying loudly. John walked up to the boy, knowing full well that perhaps his actions might be mistaken. Though seeing the child's distress, he felt he had to stop what he was doing for a moment. "What's the matter?" he asked the boy.

"I want my mummy!" said the boy who must have been, John judged, to be around seven or eight years old.

"Where is she?" asked John, "I'll take you to her."

"I don't know. I want my Mummy!"

John looked around him to see whether he could see any sight of a woman who might qualify as the child's 'mummy.' But there was no one. Finally he saw one woman walking down the sidewalk.

"Is that your mummy?" asked John.

"No, I want my mummy!"

John was at a loss as to what he should do. The child couldn't be left alone, but on the other hand, perhaps the mother had left the child there and was expecting to pick him up later and if John moved him they might be separated.

"Do you know where you live?" asked John.

The little boy shook his head.

"Where did you see your mother last?"

The boy didn't move.

"Did your mother leave you here?"

There was again no response.

"Well, you know, I can't help you unless you can tell me where you live, or when you last saw your mother."

"I want to cross the street, will you cross me?"

John didn't know what to do for the child, so he decided to take the child across the street as he wished.

When he had taken the child to the other side the boy ran to a house and knocked on the door and was immediately admitted.

How easy it was for the boy to find his mother, when just a moment before it seemed almost impossible, thought John. The thought of helping the boy, even in such a small way, made John feel very warm and relaxed inside. He was less depressed than before as he walked into yet another store.

"How should I know where your hoodlums are, am I supposed to be some kind of prophet or something? Why don't you go to your bars and dice houses and leave poor people alone. God knows we have troubles enough of our own."

There was something about going to places like that that didn't exactly appeal to John. He had never liked the gambling place in Varner's Junction and how that poor black man looked when he was thrown out by Miles Bon. Gambling places were associated with pain to John, and he would have given almost anything to have been able to have avoided such places. But if it was the only way that he was going to find Jefferson, then he must take some kind of risk. And so he went into the first shady establishment that he could find.

It turned out not to be a gambling house but a place where odd sorts of people were just sitting around. The light was dim and there was a peculiar smell about the place, like dirty clothes. He noticed that several people looked at him when he entered. Their gazes were blank, as if their minds had been appropriated by some aliens from another planet. John sat down and soon a man came over to him and asked him what he wanted. John asked for a sandwich. The waiter cocked his head, smiled, and walked away. John wasn't certain whether this was the right place to get information as there didn't seem anything threatening or connected to active criminal behavior. Instead there was a fuzziness that didn't seem at all appropriate.

John began to notice some of the other men in the place. They all seemed to have their eyes opened very wide and with most peculiar expressions on their faces. One man that John was looking at noticed that John was glancing at him and got up to go over to John's table. It was then that John noticed that the appearance of large eyes was owing to a cosmetic application on the eyelids and under the eyes.

It was something unlike John had ever seen before. The man sat down and said in a very low voice, "Have a smoke?"

"No thank you," said John, wishing that his sandwich would come.

"I saw you sitting here all alone. You're new in town aren't you?" he said, putting his hand lightly on John's arm. John didn't know exactly what was happening, but he wasn't staying around to find out. "Sorry, I've got to go," said John as he got up and left.

John pushed on with dogged determination. There were two more bars where he found nothing, when he came upon a place with three pool tables.

"You a friend of his?"

The tone of this question was such that John felt that he should be evasive.

"You might say that I'm trying to locate him."

"You're awful young to be a hit man," said the other. John didn't reply.

"Well one thing's for certain, unless you were one of us, you wouldn't be after him, now would you," the man chuckled as he said this, in an almost demented fashion.

John felt suddenly a little nervous, as he had in the first bar, but this time fearing for his bodily safety. He made a movement as if he was considering to leave, when the man, sensing this, put his burly hand on John's arm and said, "Where are you going, you haven't finished your drink."

The way in which this statement was delivered made John think it was more prudent if he stayed and finished his drink—though he was quite unnerved. He reached for the cross around his neck and held it in his left hand.

"You know if I were you, I'd call the U.S. Marshal's office. That's where he's in real good, you know. The Marshal and him are like that," the man made a gesture bringing his index and middle fingers together, "Why he's supposed to be responsible for arresting Coody and Bogs, that son-of-a-bitch nigger."

John quickly finished his drink.

"You do that, no joke, and you'll get that guy. Just call up. They know where he is."

***

Myra Dow was relieved when she heard the key go into the lock and saw Jefferson's face enter the room.

"We did it!" he exclaimed.

"You got the killer?"

"He's being arrested as we speak, and they're nullifying the arrest warrant for John, which should be completed within hours. And then everything will be as it should be."

"You're all done?" she asked with a trace of uncertainty in her voice.

"Yes, we're all done, there's nothing for us to do now but pack up and leave, as soon as I finish up a few small details with the Marshal tomorrow."

Jefferson then proceeded to tell Myra all about his phone calls to Bella County and how Julia and John had planned to meet at the station and then the abortive ambush which must have been set up by the telegraph operator. He also mentioned the sighting of John near Varner's Junction.

"I'm thinking that maybe he's coming to Savannah," began Jefferson. "I hope not, because things are getting dangerous around here."

"Yes," agreed Myra absently.

"I can hardly believe it's all over. I'm so happy. Now I can get out of this city. You know this place can sink into your skin like slime if you're not careful."

But Myra didn't answer. She merely walked over to her bed and lay down.

Chapter 8

"John makes a Phone Call"

At first the idea had seemed rather flip to him. Imagine, calling the Marshal's office, when he, John, was a wanted man! That would be very cute, getting caught by calling the Marshal himself and asking where Jefferson was. What a giveaway that would be! They'd pick him up in no time.

But the more John thought about it, the less ludicrous it sounded to him. Perhaps he could disguise his voice. But that was stupid; they wouldn't recognize his voice disguised or otherwise. Perhaps he could invent a phony cover story. He could say that he was Jefferson's brother and that he had heard that Jefferson was in town and he wanted to pay him a visit. Then when he got the address, he could just go over to see his friend at a time when he could be sure he wouldn't be seen.

It all seemed perfectly plausible to John, so he made a phone call to the station, and found out that the man he wanted to see had left for the day and wouldn't be back until the following day at eight thirty. There was nothing to do but wait.

The next morning Jefferson called the Marshal to see if he were free. Timay said, "I'm free for you. Come on over. That nullification order has been approved by a federal judge. There are just some forms to fill out."

Jefferson expressed his gratitude and told the Marshal that John had been seen in Varner's Junction, and if they got any news of him in Savannah, that he should be sure to give Jefferson a note. Then Jefferson left the public phone and started across town.

Shortly after Jefferson's call, John rung the Marshal and was put through by the efficient civil servants in short order so that the wait was only a few minutes. John was very unsure about what to say.

"Yes, this is Lincoln Brown, and I'm a relative of Jefferson John Brown. I heard that he was in town and I was wondering where I might find him?" Why had he said relative, he had wanted to say brother. They might not give such a sensitive address to any relative; he had meant to say fraternal relative.

"You say you're a relative of Jefferson's?"

"Yes sir, I'm a brother." Would this be his first error? But perhaps after his initial mistake, he should have shut up or tried another approach?

"And you heard he was in Savannah?"

"Yes sir," replied John, who was unsure what he would say if asked how he knew that he knew this information.

The Marshal, despite his information just moments before from Jefferson, didn't have any idea that the caller was really John Dow, but thought that perhaps this man was another fellow who was going to give himself up to Jefferson and so wanted to arrange a meeting with him for that purpose. And because they needed all the witnesses they could muster, he was especially careful to keep this fellow on the line and make a deal if he could.

"So you've found things a bit hot, is that it?" asked the Marshal.

John didn't know what to say. Was his routine *that bad* that the Marshal saw through it immediately? Was he sending men after him right this minute? He knew he should hang up, but he didn't.

"I don't know what you mean, I'm Lincoln—"

"C'mon, now don't fool around with me. Jefferson doesn't have a brother. Do you want to give yourself up, or don't you?"

This assertion by the Marshal that Jefferson didn't have a brother was a guess on Timay's part, but it seemed to John that this man on the other end of the line had him figured out completely. It was all over for him. He thought that he was being clever, but men like this Marshal had him pegged immediately.

"What makes you think—" began John in one last feeble attempt at maintaining his cover. But the Marshal wanted another witness for the State's case against the men they had already brought in, and was anxious not to lose this one.

"Now don't get me wrong; we will give you an easy time of it. There'll be no problem. There are no rubber hoses here. You want to meet Jefferson, fine. We can arrange a meeting to pick you up and take you here to meet him. If you trust *him* more than *us*, well then that's fine. It can all be arranged. We'll treat you well here."

John didn't know what this man was talking about. Why would Jefferson betray him? Had everyone deserted him? Was he completely alone in the world? Suddenly a terror welled within his breast and he needed to talk to someone, because he couldn't face doing anything at this moment. He ought to hang up the phone, he knew that, but somehow he couldn't.

"Now, I know how sometimes you feel more at ease dealing with your own kind, know what I mean?"

No, John didn't know what the man meant, nor was he particularly interested at that moment in what he meant. He just wanted to go somewhere safe and comfortable and rest until this tightness within him went away. He couldn't think except with sporadic, unconnected portions of his power. Nothing was right for him. Everything was centered upon that tightness.

"Now what kind of information do you have? Did you work for Wyse, or Daniels?"

Now John, even in the state he was in, could tell that this man must think that he was someone else. For John had never heard of Wyse or Daniels. Perhaps there was some kind of mistake? Suddenly he was filled with a tremendous enthusiasm as he joyfully proclaimed, "I think you've got me mistaken for someone else, I don't know what you're talking about."

"Oh, c'mon, don't play games. You're in the organization somewhere."

"Nope, you must be thinking of two other guys," said John, smiling to himself at this man's mistake. "I'm just a friend of Jefferson's paying him a social visit. I know him from Varner's Junction, in case you don't believe me. I know he works for Samuel Beauchay, and he is here solely to help out a friend of his that's in a jam."

This information was highly specific and such that no one connected with Dodson's mob would have access to, so that Paul Timay tended to think that his first impression of this mysterious caller (namely as someone who was trying to get the best terms for a surrender) was not correct. But who would know such things about Jefferson, since they were secret? Only he and Jefferson knew about it *unless*—the Marshal's keen sense of induction brought together the various scattered facts that he had at his disposal and instantly concluded that perhaps this man wasn't with the mob at all. And because Jefferson had told him that John Dow might be coming to Savannah soon, Timay surmised that this caller was perhaps that person! He was calling in a clandestine fashion so that he might escape detection (as John probably didn't know he was free now). How could he? The papers were still sitting on his desk. John was calling to obtain the address of his friend. Shouldn't he tell John that he was a free man? But no, that must wait. Jefferson had worked so long for his friend that the news should come from his lips instead of his own. Yes, that would be best. He would give the boy Jefferson's address and then alert Jefferson to that call when he came over, which was within the hour. This would allow his compatriot to prepare for the visit. Yes, that would be the best thing to do. The Marshal smiled as he thought about how pleased Jefferson would be when he found out the news.

"Well, I'll tell you, he's staying in the Adelphi Hotel, room 36."

John was about to reply, when suddenly their lines were crossed and the connection was lost. He thought about calling back, but then decided that as he had the necessary information, he wouldn't bother. Instead, he would make his way to the hotel and at last see the man from whom he had for so long been separated.

Chapter 9

"What Befalls Rod and How he went to Bed"

With his stomach full of food and his head reeling with drink, Rod Dodson staggered back to the little attic room that he used for his office with the contingency known as his *body guard*. Rod had been more thirsty than he usually was and consequently was a little out of temper.

The group sat down and Rod got out a deck of cards and began to play solitaire while the body guards sat down. One of his goons, a blonde haired guy with big biceps, picked up a comic book that was part of the reading material in the office. (He couldn't read, but he liked the pictures.) A second, slight man with greasy black hair took out his six inch knife with a curved point to clean his nails. And the third bloke who had very closely cropped brown hair sat down and looked at the wall and began whistling Dixie (which was only very slightly off-key).

They didn't talk as each was completely enraptured with what he was doing when suddenly Rod saw that he was going to lose the game of solitaire and that made him furious. Rod pursed his lips, lifted his right hand and pushed all of the cards, and anything else in the way, onto the floor with one broad movement of his arm. At the same time he screamed, "What are you lazy slobs doing, just sitting on your duffs, like a fat-assed bunch of monkeys?"

All the men were silent, except the man who had been whistling, who found it hard to stop a tune right in the middle, especially as he longed to feel the quiet comfort of the final cadence, toward which the entire song was approaching. It was a sweet order that seemed to make everything worthwhile: the song, the day, his life—everything.

But unfortunately, Rod didn't see things quite that way. To him the whistling was indicative of gross insubordination. He pursed his lips, picked up a metal paperweight (that had survived the solitaire purge) and threw it at the whistler.

The body guard was at peace and so was quick to duck, as the missile whose uninterrupted force carried it to the adjacent wall where it hit the head of a mounted feral hog with such force that the hog's head fell to the floor, breaking off the main tusk. Goon-two dropped his knife and inhaled so sharply that it sounded like a grunt.

"That was my prize!! You idiot! Did you know that thing was a present from my mother!" screamed Rod as he pounced on the whistler for having ducked and started punching him in the head. The whistler was in a bind. He didn't want to lose consciousness, but then he didn't want to lose his job, either.

Just then the door opened. Rod stopped what he was doing and looked up. It was Coody, a man they had not seen for some weeks.

"Coody!" said the big bicep man.

Rod got up and walked over to Coody and put his hand on his shoulder. "They told us that you were in the pokey."

"I was. I escaped."

"Well, that deserves a drink, get out the whiskey."

The body guards, fully aware of how much Rod had drunk, were a little slow moving at fulfilling his command.

"Hurry up, I say, break out some glasses, while we hear the story of this fellow here, who's just gotten out of the old clinker."

"But boss—" started bicep man.

"Did you hear me!" bellowed Rod in such tones that there was sudden agreement, as the same fiery irrationality flashed in his eyes.

Glasses were then distributed and the company drank up. Everyone could tell that Rod was extremely nervous and that at any moment could fly off again, but still he insisted that they talk about the most trivial and inane subjects.

"What kind of food did they serve you?"

"Nothing really, just soups, and stale bread."

"I'm glad of that, because that means you didn't squeal, right?" As Rod talked he took a knife out of his desk and started throwing it at the top of his wooden desk so that the point would penetrate and hold the weapon straight up.

"No, boss, I didn't say a word," Coody grimaced.

"Liar!" screamed Rod as he stood up and threw the knife in the direction of Coody's foot, so quickly that he didn't have time to move as the blade cut into the side molding of the shoe, splitting the side slightly, and causing minor bleeding.

"Now listen Coody, it doesn't do any good for you to lie about your pigeon stooling—we know that they took you in there and you sang like a goddamn canary; what I want to know is what you told them!"

There was a noticeable strain in Rod's voice. He was tired and drunk, but at that moment he was focusing all his power upon one simple task of examining this witness and endeavoring to make him talk if it was at all within his power to do so.

"Honest, boss—"

"Hondo, give me your gun," said Rod, as he took the weapon of the whistler and emptied all of the chambers except one. "Now you know the game, Coody. I spin this around just like roulette, and where it stops, nobody knows. But you better hope that it stops in a convenient place. Because I'm going to ask you again and each time you give me crap, I'll pull the trigger, until one time, there won't be any Coody to give us any more of them stories."

Rod spun the chamber of the gun.

"Look, I didn't tell them anything important. They found the money that I had and they wanted to know what I was going to use it for, so I told them it was a payoff for a bootlegger."

"The money for the contract, you told them was for a payoff?" screamed Rod as he pulled the trigger—there was only a click.

"That was one of the dumbest things you could have done. Do you know that? I mean really stupid—only a complete—" Rod got up, but staggered as he felt the effects of the alcohol.

"You mean to tell me—" he began again, but stopped as he walked towards the wall and casually pulled the trigger of the gun again (it was pointed towards the outer wall) and this time it went off, surprising everyone, not the least Coody, who was beginning to wonder whether coming back had been the smartest thing or not.

"No, I think that was a splendid idea, don't you boys?" he asked his body guards, who all agreed that it was very perceptive of Coody.

"Yes, you led them right off the track, all right." Then Rod turned around, leaned back against the wall, and finally said after a long pause, "Who did it? Who brought you in?"

"A nigger named Jefferson something or other. He's piled up in a hotel near here, I know the place, they kept me there awhile before they took me in."

"You say you know the place? What's the name?"

"I don't know, but I sure as hell could finds it again. Yeah, that would be no problem."

"I take it you have a dislike for this nigger?"

"Sure ah do."

"How would you like a hundred bucks to put him away?"

"I'd do it for fifty, but I'll take a hundred. It'd be a pleasure."

"Well go to it, boy, I always likes to see a man who's happy with his work." Then Rod let himself slide down the wall slowly until he was sitting on the floor. He was very tired. Suddenly there was no fire left in him and he just wanted to go to sleep.

"Well, get out of here then, Coody, I'm going to sleep. Hondo, you set a guard outside my door."

The body guards helped Rod to his feet and lead him to his bedroom. On the floor was the mess of things that had been once on his desk. On the floor was the feral pig with his main tusk broken off. The head was on its side. The glass eye seemed to look up at them, its secondary tusk still intact.

The room was quiet once more. Rod had gone to bed.

Chapter 10

"Our Hero is Surprised"

John looked up the number of the hotel in the phone book and considered phoning first, but then decided to go in person instead. He had a little difficulty in finding the place. Soon he had the old dilapidated structure in view. How long he had waited for this moment.

The door opened and to John's surprise the occupant was a woman.

"Yes?" said Myra.

"Oh, I'm sorry ma'am, there must be some mistake, I was looking for someone else," John was highly embarrassed as he backed away.

"Who were you looking for?" said Myra.

"Just a friend, a man named Jefferson," said John.

Then Myra knew that this boy standing before him was none other than John Dow, the man who had been the object of all of their labors. "John?" she ventured.

This shocked Dow, who stopped his retreat and couldn't believe his ears.

"You are John, aren't you?" asked Myra.

"Why, how did you know?"

"Come in, Jefferson's out right now. But he should be back soon."

It was all mysterious. How did she know about him? It was almost as if this woman was a reincarnation of the dwarf, but no, that couldn't be. She had mentioned the name of Jefferson. But might that be only a decoy designed to lure him into her trap?

John went inside.

"You must be wondering who I am," said Myra once John had entered and taken a seat.

"Well, the thought did cross my mind," replied John.

"Well, I know you don't remember me, but you may recognize my maiden name; I was Myra Dow."

This news couldn't have caused a more disconcerting confusion than if she had declared that the world was going to end that day, or that she really was the dwarf in disguise. But to say that she was Myra Dow was beyond anything that he had expected in this life. This woman twenty or so years older than himself was definitely black, though with light skin. She was his mother.

There she was, sitting in front of him. She wasn't too aged, he thought (Myra had indeed taken a turn for the better the last month or so since Jefferson had come into her life).

Her height, figure, and weight seemed good and the more he saw of her, the more John thought that he liked the looks of his mother. Still, there was a strange feeling within him in regards to her. It was an almost resentment that she had once given him up. Certainly he had been *happy* in the Beauchay house, and his life there had been very pleasant, but he still wondered why she had not chosen to keep him so that he might have grown up with her? He never had a mother, or any woman figure except Jessy, who had been very special in her own way, but still it had not been the same as having a real mother. It was something which he now fancied that he wanted more than anything else in the world: a real live mother to be close to, to be tender to him. He knew rationally that he had probably been given a better opportunity in life by having been brought up in the privileged Beauchay household, but then what had that privileged upbringing gotten him in the end? A murder charge, and a woman who had betrayed him. What he wouldn't trade, he thought, for the opportunity to have lived a few years with his mother. So he felt a longing for Myra, but at the same time he was forced to act distant. He had to put up defenses between them so that he might not risk being hurt once again. The conflict of these two emotions brought a hollow feeling inside him, and he merely stared at Myra, the growing tension beginning to show in his face.

Myra got up and walked over to John and hugged him. John allowed himself to be hugged. Then she brought a chair over so that she was right next to John.

"Oh I have so many things to tell you, John, I don't know where to begin," she said as she sat back down again. Then she noticed his expression and sensed that he was thinking about her as his mother. This was something that she had momentarily forgotten, and now was demonstrably made to see that this boy was looking at her through false lenses.

"I don't know what you're thinking, John. But in case you're thinking what I think you are thinking, I want to tell you here and now: *I'm not your mother*."

These words had almost as much effect upon John as the previous words *I'm Myra Dow*. Certainly she was his mother, if she truly was Myra Dow. Everybody knew that his mother was Myra Dow. Why else would he have the name of John Dow? Could there be that there were two Myra Dows and this one was not his mother, but the other—the whole perception was getting out of hand, how. . . how could it. . . .

"The whole story is a rather complicated one, but I'm not your mother, though everyone in Bella County thought that I was. Your real mother was embarrassed at having a child out of wedlock, so she paid me some money to leave the county so that people might think that the baby was mine.

"That woman I'm sure loved you very much, but because of her social rank and her unmarried status, she was unable to care for you so she decided to put you in the best home that she could find, and so you were brought up in her brother's house."

John suddenly dropped his chin.

"Yes, your mother is Dorthay Beauchay."

Dorthay Dodson, corrected John in his mind. The name had been almost taboo in the house for a long time. Mr. Beauchay never mentioned her, and he was sure that there was great animosity because of her marriage to George Dodson. Dodson was such an evil man, but he had always imagined his wife to be different, from the little that Jessy had told him. Jessy was the only one in the house who didn't follow social taboos. Mrs. Dodson seemed like an okay person in his experience with her—which hadn't been much.

John felt a strange sense of happiness at this news. This was because he was a *Beauchay*, in a sense. His mother was a Beauchay when he was born and he was brought up in the household. All his life he had secretly envied Jason, who was a Beauchay by blood and by upbringing. And now he, too, would share the same characteristics. John was a part of the entire Beauchay heritage—

though being *out of wedlock* did count for something. It meant that he could not take on the *name* of John Beauchay. He would not be in the line of inheritance. In one way he was a Beauchay, but legally he was not.

John was looking down at his folded hands when he asked, "And what of my father? He was always a mystery." Then John shook his head slowly. "For some reason I've always focused upon finding *you*. I wanted to get to know my mother. I don't know why I've concentrated on her: that distant person who brought me into the world." Then John had to stop. He was losing his composure.

Myra put her hand on John's shoulder.

"I want to see her," said John. "I will go back as soon as it is safe and talk to her." Even as he said these words, he reflected on what Myra had previously told him, *I'm sure she loved you very much*—how could this be true when she had left him and though she had lived so close, had never communicated to him that he was her son? There was never any indication at all, and now if he confronted her perhaps she wouldn't want to talk to or see him.

If she had loved him so much why hadn't she taken him aside at some time and told him directly that she was his mother and that she loved him? Perhaps she feared that he would embarrass her publicly, or that he might try and disrupt her home life, but surely she might have let him know in some way. However one might want to spin it in one's mind, the stark fact was that she paid another to take the discredit for having given him birth. *Discredit* because of social customs. He was a bastard. Victor and the others had been right. John was dirty because of something that his mother did. Dorthay Beauchay had broken the rules and didn't want to pay the price. So she paid someone else to do so. Maybe that's the way of the rich.

The reason Dorthay didn't want to have anything to do with him was because he was a *mistake*.

John looked up to the ceiling. How can a human life be a mistake? Wasn't there something special in each person that gave them worth and dignity? Jefferson had always told him so. He had to confront her and get these thoughts out in the open. He had to do this even if he accomplished nothing else in life. John took a deep breath and looked up again to Myra.

"I'm afraid it will be impossible for you to see your birth mother, John. You see, Dorthay died just a little while ago."

The words didn't penetrate at first, but then he came to understand, through all the confusion he was beginning to see that though he now knew who his mother was, it would still be impossible for him to confront her with his questions. It was now and forever impossible, and there wasn't anything he could do about it.

At that moment John felt an intense hatred for Dorthay Dodson. He hated her first for leaving him, secondly for not ever communicating anything about his birth to him, thirdly for marrying George Dodson and so obscurely linking him to that awful man (who might be construed as his step-father, after a fashion) and lastly for dying before he had a chance to walk up to her and tell her what an awful person he thought she was. "I spit on you, mother," said John to himself. "I'm *not* your flesh—I'm the same person that I always was—this hasn't changed a thing-do *you understand mother, you haven't changed one thing about me. I knew who I was, and that me isn't any different now than it was before,* all I know now is that it doesn't matter. In fact, what matters is my understanding of who I am, and that idea hasn't been changed by you one iota."

There was no real reason for John to cry. One doesn't cry over a despicable person. But he felt deeply that originally this new information may have changed his name, if he wanted it to—but now the thought was repulsive to him. John grimaced and looked at Myra square in the eye, "Do you know who the father was?"

"I don't know. Jefferson had an idea, but I'm sure that he doesn't really know for sure."

"Who's the principal suspect?"

Myra paused and then said, "Jefferson and Jessy think that it was a traveling salesman who spent a lot of time with Dorthay when the house was essentially empty."

"Was he black?" asked John immediately.

"Yes. But he was interracial because that was the only way a salesman could make it in those days."

"Was he *passing*?"

"I don't know. But here in the South, you know the rules. He was black and so are you."

John felt confused.

"You know, John, that a person is not only who their parents happen to be.

Blood is not everything. It is not even the most important thing."

Myra took John's hands and sat him in her lap. "You are a good person, John. The way Jefferson has talked about you. It was as if *he* were your father."

"Jefferson raised me. He's the most important person in my life."

"And you admire him."

"He is the best person I've ever met. I've always wanted to be like him, but I've always known that I'd fail because he has a college degree and is so smart."

Myra nodded her head. "Yes, he's brilliant. But more than that, he has a big heart."

John thought about how he had obsessed on his mother for so many years but had given hardly a thought about his father. Why was this? Well, perhaps because the rumors that had been floated all his life had suggested that either Samuel Beauchay or Jefferson John Brown was his father, and either of those alternatives would have been just fine with him.

Perhaps it was better not to focus on his birth parents but instead upon those who raised him: Jefferson and Jessy. Those who raise you are your *real* parents. There is always a confusion in understanding parenthood. What makes a parent? Is it engaging in the sexual act? What does that confer? Genetics or whatever (John had not been attentive to that part of his studies).

John did not know his biological parents and never would. And what he did know was that they were *not* nice people. Dorthay Dodson was part of the evil force infecting Bella County and beyond. The traveling salesman was only out for his own pleasure and damn the consequences.

John stopped here as he thought of Cindy Pancroft. He was no better than his biological father. He had not considered what he was doing. What if he had brought an orphan into the world without the luxury of the Beauchay farm income? He was convinced that he hadn't, but that was blind luck. He was just as guilty as the man who had gotten her pregnant.

John hugged Myra and buried his face into her bosom. Then he looked up to her with eyes of hope, "Mother, I mean Myra, I do have a father. And I'm lucky to have him. I've been such an ungrateful bastard."

Myra stroked John's hair. She almost wished she had been John's mother. She had never had a child. As she put her fingers in his hair and lightly scratched John's scalp, she tried to imagine all that he was feeling. The two remained as they were for a time when suddenly their solitude was shaken.

A key turned in the lock to the door of the apartment. Someone was entering. John jumped up to his feet in case there would be a fight. But there would be no fight. The man opening the door was Jefferson John Brown.

Jefferson's meeting had been kept very short as the Marshal had told him about the phone call.

"John," exclaimed Jefferson as he ran to John and hugged him. Myra walked over and Jefferson gave her a hug and kiss.

The three of them stood together as if they were a marble statue.

"Have you *told*?" Jefferson asked Myra.

"I told him about his mother, and that's all," she said. Then Jefferson took charge and moved John to the center of the room and reached out to put his two hands on John's two shoulders.

"John, my boy, I have the honor of telling you that we captured the real murderer of Victor Stuart. The warrant for your arrest has been legally nullified. And now you are a free man. How does that feel?"

John didn't say anything but walked around to sit down. The emotions of the past moments were beginning to overwhelm him.

When they were all seated, Jefferson told John about his work with the U.S. Marshal, Paul Timay, and without going into detail, how they had worked together to break the case. Then he told him of his phone call with Julia and how the mix-up at Atlanta had occurred. After he was finished, Myra suggested that they have some coffee, but John couldn't move. He just remained in the chair.

Chapter 11

"Time to go Home"

After a time, John decided that he wanted to return to Varner's Junction and see everyone (though particularly Julia) and so he declared his intentions of leaving that afternoon.

"That's fine, John, but you'll have to forgive us if I don't go with you just now, as I have a few last details I have to clear up first."

John said that he understood and so he talked awhile with Jefferson and Myra before making his way to the train terminal to buy a ticket home.

What a good couple Myra and Jefferson made, he thought. He wondered whether they might get married. Jefferson still had many good years left and he might even have children, something that John was certain would please his newly recognized father. How he longed for his father's (Jefferson's) happiness. Jefferson was not just a close mentor, but was now fixed in his mind as a father figure. Though Samuel Beauchay had been very nice to him as he had grown up, still there was only one man who really did the work of raising him, and that was Jefferson.

Jefferson was such a gentle man, who was mild, yet strong. Whenever he had a problem, Jefferson would always make John try and figure it out for himself by asking him, John, questions. Perhaps it was the habit of these questions that had make John come to the questioning of himself that he had undergone.

***

It was January. It had been only a few months before the end of summer that John had been anticipating the county fair. So much had changed in so short a time. He was basically the same person, but now he possessed a strength and a certainty that he had never known before. There was no knot of anxiety in his stomach anymore. He felt better than he had in quite a while. It was as if he were about to start all over again. Yes, this time, everything would be perfect, nothing could go wrong. His life seemed destined for happiness.

How lucky he had really been throughout his entire journeys. He had not been seriously ill, and he had stayed in one piece. He had even improved in many ways. Now that the pressure was over, he thought that his life of the past months might even be considered enriching. What freedom he had realized on the open road. What a pure exercise of the self he had known. Now he would go back to Varner's Junction and ask Julia to marry him. But was this what he really wanted to do? The romantic appeal of the open road again flashed before him. Perhaps this was not the time to tie himself down? But then he thought again, when he was on the road, he hadn't been very happy being all by himself. It was difficult and lonely, and he had longed to be with his Julia. It was only now that he was sure that his existence as a fugitive was over that the remembrance of it was pleasing to him. And how could he ever think of life with his Julia as anything but fulfillment? Objectively speaking, she was everything that he had ever wanted. They had grown up together and were good friends as well as being in love. He knew that he could continue to grow with Julia, and didn't have to stay apart from her. Yes, a life with his sweet lady was what he desired.

How would he make his money? Perhaps he could get a job with either the Vanderkamps or the Beauchays as an overseer of some sort on their land. Maybe he could work under Jefferson? Already, his mentor had taught him much about running a farm the size of the Beauchay's. John could build a house near the edge of the woods on the Vanderkamp land, as they had some land that was too rocky for crops, and he and Julia could live happily ever after.

All these pleasing thoughts went through John's mind as the train moved endlessly from stop to stop, though John was completely unaware of the progression of things past the window.

There was definitely a change in his feeling as he sat in the train knowing that he didn't have to fear anyone recognizing him, as had happened on the bus. All that he had to do was relax.

Suddenly, there seemed as if there were endless possibilities for him and that if he chose any one of them, he would be needlessly limiting himself. How completely happy he was now. Just a few hours before, he would have been content to have had the one simple possibility of being with Jefferson and trying to find Victor's real killer. But now that he had been apprehended, the whole process seemed to have generated new feelings of exploration and curiosity. No longer was he strictly bound in his actions to what had happened to him in the past. Now he would be free to explore and delight in things that he had been prevented in doing when he was bound by his fugitive status. In his running, he had discovered new possibilities for experience, and now he was determined that he would explore them. He would endeavor to learn.

This feeling was in no way conditioned by anything that he had ever experienced. It was a natural, spontaneous impulse that arose within him, from where he knew not. It came to be while he had been running, but it frightened him. He had to keep it under control—like the dwarf and the metamorphic old lady.

John had a thirst to know himself more deeply. And in order to fulfill this, he had to position himself in the world with all its waves and shallows. Could he still do this if he settled down as a husband to Julia? John was of two minds. On the one hand, it made sense to him to go after a person who had been a life-long friend and with whom he could grow to be the best person he could be.

But then even as logic dictated this direction, another Dionysian impulse came forward to say that he couldn't stay in Bella County—at least not just yet. He had to go away and follow this impulse wherever it led him. Would he do it solo or with Julia? The key was that he had to get out of the county and find his own way. Jefferson had left the county and gone to Boston. But after a spell he had, in steps, returned to Georgia: Boston to New York to Baltimore then back to Varner's Junction. It had been a rough road, but it had made a difference. Shouldn't he, John, do the same? How exciting it would be to go about on this expedition with his Julia at his side, and together they would play, unrestricted by endpoints which signified winners. They would explore life together, not as a pastime which children often engage in, which combines uninhibited self-expression with the adventurous urge to explore and experiment, but as a quest to discover who they really were.

These impulses were original and felt spontaneous. They sprung from that essential self that one feels inside one's mind. John thought that when he was young and he played that all he could concentrate upon was the activity itself—there was never any thought about the *self*, as it was assumed.

Then he became older and he began to be taught things in his studies. These activities brought him outside of himself. He had to live with others. Sometimes the community was cruel to him. They made him question his very identity—not just the important stuff: his values and competencies, but also his racial self. He was a bastard and a black in a society that showed hatred to both (even though both were regular and natural).

It made no sense. And it was Jefferson who helped him to understand the nature of this irrationality. Racial identity was partly physical: skin color, hair color and texture, facial bone structures like the formation of one's nose. Racial identity also had to do with the social roles one was put into just because of the tag of "black" or the tags that identified the Martinez family where they lived. These were random and therefore false tags. Neither the physical features nor the default social roles had anything to do with *who one was*. But then why was it so prominent in his upbringing?

It was true that John adored Jefferson, and yet at the same time he accepted the norm that black people—those who were captured by force in Africa to come and become property in America—were somehow inferior. This is why John had fought so long to identify as white. How could John hold such contradictory thoughts? On the one hand, Jefferson (a black man) was the most learned and ethical person he had ever met. John accepted this. Yet on the other hand in some way John also accepted that black men were somehow inferior. These propositions were not consistent.

Now that he knew for sure, blue eyes and all, that he was judged to be black by his society, John had to come to terms with this. His father figure, Jefferson, was very dark skinned. John loved him. John remembered the truck driver and how he had felt camaraderie with him. But then he had been raised in a household that was clinging onto the vestiges of the Old South in which those of African descent were thought to be an inferior species. This dogma allowed those from Africa to be owned as *property* the way one owns a mule.

Now that John was clearly black, did this change anything? How could it? Then why did he suddenly feel different?

The train jerked, throwing John slightly forward. It was slowing down for Varner's Junction.

Chapter 12

"For the Reader's Entertainment: a Few Short Interludes"

It was the late afternoon, and his brothers had nosily returned from school as William Dodson walked slowly out to a large crab apple tree that was in their front yard. He reached up and pulled several dead branches from the tree. He had examined to some degree the book and papers that his father had left to him. It did not take him long to realize that his father was in control of a large, growing enterprise. Things were just beginning to happen in a way that would make everything that they had done in the past seem as small preparation for the looming future.

His father had certainly a good sense for what would turn out to be valuable, William noted as he looked at the dates of various transactions that had been made. William marveled at how his father had been able to succeed in the way that he had. It took a certain amount of daring and the ability to go as far as people would let you, felt William. You've just got to wait for the public to stop you. His father had chosen a very influential position in town to give him a power base from which to work, but if he, William, was to carry on in his father's tradition, he would have to get a larger position: like state senator, or United States Congressman, from which he could wield tremendous influence in his region from seats on committees and advance information that such public servants are privy to.

There were never any questions as to ethical maneuverings in William's mind. His father had merely exploited the laws of the life, which William intended to continue exercising. When he had been small, his father used to take him out in their fields and after they had walked awhile they would stop and find some stick or stone to use in some pastime or other which they would invent. But no matter the game, it was always a competition. His father might give him a little handicap to make the competition fairer, but if William ever came close to actually winning one of these events, his father would suspend the handicap and go *all out* to defeat his son. Life was about winning.

Sometimes their play banter was to chat about playmates of William and their weaknesses. His dad wanted to assist William in being able judge his opponent so that there was no chance for failure. That was the worst outcome of all.

The second rule was to be productive. Many of the other young children would waste their time climbing trees or playing sports where there was no betting. "Vain pastimes are for losers," his father used to say. "The imagination is not for silly stories of witches and goblins. Instead, it should be devoted to calculated self-interest. For after all, which interest do we really care about? Nobody's but our own. And the only way to exercise your interest effectively is to gain power through exploiting the weaknesses in others." It was a beautiful philosophy to which William vowed devotion.

William believed it to be true that to be something, a man had to keep creating opportunities for himself, and not ever allow himself to sit back and relax. That was the way of the Old South. They sat back while the rest of the country economically ravaged them morning and night. But what he would be was someone who moved so fast that no one would be able to get the upper hand with him. When his father was ready to fully step down and give all his money to him, he would be ready for it. He would study the operation so that he would know it as well as his father. When his father returned, he would be surprised at how much his son had learned, and how he had ideas of his own. This would demonstrate to his father that his son was a doer.

There was a call from the house. Inside were all his siblings who were not self-reliant. They were weak and so not his true kin. He would go in and make them dinner. Then he would put them to sleep early so that he might continue to study the papers his father had left him. The morning would not come until he had mastered them.

***

The events of the past days had been quite a bit for Samuel Beauchay, especially since he was feeling rather ill. He had put himself to bed and was being cared for by Jessy, who regularly checked on his condition. He was also depressed spiritually. Everything was changing, it was true, but not exactly along the lines that he had once envisioned. The county was getting bigger, but not really any better. No one knew or cared about anybody else anymore. And now it seemed that Charles Vanderkamp had lost his land in some sort of real estate swindle.

The scheme seemed airtight. It was a well-constructed scheme. Though the Vanderkamps had gotten a temporary injunction, it was on a short time-clock. In a month, at most, they would be evicted and their property would be transformed into a textile factory.

The pollution would harm Beauchay's crops and so his property would go down in value. He might not any longer be able to sell wholesome produce. The cotton wouldn't suffer much but the other cash crops would.

The county would be changed from agricultural to industrial. Other farms would be sold and other industry would come in. The lakes and streams would be fouled with the tailings of these mechanical monsters. The future looked dim.

Samuel had always known that the South would have to get up and compete with the North, but did they have to do it this way; did they have to become just like the amoral industrialists that were so odious and foreign to everything that was truly Southern?

How backward the farmers still were in Georgia. And yet they were not so backward that they couldn't find a sneaky way to defeat his proposed coalition of southern planters. They had used the parliamentary process to its finest perfection in obstructing his ideas and implementing their own proposals. They were all style over substance. And all seemed to be for nothing. All the effort that he had expended on several fronts, all for the betterment of others, betterment which he received no support for from others, which he had to spearhead himself as he vainly but bravely fought to instigate and preserve what he believed to be right.

Somehow there must be a modicum of solace in this. There must be something that is better for the effort, though to his sadly subjective eyes, such accomplishments were invisible.

Samuel got up out of bed and walked over to the large window at the far end of his bedroom. Here the morning light would stream in and prompt him to arise and face the day. But now that it was late afternoon, the light was in the other direction. He was looking back to the past as he gazed to the east. He now knew that Jefferson had found the real killer of Victor Stuart. John was officially innocent. This problem, for some reason, had never really captured the imagination of the man—perhaps it had just come at a bad time. But he was never really confronted with the reality that John Dow (or John whatever) was really charged with murder. He knew it to be a fact. And he was fond of John, of course, but it seemed to him that events were controlling themselves and that there was no room in this contest for himself.

Instead, he found himself to be a passive bystander watching, and not really seeing, so that even the news that John was not guilty didn't surprise him. Though, naturally, he was pleased, it was not a space that occupied much of his attention of late.

Samuel Beauchay was sick. Would he die just as his sister? He had already lived longer than most Beauchay men, and his time was most likely long overdue. But somehow it seemed like such a hollow thing to die. It wasn't at all a pleasant thought. Not because it was terrible and frightening, but because it just seemed like such an anti-climax to everything: another event with no relevance to what was really happening—happening without Samuel Beauchay. When he had tried to act, it had made no difference. Dodson had won, and would have won if Samuel had dropped dead years before. The crops were in a depressed market despite all his efforts to bring about a reversal, he might as well have not tried at all—what good had it done in the end? The end (what a comic phrase—ironic would be more accurate). For the very word implies that there was *something to end*, and how could there be any end for a man who was nothing, who did nothing, and whose actions amounted to nothing?

No, there could be no end, for he couldn't honestly say that there would really be an end to anything. For what was there to begin with? He had been born an heir to an estate that had been built by others. They had mismanaged things and a war had been fought. Still, there were tangible assets. Though they were in constant decline, they still existed. He had been the caretaker of a declining business. He had been the witness to a declining civilization: the proud South. It was all over. Now what was left was impersonal motion and random movement by actors who were foreign to him. It was like the fall of Rome. The barbarians were at the gates. There was no longer any use at attempting a purpose. But failing completely to affect anything, perhaps it would be better just to die.

But it seemed so sad to him that he should die without there ever having been anything positively done by him. It was this that made him want to cry out in his loudest voice. But it was also this sense of artistic irony that made him want to live.

***

The train trip from New Haven to Varner's Junction was a circuitous route passing through New York, Philadelphia, Baltimore, Charlestown, and Atlanta. There were many train changes, but it was a trip that Jason Beauchay thought he should make. This was because his father had telegraphed him that he was very ill. Of course he would come home in this event. This was serious business since if his father died, the entire estate would be up for probate. Jason had to return in order to protect his interests.

Yale was still in session, but Jason had communicated to his professors the urgency of the situation and they were amenable. Jason wasn't sure whether his father's papers (his testament) were in order, but naturally this wasn't the only motive for his making the trip; he mildly missed his home, and he did want to see Julia again.

Book Twelve

A Farewell to the Reader

The series of plays and discussions of my own experiences is now about to end. It seems particularly appropriate to state my sincere approbation at the quality of the patronage that has stayed with me all this way. We have enriched each other, and I must say that from my side I would welcome the opportunity of going to the theater with any of you to some future production.

Most especially pleasurable has been the intimate rapport that one acquires when keeping close company with anyone for such an extended duration. I hope that these short essays haven't been too tedious and that some of the concerns of the designer have been communicated in a most informal fashion (as informality has been the touchstone for all of our pre-theatre chats).

At such a time as this, I believe that it is appropriate, as well, to think about the shape of that which is past. True, one can't concentrate upon shape until the entire sequence has been revealed. But soon this will be the case. Then there will be total revelation. At that moment, I hope that the most honored patron (as you all are) will take time and try to discern just how various components of the dramas fit together with regard to the categories that have been most modestly suggested in the previous discussions.

When experiencing the drama, one's sensations are affected and one takes in the series of events without prejudice as the audience accepts as much as possible so that the action may proceed. It is at the *end* that one of the most important moments in appreciation occurs: the reconstruction of the artistic shape. The artistic shape is that which the creator has used by way of constructional strategy in marking a beginning, middle, and an ending to his or her artifact. It is the composition of the work. Often after just viewing a painting one will look at the subject matter, then be affected by the colors and the linear balances which suggest the emotions in the scene. But after this experience has passed, it is often the case (if the viewer finds that the painting warrants it) that she will observe the various constructional aspects beginning with the composition. After this, she may want to observe other constructional factors such as brush strokes, underpainting, modeling, types of paints and pigments employed, etc. Finally, the pre-constructional considerations must be examined, such as genres and schools of painting, sources and influences, and questions concerning audience and author. Such seems to be the logical process that one follows when coming into contact with an art object that captivates him or her.

It is now my suggestion that the reader follow this procedure regarding this work—with this special observance: that when the effort seems completely uninteresting, or unrewarding in the dividends received per hour expended, then the searching should stop. A work of art should cause a student to want to continue studying it *ad infinitum*. For it should be remembered that a work of art becomes a part of the patron as well as the artist.

The artist, as has been said earlier, only suggests certain things, creating an outline, leaving the remainder of work of art to be constructed anew by each observer. The role as patron thus becomes a creative one. A true patron cannot let the artifact come to her or him as a passive recipient, but must enter into a relation with the creative process sketched by the artist and as a partner with the artist, create the work in a unique way for him or herself. In this way, each work of art becomes extremely personalized. Even as you have been reading this text, the process has been taking place. It is in this relationship that we are able to say to ourselves that we *like* one particular play more than another. What this really means is that we bring more to the favored play and enter into the process of creating it more fully. Because the nature of an artifact is as a constructed thing, this process allows us to participate in the order that the artist wished to impose upon a problem, or situation. The psychological release we feel must be related to our participation in the mental process whereby order is affirmed *or* it has to do with our feelings that are evoked as a result of tragic circumstances so that instead of order, chaos is affirmed.

Regardless, our own personal situations are put into perspective regarding the ordering that we have helped create. When this creation is of a small scale and of a low genre form, then the affect will be less than when the scale is larger. For when the scale is grandest there is the greatest demand upon the audience. In this case, the reader must work very hard to finish the artistic creation. But once achieved, it will have a profound effect upon the individual life of a person, for he has been a partner in constructing a masterpiece. Then, all the pains and energy (soul) that the artist put into the work will be felt by his partner (the reader). Together they will have invested much and received many-fold more than they originally invested. For a great piece of art will permanently enrich one's life.

This designer isn't making any such grand claims for his modest work, but he hopes that the reader has found the journey profitable and worth the investment of further time in the external examination of the constructional and pre-constructional aspects of this book. Regardless, this old man wishes each of you the *best* always, and has enjoyed the honor of being your "partner" in the creation of this drama.

Exhibits:

Still, she never repented that she had given up position and fortune to marry Will Ladislaw, and he would have held it the greatest shame as well as sorrow to him if she had repented. They were bound to each other by a love stronger than any impulses which could have marred it. Many who knew her thought it a pity that so substantive and rare a creature should have been absorbed into the life of another and be only known in a certain circle as a wife and mother. But no one stated exactly what else that was in her power she ought rather to have done—not even Sir James Chettam, who went no further than the negative prescription that she ought not to have married Will Ladislaw.

George Eliot, *Middlemarch,* from "Finale."

He yielded his right hand to her.

"What is your name?" he asked, trembling all over and feeling that he was overcome and that his desire had already passed beyond control.

"Marie. Why?"

She took his hand and kissed it, and then put her arm round his waist and pressed him to herself.

"What are you doing?" he said. "Marie, you are a devil!"

"Oh, perhaps. What does it matter?"

And embracing him she sat down with him on the bed.

At dawn he went out into the porch.

"Can this all have happened? Her father will come and she will tell him everything. She is a devil! What am I to do? Here is the axe with which I chopped off my finger." He snatched up the axe and moved back towards the cell.

The attendant came up.

"Do you want some wood chopped? Let me have the axe."

Sergius yielded up the axe and entered the cell. She was lying there asleep.

He looked at her with horror, and passed on beyond the partition, where he took down the peasant clothes and put them on. Then he seized a pair of scissors, cut off his long hair, and went out along the path down to the river, where he had not been for more than three years.

A road ran beside the river and he went along it and walked till noon. Then he went into a field of rye and lay down there. Towards evening he approached a village, but without entering it went towards the cliff that overhung the river. There he again lay down to rest.

It was early morning, half an hour before sunrise. All was damp and gloomy and a cold early wind was blowing from the west. "Yes, I must end it all. There is no God. But how am I to end it? Throw myself into the river? I can swim and should not drown. Hang myself? Yes, just throw this sash over a branch." This seemed so feasible and so easy that he felt horrified. As usual at moments of despair he felt the need of prayer. But there was no one to pray to. There was no God. He lay down resting on his arm, and suddenly such a longing for sleep overcame him that he could no longer support his head on his hand, but stretched out his arm, laid his head upon it, and fell asleep. But that sleep lasted only for a moment. He woke up immediately and began not to dream but to remember.

***

He awoke, and having decided that this was a vision sent by God, he felt glad, and resolved to do what had been told him in the vision. He knew the town where she lived. It was some three hundred versts (two hundred miles) away, and he set out to walk there.

> Leo Tolstoy, *Father Sergius,* part v, tr. Louise & Aylmer Maude.

> Javert answered, "Take your revenge."
> Jean Valjean took a knife out of his pocket, and opened it.
> "A surin!" exclaimed Javert. "You are right. That suits you better."
> Jean Valjean cut the martingale which Javert had about his neck, then he cut the ropes which he had on his wrists, then, stooping down, he cut the cord which he had on his feet; and, rising, he said to him: "You are free."
> Javert was not easily astonished, still complete master as he was of himself, he could not escape an emotion. He stood aghast and motionless.
> Jean Valjean continued: "I don't expect to leave this place. Still, if by chance I should, I live, under the name of Fauchelevent, in the Rue de l' Homme Armé, Number Seven."
> Javert had the scowl of a tiger half opening the corner of his mouth, and he muttered between his teeth: "Take care."
> "Go," said Jean Valjean.

> Victor. Hugo, *Les Miserables,* "Jean Valjean takes his revenge." Tr. Charles Wilbour, p. 494.

A double tale will I tell: at one time it grew to be one only from many, at another it divided again to be many from one. There is a double coming into being of mortal things and a double passing away. One is brought about and again destroyed, by the coming together of all things, the other grows up and is scattered as things are again divided. And these things never cease from continual shifting, at onetime all coming together, through Love into one, at another each borne apart from the others through Strife. (So, in so far as they have learnt to grow into one from many), and again, when the one is sundered are once more many, thus far they come into being and they have no lasting life; but insofar as they never cease from continual interchange of places, thus far are they ever changeless in the cycle.

> Empedocles, *Simplicius Physics*. 158, 1-13. Tr. G.S. Kirk and J.E.Raven.

But what about the cat? It is an ancient animal that had its birth in mystery and lives within the same aura. For death is no escape for a cat, it lives nine times so that it must face defeat anew. There is no giving-up, for resignation is only a self-indulgence that cowards can enjoy. The cat speaks the word, for it is only a metaphor of those nameless mysteries that make up God's creation. Even as the cat survives the world, so God survives everything. It is within this order that all its component parts must be seen.

> Notes for a book written by Jefferson John Brown, while in college.

"No act is of itself only, but is a part of a larger process which grounded in the Almighty"

> Engraved message on a medallion that once hung on the neck of Peabody's cat, John.

Lift ev'ry voice and sing,
Till earth and heaven ring,
Ring with the harmonies of Liberty;
Let our rejoicing rise
High as the list'ning skies,
Let it resound loud as the rolling sea.
Sing a song full of the faith that the dark past has taught us,
Sing a song full of hope that the present has brought us;

Facing the rising sun of our new day begun,
Let us march till victory is won.

Stony the road we trod,
Bitter the chast'ning rod,
Felt in the days when hope unborn had died;
Yet with a steady beat,
Have not our weary feet
Come to the place for which our fathers sighed?
We have come over a way that with tears has been watered,
We have come, treading our path through the blood of the
slaughtered.
Out from the gloomy past,
Till now we stand at last
Where the white gleam of our bright star is cast.

God of our weary years,
God of our silent tears,
Thou who has brought us thus far on the way;
Thou who hast by Thy might,
Led us into the light,
Keep us forever in the path, we pray,
Lest our feet stray from the places, our God, where we met Thee,
Lest our hearts, drunk with the wine of the world, we forget Thee;
Shadowed beneath Thy hand,
May we forever stand,
True to our God,
True to our native land.

> James Weldon Johnson, "Lift Every Voice and Sing"
> (1900).

. . . I believed in each of us there was a wound, an emptiness that would not be filled in our lifetime. But we could not stop if we wanted to, or go backward.

> Charles Johnson, *Dreamer* (1998): 236.

Pisces

Projection

Chapter 1

"The Bath of Rod Dodson"

Ever since the news of the abortive Daniel's hit, Rod was in very poor spirits as his energies began to become dissipated. He dwelled upon the miasma about him. His only comfort was of the southern (alcohol) variety and his rages had become more and more frequent. Often after one of his fits of anger, he would take his bottle with him to the bath tub and sit there, drinking in the hot water until he was sufficiently relaxed to sleep.

He had worked hard for his money, which was considerable, and now all seemed to be threatened. He had left a very good import-export business in Texas to come to Georgia at the insistence of his brother. George said that he was needed for operations in Savannah, which would satisfy his wildest inclinations. Well, neither his savagery nor his predispositions were in good form at the moment, so he had good reason to feel somewhat put out by the whole thing.

One evening when Rod was in the bathtub, there was a clamoring behind the bathroom door inside the main office. Rod sent his current woman to see who it was. She moved without haste, as she was the type not to become nervous about anything. She was much like his late wife, Bea, who was also a person who seemed never to care even if someone could prove to them that the world was going to end the following day.

"I want to see Rod," said the voice somewhere in the main office.

"Well, you'll have to wait," she said. "He can't be bothered just now."

"Well he'll just have to be bothered. This is important."

"Sorry—" she began to say when the man pushed her out of the way and went into the bathroom where Rod lay almost asleep.

"Rod," said the man, but getting no response and seeing the condition of the other, took his bottle away from him and filled a bucket full of cold water and dumped it over Rod. This achieved the desired effect of putting Rod into a rage as he rose from the tub, screaming and swearing at the fellow and demanding his bottle and a gun so that he could shoot this rascal who interrupted his repose.

"Damn it, Rod, you haven't been opening your mail, so I have and you got this telegram just today from Big George."

"A message from Big George?" intoned Rod in surprise as he snatched the telegram from his man and quickly read it as the water from his hair dripped on the paper and soon dissolved the thin sheet. But Rod had finished the note. George said there had been some mistake. Of course, there must have been a mistake. For how could he have ever suspected his brother of betraying him? But it had been so easy. He had sent the notes to his brother and he hadn't answered, and his courier had said that he knew that George was in the house, and that he had even seen him there, but he didn't want anything to do with answering a message from Rod. When he had tried to call his brother, the line never was connected. With all these pieces of evidence, it had seemed certain to him that his brother had, in fact, acted according to how the rumors had declared that he had acted. How was Rod to know that his brother had been on a business trip? George never told him anything about what he was doing until he had already done it—unless he wanted Rod, himself, to do it for him. The situation made sense, though. His brother hadn't been after him, but circumstances had made it seem that way. Something had to be done, and quickly.

"When did you get this message?"

"Just now, I was going over your mail as you haven't done it for the last couple days, and I thought that there might be something important."

Rod wanted to reprimand this fellow for going through mail that he had no business seeing, but at that moment the response seemed particularly inappropriate.

"Is Tom here?" asked Rod.

"No, he's over at the other house."

"Well, someone get him, I'm going upstairs."

Thus saying, Rod started upstairs, but feeling a bit cold, he turned around quickly and dried himself and got dressed first. Even urgent things could wait, sometimes.

How stupid he had been. Instantly he felt sober again and on top of all his affairs. The last few days when he had been gradually letting go, including the last twenty four hours, now seemed behind him. He was again the man in charge in Savannah. He had to intercept the man who was going to kill his brother.

Rod got properly dressed and combed his hair. When he had finished, Rod returned to the main office room and waited for Georgia Tom. Shortly, Tom arrived with the lowly go-fer.

"What do you mean you can't find him?!" screamed Rod.

"Just what I said, he's a loner, and a bit kooky. I'll be damned if I know where he is," said Tom.

"What do you think I keep your fat rump around here for if you can't deliver the goods when I want them?"

"What can I say boss? I mean you sends this guy out and so he gets some money and a promise for more when he's done, there's nothing said bout him reportin' to me or nothin'."

"I want that man."

"But Boss—"

"Listen, Georgia Tom, you are a fat, overpaid little pimp, and I'm not going to listen to your excuses on why you can't do something. What I am asking you to do is to get me my man; you understand? Tell him we *don't* want the hit."

"But Boss—"

"You have one day to bring him back to me, or you're a dead man, Tom."

Georgia Tom didn't reply to this, but merely turned around and walked out of the room, muttering to himself.

When he was gone one of the body guards said to Rod, "Do you think he'll get him?"

"He'd better if he respects his hide."

"It's a pretty tough assignment, boss," said Hondo softly.

Rod was gathering the papers on his desk and the man thought that Rod didn't hear his comment. Then Rod rose and looked at the other. "Yes, it is tough; that's why we're going to meet

Big George before he gets to town. I figure he's driving and will be here any minute, so we'd better hurry up if we're to be successful."

They all got up and checked their guns to make sure that they were loaded and ready for action. Rod put on a coat and hat and headed down the stairs.

If George had been gone for such a long time, it must mean that something big was coming through—something for which they had been waiting. Rod remembered when they had just opened operations and they had pushed out some small operators. "Why don't we hit Daniels?" Rod had said.

"Because we're not big enough," George had replied.

"But if we knock him off, then we'll have this whole area to ourselves."

"And do you know how long we'd have it? There are several good reasons why it's to our advantage to live with Daniels for the time being, and even work with him. First of all, he's established and the town is free from outside influence while he's here. We don't have to fight nobody. Secondly, we couldn't hold all of his operations yet, so if we tried we'd get busted. No, I'll tell you, what we have to do concerning Mr. Daniels is to *get in* with him, but stay separate. We will divide up the pie. And then when we're real cozy, we hit him and good—but only when we know we can handle it, without outsiders coming in."

This fact had been repeated to Rod so that he knew that his brother didn't want to move until everything was right. They had been operating for many years, making a good profit, but not making the kind of money they would if they were the main organization on the eastern half of the state.

Now, George had told Rod that he thought that it would have been a good idea to murder Daniels and so Rod had arranged for an expert to do the job. Rod had hired a man he had confidence in—complete confidence.

But somehow, the contact had been taken and there had been some sort of tip-off to Daniels who must have negotiated with the man himself and paid the hired killer to eliminate Rod but to make it look as if it was George all along. This strategy on Daniels' part might stop a gang war. But it might cripple the Dodson operations. But it was quite a gamble. If George were at hand, it would have been futile. But George had been out of town. How could Daniels have known that?

He couldn't have, it was just a lucky occurrence for him that all the events had worked together as they had. Rod had fallen for the story—he had failed to trust his own brother, and now he must make up for his mistake. If only George would have stayed in Varner's Junction instead of going to Savannah. The killer would be surveying the area around the two houses, most likely so that it was essential that George not come around, or it might be the end for him.

Rod and his three body guards descended the last flight of stairs and paused at the front door for Rod's orders. Rod decided to keep one of his body guards next to him and spread the other two out in an effort to spot George and defuse the threat. Rod and his one guard would head forward by foot towards the cathouse. Rod wanted to pause and repeat the plan again. The alcohol was still in his body. As he stood there at the foot of the stairs, Rod repeated to himself that there must be a big deal brewing. Why else would George have gone on such a long trip without telling him what he was going to do?

Perhaps they were finally going to make it *really big*, and get the kind of power that Rod was always confident that they could acquire. Rod was more impatient than his brother who preferred to go safely, one stage at a time.

Rod left his lofty thoughts. There wasn't much time. They had to act now. Rod opened the heavy oaken front door and then emerged—pausing a moment to take in the night air. He then walked down the steps of the porch stoop. But just as he and his body guard stepped down to the street, there was an instantaneous burst from several machine guns. The body guards were taken by surprise. Two went down in an instant. The third was quickly felled. None had returned a single shot. Rod turned to get back into the building, but he was too slow. He was hit by twenty-five bullets in the back and skull. As he fell into the door that he was vainly trying to open. Rod tried to say something, but no words ever came forth.

Chapter 2

"The Homecoming"

When John saw his home looming before him, he could barely contain the mixture of reactions that he felt. He tried to think of something that would sum it up, but could only manage to spring from his seat and dash to the door between the cars and open the window so that he could see the station in a clearer way.

All the thoughts that he had been having suddenly played back, like the film on a movie projector being rewound at a fast speed so that all the images and sounds were a blur of exciting speed.

As quickly as he could, John made his way to the Vanderkamp Farm. As he walked, he took in the familiar scenery. In town, there were several newly paved streets. This was a change. But once he got out of town, it seemed all the same to him. In moments he would see Julia. He would behold the woman who he had waited so long to see. She was the person he had thought about so much that she hardly seemed as if she could really be a person, but rather an ideal that he had constructed to help him in his loneliness. The Julia of his mind was someone too good to be an actual person. Could she disappear like the dwarf and metamorphosing old woman?

But an actual person, Julia, turned out to be as she came to the door, answering his knock. It would be an understatement to say that Julia was happy and surprised at seeing her lover, but her words would express no more than, "Well, John, it certainly took you long enough!"

John smiled, but was at a loss for things to say. So instead he reached out and took Julia's hands in his own and pressed them fondly. How he longed to throw his arms around her and hug her while he showered her face with soft kisses, but he felt that no matter what he did, he couldn't express the extreme tender closeness that he felt. Perhaps the pressing of her hands was as expressive as anything that he could have done at that moment.

"Come in and sit down," managed Julia, when she realized that they were just standing in the doorway.

Down the hall, John could hear the sound of footsteps. It was Martha Vanderkamp coming to see what all the noise was. She was becoming a fragile woman who sought quiet, so that the slightest interruption made her nervous. She also wanted to be control of any noise that occurred in the house which she would soon be forced to abandon.

Julia, hearing her mother coming, called to her, "Mother, come quickly and see who's here."

"Julia?" answered her mother, as she saw her daughter at the end of the hall with a young man, who she instantly recognized as John.

Now it should be explained that Julia had already informed her parents that John had been cleared of all charges and the real guilty party, Miles Bon, had been apprehended. But as to the other news, that is concerning John's birth, Julia's parents were in complete ignorance, as was Julia. However, at that very moment, Charles Vanderkamp was paying a call on his neighbor, Samuel Beauchay. The occasion of the visit was that Charles had heard that Samuel was ill. In the course of the conversation that followed, Charles let Samuel know in no uncertain terms that he believed his daughter was in love with John Dow. Further, Charles wanted to know what Samuel thought of such a situation.

Samuel replied that he considered John to be a fine lad, though a bit thoughtless at times, and it seemed that he never thought about things ahead of time. This was due to the fact that John oftentimes merely acted on the impulse of the moment. But besides that, John had many virtues that were valuable such as kindness, honesty, courage, and compassion.

"But the thing that worries me, if you want to know the truth, is whether he's—well you know, whether he's *colored*."

"What do you mean?"

"Well, you know, his birth. I love my daughter and I want to make her happy, but you know I just don't believe in marriage between the races, it doesn't seem natural to me, Samuel."

"Well, Charles, I suppose I can understand your point. Certainly it is one that is shared by most people I know—most people don't think it's wise to mix different types of blood."

"Exactly."

"Yes, I know that most people agree with that—especially the white land owners. But you know, it's always seemed strange to me that a Negro woman was good enough to lie with and to get pregnant, but not good enough to marry. That has always disturbed me. It doesn't seem to square with what most people believe about being consistent in their thinking. But maybe I just don't understand the situation properly."

Charles didn't reply. His neighbor was ill and he wasn't going to get into any arguments about it.

"But to tell you the truth," began Samuel again, "I don't think John is black, in fact I have reason to believe he's as much a Beauchay as I am. . ."

And then Samuel proceeded to tell Charles the story of John's birth and how he didn't think that the biological father was a black man, but some Greek or Italian. This seemed to relieve Charles. Though Charles seemed sanguine, Samuel was rather sad, somehow, over the entire course of the conversation.

***

"Would you like to take a walk?" suggested John.

"Yes, I'd love to," responded Julia, as her mother's presence had a somewhat restricting influence over the progress of an open conversation. Mrs. Vanderkamp, who hadn't the advantage of her husband's enlightenment concerning John's background, still thought of him suspiciously and as one who she didn't want her daughter to become serious about. What she was frightfully anxious about was that Julia might do something foolish, like accept an offer of marriage. This is why the mother wanted to be present so that she could control the direction of the conversation and thus deny John the chance to pop the question.

This was a role that she could execute within the parlor of their house sitting between the two young people. However, it would not be possible were the two to take a walk. All that was left in that event was to invite herself along. But perhaps that would not be a very good idea. Besides, it was only the first day that John had returned and surely he wouldn't try anything like that on a short little walk. But just to make sure, she asked Julia to be home in an hour to help her with the supper, as they were having a difficult meal to prepare.

"Did Jefferson tell you about Atlanta?" asked Julia as they walked toward the direction of the Vanderkamp Lake. It was mid-afternoon and the sun was moving down to just atop the trees on the island.

"Yes, it was a fortunate thing your train was late, or I might have been the one on the pavement instead of that unfortunate man."

"It must have been the telegraph operator," she said. "I could think of no one else." Then she added cautiously, "I hope that you never suspected that I had anything to do with it."

To this John merely replied, "I didn't know what to think, Julia. It was very hard you know, my running all the time. In order to survive I had to become a very suspicious animal."

"Yes, I understand, there's so much I wanted to tell you while you were gone, but you know, I'm so excited about your being back that I can't think of any of the things that I wanted to say."

Then John put his arms around Julia and kissed her on the lips. She was tense at first, but soon warmed to the embrace, which she allowed to continue for some time.

Then John asked, "While I was gone, did you, I mean, were there ever any—" John couldn't finish his sentence. "You may think this is a stupid question," John paused. He loosened his embrace and walked Julia over to a bench in the garden. He thought of Maria, and of the strange old woman, what he wanted to ask her was whether she had been seeing any other gentlemen while he was gone, and if she had begun to like any of them. He knew that he ought to expect that she did see some men, as she was the most popular girl in the county, and after the death of Victor, everyone thought that she was free again. John expected this (though he wouldn't have been saddened in the least to have found that this wasn't the case) but what he wanted to know was whether she had taken a fancy for any of them and whether she had kissed any of them? Such a question couldn't be asked outright, because John knew that it would be an insult to his lady's character to even insinuate such a thing. No, he could not bear to think such a thought. It didn't make any difference to him whether she had seen other men and kissed them or not: she was a young, attractive lady and it would be only natural for her to have entertained gentlemen and taken an occasional kiss.

Yes, only a natural event, in fact, it would be most unusual if it hadn't been the case. But even yet, it was not altogether impossible that she hadn't. Not that it made any difference in the slightest—no, any answer she gave would not affect him one way or the other in his feelings for her. He would still love her with the same passion, but he ached to know if there had been someone else in his absence.

If he had been Jefferson, a man guided by his reason, he could tell himself that it didn't make any difference that she, Julia, was faced with a situation where in all probability she would never see John again and so it was not called for in any event for her to show signs of fidelity that he might expect if he had only taken a casual trip of some kind. No, rationality told him that asking such a question could only lead to a disagreement, and that wasn't good. Self-control dictated to him to be silent.

But he wasn't Jefferson—this he plainly felt as his entire breast was seething with emotion which longed for expression. He could bear this anxiety no longer. He had to know. John, who had been looking down during this battle within himself, turned back to Julia who was seated but a few inches away from him, "What I mean to ask is, while I was gone, did you see other men?" John paused momentarily, half-hoping for her to say, "Oh, no John, darling, I didn't see anyone except my own dear family, how could I look on anyone except you. . ." or something to that effect. But instead she was completely silent, inferring that what he was surmising was true, as *silence* means *consent*—no matter, he thought. Still, he continued, "But I wonder, or should I say, I *hope* that you didn't become overly attached to any of them." The question wasn't exactly the way that John would have preferred to have phrased it, but for the time, it would do.

John then looked at Julia for an answer.

"Do you want me to say something?" replied Julia as she tilted her head.

"Well, yes, "answered John, thinking that his statement had been quite clear. He wanted to know how many men she had seen and if they had exchanged any signs of romantic affection.

"What do you want me to say?" Julia had her hands in her lap with her right hand grasping her left so that the knuckles were white. John did not notice this.

"The truth. What else?"

"Do I ever tell you *anything* else?" Julia spoke in tones that barely contained her anger.

"I hope not," he replied, though even as the words had escaped, he knew that he had said the wrong thing; he never doubted her honesty, that wasn't the question. He trusted her. What he wanted to know was whether she had been faithful to him—she was confusing the issue by talking about honesty.

"That's not what I meant," he tried to say in correction. "It's just that I know that you are a desirable girl and that, well, I have been gone for a long time. . ."

"I'm not sure at what you're driving at, but are you asking me whether I still love you?"

"Yes."

"Well, then, I do."

"But that's not all."

"What else do you want to know?"

"Have you loved another since I left?"

"No, I haven't *loved* another man, if that's what you mean— not in the way that I love you." Julia wasn't trying to be ambiguous with her answers, but she didn't see why they had to talk about other silly things like whether she still loved John or not. If she didn't love him, why would she have shown so much concern over him? He was certainly being mysterious in his questions. She had an idea about what he might be asking, but she didn't want to try and make an interpretation if at all possible, because she wanted to talk about themselves and not about other people. That was a topic that tended to separate people, and at that moment she wanted to be close to her man, not distant.

"Doggone it, Julia, you know what I mean. I want to know what you've done with other men since I've been gone," said John, turning to Julia and opening up his arms.

"Done?" Julia coughed. She brought a fist to her mouth to show her breeding.

"Have you been going out? Have you gotten sweet on anyone? Have you shown them affection by kissing or like that?" John twisted his palms so that they were raised to the sky. His mouth hung open.

"You certainly pick odd times to ask your questions," said Julia. "Here we were, in what I thought was a romantic situation and then you break it with a question like that. What am I supposed to think except that you weren't really involved in the kiss just now, but were thinking about other things," Julia stood up from the bench, "You weren't really kissing me but planning a series of questions." Then Julia crossed her arms. She stood above John and looked down on him.

John looked up at her and then down to his feet. He felt terrible, he should have restrained himself as his first impulse had dictated. Now Julia was angry with him, and it was his fault.

"I'm sorry, Julia, it's just that I don't want to force myself on you, that's all. I know that I don't have much, and—"

"So *that's* what you think of me, is it? That I weigh the price tag of each boy that I know? What would that make me then?" Julia raised her hands above her head in exasperation.

John was confused. Everything that he was saying was coming out wrong.

"You know that's not what I meant—it's just that—forget it," said John standing. He moved to kiss her, but she wouldn't permit it.

"I think it's time for more walking," she said, walking away from John. John reluctantly agreed and after a while ventured to take her arm, which she didn't refuse.

"I've seen other boys, of course, my parents are very social, as you know, and in Atlanta with my Aunt Margaret, I went to several parties. But my only romantic attachment, the only one I love, has *just* come home to me."

So answered Julia, and nothing more was said about it.

Chapter 3

"Some Unfinished Business which must be Attended To"

"You know it's getting dangerous around here; I don't like it," said Jefferson to Myra.

"The top is going to blow any second; I know that," she replied.

"I want you to leave, while you still are safe."

Myra didn't answer, but sat eating the chili that they had heated on the hotplate in the room.

"You know there's a few things that I still have to finish for Marshal Timay here. You know I owe it to him. He's helped me, so I want to help him. Besides, we're friends. I like him."

Myra stopped eating and took her half full plate over to the garbage and threw it out.

"I'm going out for a walk," she said.

"Do you want me to go with you?" asked Jefferson getting up and walking toward her.

"I'd rather go alone," she said.

"Be careful," advised Jefferson.

Myra was upset, Jefferson knew this. He knew that she didn't like the idea of his staying in the city while it was so dangerous. People in the mob knew that he was working with the authorities and that they might decide to pay him back for the work he had been doing.

Jefferson didn't like putting his life in danger, but he had gotten himself into something and he couldn't just get out when his personal goals had been fulfilled. That was foreign to every instinct in his body. He had helped John, but in the meantime he had become involved in something bigger: he was helping to rid the city of at least part of an organization of men dedicated towards perpetrating crime. These were people who made life more difficult for everyone. They had caused countless cases of extreme misery. He wanted to let Myra understand that he couldn't merely look after himself, as much as he wanted to, because what he was involved in was bigger than himself. It was as if his personality and selfish aims must be subordinated to *the cause* in which he found himself involved. They were trying to rid the city of corruption, and attempting to get the perpetrators as high up as they could—already they would have Wyse, Marsh and perhaps Georgia Tom. Getting the Dodson brothers was beyond what he could do. If they were ever to go down, it would be due to fate. But at least he had been able to do some good.

When you get the leaders, the other followers will go elsewhere. Jefferson remembered the frightened look on some of the people's faces when he had first tried to locate Georgia Tom—that look of fear was unnatural.

What he wanted to do was relieve those people of their unnatural fears, and free them of some of the suffocating fabric of crime that was all about them. He wanted to explain some things to Myra, who he had grown very fond of recently. She had changed a lot since he saw her washing in the bordello. She was still the person who saved his life. But when a man looks at a woman in a romantic way there are other factors to consider as well as Aristotelian goodness. When Jefferson saw her at the bordello he thought that she was a woman who looked more her age and was not very happy at her position in life. Now, he thought she was relatively happy and he took the liberty of thinking that perhaps he had something to do with it. One thing that he just realized was that though he wanted her to leave the city, she really didn't have anywhere to go. He didn't want her to go far away; he wanted to be near to her, but a man couldn't expect such a thing unless he makes certain promises to a woman. But he was an old man. It was too late in life to start a family—and yet. . . . maybe?

When Myra came in, Jefferson went to her and helped her off with her coat. Then he kissed her. Jefferson was never a passionate man. He was a philosopher. But this time his kiss was more than just a light peck. It came with some duration to it.

They reluctantly broke their embrace.

"Sit down," he said. "I have something I want to discuss." She sat down and held his hand. "What I was trying to say earlier was all mumbled because I hadn't thought things out clearly. I was trying to tell you that I thought it too dangerous for you to be in the city and that I worry about you being taken and beaten up or worse some day or night. I wouldn't want that. If that happened, I'd always blame myself." He paused as water filled his eyes so that he bowed his head attempting to hide the fact. "Believe me, I'd never forgive myself."

Myra pressed his hand.

"That's why I want you to go. I don't want to risk your safety."

"But what about *your* safety?" returned Myra.

"I'll take care of that. The Marshal suggested that I ride in a police car to and from his office from now on for that very reason. He says that the cover on this place was destroyed when that other guy escaped, and that I need some more protection. So I agreed, I don't want to take any unnecessary risks. But with you it's different. You don't have to be here right now. You could and should be somewhere that's safe."

"Well if you *really* want me to leave, I suppose I could," she said.

"Yes, I'd like that, not because I want to get away from you, for you see it's not that, but, well I just don't want to see you hurt."

"I do have some relatives in Memphis I could go back and stay with," she said.

Jefferson paused slightly, "I don't want you to go to Memphis, I want you to go to Bella County."

"But—" she began to protest. Jefferson reached out for her hand. She gave it to him and he pressed it between his two palms.

"You didn't let me finish. Look, I know that I'm an old man, and not much good, but I figure that I have at least ten good years left in me, and maybe a few more if the Good Lord sees fit—what I'm trying to say, and I'm afraid rather badly, is that I want you to return to Bella County as my wife, if you'll have me." As Jefferson pronounced these words, he felt a tightness in his throat.

Myra took her hand away from his momentarily. She looked towards the wall, then she turned and lifted her hand to touch his face, but before she could say anything, she put her hands around Jefferson's neck and put her head on his shoulder and began to cry.

Jefferson felt a new sensation come over him as he held her throbbing body. It was something he had not known for many years. He became acutely aware of his situation: sitting in a hotel room with a woman who was crying on his shoulder, a woman who would be his wife—the situation was exact in his mind as he imaginatively pictured the drawing of them together: simple and direct lines, but though Jefferson generally preferred complex compositions, he was truly captured by this purity of the sketch in soft, dark pencil.

Chapter 4

"A Chapter which Contains some Violence and Destruction"

George Dodson went to the place where he thought that Rod might be, but found that his brother was not there. There were only two places that Rod habituated, so George went as quickly as he could to the other. When he arrived at the house, he saw the crowd of people gathered around, and some policemen.

Has there been a raid, he wondered as he made his way through the crowd, until he saw the bodies lying on the cement. We've been hit—suddenly he searched the sidewalk for his brother, who he feared might be among them, but he didn't see anything, though there were some police on the steps indicating another body. George pushed through the police.

"Hey buddy, where you think you're going?" put one of the uniformed officers.

"I've got to get up there."

"You ain't going nowhere."

"But that may be my brother."

"I don't care if it's the Mona Lisa—"

But then George squirted through and made his way up the steps where he could behold the sight of his brother, who though he was face down, George recognized instantly.

Dodson bent down to his brother and put his hand on his shoulder.

"Hey buddy, what do you think you're doing?" asked one of the policemen, but George didn't reply but held his brother's shoulder and stared at one of the bullet holes in his neck.

"Hey, you got to get out of here," said the policemen again, pulling George up by the collar and pushing him back down the steps, but this time George didn't offer any resistance.

Things were bad in the city. He hadn't realized that so much could go wrong with a simple contract, but somehow Daniels must have found out about it and hit Rod first. But all this talk about killings was confusing to George. His brother had sounded as if he was afraid of him killing or wanting his brother dead. How could such an idea have started? Obviously the climate of the city was taking its toll and soon there would be open warfare. This would be senseless, especially since Daniels would probably win. So George decided to go and make some kind of truce with Daniels.

Even though the other man had just killed his brother, something that George didn't at all take lightly, still a war right now would destroy everything that he had worked so hard to build. Rod wouldn't have wanted George to sacrifice that had he still been alive, so George had to make best with what he had. Daniels wouldn't believe him, of course, but he might do something to make the other man agree to his point of view. Perhaps he could say that Rod had wanted to squeeze them both out and that he, Big George, had come to the city to straighten things out when he found that Daniels had already beaten him to it.

With all the rumors floating around, as George suspected, such a story might be believed by Daniels. There would have to be a certain amount of readjusting in the line of command, now that his brother was dead. He could move up Sig, but then he never really trusted Sig. George thought that Sig had his eyes always on higher things and would never be satisfied once he got so close to real power. Sig would not accept being relegated to second place. No, it would be better to put someone like Oscar in there until his own son was old enough to stand the tension of the operation. With William at the helm then perhaps George would fade himself out and let his son run the entire operation. That would be fitting, he thought, as if they were building an empire—a dynasty.

George got into his car and tried to start it, but found that it was out of gas. That's strange, I thought that I just had some gas put in a while back, someone must have siphoned it away. He could walk to a gas station, but news of this hit would be soon reaching the other building and it would be essential for there to be someone assigned to ensure that there was no panic or desertion among the ranks.

Walking to a gas station would take too long. He'd take a cab instead, being as there was one sitting across the street with the driver asleep. He would go and wake the fellow up and make him take him to the second house in a hurry.

"Hey there, 146 Marmot, and be quick!"

The man grumbled as he opened his eyes and stretched. "There's a tip if you can get me there in five minutes," said George.

He would rally his men in that one house and forget the old one, for the time. There was a bad feeling about that place. George was concerned about a shipment of booze that they were getting from the Caribbean. It was first class rum which they would have to cut and re-bottle for sale. They had lost some men recently and George wanted to make sure that the task would be carried out according to schedule.

There was also the question of all the things that had to be done in Varner's Junction. His house needed someone there to look after it; George was putting a considerable sum of capital into the construction of this grand mansion. It would be a symbol of his ascendency. The grandeur would stick it in the face of the old families who lorded it over him. George chuckled: they and their *history* would soon be relegated to stories of the past as the new order was charging ahead. And George was leading the charge.

The name of Dodson had been scurrilously attached to money for a much too long time, and now it was time to change all that. He had been in the county as long as most people, and he felt that it was time for them to think of the Dodsons as the new *established family*.

He ran through a *to-do checklist:* there was his wife who needed burying, and his defunct bank which needed to be re-invented with different terms of ownership. It seemed that everything was coming up at one time to try and confuse and defeat him, but George was made of sterner material than could easily be rent at the slightest crisis. No, he would not let these circumstances in any way get the better of him. For a strong man makes his own opportunities, and George knew that he was as strong as they came.

"Hey, Cabbie," said George, not recognizing where they were. "This isn't the way to the address I told you."

"It's a short cut, you said you wanted to get there in a hurry, so I'm taking a short cut, do you have any objections? I'll go back to the other way if you want."

George wasn't even going to reply to such an insolent remark, but made a mental note that this fellow was surely not going to get any tip from George Dodson.

The cab rolled on and George decided that he would put Georgia Tom in temporary control of things, suspending all activity for a few days until Oscar could make his way back and assess the situation and get in control. He would move Marsh up to the supervisor of the industrial park and then move someone else in for Marsh's job—perhaps that character, Bon.

Yes, things had been certainly set back a bit, but not by any means lost. Now that his thoughts were in order as to what he was going to do in the next few hours, George was in ascendency again. In other words he would arrange affairs temporarily and then return to Varner's Junction where he would attend to his obligations there and send Oscar to Savannah, etc.

He could now devote himself fully to his sorrow that he felt for his brother, but before he immersed himself very deeply, he noticed that the taxi was now well off the area where the other house was located. And moreover, it had taken seven or eight minutes, a time in which the cabbie could have made it going the regular way.

"Say are you sure you know where you're going?" asked George.

"Listen," said the driver pulling over to the curb, "I know what I'm doing. Now you get in the front seat." So saying, the man pulled out a gun and pointed it at George. It was then that George realized that he was in serious trouble.

"What is this, are you trying to rob me?" demanded George.

"Nope," said the driver. "I'm going to kill you, but the question is whether you go quickly or slowly—I mean I could shoot off your knee cap right now, and that would be very painful, but you wouldn't die from it. You'd just sit there in pain. What a pity that would be, eh?"

"Is this some kind of joke?" demanded George, knowing full well that it wasn't, but desperately trying to do or *say* something that would give him a chance to think. If he could only have a little time.

"If it is, then it's on *you*, isn't it?" said the man, smiling. It was obvious that the cabbie rather liked his task, and this frightened George.

Thinking that he could get more time by going along with what the man demanded, George got in the front seat.

"Now you stay on your side of the seat. This gun is aimed at you and if you make any sudden moves you'll just get it early."

They drove on, and George's mind was racing. It seemed to him that if he waited until the end, then there would be no chance at all. As it was, the driver was in a vulnerable position and he, George, would have his best opportunity if he acted quickly. What he had to do was wait for the best moment, when the fellow's mind was completely occupied, and then jump him. It would be a risk, but it would be a risk that he would have to take.

As they came out of the side street maze, they pulled onto a main road that looked as if it was leading them out of town. Ahead was a five-way-stop intersection. As the car approached, George noticed that there were two large trucks barreling along at high speeds coming in different directions—each wanting to make the intersection first and ignore the stop signs. The driver of the taxi became intent momentarily on beating the trucks to the intersection so that they wouldn't have to wait, either. George looked quickly behind them and saw plenty of room behind. There wasn't time for thinking: George leaped at the driver, whose attention was momentarily on getting across the intersection. The man instantly reacted to George's advance and tried to slash him across the head with the pistol, but George blocked the blow with his arm and grabbed the other by the wrist. The trucks were honking their loud horns. Then there was the deafening sound of squealing brakes.

The taxi jerked forward and spun around as the driver pulled his foot off of the gas pedal and hit the clutch and brake at the same time, causing the car to go into a skidding spin.

George wrested control of the gun from his would-be assassin. George sneered and crowed, "All right now it's all over for—" but before the words all came out, one of the trucks that was trying to stop rammed into the car. The impact was devastating. It lifted the car into the air a few feet and threw it back thirty yards, whereupon it rolled over three times and then hit the wall of a solid brick building. The force of the impact instantly smashed the vehicle so that it resembled a crumpled ball of paper. There was an awful smell of fumes and another resounding crash as the first truck was struck by the second, causing them to wrap around each other. Then the taxi carrying Dodson and his assassin exploded. However, both driver and passenger were already dead.

Chapter 5

"Some Thoughts about Marriage, Happiness, and Waiting"

"What a lot of details there are to a marriage," began John as he and Julia sat in her house, discussing their forthcoming nuptials. "Couldn't we just have a ceremony and be done with it?" he asked. He and Julia had discussed the details of their ceremony several times at length. She spoke to him for the fortieth time about whether she should have a very high or medium high collar to her wedding dress. It wasn't that John wasn't interested. He was interested extrinsically—because Julia was. He had never given any thought about the need for planning. After all, he had never attended a wedding in his life.

In his mind, he thought that perhaps a wedding ought to be simpler so that the parties could concentrate on what was being said rather than on anything superfluous. However, he fully realized that it would be Julia's big day, and that it would be selfish for the groom to deny it to her, so he listened and quietly gave his opinions as to whether her hair should be up or down, and just what time of the day would be best, and who should be invited, etc.

Julia would be wearing her mother's old wedding dress, as they didn't have much money at present (though Samuel Beauchay had offered to help with expenses). Beauchay felt a new bond toward John, as *almost* a full Beauchay. The Vanderkamps were inclined to only accept a token amount of money. They decided to keep the reception to a small occasion. It should be emphasized that the attitude of the two Vanderkamp parents had changed considerably since they heard the news that John was not only a free man, but that he hailed from the Beauchay family—though the information-chain about Dorthay was intended to stop with the neighbors, news like this never stays under wrap. Dorthay's illegitimate son soon became common knowledge. Indeed, the spreading of the news occasioned Martha Vanderkamp to change her attitude the most on the suitability of John as a son-in-law. She now was as much in favor of the ceremony as before she had been opposed to it.

"We might not have a very big ceremony, but land sakes, it will be a grand one," she would say. She happily worked on altering her old dress for her daughter as it was in excellent condition and the fine Flemish lace made it a handsome gown in its own right. Everything seemed smooth for these two happy loved ones who were lost in the ecstasy of dreams about the wonder of a life together.

John spent his days working for his "uncle" or so Samuel wished now to be called. Samuel had offered John a six-month temporary job helping Jefferson and learning how to handle a large farm. John would work under Jefferson. "Farm management is a growing area," Beauchay proclaimed. "With some full-time experience under your belt you'll be able to sell your skills to the highest bidder."

John spent the evenings talking to Julia and her parents, who were about to return to court to see whether the foreclosure might be overturned. Mr. Vanderkamp was pessimistic. Mrs. Vanderkamp was optimistic. Julia didn't know what to think. At any rate, they would schedule the wedding before the court hearing. It was generally thought that the wedding would be happier while the Vanderkamps were still in their house. Already, Charles was negotiating a contingency plan to rent a small house in Varner's Junction near the old bank.

As it was, the wedding might signify the last event to be carried out at the old house, were the lawsuit to go against them. It might represent a grand exit. Thus every detail must be worked out exactly. There would be no second chance.

Yes, it was a great occasion for all involved, and John expected that Jefferson would be coming back and helping him with his end of it, as often times he felt rather left out of the whole thing. It would be only two days until Jefferson would arrive from

Savannah, a newly married man himself, completely prepared to tell John all about the hazards that he was about to face.

It was a happy time, and yet at the same instant a nervous one as well, because so much would be changed in such a short time in regards to his entire lifestyle that it hardly seemed possible that such a thing could come about. Would he change? Where would they live? Two possibilities presented themselves: first, Samuel Beauchay might let them live in his house for the six-month probationary period; or second, Samuel Beauchay might let them live in one of the abandoned share cropper houses with some fixer-up money. Marcel Beauchay had employed share croppers while Jefferson preferred paid labor on the *piece work system*.

Would John be able to make enough money to support his wife? He would have preferred to have had a little more time to actually start earning wages and be able to put something away before he made the final step, so that he might feel somewhat more secure about it all. But owing to the fact that the Vanderkamp's financial position was so insecure, and that they wanted the wedding to be in Bella County, it was necessary to have a very short engagement and proceed quickly.

It was middle afternoon when the last mail was delivered to the post office, also known as Ike's store, and the people in the immediate area started filing around as if they were expecting something, though most went away disappointed. The volume of mail wasn't too great that particular day. Still, it took Ike and the teenaged boy he had hired some time to sort all of it and set it in the little stacks, as he did for his delivery boy to take when he was filling orders (one of the ways that Ike kept his business brisk: free mail delivery if you buy from him).

"When you going to give up da store business Ike, and jist become a mail man?" laughed Jake as he set up another game of checkers after winning handily.

"Yeah, I think you spend more time at them thar letters sometimes than ya do on your reg'lar custimers," added Ed

"You know they're goin' ta have t' open an office soon, thar's jist gettin' ta be too much of this gull derned stuff fer me or anyone else, part time."

"You'll lose half of your business," warned Ed.

"That's right, I only play checkers here, sose I can get my biannual letter on time," retorted Jake.

"You two are a team, I can't compete with a conspiracy."

They laughed and continued with their game until Ike had finished with the letters. Then Ike pulled up a chair and watched the familiar situation with interest. Most of the games, it seemed to Ike, looked the same. And yet he couldn't for the life of him tell what it was that was similar—as there always seemed to be some difference, though he was not quite certain what it was.

"Is that Dodson funeral going to be today?" asked Ike.

"Yes, later on this afternoon, I think," replied Ed.

"D'ya think there'll be many people thar?" asked Jake.

"I think so," said Ed. "He was a pretty important man around these parts."

"Well, I never liked him and I wouldn't go if you paid me. That Dobson fellow is or rather *was*, no good. Always said so, ever since he first came to work in my store as a delivery boy. You know I never told you this, but I think he used to cheat on the tips he got from customers."

"What do you mean?"

"Well, he'd go and deliver somewhere and not bring along enough money for change so that when they handed him the money he'd come up a nickel or a dime short every time. Then he'd offer to go back to town and get it for them, but most people would just say forget it and keep the nickel as a tip. He got several extra dollars a week doing that."

"Yep, he was a real business man all right," said Ed, almost admiringly.

"You know, even though he's dead, I don't think we've heard the last from him somehow," said Jake.

"What are you, Jake, loco? That feller was smashed to bits in a car accident. Car stalled or something, don't you remember?"

"Yeah, I remember, I was jist thinking about animal traps I guess," said Jake, taking a cracker as he studied the board.

Chapter 6

"A Chapter which may Prompt the Reader to Purchase some Black Crêpe"

As he stood above the graves, Samuel Beauchay thought back to those days in Texas when had only just buried his wife, and how to some extent, it was his passivity and desire to stay in the hotel room that had allowed his sister to go out on her own and find such a man as George Dodson.

She had had other men interested in her, some of them quite fine gentlemen, as he remembered. But somehow she had chosen George. That choice really separated himself from her forever. This was because her husband and himself were irrevocably opposed. They could never get along together. They represented different points of view that could never coexist, but were destined to struggle until one of them had won.

But which one of them had won? Certainly it was Samuel Beauchay who was standing over the graves of the two, on the field which he had attempted to use as a lever to hinder Dodson's rise to power. In that deal, Dodson had won. But who was standing over whose grave? In the end, Samuel's way was enduring.

Certainly he felt that there was a sense of being stronger than the dead, mangled body which lay in the wooden box. But there was another sense that such a triumph didn't mean a thing, and that the real triumph had occurred earlier. And now that Dodson was dead, there was nothing that Samuel could ever do about it. In that way, Dodson was the eternal victor. He had died when he was ahead, and so would always be ahead.

But was it Dodson who he was fighting all this time, after all? This thought didn't come into his mind distinctly, but he wondered whether now that Dodson was dead, if he, Samuel Beauchay, could now undo some of the changes that had occurred to which he had been so opposed? These changes had been effected by Dodson. Now that they lacked a protector, might they fade away? There was a possibility of undoing what Dodson had sought to accomplish. For example, he could get a cadre of like-minded gentry farmers to create a town council and then from that position enact zoning ordinances to stop the textile manufacturing plant. And when the bank was reinstated, new procedures for electing officials of the bank could be instigated. Then there were new gambling ordinances, and stricter control of alcohol. All these and others might now be enacted without anyone to mount any opposition to him.

There was still hope that all that he had tried to build up, all the changes that he had tried to effect, working gradually within the respective systems, a little at a time, patiently, might now be realized.

Samuel leaned against his cane that he took because he was very weak, being still quite ill and feverish. This was not an event he would have chosen to attend. But one-half of the funeral was about his sister. There was no way he could stay home. It didn't matter to him how bad he felt. What mattered was that his sister, who had been lost for so many years to him, was now finally dead. What a miserable life she must have led, not having any servants, forced to be almost a slave. George had been cruel to Samuel's sister. This was difficult to continence, but a funeral service was not the place to be thinking evil of someone. George must have, in his own way, thought that he was doing some good? It was just that he, Samuel, was unable to recognize what his intention really was.

How close he had been to his sister when they had been children. She was always the perfect girl, he imagined. They would pretend that they were husband and wife and go about the business of running their imaginary estate, in the grand Southern Style. Even when he had grown older and found out that brothers don't marry their sisters, he still remained very close to his sister. They were good friends as well as being related. Dorthay always had an interesting opinion on things. She was such a cultured person, so delicate and fine—so unlike her—

They piled the dirt on ceremoniously and the late afternoon sun shone from the west, covering the scene with glazes of yellow and orange in thin layers that only served to accent some tone of underpainting that is already present in the dirt, rich in red clay. As they shoveled more dirt atop the wooden caskets, there was an echo from the resonance of the largely empty boxes (*hers* because she had almost completely rotted by the time of her burial, and *his* because his mode of death left little to fill the pine box). Soon hired laborers would do the real work and the remains of Dorthay and George Dodson would be out of sight.

Samuel turned around to go. His limbs were very weak, but he didn't ask for any help. He would make it by himself, and so the gathering departed each to their separate homes to continue their lives without the influence of George Dodson. And to Samuel he would now be without his sister (though he had in all practicality lost her years before when she married George).

As Samuel climbed into his buggy and alerted his horse to get going, his mind drifted to John and his upcoming marriage. Somehow, Samuel felt a great guilt at how John had been treated. True, he had been raised as one of the family, but still there had always been that aura about him as being illegitimate. He had never been treated as quite on a par as Jason, by himself, or by others simply because of some accident of birth.

But now John was being re-evaluated by others just because his mother was a Beauchay instead of a store clerk, Myra Dow. What is the fairness in that? John was John no matter who his parents were. Of course. But this again wasn't getting to the problem; that was something that Samuel couldn't do as his mind wandered about continuously.

One day when he had been little he had tried to take out Marcel's horse, as it was supposed to be the meanest horse around. This, of course, wasn't allowed, but he had done it on the sly, at night, when Marcel wouldn't know.

Everything had gone perfectly when suddenly they came to a jump and he was thrown from the horse and landed with much pain, but fortunately no lasting injury. The horse had run away and he knew that he was really going to be beaten by Marcel for disobeying him and stealing his horse. "Do you know that they hang horse thieves?" Samuel could imagine Marcel screaming at him. And there wouldn't be anything that he could say in response. So he had ambled home in the dark, fully expecting that the next morning he would get the walloping of his life and a moral lecture from his uncle. But much to his surprise, when he returned, he found that the horse was waiting for him at the barn. Thus, Samuel could bring him in and hide him as if nothing had happened.

The trick seemed too good to be true. But it was. His uncle never found out. Samuel thought over and over about the fall and tried to discover the reason *why*. He pondered this as he groomed the horse for the night.

When he was finally allowed to ride Marcel's horse a year later, he rode it flawlessly. His uncle was so surprised that he almost swallowed his cigar. It was then that Marcel decided that little Samuel would be a racer, a fact which became impossible, as far as state and regional races were concerned, because he was too tall. As Samuel grew in stature, it became clear that despite his skill, he would only be capable of being competitive for local races. What a horse Marcel had, and how surprised Samuel was by those chance events from his own childhood.

Samuel had excelled in the manly skills of riding, hunting, and fishing. His own son, Jason, had not. John had. In this way, it was as if John were more his son than Jason was. As Jason had aged, Samuel recognized that he was not an outdoor boy but a conniving person. In the details about college, Jason had created a series of small lies about himself on the college application. Samuel might be able to wink at such exaggerations—especially to Northerners. But Samuel did not like his son's dealings with Victor Stuart. They had been hanging out at the race tracks and at The Marsh in town.

Samuel knew that he should have gotten involved, but then that was during the period that he thought that he might be able to salvage his scheme for an agricultural cartel among planters in Georgia. Besides, when he had grown up, parents gave their offspring space.

Soon it would be night and he would be able to go to sleep. He was so tired of late that it seemed to him that all he did was sleep. An industrial plant, fabricating finished textile goods, was coming to the Vanderkamp farm. A sub-division of new houses was planned for the old golf course. Samuel wanted to scream to the heavens against such a future. The rivers would become polluted, the air would turn black, and the pace of life in Varner's Junction would change for the worse.

When Charlie Vanderkamp and he were boys, they would go swimming in the rivers and lakes. This would no longer become possible when the water became foul with manufacturer trailings. It had happened to countless towns in the North and some in the South. And the population would increase with the workers in the mill who would be housed on the golf course.

The whole scenario took him by surprise.

Then there were the automobiles. These were becoming increasingly popular. It was another step away from nature. A horse was a natural creature. A buggy was made of wood and nails: all natural. A horse could travel on a dirt path or cross-country on no path at all. A buggy was less free, but was still more flexible than these Model-Ts. Samuel believed that they would ruin the county just like the textile plants. The sad fact was that no one would realize it, because it would all happen *one small step at a time*. Then nothing would be left except paved roads, dirty air, and busy people who didn't understand what it meant to sit on the veranda and think leisurely about something, not hurrying but taking all in measured cadence.

The western part of the county was a grand place to live, the best land was there. How he remembered the family tales of when the Beauchays had been the newcomers. This history came from the stories old Col. Rutherford and his Uncle Marcel, who used to tell about how the established families on the eastern side wouldn't have anything to do with them. And now all those proud families were gone, or most of them. The Stuarts would be gone soon, as they didn't have any money, and in the present credit situation, they couldn't hold out much longer—where had they all gone?

The buggy was going over some rough spots in the road. The bumps made him feel nauseous. It was the gravel roads sprayed with tar; they weren't meant for wooden wheels, but rubber ones.

I think the paved roads aren't as good either, they're ugly and revolting, and I wouldn't want to travel anywhere on one; I pity the people who do.

Samuel endured his journey home alone.

Chapter 7

"A Slight Disagreement Between the Lovers Occurs"

"Now listen to her, Charles, she may have something, land sakes. It doesn't hurt to listen to someone."

"I will not, not when she talks nonsense."

"But it may be true, father, and if it is—"

"I won't listen to it! Do you think I'd join something like that if I thought that *he* had anything to do with it?"

"But Daddy, it wouldn't be your fault, I mean, lots of other people—"

"I don't care about other people. I made a mistake. I was willing to quit, and then you and your mother ganged up on me and forced me to go through with this legal business, so that's what we're doing—though if you ask me we're throwing good money after bad, but I'm doing it. But let's not have any of this other; I won't stand for it."

With that, Charles Vanderkamp went outside to see the sun as it hung just above the horizon. He would not talk to anyone for hours: both Julia and Mrs. Vanderkamp knew this.

"I'm sorry, Mother, but I just know that there's a lot of talk."

"I know dear, but you know how sensitive of a subject the whole thing is. A man doesn't like to admit that he's made a mistake. It's hard for him. Men are just like children in that way: they want to claim that they're right even when it's thrown in their faces that they aren't. But men aren't usually as clear headed about things as women are. You know, you and I can look at the situation objectively. We aren't burdened with masculine pride and emotion. But men are weaker than we are, and they often only see things from the point of view of how they are appearing to the rest of the world. They think that we'll love them less for making some silly mistakes, and so they try to convince you that they knew something like that would happen all along, and that someone forced them into it. It's usually the wife who gets blamed or they try and tell you that they really didn't fail at all. It's the only two options open to them. I do believe that they don't see anything else."

Julia got up and walked to the window and parted the curtains of the dining room window. This was where she grew up. It was home. Then she turned back to her mother, "But if this company that's investing in our land, or trying to take it from us, was owned by George Dodson, as most people think, then, I'm sure, at the very least, the case against us will have to be held up in court for some months, and maybe by that time we can get a firmer case, or some money, or something—this is the opportunity I think we've been waiting for."

"Oh, I hope you're right, dear. Land sakes, we certainly could use a god-send right now." Martha rose and walked to her daughter.

"I think it can work, but you see, Daddy has the land in his name, and we can't do anything about getting another writ on this new clause unless he signs it and agrees to it."

"That will be hard," replied Martha.

"I know, but doesn't he want to keep his land? *Our* land?"

Martha Vanderkamp moved closer to her daughter and put her hand on her shoulder. This girl was everything that she ever could have dreamed of having. While her husband preferred Rodney (she thought), she had a leaning towards Julia, who matched her gentle, kind nature with a sharp mind and an aggressiveness that she had also felt when she was a young girl. But now, after years of marriage, sometimes the things that seem so urgent to one in youth take a different turn and seem more as problems that are to be managed rather than conquered. These were things that a woman learned in order to survive in the world of the fragile male pride.

"Yes, dear, you know we all want that, and so does your father, you know that."

"But then why won't he listen to reason?"

"That's a lot to expect of a man, Julia."

Julia looked confused.

"Honey, men are our protectors, they work hard so that they can feel indispensable. They become so proud if they can provide enough for us that they become simply adorable. And there are so many nice things about a man. He can make a woman feel very-special. So if you have a good man who is faithful and dependable, then you should overlook that fragile ego. It's a fair trade. And if you are good at manipulation, you can have your way and make him think that it was his idea all along!" Martha Vanderkamp hugged her daughter and kissed her on the forehead.

Then she straightened her dress. "Regarding the estate, dear, we have to make sure that your father does everything in his power to keep this land. I rather think he is too apt to give up without a fight. This is not to say he is weak, but that he feels he made some bad investment decisions and his honor requires him to accept the consequences of his actions." Martha turned to go when she stopped and turned her head. "We may end up losing our home, Julia, but not without turning over every means possible first."

Julia nodded. "Yes mother." Then Martha exited the room and this left Julia with some time to ponder what her mother had said. Julia knew that her father was having a hard time of it and seemed to need the support of his women folk. This did not bother Julia because she had never considered men to be infallible. Every person, man or woman, had good qualities and bad. The mark of a good marriage is when the strengths and weaknesses were complementary. The result would be better than either one singly.

Her mother's opinions of this didn't square with her knowledge of John, for example. John didn't have such a high opinion of himself. He was a modest man who was far better than the persona he gave to the world. He wouldn't create an argument over a simple demand, and then dogmatically hold to it no matter what the consequences.

Julia walked into the dining room. She strolled over to the china cabinet and lifted out a Wedgewood plate that sported the date of 1842 hand-painted at the base on the reverse side. What would become of all this? It would probably be sold along with the house and land. Would she ever be able to afford such luxury? Did it really matter? Then Julia turned to the tall east-facing windows. Her mind was full. Then she saw John, who was coming to see her.

"Well, this is a surprise!" thought Julia as she exited the room towards the front door which she opened just in time and John stood there with his hand raised, about to knock.

"I had some time off, so I decided to come and see how you are," said John with a smile.

"Well, I'm fine, but I'm afraid that the farm thing has my father down some."

"That's natural. It's a difficult time—for all of you."

Julia smiled. She took John's arm and guided him towards the lake, as it was one of her favorite places to sit and talk with John.

After they had talked for a time about little things, thoughts and whims, Julia suddenly mentioned, "You know I've been thinking. We need to do some practical planning together."

John nodded. *Planning* was not one of his strong suits.

"Perhaps you could take one of the old shacks near the lake that they used to rent out when there was share-cropping? You could fix it up for us."

"Well, what if we have to move?" John stumbled. Was he saying something cruel? "I don't mean to say you will. I only mean—"

Julia took John's hand. "I know. It's a real possibility. When you engage in planning, you have to be realistic and not idealistic."

John nodded, though he was not entirely sure he understood her meaning. So he took a breath and began again, "You may not have it for long, what would be the point in going to all the work of making a house, when we might have to give it up right away?"

"Well, you know there is the old caretaker's shack. We could modify that, without very much effort, until we saw what the verdict was going to be."

"I don't know. Wouldn't it be better to either fix up something on the Beauchay farm or to move into the house? I mean, when Jefferson gets back I'm going to apprentice under him for skills as an estate manager. Mr. Beauchay says there are always good jobs for estate managers. Until then, I'm acting as a carpenter until the weather gets warm again."

Julia and John were sitting on adjacent rocks that were next to the lake. The light was beginning to fade a bit as it does early in the day during winter. "Well, I've been thinking. This world we've grown up in is fading. Who knows if these large farms will continue? Maybe it will be like it is up North with 40 acre spreads becoming the norm? There is no more slavery. Share cropping is no longer practiced in Bella County. There are now machines for picking cotton." Julia didn't look at John as she talked.

"What are you saying?"

"I'm saying that we have to keep our options open. We don't want to be tragic figures like my parents. We have to prepare ourselves for the future and not the past."

John looked at Julia, whose gaze was on the island in the lake. She was thus a profile against a setting sun, which created a silhouette. "What does this have to do with us?"

Julia continued to look at the island. "Everything. We need a backup plan."

"A backup plan?"

"Yes," replied Julia, still looking at the empty island.

"What sort of back up?" John was getting anxious.

"I propose that while you do your apprenticeship with Jefferson that I hone my skills that would permit me to be hired as an executive secretary."

"Executive secretary? What's that?"

"Well, as more and more businesses replace agriculture as the mainstay of Southern life, they will need office workers. These exist within tiers. On the bottom level are the go-fers. Next are the typists, then the office manager, and at the top is the executive secretary. These are the careers open for a woman. At the first level you need to just to be able to remember what they tell you to do and do it on schedule. Next you need to type. I can type 60 words a minute with few mistakes. Then you need to be able to execute the designs of the boss. Finally, you need to take dictation in shorthand, correct the boss's mistakes, know some elementary accounting, and basically act as his second-in-command."

John looked at Julia, amazed. Where did she learn all this? While visiting her aunt in Atlanta? Who was this person on whose finger he would place a ring?

Julia then turned back to face John, "Except for the shorthand and the accounting I think I'm executive secretary material right now. I saw a correspondence course in a magazine a few days ago and for five dollars I can fill my gap."

"I'm sorry, but what does this all mean?" John was confused.

"Varner's Junction is changing; Georgia's changing. We've got to be prepared."

John was startled by these words. What was she saying? Did she imply that he wasn't man enough to care for her? Isn't that what a husband was for? At the very least he could work a twelve-hour day in the fields. He had a strong back. He had proved that during his sojourn with the Martinez family. But then how did they live?

Was Julia willing to forgo the luxuries with which she had grown up? Even her own family would not be living that way much longer. This was a different world.

Julia got up. "You know John, things are changing. Why, just nine years ago women got the right to vote. It is not uncommon anymore for women to work in factories and do office work. And I'm sure you wouldn't turn your head away from a little more money each week in our bank account."

"That is, if they re-open the bank," returned John.

Julia smiled but continued to pace around John, who was still perched like a toad on the rock.

"Well, I don't know. I have to think about that one. I'm not a quick thinker like you are, Julia. But when I make up my mind I like to think I won't change."

Julia nodded her head. "Perseverance, loyalty, and fidelity are all fine character traits. But sometimes we have to be flexible, too."

John pursed his lips. He wanted to change the conversation, "How did you feel when you found out that my mother was not Myra Dow but Dorthay Beauchay?"

The pivot disturbed Julia. "What does this have to do with my being an executive secretary?"

"Nothing. But tell me. What did you think?"

Julia decided to sit down again on the adjacent rock. Twilight was approaching as the sun spread out flat and rosy again. She looked down to her shoes and then up again. "You know it didn't matter to me. None of this stuff matters to me. I grew up with you. I know you inside out. I don't care whether your mother was Myra or Dorthay."

"Do you know who my father is?"

"Nobody seems to. It's a mystery. My father told me they thought he was Greek or Italian. What's the big deal?"

"Well, he's *not* Greek or Italian. This is from Myra, who should know since she took some money to walk and *take the blame*." John decided it was his turn to stand up. He walked over to his fiancé and said, "My father was black. To be more accurate, he wasn't as black as Jefferson. Jefferson's 100%. My father was some mixture. That means in the rules of the South that I'm black, too." John delivered these words while walking away from Julia. Then he pivoted and came back to her. "Are you prepared to marry a black man?"

"I'm not marrying a black man. I'm marrying John Dow, who I grew up with and love. It doesn't make any difference whether your skin is darker than mine or our hair is of a different texture or our faces are molded different. Why, most men's faces are different from women's. This is not who *you are* any more than what I look like *is me*."

Julia arose and stretched out her arms so her hands rested atop John's shoulders. "Why, my mother looks different now than she did in the early daguerreotypes that captured her youth. But inside she's the same person. The packaging on the *outside* is not the person on the *inside*. It is the inside that counts, and on that score, my darling, you are the best."

John pulled Julia to him and hugged her hard. He shut his eyes, and didn't want to let go.

Chapter 8

"Destination: Varner's Junction"

Before they were married, Myra had made Jefferson promise that for as long as they were in Savannah that they would only go places when they were escorted by police for protection. This was because the murders of the past week had been bloody and there were many people who might wish to take their revenge out on Jefferson. Sigmund Wyse had been arrested as well as Miles Bon and Bill Marsh. They didn't have anything on Oscar Whren as yet, but Marshal Timay was confident that he could get the others to talk against their "comrade."

Also, some lower order fellows had been taken, though a major exception was Georgia Tom, who was at-large, with a warrant outstanding for his apprehension. Jefferson had completed all of his business. All his depositions had been made and he had helped as much as was possible so that it would be time for him to return to the place which he had called home for most of his life.

It was a proud moment at the station as the Marshal was there to see the happy couple away.

"I hope this isn't the last I see of you, old fellow," said Marshal Timay.

"No such luck," replied Jefferson. "And watch who you're calling *old*, you know now that I have a wife, it's taken ten years off my age. I think I'd take you wrestling two out of three falls."

"I'll have to take you up on that. Next time you're around, I'll risk you a ride in one of our squad cars against a ride on one on those country mares of yours."

"You're on. But I won't give you any handicaps."

They both laughed.

Then the train whistle blew and the conductor told everyone to hurry up. The Marshal shook Myra's hand, "I hope you'll both be very happy," he said.

Myra smiled, "Thank you."

Then the conductor yelled, "Board!" And they quickly mounted the steps to the Jim Crow Car as the train began to pull away.

Myra and Jefferson sat themselves down and watched the city disappear from sight.

"Sorry to go?" asked Jefferson.

"Not on your life," said Myra so seriously that Jefferson began to laugh. "It's not funny. I had a bad feeling about that city. I think that if we'd stayed much longer, that we might have gotten hurt." Myra cleared her throat, "I mean *you*. I was scared that *you* would have gotten hurt."

"Our fears are always twice as bad as what actually happens to us," said Jefferson.

"That may be, but I'm glad to be gone just the same."

Jefferson was also happy to be gone, but for a different reason. He was anxious to take his bride to the estate and settle down to a life which would be fuller than any he'd ever known. It seemed that this trip that he'd taken on behalf of someone else had in the end benefitted him to the greatest degree. He felt that he knew himself better, and had a greater sense of peaceful direction. It was as if the turbulence was finally subsiding. Now would be a time when he could really begin to learn what tranquility was all about. All this had occurred without his philosophical questions. But he was still convinced that had he not engaged so long about such matters, he wouldn't understand his present situation as he did, and wouldn't know the know the real meaning of what it meant to be at this state in his personal outlook.

He looked at his wife who was sitting next to him. How beautiful she looked, he thought. Her face was imprinted with all of her personality traits which he had come to love. It was a face of loving concern, a visage which openly displayed her warmth and eagerness to be helpful. Jefferson reached for her hand and squeezed it gently.

Then there was the final education of John. Jefferson had always looked upon John like his own son. This planting, growing, and harvesting season he would teach John everything he knew about farm management. It was a natural, peaceful calling that he felt would suit John just fine. Oh, how the next nine months or so would be so wonderful! There would be his new wife and there would be the commencement in the education of John. What more could a man dream of?

Soon, Jefferson was called by that persuasive natural impulse (which beckons us all periodically to make done with that non-nutritive matter which our catholic bodies so prudently select as useless by-products). And so he excused himself and made his way to the back of the carriage where he hoped to satisfy this mission. However, when he arrived at the appointed door he was cautioned by a man standing there. "I was just in there, the door is broken; you see this latch on the outside?"

Jefferson nodded.

"Well, when you go in there it locks, and you can't control it from the inside: something's broken. I was in there for five minutes banging on the door before someone let me out."

Jefferson looked at the door. Clearly that wouldn't be a very good situation, to be locked in the toilet.

"If you don't believe me, go on and try it yourself, I'll stay out here and open the door for you."

"That's all right," said Jefferson, not really wishing to test the facilities. "I think I will try the one in the other car."

"They really ought to fix those things, you know. I don't know what's happening to the railroads these days."

Jefferson made his way into the other car. There were only two Jim Crow cars so this was his only other option. The philosopher moved with dispatch. However, if he had been empirically attentive, he might have gotten a glimpse of a man who (upon seeing Jefferson) quickly hid his face behind a newspaper.

The man was Coody.

Coody had followed Jefferson ever since he had been commissioned by Rod, and had been unable to do anything in Savannah because Jefferson had always been either with people, or as lately, with the police.

But it's hard for some men to forget humiliation and disgrace, and Coody was still keen on his mission even though with Rod dead he would make no money on this job. He took an acute personal interest in the assignment. How he had thought about ways to kill Jefferson as he had spent hour after hour on the floor of that apartment, and later in jail. This was all because of one man, a man who had tried to make a fool out of him, a man who had made him tell more than he had wanted to tell. Coody didn't feel as if he lacked reasons for wanting Jefferson in a stationary horizontal position, permanently. In fact, he was well equipped to do the job, as he had wire, a knife (with a triangular blade designed for quicker, more profuse bleeding) and a .38 pistol. Coody wasn't sure *how* he was going to do it, but he knew that he wanted to get him on the train. The element of surprise would be in his favor.

As Jefferson returned, Coody slid from his seat and followed him. If Jefferson had turned around, he would have seen his assailant and been able to take some kind of action, but instead Jefferson walked blindly on. Perhaps between the cars, thought Coody as he put his hand on his pistol and held it ready, hidden by his jacket.

Jefferson opened the door to walk between cars, when fortunately two black nuns were also passing on the same journey, presumably taking the advice from the same fellow—if he was still there.

Having missed the opportunity between cars, Coody thought about another venue: right in front of the other toilet. The view was blind from the rest of the car and he, Coody, could hide the body in the toilet. But owing to the presence of the friendly guide to the toilet, who was standing outside the door just waiting to tell someone else his story, Coody was forced to turn around and return to his seat without talking to the toilet master.

There would still be plenty of time. It would be foolish to risk failure at this early stage.

Coody waited for Jefferson to make another trip through the car (as the refreshment car was in the same direction), but Jefferson never did. This situation wasn't very good at all. Coody began to scheme.

Jefferson and Myra sat quietly, watching the scenery pass and commenting on it and how they remembered this or that. There seemed to be so much time before they were to arrive to their new life together. This tension made them impatient. But then they so enjoyed each other's company that time seemed to transform: they could keep themselves company forever. This dynamic gave them tranquility.

"I'm a little hungry, would you like something to eat?" asked Jefferson.

"No, I'm not that hungry, besides I never like buying food on the trains, it's so much more expensive. I can hardly enjoy what I'm eating because I know it costs so much. But you go ahead if you want to, don't let me stop you."

"You really think it's that much more expensive?"

"I'm sure of it."

"Well, I don't care. I'll get something for you, no matter what it costs."

"I'm not really that hungry just now."

Jefferson turned his head to the window across the aisle. He lifted his nose and scrunched his eyes. Then he moved his jaw forward and back, "Well, then, I think I'll wait too. It's no good just eating alone."

"I don't want to stop you, if you really want, I'll have something."

Jefferson started to get up, but then sat down, "No, it's not too long before we get to Varner's Junction, we'll get something then. I don't want to become a fat old man."

Myra laughed, "That's something you'll never be," and she kissed him on the cheek.

In the other car, Coody thought that if Jefferson didn't go to the club car, then what he could do would be to hide in the toilet in the other car. When the train stopped he would open the door slightly so that he could see who was exiting and then make his move and knife him. Then Coody would escape back within the toilet, lock the door, and climb out the window, which he'd already have opened. As the window would be on the other side of the train, he could hop over to the opposite platform to make his escape. Perhaps he wouldn't be seen and he could walk casually away. Or perhaps he could re-board the train in another section, whatever seemed best at the time. The plan was perfect. There was nothing that Jefferson could do to prevent it. He'd surprise him, pull him inside, lock the door, stab him, and make his escape.

"Did you see that Burma Shave ad? Well, that means we're almost there," said Jefferson.

"I'm rather excited, aren't you?"

"I'm always excited to be around you, sweetheart."

Coody had waited so long for this opportunity. He wasn't going to let it slip away, even if it meant personal risk to himself. This was too important. He smiled as he thought of forcing the knife into the soft flesh and seeing the expression of surprise on that black face as it contorted in pain and the blood would begin to flow.

The train began to break for Varner's Junction and the people who were going to get off got up and went through the routine of gathering their things into piles that could be lugged off the train.

"Well, here we are," said Jefferson rising to get Myra's things, as his few things were packed into one of Myra's cases.

"Be careful with those, they're heavy," warned Myra.

"I know. I put them up there," said Jefferson as he took the cases off the overhead rack.

Coody got up and made his way to the toilet. Just then a thought entered his head: what if it was in use? How awful that would be. What would he do then—perhaps he should have thought of another plan, a person should always have several plans at his disposal in case some unforeseen occasion should arise. Coody became very nervous and rushed to the toilet, but to his relief, it was vacant. He went inside and put his foot slightly in the door jam so that he could peep out from the thin crack.

Jefferson got the bags together as the train was pulling to a halt. "We'll have a little wait to get out, with that one ahead," said Myra, pointing to the rotund lady with her equally plump mate. They were traveling with hopelessly bulky trunks that the man, even with the woman's help, was just barely able to manage.

The sight was slightly comical and made Jefferson chuckle as he looked at Myra who had the same reaction. The two would be constantly trying to shift the weight so that they could manage it, but when they had gotten one bag in position the trunk would be awkward, and when that was righted, one of the bags would slip down. But still they plodded forward, bumping into people and seats as they made their way to the front of the car and the unconfined freedom of the train platform.

"You'd think they'd make two trips," said Myra.

"They couldn't do that," said Jefferson sarcastically, "we only have five minutes or so, if they want to use up the maximum time then they better do that in one trip."

Finally, the comical duo made their way into the narrow corridor which led to the door. Coody could see that behind these two oafs with their swinging trunk were Myra and Jefferson. He put his hand on his knife to make sure that it was ready.

The dynamic duo banged their way against the doors and windows when the man, trying to stop a case from falling, slammed his trunk against the door, knocking Coody to the floor and swinging the door open. The man quickly responded and caught the door handle with his elbow and pulled it shut.

"Some people don't know when to close doors," he said, as he banged his way out through the exit.

Myra and Jefferson followed quietly behind, somewhat anxious to get out of the train.

Meanwhile Coody was beside himself as he got up and tried to open the door. It was caught, and he could not open it from the inside as the infamous latch, which had been described already to many of the passengers, was holding him a prisoner. He frantically twisted and turned the handle, but to no avail. His quarry was getting away. He had to get out. He would take any risk now; just let him get him. Coody began to pound on the door forcefully to try to break it, but whereas railroad workmanship might fail in mechanical workability, no one has ever accused them of failures in strength; the door was immoveable.

Standing on the platform, Jefferson put down their own bags, "Now, do we have everything?' he asked routinely as he went over in his mind the way that they were going to get home.

"Oh, my scarf," said Myra, remembering putting the white scarf on the upper rack as they had left Savannah.

"No problem, be back in a second," said Jefferson, springing back on the train.

"Hurry, I don't want the train to leave with you," said Myra, who had visions of the train taking Jefferson away from her.

Jefferson passed by the toilet door and smiled as he heard someone struggling to get out. That could have been me, he thought as he retrieved the scarf. Then, as he walked back, he put his hand on the toilet door latch. If I was in there I'd want someone to help me, he thought. Jefferson cocked his head and smiled. The thought of someone locked in the toilet was rather comical—to someone on the outside.

No sooner had he released the latch than he saw the face of Coody, which he instantly recognized. Jefferson froze a moment as Coody tried to grab him, but Jefferson struggled with him, twisting about, trying to get him to the floor. Jefferson forced Coody to one knee, when the other pulled his knife and pushed it into Jefferson's left kidney. Jefferson recoiled with pain as he fell forwards against the side wall. Coody was quick to his feet and again he thrust the knife into Jefferson's body, this time from the front, tearing the stomach and abdomen. Suddenly Coody was *made* when he was spotted by a man who was walking between cars.

"Hey, what are you doing," yelled the man. "Murder, Murder!" screamed the man. Instantly there was panic as Coody dropped his knife and tried running through the car, but he was stopped by a large black man who felled him with a single blow to the temple.

"Murder, Murder!" continued the men.

Instantly Myra knew what had happened. To say she *knew* would be slightly inaccurate; she feared what had happened, and felt that it was Jefferson. But even when she saw him lying there bleeding with the knife beside him, she really didn't *know*, or *accept* that he had been stabbed. It was a sudden change of events so incongruous that she couldn't understand very much of what was really happening, except that she had to help him, and save his life.

Jefferson was lying on his back as his hand was groping around his chest as if to grip something, then he remembered, and smiled as he opened his eyes and saw Myra, slightly out of focus as everything was blurred at the moment. He felt no real pain, just a terrific weakness and numbing dizziness.

Myra began ripping off Jefferson's shirt to find his wounds so that she could do something about the bleeding. His life depended on her calmness, she thought, and so she worked as quickly as she could. But the light was getting dimmer, as the throbbing in his head began to annoy Jefferson so he shut his eyes to escape the pain. He sensed Myra's presence and his lips stretched into a slight smile; he tried to talk, but he couldn't say anything.

He felt her fingers touching his skin.

Chapter 9

"Victims of Death"

It seemed impossible to John that Jefferson was dead. John had gone to the funeral, and had seen Myra. These were facts that he could assimilate, but the reality that Jefferson wouldn't *be there* in case he ever wanted to see him or talk with him had never really struck him with as much dread as it did at that moment. John felt scared. What if there was trouble ahead? Where would he go? Who could he ever talk to in the same way as he had talked to Jefferson? There could be no one. The bluntness of the negation hit John as nothing ever had. Jefferson's no longer existing was something that couldn't be true. Jefferson was too good. How could he cease to exist? He must be somewhere; Jefferson couldn't die. If there were any purpose to anything, then Jefferson must still live in some form. Jefferson had been a Christian. Christians believe in eternal life for good people, but this was of little solace to John as he knew that whether Jefferson was existing in some other reality or not, he wouldn't be around to be a father to him.

John had lost his father.

There had been so much that he would have liked to discuss with Jefferson, about his travels, about things he'd learned—problems that he wanted to test out and see what Jefferson thought about. It was all so sudden; one day he was alive and the next he was dead.

It seemed to John that people should sort of fade away gradually so that one could get used to the idea that they might die, but to die so suddenly, so violently; it was not something that he could understand. He had never even had the chance of thanking

Jefferson for all that he had done for him. If it hadn't been for Jefferson, John would be a life-long fugitive. He would be living with the dwarf and the mutable old lady forever.

But Jefferson changed all that. Jefferson was dead so that John could have a life. Jefferson was so smart, but unlike other smart people he had met, like Mr. Russell, Jefferson was a kind and compassionate man. That was Jefferson. But why did all the good people have to die? How painful it was to those who remained.

And selfishly, John wanted Jefferson around to launch him into adulthood. First, John was to be apprenticed to Jefferson for six months. Second, he would have given John advice on how to be a good husband. What was John going to do?

There had been a big hole in the cemetery ground. John had paid particular attention to this pit at the funeral. It went down six feet. It was at the far end of the cemetery on a downward slope that inclined the existing land into rain-induced gullies that marred the existing graves. This was an especially marked-off area. It was for black men who held special status. It was separated from the main white cemetery by a little brook that meandered about. No one attending the funeral, including John, gave the separation any heed.

Instead, what John thought about was a body in the ground, lying in cold deafness to all but the termites who even now may be at the box—as the regeneration of the chemical structure quietly proceeds: everything continues. Each of us, John thought, has to continue. The end of his mentor was even more tragic because in so many ways the end was not an end at all. It was only a part of something else. Jefferson was a part of the natural rhythms: people die all the time. But John never gave such heed to them as he had to Jefferson's death. But over the world there must be someone dying every minute in the day, so that while John was calmly living, in the same moments others were in the embrace of their ultimate finitude. The stench of the dead and those who mourn them with their crying is an ever present reality that he had never thought about.

But a person couldn't dwell on such things or he would be continually depressed. John had a wonderful life to look forward to. And it would be his duty to try and achieve all that he could, as that's what Jefferson wanted for John. And as Jefferson had spent so much time trying to secure John's freedom and happiness, it would be a dastardly act of ingratitude not to diligently go forward.

If John could live a life in keeping with the model of Jefferson, then maybe his murder would not be entirely in vain.

It was early morning and John had decided to make a solitary visit. There were no wildflowers because it was still winter. John looked about and found a red colored pebble the size of his thumb and laid it at the base of the headstone.

The dew was still heavy and John's feet were getting wet through his Sunday shoes. There was something about the morning and its quiet that turned one's thoughts to somber reflection about topics that John never really had time for the rest of the day.

There was so much about death that John didn't understand. It was such a mystery. However, had he been to someone else's funeral, he might compartmentalize the events and set them aside. But now what he most wanted to do was to question Jefferson about the meaning of everything. But Jefferson could not hear him. John longed to listen to the wisdom of the man who seemed to know so much about everything. Every time that John had come up with what he imagined to be a very original thought or question, Jefferson would tell John how earlier thinkers had considered the same thing from different positions. What John had taken as so original was really not. It had already been considered in the erudite mind of Jefferson.

John looked down to the newly turned dirt that was muddy with the dew. Is that the way the world treats genius? How sad to live in such a time and place.

And yet Jefferson had been more than a thinking machine. He was also the kindest man John had ever met. Jefferson had such reason to boast at his superiority, and yet he had been a gentle, humble man. This was the sort of person that John wanted to be.

John walked over to the edge of the colored section of the cemetery and climbed onto the fence post that jutted out at an angle from the ground, and though he was in his good clothes, he felt that he had to sit on that post, as if it was designed to bear his weight at that moment.

How quiet the world could be sometimes; it was a stillness that he didn't often take time to recognize. There was something sacred about that silence, like the tinkling of the spheres in harmonious melody. It was this symphony of quietude that rested below everything, yet was so rarely felt. His future rested with Julia; he knew this. There were so many uncertainties that sometimes thrilled him, but others often caused him fear. It was an odd type of non-object-directed nervousness that could only be described as anxiousness in general.

John saw a cat running after a mouse, then the mouse stopped, and the cat poised itself in front of the rodent, which began to hop about as the cat playfully batted with its paws as if in a game. John smiled. The pair went at it for a minute or so before the cat decided to end the game and pounced upon the mouse and killed it.

John got down from his perch and walked home.

Chapter 10

"Getting One's Due"

As Jason sat in the waiting room of the lawyer's office, he went over the various arguments in his mind. He had come home just in time. His father was very sick and might soon die. In all the excitement about this stupid marriage between John Dow and Julia Vanderkamp, there was a rumor that his father might decide to leave some of his property to that empty-headed bastard.

It hardly seemed right that when a person goes away to college that he should have to submit to such alterations when he returned home. How it was that John had gotten off the hook for the murder charge, he'd never know. John deserved to swing on the gallows. Jason had half a suspicion that something underhanded had been done to free him. This was because not only was the charge dropped, but then they worked up some cock and bull story that claimed that John was his half-cousin!

Imagine what nonsense: John, the nigger bastard, being anyone's cousin, except some old drunken coon somewhere. Well, at any rate, everyone was so shaken up by the death of George Dodson that they would swallow anything. And the coincidence that Dorthay Dodson had conveniently died so that she could not deny the story was more than Jason could stand. Jason did not believe that this could have occurred by chance—there had to have been a design. But how had he missed it? Of course he couldn't keep track of everything, being so far away from life in the county. It was impossible. Perhaps he wouldn't go back if he was going to be cheated out of everything he deserved each time he left for college term. If that were the case, then at the end of four years he'd be a much poorer man than when he started. No, it became clear to Jason that he had to invoke a change of plans.

A stupid sheepskin didn't count for squat if he were to lose a nickel in his father's estate. Jason needed every penny so that he could build his empire. As Jason sat in the stiff-backed wooden chair, he suddenly became aware of a spider's web in the corner of the room. It was a beautiful web. Mr. Russell had told them that spiders' webs were created rather ingeniously. The long threads were not sticky. They allowed the spider to traverse the web at will. The cross threads were sticky and would capture flying insects until the spider could confront his prey and suck out its innards.

Jason smiled at the spider's web.

Most weak-willed people would scoff at him. Jason knew this. Even his own father, when pressed, would not embrace his own son for who he was. This was why Jason always had to create a persona that he knew daddy would approve of. And his father was so daft that he accepted the act without question. Jason was counting on this as he was about to press the attorney for a change of the term of distribution in the will to include mental incompetence. Charles Vanderkamp had been duped out of three-quarters of his net worth by his own stupidity. It was easy to fleece those in the latter stages of life.

Who had done it? Probably someone connected with George Dodson. But George was now dead. Who was left? William. Jason had met William a few times. The two of them hit it off well. William was younger, but he was no nonsense. He had a goal and was ready to stick to it. This interested Jason. After he could strike the best deal he could for conditions of competency and a pre-death ownership hearing, Jason decided he would find William and have a very long talk with him—perhaps over some whiskey. Being younger, William might not have learned to hold his liquor.

Then Jason might be able to forge a relationship with William so that Jason was the favored party. William had so much already from his father that he would need an incentive to bring Jason into the business. Jason had just the ticket: the Beauchay family estate. When his father was found legally incompetent, the time would be ripe to take it all away as soon as possible. Jason smiled broadly at the prospect. There would be no going back to college. The future was *here* and *now*.

Then the great walnut door opened and the lawyer walked out. The man was silver-haired and nattily dressed. He grinned as he strode forward to shake Jason's hand.

"How are you Jason? Do you like school?"

"Very well on both counts, sir," replied Jason with a smile that showed teeth.

"Come in to my office, won't you?"

And so Jason went inside the handsomely decorated office and presented his case.

Chapter 11

"The Marriage: Wherein our History draws Nearer to a Conclusion"

As John took Julia in his arms to seal the vows before all the friends who were watching, he felt rather as if he were being made a spectacle of. He had wanted to have a very quiet ceremony with only a few people, though Mrs. Vanderkamp had insisted that they have a big to-do. Circumstances proved influential, and by estate standards it was a modest affair. And though John was certainly proud to be Julia's husband, he was somewhat shy about the idea of repeating such private vows in front of 150 people. And then kissing Julia, something he had done only infrequently before, and then in strictest privacy, in front of all those people. It seemed almost exhibitionistic to him, though he knew that this was not the case as it was tradition and customary, etc. But still such a long kiss as this made him uncomfortable. Because of this he was trying to break free, but Julia was holding to it. The duration seemed like minutes to him, when actually it was only a second or two.

But then it was over and they were shaking everyone's hands and saying thank you and how lucky they were and how they knew that it was just the right time for a wedding etc., during which John's mind began to wander somewhat towards what was to follow later. He pictured that delightful experience whereupon he might taste the full creamy delectable sweetness that is the fruit for the groom after his arduous wait through the ceremony and the shaking of hands. It was a powerful lure which his mind fondly lingered upon, despite all efforts by himself to push it from his thoughts.

Overcoming his efforts, the image would return in fuller force than before, making him anxious to be done with all this fiddle-faddle and get to what he had long been waiting for: that prize which his mind had been dreaming about ever since the reception had begun, that still perfect, untouched, tender, delicate, sensuously delightful experience of . . . cutting and eating the wedding cake!

John's fondness for cake went back to when he was a boy, and now he longed to get to it, as it stood tall before him. It was just waiting for the groom to put the knife to it and make the reception official.

In fact he had nothing to eat that entire day, and he was ravenous. "You can't eat on your wedding day," Jessy had told him.

"Why not?"

"Because you're too nervous, that's why."

"But I'm hungry."

"It will just give you a stomach ache."

"No it won't."

"Listen young man, don't you go tellin' me 'bout what's gives you a stomach ache. Why I remembers when youse was just a youngin and youse come in and try and eats everything in sight, sometimes. I just had to stops ya, or you'd start crying louder than a wet cat. Now that wouldn't do at your weddin' now woulds it?"

How does one argue with a woman like that? It was impossible, so John had gone *without* that entire day. He was just waiting for the chance when it was all over, when he would be able to taste the sweetness of something on his palate, and his ravenous appetite would be satisfied. For it seemed that with hunger, which it may be remembered that he had suffered for almost a month in the lumbering town without undue complaint, that when it is self-imposed, one can do without for long periods of time and not complain. But when the cause for the lack of nourishment becomes an external factor, then the hunger almost increases by the same proportion that the external force of restraint is exerted. And so it is quite fair to assume that John was as completely hungry as can be, in the strongest sense of the word.

"Well, I guess this is your big day," said a man that John didn't know.

"Yes sir," said John, shaking his hand.

"You sure got a fine girl there." He squeezed John's hand too tightly. Was he trying to test to see whether John was a real man or not, in folksy southern tradition?

"Yes sir," said John, trying to conceal the pain that he was feeling.

"Yep, I've known Julia since she was knee high."

"Yes sir," replied John once more as the man had loosened his grip.

"You're going to be mighty happy." The man had a broad smile on his face.

"Yes sir." John was eyeing the cake again. They wouldn't break tradition and cut it before he was through with the line, would they?

"Where are you going to live?"

"Yes sir," said John absently, trying to get a glimpse of the cutting knife.

"What was that?" bellowed the man in a tone that John couldn't discern as being a laugh or a sign of anger.

"Ah, well—" started John, not knowing quite what he was going to say, but feeling certain that it was expected that he say something.

"This husband of yours is really a card, do you know that, Julia?" said the man, indicating that he had been amused.

John sighed and smiled as his hand was once more gripped by the wet palm of a woman, who had either just cleaned fish or had extremely clammy hands.

Soon it was time for cake. John gave himself a big piece. There was more chit chat as people stood holding plates and getting frosting on their face which they could only extract with the back of the hand holding the fork. This merely transferred the issue from one venue to another. It was an old Southern tradition.

When it was all over and the dances had been completed and the laughter finished and all the commotion suffused into the collective memory, John wondered about how people all seemed to change on special occasions. The guests took on roles as if they were in a drama. This new actor was hardly recognizable in the midst of it all. They were smiling and pretending to be gay. Perhaps it was just the nervousness of everyone. He had been the object of such scorn for so long that he felt that perhaps they were making it up, or trying to at any rate, by being overly friendly. How much had this to do with his Beauchay connection now being common knowledge? How much was it due to the new rumor that his father had been a Greek instead of a man of mixed African ancestry? It was easier for them to accept him as a Greek. John clenched his teeth as he thrust his jaw forward. He didn't like this part of the script. It was phony.

***

How much of this analysis was correct, John couldn't be sure, as he had never gone to a wedding before and had little interest in so-called formal occasions. Perhaps these conclusions were all in his hypersensitive mind. There was no way to know and no Jefferson to help him through it.

Instead, John looked to his right and gazed at his bride sound asleep beside him.

She would become his new partner in heady speculation. Though neither of them had the prized college degree that Jefferson had earned, still if they could develop ways of exploring problems together then they might become even better friends. And wouldn't that be grand?

Mr. Beauchay couldn't very well let John be the farm steward. John wasn't qualified. The apprenticeship with Jefferson could no longer be. Since it was technically the beginning of spring, there would be a lot of hours of regular labor for which John could earn a wage (a reform that Jefferson had instigated). This would take them to late May. Then they'd have to re-assess. That was a longer span than he'd often had on the road at a new stopping point.

Again, he looked at his sleeping bride. He felt hopeful.

Chapter 12

"In Which the History is Concluded"

The next Monday brought news from Atlanta. The foreclosure of the Vanderkamp farm was legally affirmed. Charles and Martha Vanderkamp were given 60 days before they would have to vacate the property. Samuel Beauchay came by with his son, Jason (who had decided to drop out of college) to help Charles and Martha go into town and further explore a new place to live. Jason was driving the buggy with Samuel and Martha beside Charles on the second seat.

"Three generations. This land. And I lose it." Charles was losing more than his land.

"Darling, we will be fine in town. We can drive on the new paved roads. They say that in three years all the roads in town will be paved." Martha kissed her husband on the cheek.

"Damn the paved roads! I want our land back. It's been my life."

"Well, we have to move on, dear. There just isn't another way. It's the times. We have to go with them. President Hoover has said so on the radio."

"President Hoover be damned. He's a northern Republican!"

Samuel put his arm around Charles, "Hey, we've got to be realists. Do you think I'll be on my place next year? We're starting the spring planting now, but I can see the writing on the wall. This county's changing. This state's changing. This whole country is changing."

"Don't I know it," was Charles' reply.

Jason, who was driving the horses, could not suppress a slight grin.

***

"Ya know what gits me," said Ike, thinking about the golf course, "is who is going to git all that money that Dobson had."

"Probably his kin, who else?" said Jake.

"But supposin' he didn't make no will?" replied Ike.

"Don't talk foolish, Ike, course he made a will. Anyone with that much money has to had a will," said Jake.

"C'mon, make your move," said Ed, as he had his friend in a bad position on the checker board.

"I don't know. First, that it seems kinda odd that someone who had all dat money should all of a sudden be gone," said Ike philosophically.

"I know what you mean, Ike," said Ed, "it's almost *sad* that a feller who had built up so much should suddenly go, and all his work fall apart."

Jake didn't say anything, but studied the board.

"I was jist a wonderin' whether now that Dobson's dead, that maybe I could buy that old golf course property."

"Now what would you want that fur, Ike?" asked Jake.

"Don't know, but I always fancied that it was a mighty choice bit of land, that's all."

"Take my advice and stick to shop-keeping," said Jake.

"That's just like you, Jake, you have no imagination. It's true; you jist don't have no imagination."

"That may be, but I still wouldn't buy no golf course property."

"C'mon and move," said Ed as his victory seemed certain.

"I think it's a beautiful little stretch," said Ike, a little hurt by Jake.

"Sure it's fine, Ike," said Ed. "Remember when we went out a-scouting it?"

"Sure do," laughed Ike. "I always had a feelin' 'bout it."

Then Jake quadruple jumped Ed's men, ending the trap and the game. Jake smiled broadly, "Want to play 'nother game?" asked Jake. Ed couldn't respond. He hadn't seen the trap. He had played so many games with Jake that he thought he knew him inside-out. But this was a shiner. How had it happened? He had been so sure. . .

***

The man took up a drink and passed it over to the young man. "So what's this all about, eh?" They were sitting in *The Marsh*. "What did you say your name was?"

"William." The oldest Dodson son was wearing a white shirt with Arrow Collar. He had a black bow tie and a grey sweater. His straight, thin, dark brown hair was parted in the middle and oiled down. His face was stern.

"Billy?" asked the older man with a smile.

"No, William." There was no change in the facial expression.

"All right, William, why should I listen to you?"

"Because I control Big George's holdings. You see, he was prepared for any possibility."

"But your organization's finished." The older man began playing with his light brown moustache. His smile had turned to a smirk.

"That's what you think. I've done some re-organizing, and we'll be still quite effective. Remember, I'm the only one who has the contacts for the booze, and we still have friends. I think you ought to think my proposition over."

"A partnership?"

"Yes, and this time, we'll draw up some terms so that there is no misunderstanding. You realize that all this shooting that went on was absolutely useless. The only ones who gained were the cops—as if they needed a helping hand from us?" He paused. "You know they put a lot of our men under ground and behind bars."

"Mostly yours."

"Mostly mine, but it doesn't matter whose they were. A loss to me is a loss to you. Get it?" William leaned forward. He took out a cigarette, put it in his mouth, and lit the match off his left thumb nail.

The older man smiled at the trick. "I get that you tried to knock me off."

"All this will be taken care of in our new agreement. Look, I've got tremendous plans for consolidation. The trouble before was that everything was too loosely arranged into a myriad of small companies. I plan to merge these into larger ones which are real—you know?

"These would be companies which have actual assets, like the textile mill that I'm building on the old Vanderkamp farm, and the housing development that I'm building so that the workers have a place to live. I'm calling that firm Georgia Construction. They will also build the physical building for the textile factory. These real companies deflect attention. Then we got some cover when someone comes sticking his nose around here."

Daniels was quite impressed by this young kid. He felt that this boy was smarter than his old man, and perhaps more dangerous as well. But he also knew that if he made an enemy of him that it could mean his eventual demise. Therefore, he smiled and agreed to consider the proposal. He planned to accept, but he had to keep to form and not seem too eager. He couldn't let this kid get too far out of control.

***

It was evening. John and Julia were alternating their living between the Beauchay house and the Vanderkamp house until John had finished the repairs on a small shed that used to house share croppers who worked the fields. John thought the work would be done in two or three weeks. Then they would move in there until the spring planting was done and the crops were secure on the Beauchay fields.

Samuel Beauchay had not replaced Jefferson. He talked about selling the land after harvest. For the time being, he and Jason would take on the managerial role overseeing everything.

John and Julia were walking toward town. It was always interesting to see the civic silhouette as the sun set. "Rodney can't come to give his input on the new house," said Julia.

"Why's that? Too engaged in his studies?" asked John.

"Too engaged in sports. Rodney is not fully cognizant about what's going on. This despite copies of the same letters I received. He's trying out for the baseball team. I swear, I think they should have a special college for athletes where all they do is play games."

"I thought they called that childhood," put John.

The two of them smiled.

They walked for a while without talking. Then Julia said, "My aunt said that after we've put the Beauchay crops into the ground that we can stay with her while you and I try out Atlanta."

John looked up to the sky. It was getting darker. "Well, you finished your short-hand and accounting courses."

"Yes, and Aunt Julia has some opportunities for you, too."

John thrust his jaw forward. "Not much of a city boy."

The two stopped and Julia turned and looked at John straight on. "You know what you are John Dow? You are a survivor. You have proved that. You're like Jefferson. He was a survivor, too. That's partly why I married you. You are a strong man and a kind man. The two don't often go together. But they go together in you, and I love you for it."

Then Julia took John's face in her hands and kissed him on the lips. John melted in her embrace.

Then they walked towards town. The view of Varner's Junction was getting lost in the blackness. It was almost invisible. It certainly had changed in their lifetime. But it would be theirs for not much longer.

The couple looked to the east, which was now in total darkness. That was the side where the first settlers of Bella had established themselves so many years ago. It was a beautiful piece of land that also engendered much conflict from the European descended conquerors who in time planted cotton and managed the land with the labor of men whose freedom had been captured from them. This created another level of conflict. And when this principle eventually became the friction point where all-out warfare was waged, then the beautiful side of Bella was subsumed in the crimson of human blood.

But that was hidden now. The couple decided to retreat back towards the Vanderkamp house where they were staying the night. Now they were positioned towards the west. There was still a glimmer of yellow sunlight in this direction.

The two lovers linked hands. Their Bella County paradise, so late their happy abode, was now only a memory. Their eyes welled in watery sadness, but they wiped them soon—Georgia was before them, and they knew not where they would go, as their future was uncertain. Soon they would be purchasing a train ticket to Atlanta for which neither of them were really prepared. Though they knew not what they wanted, the die had been cast by forces greater than themselves. John and Julia were making their solitary way into a future of uncertainty where their faith and endurance would be all their protection from life's catastrophes and the grim reality of the dark scythe's terrible inevitability.

Other Novels by Michael Boylan

Rainbow Curve (2014) Fans of baseball's history will appreciate this compelling tale about race, politics, and corrupting power and one's man's courage to stand-up. *De Anima #1*

The Extinction of Desire (2007) What would you do if you suddenly became rich? *De Anima #2*

To the Promised Land (2015) Are there limits to forgiveness: personal, corporate, and political? *De Anima #3*

Maya (forthcoming) Follow the fate of an Irish-American family through three generations in the U.S.A. It's the story of immigrants and a story of History. *De Anima #4.*

Naked Reverse (2016) There is a backdoor to the ivory tower. Find out what happens to one college professor who escapes. *Archē #1*

Georgia: Part One (2106) and Part Two (2017) A novel told in three parts. Explore racial identity through a murder mystery set in the early 20th century. *Archē #2, 3*

T-Rx: The History of a Radical Leader (forthcoming) An epistolary novel about radicalization in the Vietnam-era. What are and what are *not* legitimate tactics for social/political change? *Archē #5*

The Long Fall of the Ball from the Wall (forthcoming) A novel set in the investigation of the JFK assassination that connects this event to larger social phenomena. *Archē #6*

www.ingramcontent.com/pod-product-compliance
Lightning Source LLC
Chambersburg PA
CBHW020840020726
47497CB00005B/1185